The Postcard

Fern Britton

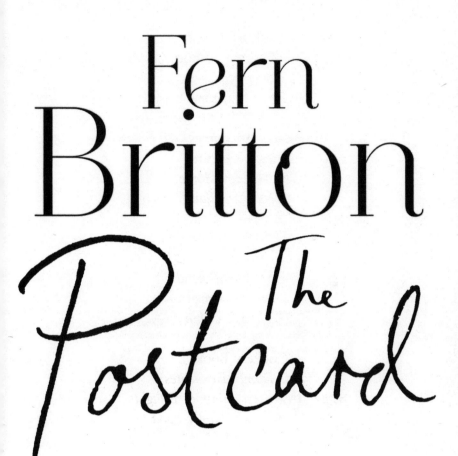

The Postcard

HarperCollins*Publishers*

HarperCollins*Publishers*
The News Building
1 London Bridge Street,
London SE1 9GF

www.harpercollins.co.uk

Published by HarperCollins*Publishers* 2016
1

A catalogue record for this book
is available from the British Library

ISBN: 978-0-00-756297-8

This novel is entirely a work of fiction.
The names, characters and incidents portrayed in it are
the work of the author's imagination. Any resemblance to
actual persons, living or dead, events or localities is
entirely coincidental.

Typeset in Birka by Palimpsest Book Production Ltd, Falkirk, Stirlingshire

Printed and bound in Great Britain by
Clays Ltd, St Ives plc

MIX
Paper from
responsible sources
FSC˚ C007454

FSC™ is a non-profit international organisation established to promote
the responsible management of the world's forests. Products carrying the
FSC label are independently certified to assure consumers that they come
from forests that are managed to meet the social, economic and
ecological needs of present and future generations,
and other controlled sources.

Find out more about HarperCollins and the environment at
www.harpercollins.co.uk/green

To my darling Winnie, with lots of purrs, Mumma.

ACKNOWLEDGEMENTS

My enormous thanks go to Kate Bradley and Kimberley Young, both very fine editors and patient ones too. Thank you for the chocolate, whip cracking and long chats about the theatre, the royal family and estate agents.

Also to Elizabeth Dawson, who is not only a great publicist but a lovely friend.

I am lucky to also be guided by Luigi Bonomi and John Rush, who never cease to give me the best advice as only agents can.

Also, to you. Thank you for reading this and being so supportive. Without you I'd have no reason to write.

All love,
Fern

PROLOGUE

The baby was crying. Penny listened. Would her mother hear? She opened her eyes wide but could see nothing in the deep blackness of her small bedroom. She rolled over to face the closed door. The perfect line of light from the landing barely illuminated the carpet. She heard the door of the drawing room open downstairs and the soft tread of her mother ascending. There was the comforting 'shush' of her mother's stockinged legs as they brushed together approaching Penny's door, walking past, then headed into her baby sister's room.

'Have you had a bad dream, darling?' her mother murmured.

Penny listened and caught the rustle of baby Suzie being gathered from her cot and into her mother's arms.

Suzie had stopped crying and was snuffling. Penny heard the kisses and imagined them being dropped onto Suzie's soft scalp and downy hair.

'Mummy's here, darling. It was just a naughty old dream. Now where's Bunny?'

Penny, five years old, tightened her hold on her own teddy, Sniffy. She pulled him into her arms and sniffed his flattened, furry ear. She whispered to him, 'Suzie has had a bad dream. She's only got Bunny but I've got you.'

Eventually Suzie was soothed back to sleep and her mother walked back and past Penny's room. Penny called, 'Night-night, Mummy.'

She got no reply.

Part One

Winter

1

Penny Leighton didn't feel right. She hadn't been feeling right for a long time now. She couldn't remember how long it had been since she *had* felt right.

She was lying in her big marital bed. The Cornish winter sun had not yet risen and she could see the dark sky through a crack in her exuberant poppy curtains. She'd thought them so cheerful when she'd bought them. She looked at them now and closed her eyes.

She had to get up. She had an important call to take at eleven o'clock. She opened her eyes and squinted at her phone. Ten to seven.

'Morning, my love.' Simon stirred and reached under the duvet to put his hand around her waist. 'How did you sleep?'

She closed her eyes. 'Hm.'

'Is that a hm of yes or a hm of no?'

'Hm.'

'Did Jenna wake up?'

Her look said it all.

'Oh dear. Why won't you wake me? I'm more than happy to see to her.'

'Then why don't you?'

'I don't hear her.'

'There doesn't seem any point in us both being awake then.'

Simon thought better than to reply. Penny had not been herself recently, quick to criticize, withdrawn and moody. He'd felt the sharp side of her tongue too often of late. He decided to make some coffee and bring it up to her but the act of shifting the duvet, even slightly, caused her grievance. 'Why do you always pull the bedding off me?' She pulled the duvet tight around her chin. 'It *is* winter, you know.'

'I didn't mean to. Coffee?'

Penny knew she'd been unkind and rolled over to face him as he sat on the edge of the bed, back towards her, slipping on his T-shirt from the day before. She reached out and stroked the side of his hip. 'I'm sorry. Just a bit tired. I'd love some coffee, thank you.' He stood up and she let her arm fall back onto the sheets.

She said, 'I do love you, you know.'

He ran his hands over his bald head and picked his glasses up from the bedside table. 'I know. I love you too.' He smiled at her and, putting a knee onto the mattress, leant over to kiss her. She put her hands on either side of his face and returned the gentle kiss. 'Coffee, tea or me?' she smiled. From across the landing came the grizzly morning cry of their daughter, 'Mumma? Dadda?'

'Shit!' groaned Penny.

Simon eased himself back off the bed. 'I'll get her. Stay there and I'll bring you your coffee.'

Penny had her coffee in the luxurious silence of her peaceful bed. Winter in Cornwall held a quiet all of its own. No tractors would be out until the sun came up. No bird would be stirring in its nest and no parishioners would be beating their way up the vicarage path to give Simon another burden of responsibility. Finishing her coffee she stretched and wriggled back down into the warmth of her covers. She'd wait five minutes, just three hundred tiny seconds, she said to herself, and then she'd feel strong enough to get up and face the day.

Unable to put off the inevitable any longer, Penny tore herself out of bed and stared into the bathroom mirror. First she examined the two spots on her chin and then the circles under her eyes. She stood sideways and lifted her nightie to see her pale and wobbly tummy. She'd seen fewer pleats in the curtains of the local cinema. Whose stomach *was* this? She wanted her own returned. The firm and rounded one that she'd taken for granted for all those pre-baby years. Dropping her nightie and shrugging on her dressing gown, which still smelt of Marmite even after a wash and half a day hanging on the line in the sun, she slopped down to the kitchen.

Jenna was in her high chair and Simon was attempting to spoon porridge into her. 'That's good, isn't it?' he said encouragingly.

Jenna opened her mouth and grinned. Pushing her tongue out, she allowed the cereal to ooze down her chin. Simon spooned it back in.

It came out again, and before Simon could catch it Jenna had put her hands into it and rubbed it into her face and hair.

'Would you like a banana, then?' he asked, reaching for a baby wipe.

Jenna shook her head. She had just turned one. 'Mumma.'

'Mummy's a bit tired,' said Simon.

Penny sat at the table. 'Too right Mummy's tired.'

'Get this down you.' Simon passed her a fresh cup of

coffee. 'A caffeine hit should make everything look better. By the way, I've emptied the dishwasher for you.'

Penny gave him a cold stare, suddenly irritated again. 'You've emptied the dishwasher for me? Why for me? Because it's my job, is it? The woman's job is to empty the dishwasher? Is that it?'

'Oh Penny, you know what I meant. It's a figure of speech. Like when you tell me you've done my ironing for me.'

'Well, that *is* for you. It's yours. Do you ever do the ironing for me?'

Simon took his glasses off and began polishing them. 'You know what I mean.'

Penny picked up Jenna's breakfast bowl. 'Come on then, monster, have your porridge.'

Jenna obligingly opened her mouth and tucked in.

Simon, returning his glasses to his face, tried a cheerful smile. 'Good girl, Jenna, you wouldn't do that for Daddy, would you?'

'Why do you refer to yourself in the third person?' asked Penny. 'Don't say Daddy, say me.'

'It's just a fig—'

'A figure of speech.' Penny popped the last spoonful into Jenna's mouth. 'Everything is a figure of speech to you, isn't it? Pass me the wet wipes.'

She expertly mopped Jenna's face and hands, hoping that Simon felt inadequate watching just how deftly she did it, then lifted her from the high chair and handed her to her father.

'I'm just going for a shower,' she said.

He looked anxious. 'How long will you be?'

'As long as it takes.'

He looked at the kitchen clock.

'Well, I can give you ten minutes then I have to go.'

'You can *give* me ten minutes? How very generous.' Penny went to leave the kitchen.

'Sarcasm does not become you,' Simon blurted.

'That wasn't sarcasm,' she threw over her shoulder. 'Sarcasm takes energy and wit and I am too tired for either.'

Walking up the stairs was an effort. Her body was not responding to the caffeine. Everything was an effort nowadays. She looked forward to nothing, she laughed at nothing, her brain felt nothing. Nothing but an emptiness that – and may God forgive her – even Jenna's dear face couldn't always fill.

She turned on the shower, stripped off her nightclothes, stood under the hot water and cried.

The morning crept on. By ten thirty Penny had Jenna washed and changed and back in her cot for her morning sleep.

Simon had gone off to his parish meeting about the upcoming Nativity service, complaining that he'd be late, and porridge bowls still sat in the sink under cold and lumpy water.

Penny was in her room dragging a comb through her newly washed hair. She badly needed a cut and a colour, but trying to find a couple of hours when someone could mind Jenna was hard. She stared for the second time that day at her reflection. God, she'd aged. Crow's feet, jowls, a liver spot by her eyebrow . . . She'd had Jenna when she was well into her forties and it had been the hardest thing she'd ever done. Harder even than leaving her life in London.

In London she had been somebody: a busy, single,

career woman; an award-winning television producer with her own production company, Penny Leighton Productions.

Now she hardly knew who she was. Again she felt guilty at how horrible she'd been to Simon. Taking a deep breath she slapped on a little mascara and lip gloss and vowed to present him with steak and a bottle of wine for supper.

She got downstairs and into her study two minutes before the phone rang on the dot of eleven. Penny took a deep breath and plastered on a cheery persona.

'Good morning, Jack.'

'Hello, Penny, how is life at the vicarage treating you?'

Jack Bradbury was playing his usual game of feigned bonhomie. He laughed. 'I still can't believe you're a vicar's wife.'

'And a mother,' she played along.

'And a mother. Good God, who'd have thought it. How is the son and heir?'

'The *daughter* and heir is doing very well, thank you.'

'Ah yes, Jenny, isn't it?'

'Jenna.'

'Jenna . . . of course.'

The niceties were achieved.

'So, Penny . . . ' She imagined Jack leaning back in his ergonomic chair and admiring his manicured hands. 'We want more Mr Tibbs on Channel 7.'

'That's good news. So do I.' Penny reached for a wet wipe and rubbed at something sticky on the screen of her computer. Jenna had been gumming it yesterday.

'So, you've got hold of old Mave, have you?' asked Jack.

'I emailed her yesterday,' said Penny.

'And how did she reply?'

'She hasn't yet. The ship is somewhere in the Pacific heading to or from the Panama Canal, I can't remember which.'

Jack sounded impatient. 'Does she spend her entire bloody life on a cruise? Does she never get off?'

'She likes it.'

'I'd like it more if she wrote some more Mr bloody Tibbs scripts in between ordering another gin and tonic.'

'I'll try to get her again today.' Penny wiped her forehead with a clammy palm. She wasn't used to being on the back foot.

'Tell her that Channel 7 wants another six eps, pronto, plus a Christmas special. I want to start shooting the series in the summer, ready to air in the New Year.'

'I *have* told her that and I'm sure she wants the same.'

'I'm not fannying around on this for ever, Penny. David Cunningham's agent has already been on the blower. Needs to know if David will be playing Mr Tibbs again or he'll sign him up to a new Danish drama. And he's asking for more money.'

'I want to talk to you about budget—'

'You bring me old Mave and then we'll talk money.'

'Deal. I'll let you know as soon as I get hold of her.'

'Phone me asap.' He hung up before she said goodbye.

Old Mave was Mavis Crewe, an eighty-something powerhouse who had created her most famous character, Mr Tibbs, back in the late 1950s. Penny had snapped up the screen rights to the books for peanuts and the stories of the crime-solving bank manager and his sidekick secretary, Nancy Trumpet, had become the most watched period drama serial of the past three years.

Penny's problem was that she had now filmed all the

books and needed Mavis to write some more. But Mavis, a law unto herself, was enjoying spending her unexpected new income by constantly circumnavigating the globe.

Penny rubbed a hand over her chin and found two or three fresh spiky hairs. She'd had no time to get them waxed and, right now, had no energy to go upstairs and locate her long-missing tweezers.

She pushed her laptop away and laid her head on the leather-topped desk. 'I'm so tired . . .' she said to no one, and jumped when her computer replied with a trill. An email.

TO: PennyLeighton@tlx.com
FROM: MavisCrewe@sga.com
SUBJECT: Mr Tibbs

Dear Penny,

How simply thrilling that Mr Tibbs is wanted so badly by Channel 7 and the charming Jack Bradbury. It really is such a joy to know that one's lifework has a fresh impact on the next generation of viewing public.

Another six stories, *and* a Christmas special? But my dear, that is simply not possible.

I wrote those stories years ago as a young widow in order to feed my family. Mr Tibbs has done his job, I'd say and I don't have the patience to think up more adventures for him.

Can you not simply repeat the old ones?

Yesterday we went through the Panama Canal. Absolutely extraordinary. Very wide in parts and very narrow in others. We are now sailing in the Pacific and stopping off at Costa Rica tomorrow. Why don't you drop everything and join me for a few weeks? Enjoy our spoils from dear Mr Tibbs.

With great affection,
Mavis Crewe CBE

Penny couldn't move. She read the email again and broke into a cold sweat. No more Mr Tibbs? Put out repeats? Go and join her on a cruise? Did the woman have no idea that so many people's careers were hanging in the balance because she couldn't be arsed to write a half-baked whimsy about a fictional bloke who solved the mystery of a missing back-door key? Anger and frustration coursed through her. She pressed reply and started to type.

TO: MavisCrewe@sga.com
FROM: PennyLeighton@tlx.com
SUBJECT: Mr Tibbs

Dear Mavis,

If we have no more bloody scripts there is no more Mr Tibbs. Do you want to throw away all that you've achieved? I certainly am not going to let you. The end of Mr Tibbs would mean the end of your cruising and the end of me. PLEASE write SOMETHING! And if you won't do that, I shall have to find someone else to write Mr Tibbs for me, with or without your help.

Penny

She hovered over the send icon. No, she needed time to think. She couldn't afford to fall out with Mavis. She must sweet-talk her round. She pressed delete and began again.

Dear Mavis,

How lovely to hear from you and what a fabulous time you must be having!

I respect your wishes to put Mr Tibbs 'to bed' as it were. He has indeed served you well and given much pleasure to our viewers.

Which brings me to a difficult question. If you won't write the next six episodes and a Christmas special, someone else will have to. Before I find that special someone, do you have anyone you would prefer to pick up your nib? Someone whose writing you admire and that you feel could imitate your style?

No one could be as good as you, of course, but this could be an exciting new future for the Mr Tibbs' franchise as I'm certain you agree.

With all my very best wishes – and have a tequila for me!

Penny xxx

She read it through once and pressed send.

'Right,' she said to the empty room. 'The office is now shut for the day'. She switched off the computer and threw her iPhone into the desk drawer. 'I am going to eat cake.'

*

Jenna always woke from her morning nap at about twelve thirty, so Penny had some fruit cake with a milky cup of coffee and flicked through a magazine, all the while feeling a creeping anxiety about how Mavis would react to the email. Mavis was no pushover and would recognize Penny's bluffing for what it was. She was beginning to regret sending it. But what was the worst that could happen? Mavis refusing point-blank to write anything? So what. Penny would do as she threatened, find a new writer, pay them a quarter of Mavis's fee, and stuff her.

She heard Jenna's little voice calling from her cot upstairs.

'Coming, darling!' responded Penny, and she put all thought of Mavis out of her head.

Penny loved Jenna with a fierceness that was almost as big as the fear she had that she was not good enough to be her mother. She would gladly die for her, but the endless hours of playing peekaboo and looking repetitively at the same old picture books, pointing out the spider or the mouse or the fairy, was killing her. There were days when she couldn't wait to put Jenna to bed and then, while she was sleeping, would be riven with the horror of not being good enough.

Repetitive.

Exhausting.

Mind-numbing.

Frightening.

Nerve-shredding.

She watched in envy as the young mums in Pendruggan appeared to revel in picnics on the village green, swimming lessons, tumble tots, musical games and the endless coffee mornings with other women trading their inane chatter.

Penny had been invited to one once. As vicar's wife she tried to do the right thing, but the amount of snot and sick and stinking nappies – not to mention stories of leaking breastpads and painful episiotomies – really wasn't her thing.

The truth was she missed work when she was with Jenna, and she missed Jenna when she was at work. Her love for Jenna was overwhelming, so big that it was impossible to connect with it, but . . .

She missed an organized diary, a clear office with regular coffee, and power lunches.

She missed flying to LA. She missed being in control of her life.

And she missed her London flat.

She had kept it on when she married Simon, telling him that it would always be useful, a bolthole for both of them, although neither of them had been there since Jenna was born.

But Jenna was here now. Here to stay. How could Penny be lonely with this beautiful, perfect, loving little girl who depended on her for everything? Penny looked at her daughter, sitting in her pram, ready for a trip to Queenie's village shop, just for something to do. She bent down and tucked the chubby little legs under the blanket. 'It's cold outside.' Jenna lay back and smiled. 'I love you, Jenna,' said Penny. Tears pricked her eyes. She angrily wiped one away as it escaped down her cheek.

'Mumma,' said Jenna. She held her hands out to Penny. 'Mumma?'

'I'm fine. I'm fine, darling,' Penny said with a tight throat. She found a tissue in her coat pocket and wiped her face. 'Now then!' She stretched her mouth into its trademark grin. 'Let's go and see Queenie, shall we? She might have some Christmas cards for us to buy.'

''Ello, me duck.' The indomitable Queenie was sitting behind her ancient counter opening a box of springy, multicoloured tinsel. ''Ere, 'ave you 'eard the latest?'

'Nope,' said Penny. 'It'd better be good because I'm starved of news. Jenna's not too good a raconteur yet.'

'Ah, she's beautiful. Wait till she does start talkin' – then you'll want 'er to shut up. Give 'er 'ere. And pull up a chair. You look wiped out.'

Penny sank gratefully into one of the three tatty armchairs that had appeared recently in the shop. Queenie liked a chat and most of her customers enjoyed a sit down.

'This chair's very comfortable,' sighed Penny, sinking into the feather seat.

'Ain't it? Simple Tony got them for me over St Eval. Someone was chucking them out.' Queenie sat down with Jenna on her lap and Jenna reached up to pull at the rope of pink tinsel Queenie had thrown round her shoulders. 'Real pretty that is, darling, ain't it? When you're a big girl you can come in 'ere and 'elp me get all this stuff out.'

Jenna crammed a thumb in her mouth and sucked it ruminatively.

Penny shut her eyes and enjoyed the peace. 'Tell me the gossip then, Queenie.'

'Well, you know Marguerite Cottage what's just behind the vicarage?'

'Oh God, yes. The builders have been making a racket for months.'

'Well, I had the estate agent in here the other day. Come in for her fags. Silk Cut. Not proper fags at all but that's what she wanted. Anyway, I asks her, "Oh, who's buyin' Marguerite, then?" and she says, "It's been let for a year by two fellas from up country." I says, "Well, good luck to 'em if they're 'appy together." And she says, "One of them is a doctor and the other an artist." So I says, "Stands to reason. These gay boys are very arty and nice-natured." And she says, "They've got dogs, too." And I turn round and say, "Well, they always 'ave dogs." And she turns round and says—'

Queenie stopped mid-flow and looked at Penny. 'Oi, Penny, 'ave you fallen asleep?'

2

The following morning Simon crept out of bed and left Penny snoring quietly. She hadn't been sleeping well at all since Jenna had arrived, but she always refused his offer to share the night-time feeds. He knew how tired *he* was with a baby in the house, so goodness knows how tired she was. Simon stood on the landing and looked through its curtainless window. From here, in the winter before the trees were in leaf, you could just see the sea at Shellsand Bay. The waning moon was low in the sky and spilling its silver stream onto the dark waves. It was so peaceful. He sent a prayer of gratitude for his wife, his daughter and his life.

Downstairs he put the kettle on and, while he waited for it to boil, he tidied up the previous day's newspapers. Tomorrow was recycling day.

He enjoyed the order of recycling and was fastidious about doing it correctly. He opened the paper box. Someone – Penny presumably – had put a wine bottle in it. Swallowing his annoyance he picked it out, replacing it with the newspapers, then opened the box for glass. It was almost full. He counted eight wine bottles, not including the one in his hand. All were Penny's favourite. He put the lid back on and stood up. So this was why Penny had been so moody. She was drinking.

Too much.

She had always liked a drink. When they first met she had never been without a vodka in her hand. But she'd settled, and although enjoying the odd glass of wine, he had not seen her the worse for wear since she'd been pregnant with Jenna.

Upstairs, he woke her gently. 'Coffee's here, darling.'

Penny opened one eye. Her wavy hair was over her face and she pushed it out of the way as she sat up. 'Thank you.'

'How are you feeling?' he asked.

She looked at him with suspicion. 'Fine. How are *you* feeling?'

'Good. Yes. Very good.' How was he to broach this new and tricky subject? 'Shall I buy some more wine today? I think we're low on your – our – favourite.'

'Are we? We polished off a bottle with the steak last night, I suppose.'

Simon thought back to last night. She had been halfway down a bottle of red wine by the time he got home. 'Yes,' he said carefully.

'Well, if you're passing the off-licence, get some.' She took the coffee cup he was proffering.

He took a mouthful of his own coffee. 'We seem to have got through the last lot of wine quite quickly. And you *are* still breast-feeding.'

She gave a heavy sigh. 'Oh, I see. Are you lecturing me?'

'Heavens, no.'

'It sounds like it.' She put her cup down and got out of bed. 'I need a pee – and, as it happens, an aspirin. I have a headache.'

He pushed his glasses a little further up his nose and looked at the carpet.

'Don't give me that attitude.' She glared at him. 'I have a headache, not a hangover.'

The morning followed its usual routine. Penny treated Simon with the cool indifference that had recently become second nature to her. (When had that habit started, she wondered.) And he trod round her as if on eggshells. Eventually he left the house to do God knew what and Penny saw to Jenna.

Jenna was washed and dressed, breakfasted, entertained and put down for her nap. She was overtired and it was making her silly and difficult. Penny checked her forehead. 'Is it those naughty teeth?' she asked. Jenna nodded her pink-cheeked face and a string of drool dribbled from her mouth. 'Poor old Jen.' Penny kissed her daughter's damp head. 'I'll get the Calpol.'

Cuddled on Penny's lap, Jenna suckled at Penny's breast while keeping a sleepy eye on the picture book being read to her. She fell asleep before the end giving her mother a chance to drink in the sight, sound, and smell of her. The overwhelming love Penny had for Jenna hurt. It also filled her with a kind of panic. She had never been the maternal type and had honestly thought that she would never marry. She had had endless unsuitable affairs with glamorous and handsome men, not all of whom were single, but she hadn't ever imagined falling in love with someone. Or someone falling in love with her. But both things had happened when she'd found Pendruggan, the ideal location for Mr Tibbs. She had been cruel to Simon when she'd first arrived, had thought him a parochial innocent, a drippy village vicar, wearing his vocation on his sleeve.

He had originally been keen on her best friend Helen,

who had just moved into the village. Penny had teased him, but Cupid had shot his arrows capriciously. The oddest of odd couples fell in love and were married. That was a miracle in itself, but Simon's God had one more surprise for them. Jenna. Penny leant her head back on the Edwardian nursing chair and looked around the nursery: soft colours and peaceful, the Noah's Ark night-light that the parishioners had presented to them on Jenna's birth, the cot given to her by her godparents, Helen and Piran, the photograph of Penny's father. How he would love his granddaughter. And next to his picture, legs dangling over the shelf, was her love-worn Sniffy, the bear her father had given her when *she* was a baby.

Penny shut her eyes for a moment and felt the familiar stab of grief. She missed her father every day. In her unsettled childhood he had meant everything to her, until he died. She spoke to him, 'Daddy, look how lucky I am. Jenna, Simon, success.' She felt her throat tighten. 'Why aren't I happy, Daddy? Can you help me to feel happy? Help me to be nicer to Simon? A good wife?'

Once Jenna was tucked into her cot, Penny felt drained; if the pile of laundry on the landing hadn't been winking at her she'd have gone back to bed. The aspirin was working on her hangover but not her spirits. She heard the sound of raking from the garden and closed Jenna's door. Looking out of the landing window she saw Simon, returned from wherever he'd been, raking leaves on the back lawn. His breath was steaming in the chill air. He looked happy creating neat piles. He stopped for a moment, aware of her gaze. He waved up at her. She waved back and debated whether to take him out a cup of tea as a peace offering.

She took the tea out to him and gave him a kiss.

'What have I done to deserve this?' he asked, pulling off his warm gloves.

'It's a thank you,' she said. 'And an apology. I am so sorry I'm being a cow to live with. I don't know what's wrong with me.'

He put an arm around her waist and hugged her. 'You're just a bit tired. We both are. Babies do that, apparently. You'll be fine.'

'Will I?'

'Absolutely. By Christmas you'll be as right as rain.'

Penny nuzzled into the comfort of Simon's old gardening jumper. 'I don't want to hear the C word.'

Simon kissed the top of her head. 'Well, there's a few weeks to go yet and Jenna is old enough to sit up and enjoy it this year. You'll bring her to the Nativity service, won't you?'

'Only if I can put her in the manger and leave her there.' She looked at Simon to check his reaction. 'Only joking. Of course I'll bring her. She'll enjoy seeing her daddy at work.'

Penny had commandeered the vicarage's old dining room as her office. Her desk sat under the big Victorian sash window through which the December sun shone weakly. She swung on her new office chair, watching the dust motes that sallied in the air. An estate agent might call this a 'handsome room with tall ceilings, wood panelling, and magnificent large fireplace'. Which was true. But it was also very cold. She thought about lighting the fire but couldn't muster the energy to find newspaper and kindling.

She opened her laptop and plugged in the charger, then fished her phone from the drawer where she'd chucked it yesterday.

There was a text from her best friend, Helen.

Hiya. Piran and I wondered if you and Simon would like to go into Trevay one night this week for a bite to eat. We'll go early so that Jenna can come too. I need a cuddle with my goddaughter! H xx

Penny read the message twice. Helen had been Penny's friend for almost twenty-five years. They'd worked together as young secretaries at the BBC and Helen had married a handsome womanizer with whom she had two children. Finally, tired of the repeated humiliation of finding the lipstick and earrings of other women in his car, she divorced him, left Chiswick, and found her paradise in Pendruggan, in a little cottage called Gull's Cry, just across the green from the vicarage. She was now happy with the handsome but difficult Piran.

Penny's eyes filled with tears again at the thoughtfulness of her friend. 'We'll go early so that Jenna can come too.' Helen knew how hard Penny found it to leave Jenna with a baby-sitter, the anxiety she felt about being apart from her little girl.

Helen understood Penny's determination to be a better mother to Jenna than her own had been to her.

She replied. '*Darling, how lovely. I'll talk to S. xxxx*'

She put the phone back in the drawer – ringer off – and checked her emails. She scanned to see if there was one from Mavis. There wasn't. What did that mean? Had Mavis read the email or not? A cold sweat of anxiety swept over Penny again. Oh God! If she didn't get Mavis to write more scripts she'd have to find a writer who could do them in a similar style. And quickly. And if that didn't work there would be no more Mr Tibbs, no more work with Channel 7, and she'd be a laughing stock in the industry, all her old foes sniggering and toasting her downfall. She shivered as a ghost walked over her grave. She remembered something Helen had once said to her, 'Just because you're paranoid doesn't mean to say people aren't out to get you.'

She pulled herself together and replied to all the easy emails, deleted the rubbish ones, and left the others for later.

She heard the back door swing open and Simon's voice. 'Darling?' he called. 'Any chance of another cuppa?'

She dropped her head into her hands and took a deep breath. She forced a smile onto her face and called back, 'Perfect timing. I'm just finished here.'

As it was almost lunchtime, the cuppa turned into scrambled eggs on toast. Jenna was still sleeping and both husband and wife were greatly appreciating the unexpected peace.

'By the way,' said Penny, 'I had a text from Helen. She'd like us to go to dinner in Trevay with her and Piran. Early, so that Jenna can come too.'

'That sounds good.' Simon put his knife and fork together, wiping the last toast crumbs from the corner of his mouth.

Simon sensed that Penny was in a better mood and felt confident enough to bring up a tricky subject. 'Penny, I really do think a nanny to help you with Jenna is a good idea.'

Penny looked at him wearily. 'No thank you.'

'But it would be such a help for you. You could concentrate on your work, go for lunch with Helen, have your hair done. The other day you were saying how you dreamt of spending the day at a spa. Massages and all that stuff.'

'I can do that when she's older but not while she needs me.'

'She'll always need you. You are her mum and a very good mum. But I worry about you and—'

'And you worry about how much I drink?'

Simon pulled an expression of regret. 'Well, yes, if I'm truthful.'

Penny carefully put her knife and fork together and folded her hands in her lap and said as calmly as she could muster, 'Maybe a little more help from you would be good. Once Jenna has gone to bed for the night, where are you?'

Simon bridled. 'We've been through all this before. I have to work.'

'I'll tell you, shall I? Monday, confirmation class. Tuesday, bible study. Wednesday, the parish council. Thursday, sermon-writing night. Friday, the bloody under 16s disco night . . . Shall I go on?'

'No.'

'And now it's almost bloody Christmas with all that entails! So which night is Penny night? Hm? Tell me.'

'Well, that's what I'm saying. We get countless offers from ladies in the parish to mind Jenna and I know you don't want that. But if we had a nanny, someone you can trust, you could get out more. See Helen. It makes sense.'

Penny put her hands to her temples and squeezed hard. What Simon said made some kind of sense, but why couldn't he see that she loved Jenna so much that no one could look after her like she did?

There was a loud knock at the front door. 'I'll get it,' said Simon, relieved by the timely interruption, and left the kitchen to walk down the hall to answer.

The knock had woken Jenna and Penny went to get her.

Jenna's dear face was pink and puffy with sleep. She put her arms around Penny's neck and rubbed into her neck.

'Hello, baby girl. Do you feel better after your sleep?'

Jenna looked over her mother's shoulder and gazed out of the window. 'Woof woof,' she said.

'Woof woof to you too, my love. Now, shall we change your nappy? Then have some nice lunch? Hm?'

'Woof-woofs,' said Jenna, pointing at the window. Penny glanced down and saw two languid Afghan hounds sniffing round the garden. One cocked its leg on the old apple tree and the other was squatting on top of a heap of Simon's raked leaves with a look of serious intent.

Penny banged on the window. 'Shoo! Shoo!'

The dogs looked up and the one who'd finished peeing wagged its tail and barked a greeting.

Hurriedly changing Jenna's nappy and wrapping her in a warm shawl, Penny ran downstairs, calling for Simon.

She found him loafing by the gate, hands in pockets rattling his small change and chatting to three men in matching sweatshirts. They were laughing together, plumes of steam escaping their warm mouths and hitting the cold air. Behind them was an enormous removal van blocking the gate to the vicarage.

'Woof-woof,' said Jenna and started to giggle. Simon, hearing her, turned and said, 'Ah, this is my wife, Penny, and my daughter, Jenna. Darling, these chaps have come all the way from Surrey. I said you wouldn't mind putting the kettle on for them. It's damned cold out here.'

Penny fought the urge to scream and said coldly, 'There are two dogs fouling my garden. Are they yours?'

The oldest of the matching sweatshirts, the foreman Penny guessed, rubbed his cold hands together then pointed to a man who was trying to open the front door of Marguerite Cottage, and said, 'They belong to him.'

A man in his early-thirties, scruffily dressed in old jeans and a T-shirt with a stripey jumper over the top, was patiently trying one key at a time from the bunch in his hand.

'Excuse me!' shouted Penny.

'No need to shout, darling,' said Simon, taking her arm. She shrugged him off. 'How can he hear me otherwise?' she hissed.

The man had got the door open and had turned to give the three removal men the thumbs up.

'Excuse me!' Penny shouted again. 'Are these dogs yours?'

The man smiled and lifted his hand in an apologetic greeting.

'I'm awfully sorry.' He came towards them and held out his hand. 'Hello. My name is Kit and I'm your new neighbour. I'm moving into Marguerite Cottage.'

Penny didn't take his hand. 'Would you please remove your dogs from my garden and clear up any mess you find? My daughter is learning to walk and I like to keep the garden clean and safe.'

'Oh yes, of course.' Kit kept up his warm smile. 'I'm so sorry.' He called to the dogs. 'Terry, Celia – come here.' The animals ambled towards him and allowed him to rub their ears.

'Welcome to Pendruggan, Kit. I'm Simon.' Simon held out his hand. 'Lovely dogs.'

Kit shook Simon's proffered hand. 'Celia thinks she owns the world. She definitely rules me. Terry is very easy-going but don't try to befriend him. If he likes you, you'll know.'

'Please don't let them come in to my garden again,' said Penny.

'Woof-woofs,' said Jenna, straining sideways to get out of Penny's arms and down to the dogs.

'No, darling, don't touch them. They may bite,' she ordered.

Kit smiled at her. 'Well, they haven't bitten anyone yet, but let's not tempt it on our first meeting, shall we?'

Penny switched her attention to the removal men who were clearly waiting for their cup of tea. 'How long will you be blocking our drive?'

'I've said they can take as long as they like.' Simon smiled. 'It's easier for everybody if they tuck in here, off the road. Marguerite doesn't have easy access. And we don't need to go out again today, do we?'

'I may want to go out,' Penny said through clenched teeth.

'What for?' smiled Simon.

While Penny was thinking of an answer Queenie, dressed in a moth-eaten fur coat and with a scarf wrapped round her head, approached them from the shop. She was going as fast as her arthritic hips would let her, keen not to miss out on a bit of village news.

'I saw the lorry and I thought, "Ooh there's me new neighbours." I like to welcome anyone new to the village, don't I, vicar?'

'You certainly do. Gentlemen, this is Queenie who runs the village shop and is the fountain of all local knowledge.'

Queenie smiled and pretended to be abashed. 'Oh, he's a charmer is our vicar. Anyways, I bet you boys are 'ungry, so I've brought you some of me famous pasties. They're yesterday's, but I've heated them up so they'll be fine.'

'Thank you very much,' said the chief removal man gratefully. 'They'll go down lovely with a cup of tea.' He looked hopefully at Penny who refused to catch his eye.

Inside the vicarage, the phone began to ring. Penny passed Jenna to Simon. 'I'll get it. And don't put Jenna anywhere near those dogs or their poo.'

Queenie watched her go. 'She's always busy, that one. I don't think you'll get a cup of tea out of her today. Eat them pasties before they go cold and I'll go and make the tea. Come up to the shop in a minute, 'cause I can't carry an 'eavy tray down 'ere.'

She patted the pockets of her original 1950s fur coat. 'I nearly forgot. This 'ere is the post what's come for the new tenants of Marguerite Cottage.' She handed over several letters. 'Most of them is the electric company and water and so on but one of them looks like a card. Probably welcoming them boys into their new 'ome.' She screwed up her eyes and squinted through her rather greasy spectacles. 'Doctor Adam Beauchamp and—' Simon stopped her from continuing. 'Queenie, this is Kit, our new neighbour. I think that post is for him.'

Queenie was unembarrassed. 'Pleased to meet you, I'm sure. Our postman, Freddie, 'e's ever so good, he asked me to look after these for you.' She handed the envelopes to their rightful owner.

'Thank you.' He took them from her. 'Those pasties smell awfully good.'

'Oh they are,' grinned Queenie. 'Come with me up the shop and I'll get one for you if you help me with the tea tray.'

'It would be my pleasure. Do you mind if the dogs come too?'

'Not at all. I 'eard you two had dogs. That's lovely. Like children to you, I 'spect. By the way I'm not just the village shop, I'm the postmistress too, you know.'

Simon watched them go and felt it safe to let Jenna down from his arms.

Penny shouted at him from the front door, 'Simon! Please come. Quickly. Something terrible has happened.' She was pale with shock.

Simon picked up Jenna and ran to his wife.

3

'What on earth is it?' Simon steered Penny with one hand, all the while gripping Jenna who was wriggling under his opposite arm, into the drawing room. 'Sit down and tell me.'

Penny sat shakily, her hands in her lap, her fingers weaving restlessly. She stared, unfocussed, at their wedding picture on the wall.

Simon waited.

'Mumma?' Jenna put her arms out and whined for reassurance. 'Mumma?'

Penny spoke. 'It's my mother. An old friend just rang. Thought I should know. She's dead.'

Simon frowned and put his hand on Penny's. 'Your mother is dead?'

Penny nodded, her face almost grey with shock.

'Is she sure, your friend? How does she know?'

'It was announced in the local paper.'

'When?'

'Last week, but she's only just seen it.'

'But why didn't Suzie tell you?'

Penny shrugged helplessly. 'We haven't spoken since that terrible lunch. Maybe she thought I didn't want to know? Maybe she thought I wouldn't speak to her if she had called? Or maybe,' she brushed a tear from her eye, 'she's punishing me just a little bit more.'

'But, darling.' Simon stood before her his hands in his corduroy trousers, out of his depth. Penny had never told him what had happened over that lunch. He hadn't known her then and she had steadfastly refused to discuss either her mother or her sister since, other than that they were cut from her life. He said, 'Maybe she just doesn't know how to approach you? Could you ring her?'

Penny shook her head. 'No. You are my family now, Simon. And I'm so grateful to you for loving me.'

'Oh that's the easy bit. You are very lovable.' He put Jenna down. 'You're in shock. Your mother has died and you need time to process it all. There's plenty of time to think about the future. How about a drink? Tea – coffee? Or would you prefer something stronger?'

Penny gave him a wry smile. 'This morning I was drinking too much, wasn't I?'

'Yes, well. I think this calls for a drink.'

Instead of the kitchen he walked towards the drinks cupboard. 'Brandy? I've some lovage cordial too – shall I put some in?'

Penny said nothing. Jenna climbed onto her lap and, putting a thumb in her mouth, stroked Penny's hair.

'Get this down you.' Simon placed the glass in front of her.

*

Penny was just seven when her father had his first heart attack. That day she had woken early, about six, she supposed. The sun was already up because it was summer. She had heard the back door open and click shut. Her father must be checking on his greenhouse.

She crept out of bed and just missed the creaking floor-board outside her mother's bedroom. She stopped and listened for anyone stirring. All quiet.

In the garden the birds were busy chatting to each other and a fat thrush was pulling at an early worm. She threaded her way across the dew-soaked lawn, past the scented orange blossom bush and under the golden hop archway into the vegetable garden. There was her father, a cigarette in the corner of his mouth, his eyes screwed up against the smoke as he tied up a stray branch of cucumber.

He jumped when he saw her and closed his eyes, holding his chest. 'Oh my goodness, Penny. You gave me a fright.' Then he laughed and she giggled as he held his arms out to wedge her on his hip, the cigarette still dangling from his lips.

'Naughty, naughty,' Penny admonished him.

'Don't tell Mum,' he said conspiratorially, stubbing it out in a flowerpot.

She smiled. She liked sharing his secrets. 'I won't,' she said.

'Good girl.' He looked up towards the house. 'All quiet on the Western Front?'

She nodded.

'Want a cup of coffee?'

'With sugar?' she asked hopefully.

'Of course.'

In the far corner of his greenhouse was hidden a little camping stove, a bottle of water, jars of coffee and sugar and a tin of Carnation milk. There was also, hidden in a large cardboard box, a bottle of Gordon's gin: another delicious secret that no one else shared.

The smell of the methylated spirits and the match as

it caught the flame for the camping stove was intoxicating.

'Do take a seat, madam.' Her father snapped open a rickety folding chair and placed an ancient chintz cushion on the seat. She sat, her bare feet, with sodden grass stalks sticking to them, barely touching the gravel floor.

'Are you warm enough?' he asked. 'You must be cold in your nightie. Here, would you like my cardigan?'

She nodded and enjoyed the warmth of his body heat stored in the wool as he draped it over her shoulders. The kettle was boiling and he made them drinks. He had two spoons of coffee, no sugar and black. She had one teaspoon of coffee, two of sugar and a large dollop of the condensed milk. She didn't really like coffee but she didn't want to hurt him by saying so.

He sat on an old wooden crate and pulled a serious face.

'So, young lady, what have you got on at school today? Latin? Quantum Physics? Or a little light dissection?'

She giggled. 'Daddy, I'm only seven. I've got reading. Sums, I think. Music and playing.'

'A full and busy day then.'

She nodded. 'Yep. What about you?'

He lit another cigarette. Rothmans. Penny thought them terribly glamorous.

'Well, I've got to show a lady and a man around a very nice house that I think they should buy.'

'Why do you think they should buy it?'

'Because it is pretty, has a sunny garden, and their little boy will be able to play cricket on the lawn.'

Penny drank her coffee. The sugar and the Carnation milk made it just about bearable. 'Can I come and see it?'

'No. Sorry, madam.'

'Is it as nice as our house?'

'Gosh, no. Ours is much nicer. And do you know why it's nicer?'

Penny shook her head.

'Because you live in it.'

'And Suzie. And Mummy,' she said loyally.

Her father stubbed out his cigarette. 'Of course. Them too. Now, are you going to help me open these roof lights? It's going to be hot today.'

For twenty minutes or so she helped him with the windows and fed the little goldfish in the pond and put out some birdseed while he pottered in the veg patch checking on the peas and lettuces.

They heard the back door open. Her mother stood on the step. 'Mike? Are you out there with Penny?'

'Yes, my love.' He smiled and waved to his wife. 'We've just been doing the early jobs.'

'Well, come in or she'll be late for school.'

Penny couldn't recall the next hour or so, although over the years she had tried. There must have been breakfast, getting ready for school, kissing her mother goodbye and hugging her baby sister. But try as she might there was a blank. Her memory jumped straight from her father holding her hand as they walked back across the lawn, to the interior of her father's car. It was big and dark green and the leather seats were warm under her bare legs. When it was just the two of them her father let her sit in the front next to him. Sometimes he let her change gear, instructing her when and how to do it. This morning was one of those days.

'And into third. Good girl. And up into fourth.'

It was a happy morning. Even the man on the radio

reading the news sounded happy. When the news ended and some music came on, her father lit another cigarette and opened his window, leaning his right elbow out into the warm air and tapping the steering wheel with his fingers. She was looking out of her window at a little dog walking smartly on a lead with a pretty lady in a pink coat when they stopped at the traffic lights. The noise and impact of the car running into the back of them was like an earthquake.

There was silence and then she started to cry. Her father asked in a rasping voice, 'Are you OK?'

'Yes,' she said through shocked tears.

'Thank God.' Her father, ashen, and with a sheen of sweat on his forehead, was finding it hard to speak, gasping for every word. Penny was scared. 'Daddy? What's the matter?'

Her father's lips were going blue and his eyes were starey.

A man watching from the pavement ran towards them and spoke through the open window.

'You OK, sir? I saw it happen. Wasn't your fault, it was the bloke behind.'

Her father didn't answer him. He was still struggling for breath but was now clutching at his left arm.

'Daddy!' Penny was frightened. 'Daddy, what's the matter?'

The man called the gathering crowd for help. 'Quick, someone call an ambulance. This bloke's having a heart attack.'

The police were very kind to Penny and a young police lady took her to school. Years later, when she was an adult, Penny wondered why she'd been taken to school at all. Let alone by a policewoman. Had they phoned her mother and she'd suggested it? That would make sense as it meant her mother could then go straight to the hospital. But who had looked after Suzie? Either way, Penny's next memory was of being called out of her reading class and being taken to the headmistress's study.

'Ah, Penny,' she'd said, 'do sit down. You've had quite an adventure this morning.'

Penny didn't know how to answer this so she just nodded.

'Your daddy has been taken ill but the doctors are looking after him. Hopefully he'll be OK but you may have to prepare yourself to be a very brave girl.' Mrs Tyler looked directly into Penny's eyes. 'You understand?'

Penny didn't understand, but said, 'Yes.'

'Good girl. Now, off you pop and be good for Mummy when you get home tonight.'

Penny spent the rest of the day in fear.

Somebody must have taken her home from school. It certainly wasn't her mother because she was already home when Penny returned.

Penny ran to her and hugged her with relief. 'How's Daddy?'

Margot unwrapped herself from Penny. 'He's been very silly. He's been smoking too many cigarettes and drinking too much gin. I'm very cross with him and so are the doctors.'

'I told him off this morning,' Penny said without thinking.

'Told him off? Why?'

Penny was afraid she'd got her father into trouble. 'Because . . .'

'Was he smoking in the garden?'

Penny said nothing.

Her mother strode in to the kitchen and wrenched the back door open. Penny ran after her but couldn't stop her finding the two cigarette butts. 'Was he smoking these?' Margot held them up.

Penny nodded and moved instinctively to protect the large cardboard box containing the contraband gin. Margot reached past her and opened the box.

She pulled out the bottle. 'Did you know this was here?'

Penny remained mute. Margot shouted. '*Did you know this was here?*'

'Yes,' Penny said, feeling like a traitor.

Her mother looked at Penny with poison. 'So *you* are responsible. It's your fault he's in the hospital. If you had stopped him, we wouldn't be in this mess but if he dies now we won't have anything. No Daddy, no money. If we are thrown out of this house it will be *your* fault. I hope you remember that.' Penny lived in fear for several days, expecting to hear that her father had died and that it was all her fault. But he came back to her. That time.

*

Penny's hand shook as she took a mouthful of the brandy and lovage. 'She hated me.'

'Hate is a very strong word. I'm sure she didn't hate you,' said Simon, reasonably.

'You never met her though, did you?'

'I would have liked to.'

'She'd have hated you too.'

40

'Well, we'll never know.' Simon had a fresh thought. 'I still can't understand why Suzie hasn't phoned you.'

Penny drained her glass. 'Why would she?'

'She's your sister when all is said and done.'

'We burnt our bridges the last time we saw each other.'

'Please tell me what happened.'

'No.'

'It might help. After all, it must be five years ago now.'

'It doesn't matter now my mother's dead.' Penny swallowed the remains of her drink and hugged Jenna tightly. 'I don't want to think about it. And it really, really doesn't matter now.'

Simon sat down next to her. 'Exactly, Penny, love, she can't hurt you any more.'

When he and Penny had decided to get married, Penny had refused point-blank to invite them to the wedding.

'But this is a chance to rebuild the relationship,' Simon had told her. 'To forgive.'

Penny had been adamant. 'I don't want them infecting my life again. I don't want them to tell you things about me that will stop you loving me.'

'You don't know that – and anyway, I could never stop loving you.'

'Believe me, they would try.'

Simon had attempted to bring the conversation up a handful of times since, but each time Penny had become tearful and finally he dropped the subject.

Penny took his hand and held it against her chest. 'I'm so lucky to have you.'

'And me you.' He dropped a kiss on to the top of her head and she released him. 'When is the funeral?'

She looked surprised. 'Oh God! I forgot to ask.'

'Will you go?'

'I don't want to.'

'It may help. The ending resolved and all that stuff.'

Penny gave a small bark of laughter. 'I don't think so.'

Penny's head dropped as she rubbed her face into Jenna's soft hair. Simon could tell she was crying. 'Darling Penny – was it really that bad?'

Penny nodded her head, not trusting herself to speak.

Simon persisted gently. 'But you have a sister. Jenna has an aunt. Wouldn't you like to have your family reunited again?'

Penny lifted her face to him. In that moment wishing she could tell him the truth but she was unable to confront the pain it caused her. 'I *have* my family. You and Jenna and Helen – *you* are my family.'

4

ELLA

It was a Sunday and it was raining in Clapham. The branches of the cherry trees in Mandalay Road were bare, their leaves long ago dropped damply onto the windscreens of the cars parked on either side of the street. Rain bounced off the slate roofs like heavy artillery fire and swilled down drainpipes, startling flat-eared cats who skittered off to their catflaps. At intervals, passing cars shooshed through the deep puddles ploughing up sheets of water to drench already bedraggled pedestrians. It was a road of good neighbours and occasional street parties. The Queen's Jubilee and the Royal Wedding were still fresh in the residents' memories. Now, Christmas trees were already appearing in bay windows, their lights flashing and twinkling brightly.

No 47, Mandalay Road was identical in design to all the others in the terrace: an early Edwardian, two-up two-down with a small front garden. Its front door and window frames were painted in a delicate lilac, complementing the pale blues, pinks and yellows of its neighbours.

Inside, Ella was lolling on a sofa that was strewn with shawls to hide the decades of wear and tear. There was little spring left in its base but it had been Ella's grandmother's and was therefore treasured. She looked contentedly at the Christmas tree she had put up that afternoon.

A pot of tea, now stewed, and a half-empty mug sat on a tray by her side. On the television Julie Andrews was yodelling. All was well with the world.

She heard the creak of the floorboards above and the tread on the stairs before the door to the sitting room opened. Her brother came in, rubbing his stubbly chin and yawning.

'What you watching?' he said. 'Shift yourself.'

She moved her legs and he sat in the space she'd created. She said, 'What do you think of the tree?'

He looked at it. 'Oh yeah. Nice.'

'One of Granny's baubles had broken.'

'Inevitable after all these years.'

'I know, but it upsets me. Each year a little more of our history gone.'

'What's made you so cheerful?' he asked, prodding her with his elbow.

'Christmas is a time for reflection,' she said primly.

He grunted and watched as Julie Andrews and the von Trapp children worked the little puppets. 'So, you hungry?' he asked.

She nodded. 'I've got fish fingers and waffles in the freezer.'

'I fancy an Indian.'

'Have we got enough money?'

'Bollocks to that. I'll put it on my credit card.'

'Are you going to eat that bhaji?' Henry reached with his fork to spear it but Ella got there first. 'Mine! I'm starving.'

Henry mopped up the last of his tarka dahl with his

peshwari naan and sat back, contentedly munching. 'God, that was good.'

'Don't speak with your mouth full; you're spitting desiccated coconut on the rug.'

He grinned at her. 'Don't care. Want a beer?'

'We've only got one can left.'

'Share?'

She nodded and he got up to get it from the fridge.

They were sitting on the threadbare Aubusson rug – another of Granny's hand-me-downs – backs against the sofa, watching a rerun of *The Mr Tibbs Mysteries* on a satellite channel.

Henry reappeared with the last tin of beer and settled himself back down. 'I rather fancy old Nancy,' he said.

'She's very glam,' agreed Ella. 'But then Mr Tibbs is very handsome too.'

'I read somewhere that in real life he's a bit of a goer,' Henry said.

'Really? He looks like the perfect gentleman.' They watched as Mr Tibbs climbed in through an open window at the suspect's house. He was closely followed by his secretary and sleuthing sidekick, Nancy Trumpet, who revealed a lacy stocking top as she slid over the casement.

'Phwoar!' murmured Henry.

Ella tutted.

'What?' her brother said.

'You know what.'

'What do you expect me to do when I see a lacy stocking top and a glimpse of suspender? My generation are sold short on all that stuff. You girls and your tights and big pants and boring bras! I was born too late.'

Ella laughed. 'So Jools has blown you out, has she?'

'No.'

'When did you last see her then?'

'The other day.'

'Where?'

'Can't remember.'

'So what happened?'

'She blew me out.'

'Ha. Why?'

'She said she liked me and all that, but . . .' Henry pitched his voice higher and posher, 'she couldn't see a future for us and anyway, she wanted to be free to see other people.'

'Like who?'

'Justin.'

'Justin no socks and loafers?'

'Yeah.'

Ella was offended on her brother's behalf.

'Well, she's welcome to that total prick.'

'He is a prick, isn't he?'

'Total.'

They sat quietly thinking about Justin and Jools and watching the television screen as Mr Tibbs slipped his penknife into the lock of the desk drawer and revealed the stolen diary he'd been searching for. The camera cut to Nancy, a lock of hair falling alluringly over one eye and a button or two of her silk blouse undone more than was strictly necessary. Henry was rapt.

'Stop looking at her cleavage.'

'I'm not.'

'Yes, you are.'

'If you must know, I was looking at the gorgeous scenery.' The screen was now on a wide shot of a Cornish beach, the wind whipping white horses off the crests of the waves. Henry sighed. 'I miss Cornwall.'

Ella sighed too. 'Yep. We haven't been back for a long time, have we?' She poked him with her foot. 'If you ever get a girlfriend you can take her down. Give her the romantic tour of Trevay – Granny's old house, our old school – and she'd be putty in your hands.'

That night, lying in her bed and listening to the rain still hurling itself at No 47, Ella thought about what her brother had said after they'd finished watching TV. She did need a job. She'd had plenty of them since getting her art degree from Swindon where she had trained to be an illustrator specializing in children's books, but none of them had been as an illustrator. She'd been a chalet maid in Val d'Isere, a nanny in Ibiza, Holland and Scotland and a barmaid in countless pubs and bars in South London. Henry had taken pity on her and offered her a room in No 47, a house he'd bought from his best friend when he'd left to get married. Henry was working his way up in a firm of commercial surveyors but he was making it very clear that he couldn't afford to have his sister as a non-rent paying guest for ever, even if she had brought her share of Granny's furniture with her.

She thumped her pillows into a more comfortable shape and sent a little prayer to her grandmother. 'Granny, would you find me a nice job? Either someone who'd like me to illustrate a book or a publisher who wants to print *Hedgerow Adventures*? Please Granny. Night-night.'

In the morning Ella felt refreshed and hopeful. The sun was shining and every rain cloud had vanished, leaving the sky periwinkle blue. She sang along to the radio as she washed up last night's curry plates and put some bacon under the grill. Henry appeared. 'Bacon? Ella, you're a darling.'

'It's the last few rashers but enough for sandwiches.'

'What sort of day have you got planned?' he asked as she plonked a bottle of ketchup in front of him.

She had good news. 'I'm going to look for a job.' He raised his eyebrows at her as he bit into his sandwich. She raised hers back. 'A *proper* job. And I'm going to send out *Hedgerow Adventures* to another literary agent.'

He couldn't hide his frustration. 'Not another one?'

'Yes,' she said defiantly. 'It's a good story and the pictures are some of my best. Every child I've ever nannied for has loved it.'

He shrugged. 'Ever thought they may have been being polite?'

'Charming! Thank you, you really know how to boost confidence, don't you? Ever thought of life coaching? Writing a best-selling personal help book, such as *Achieve The Ultimate You* by Henry Huntley, Fuckwit with Hons?'

'Ella, I'm trying to be helpful. *Hedgerow Adventures* is very charming, but it's not going to turn you into J.K. Rowling overnight, is it?'

She couldn't disagree.

'So . . .' He stood up and put his plate in the sink before doing up the top button of his shirt and straightening his tie. 'By all means send it to a new agent – but promise me you'll check out the job agencies too?'

It was lunchtime and her feet were tired. Not having enough money to top up her Oyster card she'd walked for miles, checking every job agency before setting off on the long hike up to Bedford Square and the offices of the latest hotshot literary agent she'd read about in *The Bookseller.*

The brass plaque outside was freshly polished. She walked up the short flight of steps and pushed the doorbell on the intercom. A buzzer sounded and the blackly glossy front door opened to reveal a silent marble hall with a grand staircase curling up to the right. On her left was an open doorway and a smart young man behind the desk spoke without looking up. 'Can I help you?'

'Thank you, yes. I was wondering if I could have a meeting with someone about my book.'

His eyes scanned her from head to toe and back again. Expressionless, he asked, 'Do you have an appointment?'

'No, but perhaps I could—'

'I'm sorry, but we don't accept unsolicited manuscripts.'

'I see. It's a very short story, it would only take a few min—'

'You must have an appointment first.'

'May I make one?'

'Has anyone asked to see your manuscript?'

'Well no, but—'

'Then I can't make an appointment.'

'But how do I make an appointment if no one's read my book? And how do I get someone to read my book if I can't get an appointment?'

He smiled wanly. 'It's a very difficult business.'

The phone on his desk rang and he took the call, making it clear that he'd terminated his dealings with her.

Ella was angry and felt humiliated to boot. She pulled herself up tall and walked back into the hall to let herself out.

Running down the staircase was a young woman with

her hair scraped messily back from her face and a smudge of red ink on her cheek. She was heading for the front door as Ella was struggling with the handle.

'Here, let me help you,' said the woman.

The door opened with ease under her practised touch. She smiled at Ella. 'Are you Gilda's temp?'

Ella wished she were. 'No, but . . .'

The woman spotted Ella's manuscript.

'Oh, an author?'

'Well, not exactly, I—'

The woman smiled knowingly. 'Supercilious Louis wouldn't let you hand it in? Give it to me and I'll read it. You've got your contact details on it, I assume?'

'Yes, on the front page.'

'Great. Sorry, I must rush. Meeting someone for a coffee. I'll be in touch. You never know, this just might be our lucky day. Bye!'

Ella watched as the woman walked quickly across the square.

'Granny,' she murmured, 'what have you done?'

5

In the vicarage in Pendruggan the sun was still hiding behind the cliffs – and Penny wished she could hide under her covers. She felt lightheaded. She hadn't slept well because Jenna had had her up three times in the night. Teething was horrible for both of them. Night feeds were usually rather special. Jenna and she would sit in the silence, staring into each other's eyes, sharing comfort and love. But last night had been awful. Jenna had wanted to bite down on Penny's nipples to relieve the pain in her gums but she did it once too often and Penny tapped her leg in anger. In the split second before she opened her lungs and screamed, Penny saw her look of shock and disbelief.

'Jenna, darling! I'm so sorry. Shh, Daddy's sleeping. Shh. I'm so sorry. I'm so sorry.' Penny was beside herself. How could she have hurt Jenna like that? She wrapped her up in a cot blanket and held her close as she carried her downstairs. She went to her study, the room furthest from their bedroom, so that Simon wouldn't be disturbed.

'Darling, shh, shh. I love you. I'm so so sorry.' She rocked Jenna back and forwards until she calmed a little and reached out to touch Penny's face. Penny kissed the tiny palm and smiled. 'Forgiven?'

She fumbled for her handbag, which was on the floor

next to her desk, and found the travelling sachets of Calpol. 'Here, darling, open wide.' Then she found the teething ring she'd bought the day before and offered that to Jenna too. At last peace reigned again.

Penny got herself and Jenna comfy in her desk chair and she idly turned on her computer to see if there were any messages from Mavis. There were about fifty messages. She scrolled through them. The first dozen were spam or unimportant. Then she saw Jack Bradbury's name. Three emails, one after the other, all of them with the same subject. URGENT: MR TIBBS

She felt her pulse quickening and her breathing become shallow. Her fingers were shaking. She couldn't make herself open the emails. She scrolled down to see if Mavis had replied. Nothing. A black dread settled over her. She heard the roar of her own blood in her ears. Shit shit shit. What was she going to do? Where was the old Penny who would have known what to do and would have done it? Overwhelming grief at the loss of herself bore down on her shoulders and she wept silently, her tears falling on the sleeping Jenna. She deleted Jack's emails and shut her computer down again.

And now it was just after midday and she was exhausted, but this feeling was not simply tiredness. Since she'd heard about the death of her mother an extra layer of darkness, an invisible membrane, was separating her from the world. She had often felt like this as a child, particularly after her father had died. A feeling that she didn't really exist, that life rushed around her and she simply glided through it like a ghost. Occasionally she'd reach out a hand to touch a wall or her leg, just to make sure she was real, but it still didn't feel right.

As a child, she had tried explaining it to her mother. 'You're liverish,' Margot had sniffed.

'What does that mean?'

'That there's nothing wrong with you.'

It was one of the many things she looked up in later life. Her computer dictionary gave the meaning as 'slightly ill as in having a liver disorder' or 'unhappy and bad-tempered'.

Well, she'd certainly been unhappy.

And now her mother was dead and the feeling had come back. She wandered through the downstairs rooms and hovered at the closed door to her office. She told herself that she should go in and get on with some work. Work had always been her salvation; a raft to cling to when storms raged.

'Keep going, Penny, keep going,' her father had told her when she started to learn to use her Hula Hoop. She had kept going every day of the summer holidays until she became really very good at it. It was the same mantra she had applied to her work and to every contraction that had squeezed Jenna into the world.

Keep going, Penny, keep going.

Now, standing outside her office door she said it to herself again. 'Keep going, Penny. Just open the door. Keep going.'

'Hellooo.' A stranger's voice came from the back door and startled her.

She jumped in fright.

Her heart was in her mouth. 'Hello? Who's there?'

Thank God Simon had taken Jenna out for the day.

If she was to be murdered by a stranger at least they were safe.

The voice called out again. 'Hello? It's your new neighbour. Kit?'

The bloody man with the uncontrollable dogs! She'd tell him where to go.

Penny stomped to the kitchen where she found Kit standing apologetically at the open back door with a large bunch of flowers. He smiled, not unattractively she was annoyed to notice, and proffered them to her. 'Good morning. These are from Terry and Celia and me.'

Penny's pursed lips were not the reaction he had expected but he continued valiantly, 'As way of an apology for the way they behaved yesterday.'

'I'm very busy, but thank you.' She took the flowers. 'I'd offer you tea or something but—'

He stepped over the threshold. 'That's very kind of you. I'd love a coffee. I won't keep you long as I have a busy afternoon ahead.'

Penny frowned. She had been about to tell *him* that she had a busy afternoon ahead. 'I don't have much time myself,' she said acidly.

He pulled a chair out from under the table and sat down. 'What a lovely kitchen.'

'Thank you.' She filled the kettle whilst quietly hating him.

'Are all the cupboards original?' he asked, looking around.

'Yes. Do you take milk? Sugar?'

'Black, two sugars. They look Edwardian.'

'They are.' What was this, *Bargain Hunt*? 'Here's your coffee.'

'Thanks. How long have you been here?'

'A while.' She looked pointedly at the wall clock above the Aga.

'I'm sorry – I'm being intrusive. I'm just interested in getting to know the village and my neighbours and all that stuff before Adam comes down.'

In spite of herself she was interested. 'Ah yes. Where is he at the moment?'

'Finishing off some odds and ends at his old practice – he'll be here before Christmas though. I've been sent ahead to get the cottage set up with all his little home comforts. I've got a builder coming later this morning. I have permission to put in a couple of skylights.'

'Oh? I thought all the building work had been finished.' She took a mouthful of coffee and thought of all the noise and dust she had just endured.

'I'm a painter. The spare bedroom will be my studio and the roof windows will give me the northern light that is so good.'

'Who's your builder?'

'Bob. Bob the builder.' Kit laughed at his own joke.

Penny smiled and said 'Sinewy bloke? Very brown? Favours short shorts and always has a cigarette on?'

'That's him.'

'He's known as Gasping Bob.'

'Behind his back, I hope?'

'No, no. To his face. Almost all the locals have nicknames here: Dreadlock Dave, Flappy, Twitcher, Simple Tony—'

'Simple Tony? That's a bit un-PC, isn't it?'

'Not here, and anyway, it's what he likes to be called. He's a dear man and a very good gardener.'

'I'm looking for a gardener. Perhaps you could give me his number?'

'He doesn't have a phone. He says they make him go all fizzy or something. But you'll find him in the back garden of Candle Cottage. Polly owns the house and she lets Tony have the Shepherd's Hut there. Best let Polly introduce you to Tony as he's a bit shy.'

'Is he good? At gardening?'

'Well, put it this way, a couple of years ago Alan Titchmarsh came to open the village summer fayre and Tony gave him a few tips.'

Kit drained the last of his coffee. 'Great. I'll get in touch.' He looked at his watch. 'Well, I'd best be off. Gasping Bob said he'd be here by two thirty and I know you've got a lot to do.'

Penny felt a sudden fear of being left on her own in the house. Simon had taken Jenna out in order to let her absorb the news of her mother and think more about contacting her sister. 'Go for a walk on the beach,' he'd said. 'The fresh air will help clarify your thoughts.' But now she found the company of Kit, a stranger, very important to her sanity.

'Don't go. Not yet. Bob's not known for his timekeeping. Let me make you another coffee?'

Kit looked surprised but he accepted and watched as Penny filled the kettle from the old brass tap over the butler's sink.

With her back still to him, she said, 'I'm sorry if I've been rude. I had some bad news yesterday. My mother died.'

Kit looked at her with concern. 'I'm so sorry. And it's me who has been rude. I shouldn't be here. Would you like me to go?'

'No. Please stay. She and I didn't get on very well and I haven't seen her for quite a while. But, it's still been a shock.'

'It must be.'

Penny nodded. 'I'm sorry. I don't know why I'm telling you this. It's made me feel rather numb and . . . I can't explain it.' She brushed away the embarrassing tears that had sprung from nowhere. 'It feels unreal.'

'I'm a good listener and very discreet if you want to talk?'

She shook her head. 'That's kind, but I'm fine. It has felt good just being able to say the words out loud to somebody. I am going to have to say it a lot more now, I suppose. I have to tell people that my mother is dead. It's convention, isn't it?'

'I don't know. We could practise it a few times if you like.' She shook her head and wiped her nose on the back of her hand.

He continued, 'Or we could talk about something else?'

'Oh, let's talk about something else.' She tucked a strand of hair behind her ear and rubbed at her tired eyes. 'Let's talk about you. What do you paint?'

'Ah well, I paint landscapes for myself, and portraits for money. That's why I've come down here with Adam, actually. I have a commission to paint Lady Carolyn Chafford of Chafford Hall, near Launceston.'

'How very posh!'

'Not quite as she sounds. She and her husband bought the title – feudal, of course, so not in the peerage – with the manor, but they are very nice and very loaded, so she'll do for me.'

'And tell me about your partner, Adam.'

'Partner?' A frown wrinkled Kit's clear brow then he started to laugh. 'He's not my *partner*. He's my cousin.' He sat back in his chair and tipped his head to the ceiling, letting out a deeply infectious laugh. 'Oh my God, that's why Queenie said the dogs were like children to me!' He reached for a handkerchief in his jeans and wiped his eyes. 'She's very open-minded, I'll give her that. Wait till I tell Adam.'

Penny was smiling too. 'Typical Queenie. She loves a gossip. She was convinced you were going to be the only gays in the village.'

Kit blew his nose and put his handkerchief back. 'Oh, that's so funny. Sorry to disappoint her, but Adam and I have lived together, practically from birth. Adam lost his dad in the Falklands War and so his brother, my dad, took him and Auntie Aileen in and we grew up as brothers.'

Penny's mobile phone interrupted him. Penny looked at the screen and saw it was Jack Bradbury from Channel 7. A familiar surge of panic made her clench her hands. She could feel her pulse quickening. She reached for the phone and cancelled the call.

Kit felt her mood change. 'Are you OK?'

'Fine, yeah.'

'I barely know you but I can see you are upset,' he said gently.

Penny flashed a wide smile at him and pushed the phone under a pile of newspapers. 'Just a work thing. It can wait. Want a biscuit?'

Penny and Kit spent the rest of the lunchtime swapping snippets about their lives, work and village characters.

'Just look out for Queenie,' Penny warned, 'she's not the sweet innocent old lady that she likes to pretend to be. She has a sharp business head with a love of gossip but a heart of gold. Pendruggan wouldn't be the same without her.' Penny hesitated for a moment then added mischievously, 'Let's not tell her just yet that you and Adam aren't a couple.'

'You are very naughty for a vicar's wife, aren't you!' Kit nudged Penny's arm with his elbow

Penny sighed. 'Well, I used to be naughty – before I married – but let's just say this last couple of hours have been the most entertaining I've had in a long time.'

'Intriguing. What was your life before this one?' he asked.

Penny told him about what she did, about her production company and Mr Tibbs, her thrilling time in Hollywood with the film *Hats Off Trevay*.

'That was your film?' asked Kit in amazement.

'Yep. Well, me and quite a few other people too, but it was amazing.'

'What a life you've had. How on earth have you managed to settle down in sleepy Pendruggan?'

She shrugged. 'Oh. You know. I have a wonderful husband and Jenna my gorgeous daughter. Lots of blessings.'

'You must miss the excitement of your old life, though?'

She picked up their coffee mugs and took them to the sink. 'Maybe. A bit.' She kept her back turned so that Kit wouldn't see the disloyalty she felt at having suggested her marriage wasn't happy. She and Simon were going through a difficult patch admittedly. Everything he did annoyed her. The way he ate, breathed, looked— She pulled herself up sharply at these terrifying thoughts. Keep going, Penny, keep going.

'Well, I'd better be off.' Kit was standing and tying his stripey jumper round his neck.

Startled, Penny stood up straight. 'Yes of course. Well, thanks again for the flowers and the company.'

She opened the back door to let him out and found her best friend Helen rounding the corner.

'Oh Helen, you must meet Kit. Helen, this is Kit, our new neighbour at Marguerite Cottage.'

Helen shook his hand. 'Lovely to meet you. Queenie is all agog with the news of two young men arriving in Pendruggan.'

'We'll try not to disappoint,' smiled Kit, tapping his nose conspiratorially.

Penny turned to him. 'If you want any fish or lobster, Helen is the woman to go to. Her partner, Piran, catches them all the time.'

'Sounds amazing. Adam loves my curried lobster.'

Helen beamed excitedly at him. 'Oh, Piran and I love curry.'

'Well, I must cook for you when we're settled.' Kit bent to kiss Penny's cheek and shook Helen's hand. 'Lovely to meet you, but I have a date with Puffing Bob.'

'Gasping Bob!' Helen and Penny shouted in unison and they watched Kit stroll over to Marguerite Cottage just as Gasping Bob's rusty Rascal van rattled its way towards him.

'He seems nice,' said Helen.

'He is. Very,' said Penny, and immediately burst into tears.

Helen bundled Penny back into the kitchen. 'What's happened, darling?'

'It's my mother,' sobbed Penny. 'She's dead.'

'What?' Helen was shocked. 'When?'

When Helen had heard the whole story, short though it was, she became very practical.

'You must phone your sister and ask her when the funeral is.'

'I don't think I have her number.' Penny's head was in her hands. 'And the last time we spoke it was so awful. I can't ring her.'

'For goodness' sake, Penny, she's your sister. She should have phoned you by now, anyway.' Helen stood up and looked purposeful. 'Right, where is your address book?'

Penny looked at her, pale-faced. 'In my office somewhere.'

'In your desk?'

'Probably.'

'Right. I'll get it and we'll call her.'

'I'm not sure I'm up to that.' Penny struggled out of her hair and followed her friend to the office. 'Please, Helen. I can't. I need to feel a bit stronger before I—'

It was too late. Helen was in the office and pulling at a drawer. As she did so the house phone rang.

'Don't answer it!' Penny almost screamed. 'Leave it.'

The two women stared at each other before the answerphone picked up. They listened to Penny's recorded voice telling the caller that she was unavailable and to please leave a message. She would get back as soon as possible.

It was Jack Bradbury.

He was shouting. 'Penny! *Jesus*. Don't you ever answer your calls or look at your emails? Mavis Crewe is pulling out and if you don't get me six new scripts and a Christmas special *soon* I can promise you that you will never work for me or Channel 7 ever again!'

He hung up.

Helen looked at her friend properly.

Penny shoved her hands inside the saggy pockets of

her ancient cashmere cardigan dropping her pale, swollen-nosed and red-eyed face to the floor.

It was the first time in twenty-five years that Helen had ever seen Penny Leighton look defeated. 'Open your emails,' she said.

Penny hovered for a moment; she'd got into an awful habit of hiding things and Helen would be cross with her if she knew the emails were deleted. She took a deep breath and then made her decision. She went to the kitchen and poured herself a glass of wine.

6

Helen was back in Gull's Cry, her cosy cottage across the village green from the vicarage. She'd listened to Penny as she'd sunk a bottle of wine and then eventually been persuaded to go to bed. Helen nestled the phone between her shoulder and chin and put a pan of water onto the Aga for spaghetti. 'I'm really worried about her, Simon.'

Simon, sitting in his study, phone in one hand, his head in the other, was feeling helpless. 'She's just a bit tired, that's all.'

'I think it's more than that.' Helen saw her boyfriend, Piran, walking up the path with a brace of mackerel in his hand. 'I think she should go to the doctor.' Piran pushed open the front door and Helen put her finger to her lips and mouthed 'Simon' at him before pointing to a bottle of wine and a corkscrew.

She heard Simon attempt a half-hearted laugh before he said, 'I'm not sure she needs the doctor, just a couple of good nights' sleep. Jenna's teething, work's a bit stressful, and her mother dying . . .'

Helen rolled her eyes at Piran and said, 'Simon, seriously, for my sake, could you go to the doc's with her? Tell her you've made an appointment to check on Jenna's teeth or something. Go together, the three of you. Then throw in that you're worried about Penny. Please?'

Simon fiddled with his propelling pencil, a wedding gift from his parishioners, and sighed. 'OK.'

Helen was relieved. 'Good. Is she still asleep?'

'Yes. I checked on her a little while ago and she's fine. What actually happened earlier?'

'I think Mavis Crewe isn't going to write any more Mr Tibbs scripts and Jack Bradbury is taking it out on Penny. Also, I think she really should get in contact with her sister about when the funeral is. But when I suggested that she looked so . . . well, the only way I can describe it is that she seemed to have all her legendary courage drained from her. I ran her a bath and popped a hot water bottle in her bed and she didn't argue. Just did it and got into bed. That's not like her, is it?'

Simon pushed his glasses up onto his forehead and rubbed his eyes. 'No. It isn't.'

'Can you phone the sister?' asked Helen hopefully.

'I'm not sure. Pen won't want me interfering behind her back. She never talks about them, not even when Jenna was born. I don't want her more upset than she is.'

'Understood. Let's see how she is tomorrow.' Piran handed Helen a glass of chilled Sancerre and sauntered into the small drawing room where Helen heard him turn on the television news. The water on the Aga began to boil. 'Simon, I must go . . .'

Simon drooped in his chair a little. 'One last thing, Helen: do you think a nanny might be a good idea? A little help with Jenna might help Penny a lot.'

'Yes I do. Just try persuading her of that.'

Upstairs, Penny had woken from her sleep and was furtively searching for her tablet. She found it in her bedside drawer. She got back into bed and listened carefully in case Simon had heard her. Nothing. She turned the tablet on and the stream of ignored emails plus others popped up. She deleted a fair majority and managed to answer the simple ones. The three she'd deleted from Jack, she retrieved but there were two new ones, one of which sent a flood of panic through her abdomen. It was from Mavis. The other was from an old school friend, Marion Watson. A jolly hockey sticks sort of girl who married well and became an MP. The subject line said SUZIE. Penny didn't know which to go for first.

The one from Mavis could be good, could be bad.

The one from Marion spooked her, so that had to be last.

The ones from Jack? Well, at least they wouldn't hold any surprises.

She opened Jack's first email.

TO: Penny Leighton
FROM: Jack Bradbury
SUBJECT: URGENT: MR TIBBS

P,

   Mavis has flatly refused to write any more scripts.
What are you going to do about it?
Bloody call me.
J.

Penny thought it could have been worse. It could have been the sack.

She hovered between opening the next two.
She opened the one from Mavis.

TO: Penny Leighton
FROM: Mavis Crewe
SUBJECT: Jack Bradbury

Dearest Penny,

I really cannot deal with Mr Bradbury any longer.
What an arrogant bully. Even if I were able to write
more Mr Tibbs tales, I would never again let them
go to Channel 7.

I can see now why your last email was trying to
butter me up. Oh yes, I can tell. I wasn't born
yesterday. The odious Mr Bradbury has been
leaning on you, hasn't he? No wonder you made
the wild suggestion that another writer could take
over. No no no, my dear. That is *never* going to
happen. Mr Tibbs is *my* creation and I will never
give permission for another writer to take on the
franchise while I have the copyright.

I understand this may be inconvenient for you
and Penny Leighton Productions, but all good
things come to an end, don't they?

I have adored working with you and am still
waiting to hear that you can come and join me on
this marvellous cruise. How about hopping over
for LA?

With affectionate regards,
Mavis

Penny felt dizzy. Black spots were clouding her vision. She was breathing in little rapid pants. She heard her father's voice: Keep going, Penny. She wished she had a drink but couldn't face Simon's disappointment if he caught her creeping to the fridge.

She concentrated on getting herself calmer then she opened the email from Marion.

TO: Penny Leighton
FROM: Marion Watson
SUBJECT: SUZIE

Darling Pen,

Long time no see and all that. I have received an email from Suzie, which she has asked me to forward to you. She contacted me at my House of Commons address (very easy to find) wondering if I had your contact details. Apparently she has mislaid them. I sent them to her but she wants me to be an intermediary, God knows why, given that she and I only met at sports days and the like, hence my involvement. Being a nosy old cow, I did read it and may I say how very sorry I am to hear of your ma's death. She was always the most glam of all the mothers at speech day.

Anyway, next time you're in London drop in. I'd love to show you off in the Stranger's Dining Room.

Regards,
Marion

Penny scrolled down.

Dear Penny,

Since you lost contact with Mummy and me, I have had to resort to going through Marion as she is a trusted friend of yours.

I'm sorry to break the news in this impersonal way. I would have rather phoned you or come to your home, but since I have no idea where you are, this is the best I can do.

Mummy died. She was very, very brave and was terribly ill at the end. I nursed her myself and friends and neighbours were very kind, bringing in meals. They have all said how marvellous Mummy was and how she wouldn't have lasted as long as she did if it weren't for me. I was with her till her last breath. It was so peaceful and such a privilege for me. She died listening to that lovely Schubert that she and Daddy adored. I made sure we played it at her funeral as she left the church for the crematorium.

I thought long and hard whether to contact you before the funeral but, honestly, after we last spoke I think Mummy wouldn't have wanted you there.

As you can imagine, I am exhausted with it all and, even after all that happened, feel the need to make contact with you again. We are sisters and have been through so much together. Your life has been a lot luckier than mine. You have forged a career and now have a family of your own. I couldn't have selfishly left Mummy to do what you have done. I forgive you for all the upset of the past and would like to come and visit you. Perhaps in the New Year? I am taking a little sunshine break over Christmas. Doctor's orders. Too many memories of Mummy . . . You are my only family and my dearest wish is for us to reach the hands of goodwill towards each other in my bereavement.

Yours truly,
Suzie

Penny's breathing became ragged again. She clutched at her bed sheets as if the bed was tossing on an open sea and she was to be cast into its chilled depths. Her eyes scanned the horrible words again.

Lost contact. Mummy died. Last breath. Schubert. Funeral. Wouldn't have wanted you there. I forgive you. Penny had never felt so alone. Not since she had walked away from their last meeting. How could they have held such secrets from her? And Suzie, her sister. Always on target when inflicting emotional pain. Suzie, the sister who had kept the secret that Margot, their mother had shared with her but not with Penny. But the secret had popped out over that terrible lunch a few years ago. No apology. No comfort. A secret that had blind-sided Penny. A secret she still hadn't processed. A secret she'd swept under the carpet where it could stay.

Would her father have told her the truth?

*

The memories that Penny had kept so tightly locked inside her were flashing back thick and fast, so real it was as if she'd stepped back into the shoes of her younger self. Little

Penny standing in the kitchen holding her hands over her ears as her mother scolded, '*You* are responsible . . . If he dies now . . . it will be *your* fault.' Penny still felt the pain of her mother's words after almost forty years.

She hadn't been allowed to visit her father in hospital.

'He's very ill. He certainly doesn't want the stress and noise of a silly little girl like you,' her mother had said.

Penny had watched as her mother had put Suzie's little coat on and carried her out to the car.

'Is Suzie allowed to see Daddy?' she'd asked.

'Of course. Daddy wants to see Suzie. *She's* a good girl.'

Penny would sit on the monks seat of the small hallway, watching out of the window and waiting until they returned.

'Is Daddy coming home soon?' she'd ask.

Her mother would look at her with impatience. 'Absolutely not. He's much too ill.'

Then one day the answer was different. 'The doctors say he can come home tomorrow.'

Penny was filled with happiness. 'I shall make a coming-home picture for him.' She ran up to her room and found her crayons and drawing book. She drew a picture of her father wearing his old jumper. He was in the garden and a big smiley sun with curly rays was over his head. Behind him was the greenhouse with red blobs of ripe tomatoes and long green cucumbers. She wrote *welcome home daddy xxxxx* across the fluffy clouds and along the bottom *by Penny Leighton age 7.*

She kept it under her bed as a surprise for the next day.

Penny had been waiting impatiently for her mother's car to pull into the drive. When it did, she opened the front door and rushed to meet her father. She stopped a few feet away as she saw him climb out. His perpetual suntan had faded and his clothes were loose on him, but as soon as he saw her he beamed and spread his arms out wide. 'Penny,' he said lovingly, 'I've missed you.'

She ran to him and hugged him close, his stomach soft on her face, 'Have you missed your old dad?' he asked, ruffling the top of her hair.

'I have. I wanted to see you but Mummy said you were too ill and that I'd get you over excited.' Her words were muffled by his jacket and her tears.

'Did she? Well, I think you would have been the best medicine. I feel better already just seeing you.' He took her hand and together they walked to the front door.

The daily, Linda, came out on to the step. 'Welcome home, Mr Leighton. I've got the kettle on.'

Margot had caught up now, carrying a small suitcase and Suzie. She thrust both at Linda. 'I'll do the tea. If you could just put Mr Leighton's case upstairs, in the spare room, and see to Suzie, please.'

Linda did as she was asked.

'Come and sit in your chair, Daddy.' Penny led her father to the sunny drawing room that ran the length of the house. At one end you could see the front garden and the road and at the other end the back garden. His chair was facing the back garden. Mike sat and patted the arm for Penny to sit on. 'So, Pen, have you been looking after my greenhouse?'

'Mummy said I wasn't to touch it.'

'Well, we'll go and have a look later, shall we?' He held her hand and squeezed it.

'Oh, that reminds me . . .' Penny jumped down. 'I won't be a minute.'

When she came back, Margot was fussing with teacups

and plates of bread and butter. 'Here you are, Daddy.' Penny handed him her drawing. 'I did it for you last night.'

He took it and admired it carefully. 'You've got it all just right. My old jumper, the greenhouse . . . And I love the sun shining down.'

Penny glowed with this praise.

Margot admonished her. 'Penny, don't just sit there, help with the tea.' She helped to pass round the little plates and gave Suzie her beaker of milk. 'Mummy, Daddy says we can go and look at the greenhouse together later.'

Margot looked incredulous. 'Look at the greenhouse? Oh no you won't. Either of you. The doctor has told Daddy to take things easy which means no more digging and lugging heavy watering cans around.'

'But I can do that for him,' smiled Penny, thrilled with the idea of helping her father. 'Can't I, Daddy?'

Mike smiled at his wife. 'Seeing to the greenhouse isn't hard work; and anyway, the doctor said I need to take exercise to keep me fitter.'

'No,' said Margot flatly. 'The greenhouse is too much and I'd never be able to trust you again. As soon as my back is turned you'll be smoking again and worse.'

Mike chuckled and gave Margot one of his most handsome glances. 'Come on, old thing. A man is allowed the odd bit of fun.'

She remained impervious. 'In case you have forgotten, you nearly died because of your secret smoking and drinking.'

Two bright spots of colour formed on his cheeks. 'Oh, for God's sake!' he said angrily.

'Now don't lose your temper. I'm trying to help you,' said Margot.

'Help me? Castrate me you mean.'

'Drink your tea and calm down. You know you're not to get agitated.'

Penny watched this exchange with mounting anxiety. 'Mummy. Daddy. Stop.'

Margot sniffed and sat on an upright chair, balancing her teacup on her lap. Mike looked out of the window at his greenhouse and drained his cup. 'Penny, put this on the table, would you, darling?' He handed her the empty cup and stood up. 'I'm going to have a look at my greenhouse,' he said. 'Care to come with me, Pen?'

She glanced quickly at her mother who was finding the toe of her shoe fascinating.

Penny took her father's hand. As they got to the kitchen and unlocked the back door they heard her mother shout bitterly, 'Take a good look. I've got a man coming to take it down tomorrow.'

*

Penny leant back against her pillows feeling the familiar tears pricking her eyes. Why were these memories flooding back now? Drowning her. The death of a parent? The fact that she hadn't shared the truth with a soul? The opening of old wounds? The fear of what would happen next? Or just a deep dark sorrow . . .

*

ELLA

At exactly the same time in London, Ella was wiping tears away too. Tears of fury and frustration because of her mother, her irresponsible, unreliable mother, who had left her and her not-much-older brother, Henry, two tiny children, with their grandmother and disappeared to God knew where. Ella blamed her mother for the early death of her darling granny – after all, she had worried night and day about where her daughter had disappeared to, as well as being left in sole charge of two young children. But Granny had devoted every breathing moment to making their childhood magical.

Ella thought back to a time when she was about eight years old and she and Granny were walking on Shellsand Beach looking for shells.

'I want you to find the prettiest, the smallest, the most colourful and the biggest,' Granny had said. Ella had dashed down to the rock pools and begun scrabbling through the seaweed and sand. Something caught her eye. 'Granny!' she shouted excitedly. 'I think I've found a hermit crab. Look.'

Her grandmother was settled on a dry piece of sand. She was sitting on a beach towel and wearing her usual garb of blue linen trousers and fisherman's smock, faded through sun and wear. 'Put it in your bucket and show me,' she called back.

Ella had some trouble catching the little hermit crab that sidled speedily under a cloud of seaweed, but eventually she got him and trundled up the beach, trying not to slop the bucket. 'Look, Granny.'

Her grandmother always took the time to examine treasures fully. 'Oh yes. He's a beaut. What shall we call him?' she asked.

'How about Crabby?'

'Perfect. Crabby he is. I'll look after him while you find me those shells.'

Ella smiled at the memory. How she missed her

grandmother. There was nothing to miss about her mother, who just hadn't been there.

Straightening her shoulders and wiping her eyes, Ella called Henry's mobile. 'Hey, it's me. Granny's solicitor in Trevay has just called. He thinks he may have another lead on Mum's whereabouts.'

She heard Henry swear under his breath. 'Hasn't she done enough damage? If they find her she'll swoop in and inherit everything. Granny will be spinning in her grave.'

7

Getting up the next morning, Penny couldn't remember when she'd had more than a two-hour run of sleep. She felt weak and dizzy most of the time. Her appetite had drifted and her eating had become chaotic. Jenna was the centre of her being and yet she was being grizzly and difficult and Penny had started to berate herself for being a terrible mother. Simon, who was caught up in his preparations for Christmas and all the needs of his flock, hadn't appreciated how low she was until last night.

Penny had had too much wine and accused him of ignoring the most important commandment of all. 'Remember, do unto others as you would have them do unto you!' she shouted at him. 'Would you love me more if I dressed up as Mary and slept in the garage with Jenna in the wheelbarrow? Chuck in a couple of sheep and an angel or two then we'd have your full attention?'

'Penny,' he said, 'you and Jenna are my top priority but I'm a vicar and this is one of the busiest times of the year for me.'

She clung to him, starting to cry. 'It's busy for me too. Christmas is less than four weeks away and I haven't done anything. No presents. No cards. No tree. No husband to help me.'

Simon had held her tight. 'OK, my love, OK. You tell me what you'd like me to do and I'll do it.'

'Promise?'

'Promise,' he'd said.

Penny drooped down the stairs and sat at the bottom to listen out for Jenna who was settling down for her morning sleep. Satisfied that all was quiet she hauled herself to her feet and made her way to the office. She was exhausted mentally and emotionally but, with wearying inevitability, she knew she had an email to write.

To: Mavis Crewe
From: Penny Leighton
Subject: The Mr Tibbs Mysteries

Dear Mavis,

I can't tell you how upset I am by your decision but I will honour it. In the next day or two I shall talk to David Cunningham and Dahlia Dahling's agents and let them know that there is to be no more Mr Tibbs. David and Dahlia have worked so hard on their lead characters and I know they will be as distraught as I am seeing Mr Tibbs and Miss Trumpet leave our screens. I shall have to work on a press release that will go out once all the cast and production team have received the news.

On a personal note, I can't express how much I shall miss you. Your friendship has meant a lot to me. However, as you said, all good things come to an end and I guess this is the end.

With fondest memories,

Penny.

She pressed send and quickly wrote another email, this time to Jack Bradbury, confirming that she accepted Mr Tibbs was no more and that she would not be presenting Channel 7 with plans for a future series.

In the kitchen she opened the fridge and took out an opened bottle of Chablis. She looked at the kitchen clock. Just after eleven fifteen. She reached for a wine glass. The bottle of wine was cool in her hand and, as she pulled out the cork the nostalgic smells of hot, uncomplicated summers assaulted her. She poured just half a glass. That would be plenty to take the edge off. She pulled her chair, with the soft cashmere cushion on it, out from under the table and sat down. She put the glass to her mouth and drank. The wine slid down like oil into a rusted engine. She could feel her body waking to its silky caress and took another mouthful; almost as good as the first; and another, until the glass was empty. She went to the fridge and took a last refill from the bottle. With every sip a new fear tripped into her mind: how could she ever be a good mother when her own mother had hated her? When her sister hated her so much? She sat and closed her eyes, hoping it would help shut out the memories. She knew there was another bottle in the fridge. Maybe just one more glass? The more she drank, the more relaxed she became, and the more it didn't matter. She stood up and knocked her chair backwards, making a loud clatter. 'Shhhhh,' she said to the empty room, 'mustn't wake Jenna.' She took the remains of the bottle to the fridge. Her legs felt wobbly. 'Oh Penny,' she smiled ruefully, 'you're pissed. You need a little lie down on the sofa. Just forty winks.'

*

Penny had come home from school and her mother was sitting in the drawing room looking wronged. 'Hello, Mummy, are you OK?' asked Penny.

Her mother shot her a look. 'The doctor says your father needs a holiday. *He* needs a holiday? What about *me*? I'm the one who has suffered. I need a holiday more than he does.'

Penny went to put her hand on her mother's knee. 'I'll help you. I'll swim with him and you can get some rest.'

'You're not coming.'

Penny was baffled. 'But Daddy likes to swim with me.'

'You are staying with your aunt and uncle. You have school to go to. Daddy, Suzie and I are going to the south of France where it is warm.' She pushed Penny's hand away. 'God knows how we can afford it.'

Penny didn't understand why her mother was always going on about money when she was always at the hairdresser's or coming home with a new dress.

'But Daddy can, can't he?'

'He'll have to. I certainly can't.'

Penny thought about the other bit of news. She wasn't going to join them on holiday. That hurt. She liked her uncle, her father's brother, very much and her aunt was cuddly and kind, but she would rather be going on holiday with her family. 'How long will you be away for?'

'I'm not sure.'

'Can I go and look at Daddy? If he's asleep I won't wake him. I promise.'

'You must not go near his room. I have enough on my plate.' Her mother got up and went looking for Suzie.

Penny sneaked upstairs and opened the door of the spare bedroom as quietly as she could. Her father was lying on his side, facing away from her, his breathing deep and rhythmic. She crept a little closer and tiptoed around the bed so that she could see his face. His eyes were shut but he looked a lot better than he had done. She climbed on to the bed and snuggled next to him. She kissed his nose. He opened his eyes slowly and looked at her with a smile. 'Hello, Pen.'

'Hello, Daddy.'

'I've missed you.'

'I've missed you too – and I'm going to miss you when you go on holiday with Mummy and Suzie.'

His face clouded momentarily. 'Ah, Mummy's told you, then?'

Penny nodded.

'I'm sorry, sausage, its doctor's orders apparently and you don't mind being at Uncle Nick and Auntie Dawn's do you?'

'Not really, but I'd rather be with you.'

He put his arm around her and hugged her to him. 'And I'd rather be with you.'

'Penny!' Her mother was shouting at her. 'Penny! Wake up. Jenna's screaming.'

Penny opened her eyes – and Simon was standing in front of her . . .

'Penny, have you been drinking? What's going on?'

She couldn't think of a suitable answer. He turned and walked away. 'I'd better see to Jenna. One of us has to be a responsible parent.'

*

'He looked at me with such – disappointment.' Penny was sitting at Helen's kitchen table in Gull's Cry, nursing a dry mouth and a headache.

'Well, can't you see why?' said Helen worriedly. 'Penny, how could you have done something like that when you had Jenna upstairs. Anything could have happened.'

Penny looked at her forlornly. 'I've never felt as low as this. I have no energy. I look forward to nothing. I want everything to just stop. I feel I'm going mad. Mr Tibbs has come to an end, my mother has died – wouldn't you have a little drink too?

Helen, who had had a particularly unpleasant argument with Piran not half an hour before Penny had arrived, had little patience left. 'Penny, I'm worried about you. It's just not like you to be so defeatist. Yes, it's a tough time right now but you have so many blessings to count. Your life is peachy compared to others.' She started to tick the list off on her fingers. 'A house, a husband, a daughter, a business, money in the bank, friends – what more do you want? If I were you I'd be skipping round the village green every day, thanking my lucky stars. Couldn't you use this time to take a little break, enjoy being with Jenna while she's still so tiny and get back into all the TV stuff in a year or two?'

Penny was stung. 'But if I was out for that long people would forget about me! And I know I should be grateful, of course I do. But why do I feel so unhappy? Why don't I feel the happiness I *should* feel?'

Helen felt out of her depth and said more gently, 'Penny, you must snap out of it. Go for a walk. Read a book. Go to a spa?'

'Simon says I need to get a nanny.'

'You *do* need to get a nanny.'

'I don't want a nanny.'

'It wouldn't be for you, it's for Jenna.'

'Because I'm such a useless mother?' Penny's voice started to rise in panic.

'No, no,' Helen tried to calm her. 'No one is saying that but . . .' She took a moment to think of the right words. 'But you need a break and some help.'

'I just need some sleep and for Simon to be around a bit more.'

'And you could have that *if* you had a nanny.'

Penny sat back in her chair and rubbed her make-up-less eyes with her fingers. 'I'd love a spa day.'

'Then let's do it.' Helen leant across the table and held her best friend's hand.

'Who will have Jenna?' countered Penny.

'Simon will.'

'But he's always so busy.'

'I'll ask him. Anyway, it's your birthday soon, isn't it?'

'No.'

'Well, I'll tell him it's an early birthday present. Or a late one. '

When Penny got back to the vicarage, Simon had more than a whiff of burning martyr about him. 'Jenna's had her supper and bath.'

'Thank you.'

'I'm sure she'd like a story from you . . . if you aren't too tired.' To Penny's mind he put the emphasis on the word tired to suggest she might still be full of wine.

'No, I'm fine, thank you.'

'Right.' He collected up some leaflets for the Parish Council meeting. 'Well, I'm off.' He picked up the keys to his Volvo. 'See you later.'

As the door clunked shut behind him Penny had to fight the urge to run after him, tell him she was so sorry for getting drunk. Sorry for being a horrible harridan. Sorry for being a bad mother. Anything to stop him from leaving her. She needed his reassurance, his security. She wanted him as she had wanted her father when he had finally left her.

She looked at herself in the mirror behind the kitchen door. Who was she? She looked like a mad woman. Her face frightened her.

Frantically she splashed herself with cold water, dried her hands by running them through her uncombed hair. She could hear Jenna calling from upstairs.

'Come on, Penny. You can do this,' she said to her reflection before calling out, 'coming, my love.'

When Jenna had finally fallen asleep, Penny crept out on to the landing and down to her office. She knew she couldn't bury her head in the sand and checked her emails. Nothing from her contacts or Jack Bradbury or Mavis Crewe. This is how it starts, she thought, one day the phone stops ringing and your career stops too.

She scrolled down her list of opened emails and found the one from her sister via Marion. She read it again. What kind of sister would withhold the information about her mother being ill, let alone dead? And to go ahead with the funeral, which she wasn't sure she'd have attended anyway, without letting her know. Penny's hurt balled into the back of her throat where it writhed and tightened until her body spat it out in one long wail. She sat rocking backwards and forwards on her office chair, unable to stop the noise or the tears, which now ran down her cheeks in a constant stream. She found her voice and sputtered into the air. 'Help me! Someone help me. I can't, I can't, I *can't* do this any more. I'm so tired. Please help me someone!' Her throat constricted again and more sobs followed, but there was no one to come. After some time, and experiencing the odd sense of floating outside her body that had recently been so strong, she went to the downstairs cloakroom and rummaged on the shelves behind the coat racks where she kept the first aid tin. She opened it and the familiar smell of Savlon leaked out. She found what she wanted and put them in her cardigan pocket. She went to the kitchen, filled a large glass with tap water, and walked up the stairs

She took the strip of tablets from her pocket and carefully popped each one from its foil blister, lined them up on the bedside table, then went to look in on Jenna. She stroked the sleeping face and whispered 'I love you so much' to her tiny daughter. Her tears dripped on to the warm cheek of her beloved girl, causing her to give a little reflex jump, but she didn't wake. 'Night-night, darling. Mummy will always love you. I'll always be here for you.' As she left the room she saw Sniffy on the shelf. She picked him up and sniffed him before taking him to her room.

She cleaned her face and her teeth and brushed her hair. She spritzed on a little of the perfume that Simon liked and then got into bed. She lay down for a moment and, with the scene set, she felt a peacefulness that had eluded her for months. She propped herself on one elbow and picked up all the pills, put them in her mouth one by one, taking a mouthful of water with each and swallowed. She lay down with Sniffy in the crook of her arm where he had always belonged.

8

'Can you hear me, Penny?'

Penny didn't want to open her eyes. Who was this person disturbing her?

'Penny, love, my name is Sandra. I'm a paramedic. You've taken some pills.'

Penny answered silently. Yes, I did, and now I'm sleeping. Stop tapping my hand.

'Penny, stay with me. Can you say "Hello, Sandra"?'

Penny mustered the words. 'Hello, Sandra.' There, satisfied?

'What was that? You're mumbling a bit.'

Are you deaf? I'm trying to sleep.

'Your husband's here.'

Oh shit.

'He found you and called us. He's very worried. How many pills did you take?'

Not enough.

'Penny, come on, stay with me.' The patting on Penny's arm was getting quite painful. She tried to pull her arm away but it was held fast.

Now she heard Simon's voice, anxious, 'Penny, darling. They're going to pop you in the ambulance and get you to hospital.'

'Where's Jenna?' she managed to say.

'Jenna's OK. Don't worry about Jenna,' said the

bloody Sandra woman again. 'She's with your friend.'

Simon's voice again, 'Yes, she's with Helen. I'm coming with you to hospital.'

She quite liked the feeling of being manhandled onto a stretcher and carried down the stairs. She could at least keep her eyes closed and no one was asking any more silly questions. The ambulance was comfortable but still the bloody Sandra woman wouldn't let her sleep.

'Open your eyes for me, would you, Penny?'

Bugger off, thought Penny.

'Come on now, Penny, open your eyes for me, please.' The woman started patting the back of Penny's hand again.

'What now?' asked Penny, angrily opening her eyes.

'That's it, well done,' said Sandra who immediately shone the brightest of lights into her eyes. She instantly shut them again.

When she woke next, she was in a hospital bed feeling groggy. There was a canula in the back of her left hand attached to a drip. The room was quiet apart from the beep of what she assumed was a heart machine recording her pulse. She wasn't dead, then.

Simon was sitting in a plastic-covered armchair at the foot of the bed. He looked grey.

'Hello,' he said with a tired smile. He got up and came to the bed, bending down to kiss her forehead then her hand. He started to cry. 'Oh, Pen. Why did you do it?'

'What time is it?' she asked him. Her throat was dry and her head ached.

'Almost six.'

'In the morning?'

'Yes.'

'Have I been here all night?'

'Yes.'

'Have *you* been here all night?'

'Yes.'

'Thank you . . .'

Outside, the corridor was already rustling into life. She heard a rattle of teacups as a trolley pushed closer to her room. It stopped at a door along from hers and she heard the squeak of soles on the rubber floor, a cheery voice. 'Morning, Mrs Wilson. You ready for a cup of tea, my dear?'

'Why did you do it?' asked Simon again.

She turned her head away from him and felt the pillow cool on her cheek. 'I don't know.'

'Are things so bad that you wanted to leave Jenna and me?'

'I just wanted to stop for a bit. I wanted everything to stop, just for a minute, and leave me be. I didn't want to die, necessarily, just . . . stop . . . Stop.'

'Did you think about me?'

She thought and answered truthfully. 'No.'

He reached for his handkerchief and wiped his eyes before blowing his nose. 'Don't you love us any more?'

She closed her eyes. 'It's not that. I just wanted to . . . I don't know . . . just have a bit of peace. I was, *am*, so tired.' She looked at him, tearfully. 'Please don't be angry with me.'

'I'm not angry,' he said a little angrily, 'but I can't bear the thought that you – that we – nearly lost you.'

The door pushed open and a smiling nurse came in. 'Good to see you awake, Mrs Canter. Mr Canter has been watching you all night.'

'I know he has.'

The nurse, whose name badge said Sister Mairi McLeod,

busied herself with taking Penny's blood pressure, temperature and pulse. 'How are you feeling this morning?' she asked.

'OK,' said Penny.

'Got a headache, I expect?'

Penny attempted humour. 'Yes. Which is odd considering I took so many pills. You would have thought I'd have slept it off!'

Sister Mairi frowned. 'You took enough to kill yourself. It wasn't funny for the team in A & E who had to get them out of you.'

Penny was chastened. 'Sorry.' She glanced over at Simon, who was examining his hands. 'When can I go home?' Penny asked

'After Dr Nickelson, the consultant psychiatrist, has assessed you.'

Psychiatrist? 'I'm fine,' said Penny, panicking a little. 'I just needed some sleep and now I want to go home to my daughter, she's only a baby. I don't need a psychiatrist.' She gave a little laugh. 'I'm not mad.'

Sister Mairi clicked the end of her Biro and began to write on the file of notes that hooked onto the end of the bed. Without looking up she said, 'Let Dr Nickelson decide what's what. Once he's had a look at you, you'll know when you can go home. I'm going to check your bloods again now. Hopefully you won't have done any long-term damage. You've been lucky.'

Penny wasn't sure she agreed.

At some point during the following minutes and hours Simon had gone in search of breakfast and a cup of tea and had returned with a copy of the *Telegraph* and the latest *Vogue*. He gave the magazine to Penny, who waved it away, and then settled in the plastic armchair to do the crossword. He made no attempt at conversation, which Penny appreciated; although she noticed that he was just staring blankly at the lines of text without reading. She didn't want to face any of his sad-eyed questioning. She closed her eyes and spent the time drifting in and out of a pleasant slumber.

Just before lunch – she knew it was lunchtime because the smell of mince and onions was drifting through her door – a young man in a check shirt and corduroy trousers came smilingly into the room.

'Hello, I'm Dr Nickelson. Consultant psychiatrist.'

Simon leapt to his feet and pumped hands with him. 'Jolly good of you to come,' he said, delighted, or so Penny thought, that at last there was a male in the room. Someone he could understand.

Dr Nickelson turned and smiled at Penny. 'Mrs Canter.' He shook her hand too and dragged a smaller chair up to the bedside. He had a file in one hand, which he opened and quickly scanned, reminding himself of the facts.

Penny lay silent.

'May I call you Penny?' he asked pleasantly.

She nodded.

He settled himself. 'So. Let's start with the hardest question. Why?'

Penny took a deep breath. 'I have a young baby.'

'How old?'

'Just turned one. And she's such a good girl but I get so tired. I just . . .' Her voice broke. 'I just wanted a good night's sleep.'

'Hm.' He looked at her notes again. 'With a large quantity of pills.'

She nodded. She could feel tears gripping her throat. She tried to swallow them down.

'Have you had suicidal thoughts before?'

She paused, forcing the dreaded tears not to come. 'I didn't want to die – I just wanted the world to stop for a bit. So that I could get some rest.'

He smiled again and she saw the understanding in his eyes. 'I think we all want that sometimes. You're not mad.'

The tears raced up her throat and into her eyes and spilled down her cheeks. 'Thank you,' she croaked.

'So, apart from managing a young baby, have there been any other difficulties recently?'

She wiped a trickle of snot from her nose. 'Not really.'

Simon uncrossed his legs and leant forward, passing her a tissue. 'That's not true, Penny,' he said. 'What about work? And your mother?'

Dr Nickelson kept his eyes on Penny and waited.

She turned her eyes from Simon to Dr Nickelson and all of a sudden found her tears flowing unstoppably. She tried to compose herself. 'Oh, I work in television and a programme I make has been cancelled.' She stopped.

'And your mother?' prompted Dr Nickelson.

'She, erm . . .' Penny wiped her eyes with a fresh tissue then twisted it around her fingers. 'She and I hadn't spoken for a while, and – and she died. A couple of weeks ago I think.'

'You think?'

'My sister told me a few days ago and it was . . . It was a shock.'

'I'm sure it was. Has there been the funeral yet?'

'It happened without me knowing.'

He raised his eyebrows. 'Well, no wonder you have

been feeling so low. Just one of those events – new baby, problems at work *or* the death of a parent – would be enough to make anyone feel the way you do.'

'I suppose.' She looked at Simon. 'I'm so sorry, Simon. So sorry.' Her tears came again.

He blinked his large chocolate eyes behind his spectacles and got up, bending awkwardly to hug her prone body lying in the bed. 'I'm sorry, too,' he said. 'I should have noticed how bad you were feeling. I'm so grateful that I've been given the chance to make things better for you. I could have . . .' He fought the lump in his throat. 'I could have lost you. But I know now, and we can get through this, together.'

Dr Nickelson talked a bit more about the tests they'd run. Her liver and kidneys were undamaged but she should get a lot of rest and do only the things she wanted to do. 'More long baths, walks and time to heal,' he said. 'I'll write to your GP and will see you once a week for the next month or so, after which we'll see which is the best way forward.'

'Not the Priory?' she said as another small joke.

He smiled. 'No. Not the Priory.'

'When can I take her home?' asked Simon.

Dr Nickelson looked from one to the other. 'Well, as long as you promise to ring me or your GP or even the hospital if you feel the harmful thoughts coming back, I don't see why you shouldn't go home now.'

'Really?' Simon tightened his hold on Penny's hand and her own fingers tightened in response.

'Really. I'll write a prescription and then you can jump on your horse and ride outta here.'

As soon as Nickelson had gone, Simon sat on the bed and took Penny's hand. He pressed it to his lips as he looked into her eyes. She saw his fear and his love and squeezed his hand tightly. 'I do love you, Simon Canter. I'm so sorry.' She felt a tremendous rush of gratitude for her husband and the life she still had. 'I love you. I really do love you. I promise, I won't ever try to leave you again.'

They went home, Simon settling her into the front seat and then driving very carefully to the vicarage. There was too much to say to each other, and neither had the words.

Helen was there when they arrived, opening the front door with Jenna on her hip. Penny took her beloved daughter in her arms and hugged her tight, kissing her sweet-smelling hair. Helen got them both upstairs and ran a hot bath for Penny while putting Jenna into Simon's care.

Helen watched as Penny undressed and got into the bath. 'Would you like me to wash your hair for you?' she asked. Penny nodded, and shed more tears as her friend performed this gentle and loving kindness.

'I'm so sorry I spoke to you harshly yesterday,' said Helen, keeping her own guilty tears at bay. 'I wasn't a good friend to you.'

Penny shook her head. 'You've been a wonderful friend. Always. I'm so sorry I have let you all down.'

'All you've done is make us realize how very unhappy you have been.'

'Does Simon think me very selfish?'

'You'll have to talk to him about that.'

Penny nodded. 'Yes.'

'Here, tip your head back and I'll give you a good rinse.' Helen took the showerhead and allowed the warm water to do its job. 'Bloody hell! When did you last have your roots done?' she mocked affectionately.

'Can't remember.'

'Well, that's tomorrow sorted then. We're going to get ourselves pampered.'

Lying in bed that night, Penny listened to the house gently settling around her. She heard Simon see Helen out of the front door, thanking her again. She turned and looked at the bunch of Christmas roses and winter honeysuckle in the blue jug on her windowsill. Helen had put them there, knowing that they were her favourites. Old friends and family . . . She closed her eyes and felt so grateful. Tonight she could have been in a mortuary, but instead she was in her own bed, surrounded by her true family and the scent of honeysuckle.

At her parents' house she could remember the breakfast table always had a cut-glass vase of fresh flowers perfectly in the centre, but with the atmosphere crackling with barbed comments from her mother and patient responses from her father. She would always arrive late for school having been hurried and harried and, more often than not, having forgotten some vital piece of homework or kit in the flurry. Life was chaotic and loud and tense.

But life with Uncle Nick and Auntie Dawn was nothing like life at home. Here they let her enjoy the forbidden pleasures of Kellogg's variety packs, syrup on her porridge and ketchup on her toast. At weekends Uncle Nick always cooked a fry-up, which Auntie Dawn adored. There was crispy bacon, fat sausages, mushrooms, tomatoes with fried bread, and, occasionally, black pudding. And always tomato ketchup. Their world was tranquil and structured. She arrived at school on time and without stress. When she got home there would be a hot chocolate and a snack followed by a dinner of cottage pie or ham salad or – her favourite – a packet of Vesta Chow Mein with crispy noodles. (A thing her mother called an abomination to cuisine.)

It wasn't that she didn't miss her parents, her father in particular, but she felt riven with guilt that she didn't miss her mother or Suzie more. So she diligently prayed for them all each night.

She ticked off the days in her five-year diary, the only thing she ever did put in it, and after thirty-two days her father came to pick her up.

'Daddy!' She flung herself into his arms, which felt as strong as they always had as they wrapped themselves around her.

'Hello, sausage. Have you missed your old dad?'

'I have. Where's Mummy and Suzie?'

'They're at home. We came back last night.'

'Why didn't you get me last night?'

'Mummy wanted to make sure that the house was all ready for when you came home.'

'Really?'

'Yes,' he laughed, 'really!' He patted his trouser pocket. 'Oh, now what have I got here?'

He pulled out a small camera on a key ring.

'Does it take pictures?'

'No, but look through it and press the little button.'

She did as she was told and a series of photographs of St Tropez, Cannes and Monaco appeared with each click. Beautiful women in bikinis and men in smart sports cars were enjoying themselves on beaches and outside pavement cafes.

'It's lovely, Daddy.'

'I hoped you'd like it.'
She had adored it.

*

Simon had made her an appointment with the doctor when they got home yesterday, and the feeling that someone else was now at the helm had given Penny permission to stop worrying, even if it was just for a couple of hours. And God knows how Helen had swung it, but she'd got the pair of them an afternoon at the Starfish Spa. Just three weeks before Christmas and the place was buzzing with clients, chatter, stylishly coordinated Christmas trees, and huge vases full of sparkly twigs. Penny pushed any anxious thoughts about her own lack of Christmas preparations to the back of her mind.

Sitting with a pile of magazines and a skinny latte as her colour was being mixed she felt better than she had for a while. Helen, sitting next to her with wet hair waiting for her blow-dry, winked at her and raised her cappuccino. 'Happy Christmas, Pen.'

'Happy Christmas,' she smiled back. She looked at herself in the mirror. The hour-long detoxing, rejuvenating and lifting facial had definitely brightened her skin tone and the ninety-minute aromatherapy body massage had had her snoring happily.

'Feeling a bit more like yourself?' asked Helen.

'Much.' She leant over and touched Helen's arm. 'Thanks, Hel.'

'*And* we've still got our manis and pedis to go.'

Penny looked at her hands. 'Look at these!' she said, holding them up. 'And my feet? Well, I haven't even looked at them for months.'

'Maybe the therapist could put horseshoes on you?' laughed Helen.

'Piss off!' laughed Penny.

A young girl dressed all in white arrived with two glasses of chilled champagne. 'Compliments of the season,' she said.

Helen smiled and raised her glass. 'To you, Pen, and your happiness.'

Penny felt the spike of the bubbles as they trickled down her throat. She was really beginning to feel a lot more like herself – the spa day was just a start to getting her life back on track, and the doctor's appointment tomorrow would be another massive boost. If she could just get through these two days then surely everything would be fine, wouldn't it?

On her lap, her bag began to vibrate and she fished out her phone without looking at the caller ID.

'Helloo,' she said cheerfully, mouthing to Penny, 'probably Hollywood!' Then her tone changed. 'Jack, hello.' She listened. 'When? Yes, I can come up . . . I see . . . OK, see you then. Bye.'

Helen was looking at her with concern. 'Who was that?'

'Jack Bradbury from Channel 7 – he wants to meet me the day after tomorrow.'

Helen shook her head. 'You can't go. You're not ready to take on any stress.'

'I have to, Helen. It's work.'

'Bugger work. What did Dr Nickelson say? Rest and no stress. You'd be a fool to go now.'

But Penny was conditioned to these kinds of demands. 'It's only one day. A meeting, that's all. I've got to go.'

9

Kit was sitting in the small lounge of Marguerite Cottage looking out at the rain. Celia and Terry were flopped elegantly on the rug in front of him, Celia snoring gently.

Kit was on the phone to Adam.

'Weather's been awful these past couple of days. The dogs aren't impressed, but everyone tells me it's normal for Cornwall. I thought it was all palm trees and sunny skies.'

'Mate,' said Adam, trying not to catch the gaze of the new blonde receptionist who was staring at him, moon-faced, through his half-open consulting room door, 'I can't wait to get away. I've had enough here. What are the neighbours like?'

'So far, so good. Our closest neighbour is the vicar, Simon Canter.' He heard Adam groan. 'No, listen,' he continued, 'he's married to a lovely woman, but she's having some problems, I think. According to village gossip she took an overdose the other night.'

Adam frowned. 'Poor woman. How is she?'

'She's back home now but Simon, her husband—'

'The vicar.'

'Yes. He came over and we had a little chat. He's a very decent bloke. He knew that the gossip would be all over the village in seconds, so he's telling us all what happened before the Chinese whispers begin.'

'That's a hell of a lot of people to tell, isn't it?' The new blonde receptionist caught his eye and raised her hands to form the letter T. He shook his head, trying not to let her feel he was giving her the brush off.

'No, not really.' Kit was still talking, 'Pendruggan is even smaller than we thought and it seems that everyone knows everything there is to know about everybody.'

'Oh God! I hope we don't become village fodder.' The receptionist was now openly staring at him. He got up and closed his door. 'So, how's the cottage?'

'A bit small, but plenty for us. The builder, Gasping Bob he's called, has put the new roof lights into my studio and I've been doing a bit of work in it today. Very nice.'

'And that office thing in the garden. Is it going to be suitable for my private clinic?'

'Yeah. It's OK. Two rooms, doors out onto a little porch facing the back garden and the churchyard, and it's got solar panels and running water.'

'Room for a couch and my desk?'

'Plenty.'

'Two rooms you said? Waiting room and consulting room?'

'Yep.'

'Anyone who would be suitable as my reception-ist-cum-secretary?'

'I'll look around.'

'Look for a sane one.'

'You won't have time for flirting if you're working in the GP's in Trevay as well as playing with your tinctures and crystals in the garden shed.'

'Acupuncture and homeopathy are highly effective.'

Kit laughed. 'So it's your farewell drinks tonight, is it?'

'Yep.'

'What's the plan of action?'

'I've been told to be ready for seven before the team take me out for my surprise curry and secret present of a surfboard.'

'How the hell do you know all that if it's a secret?'

'I'm very good at listening through keyholes.'

'Ha. You're a bugger, Adam.'

'Yes, but a charming one.'

The party went rather well. The curry was passable, the wine filthy, and the company dull. Carly, the receptionist, raced to sit next to him at the long table laid out in the darkest corner of the restaurant and made sure she touched his thigh or flashed her cleavage as often as possible. He wasn't sorry to be leaving the practice. Two of his male colleagues were jealous of the attention he received from female patients, while his two female colleagues were clear from the start that he had to have a nurse in the room if he was performing an intimate examination. But he had never, would never, cross the line, despite the horrible rumours that had surrounded him. No, he was glad to be leaving for a place where no one knew him.

He left them all just before midnight, disentangling himself from the tentacles of Carly, making promises to stay in touch, even though he knew he'd break them.

The next morning he was up early and happy to lock the door to his old flat for the last time. A courier had already taken his last pieces of luggage, including the surfboard, and would deliver it all to Cornwall in a day or two.

He dropped the keys into the estate agents, drove his Audi TT to the garage for them to sell (he was hoping to buy a Land Rover Defender when he got to Cornwall) and grabbed a black taxi to Paddington.

He settled himself into the first-class carriage of the Cornish Riviera Express. The carriage was less than a third full and the hush of muted talk among plush seats filled him with a deep sense of pleasure. Out of his brief-case – Burberry, a gift from the widow of a patient he'd been fond of – he pulled the *Lancet* and the latest edition of *Private Eye*. He stretched his legs out under the table in front of him and luxuriated in the emptiness of the seats surrounding him. A steward came towards him. 'Morning, sir. Will you be having lunch with us later?'

'I think I will. Thank you.'

'My pleasure, sir. The dining car is the next carriage along. I'll reserve a seat. Do you have a travelling companion?'

'I shall dine alone.'

'Righty ho, sir.'

As the steward left, Adam heard the guard's whistle from the platform and the final slamming of doors. As he prepared for the train to transport him to the new chapter of his life he heard a young woman's voice calling from outside.

'Wait! Wait! Please can I get on?' she shouted.

Through the window Adam saw the train guard, whistle still in mouth, walk past and behind him, a young woman, red in the face, wheeling a case and carrying what seemed to be an artist's easel, and saying something imploring. Whatever it was, the guard smiled, took pity and opened the first-class carriage door, situated behind Adam. Adam heard her thanking the guard in a well-modulated and cultured voice as she climbed aboard. The door was slammed shut, the whistle was blown, and at last the train pulled itself haltingly out of the station.

'Oh, phew. Oh my goodness,' the young woman was muttering to herself as she found a spot in the luggage rack for her case.

Adam opened his *Lancet* and covertly glanced at her as she settled herself on the opposite side of the gangway but facing him.

Startling red hair with tight corkscrew curls.

Mid-twenties.

Tall.

She struggled out of her coat and pushed it up onto the luggage rack above her head. She caught his eye and he dropped his gaze back to the *Lancet*.

'Phew. That was lucky.' She took both hands to her thick curls and pushed them behind her shoulders. He looked up, pretending he hadn't noticed her struggle to catch the train.

'I'm sorry?' he said.

'I nearly missed the train. My brother's car wouldn't start so I had to push it to get the thing bump-started.'

'Ah,' he said, and went back to his *Lancet* again.

She settled herself into her seat and exhaled loudly. He prayed she wouldn't be a talkative annoyance.

She wasn't. She closed her eyes and slept.

The time went by peacefully and allowed Adam to finish the *Lancet* and look on Amazon for a fishing rod. He fancied himself standing handsomely in the breaking surf, reeling in sea bass after sea bass. Whilst he was in this reverie the ticket collector, an angry-faced bull of a man, made his presence known by thundering loudly, 'Tickets, please, ladies and gentlemen. Have your tickets ready for inspection.'

Adam patted his pockets and found his ticket. The inspector pulled it roughly from his hand whilst looking at the rest of the carriage with aggressive suspicion. He clipped Adam's ticket and shoved it back at him.

His next victim was the girl with the corkscrew red hair. She was sleeping still, her mouth a little open. The inspector stood over her with his ham-hock hands on his hips, then he bent towards her ear and said loudly, 'Madam! May I see your first-class ticket?'

She jumped and blinked her eyes several times in confusion, staring as the man shifted his weight to his other foot and held out his hand, snapping his fingers as he did so.

She retrieved her bag from under her feet and went all through the purse and inner depths with an increasing panic. 'It's here somewhere.'

The man's lips curled. 'If I find you do not have a valid ticket for travel in first class, or no ticket at all, I shall have no alternative but to eject you from the train at the next station.'

'I've got it. It's – it's here somewhere.'

The inspector had lost patience. 'Right, come with me, miss. No first-class ticket, no first-class carriage.' He bent very close to her face so that she could smell the sourness of the tea he had recently drunk. 'Do you understand?' he asked sarcastically.

Adam was uncomfortable for her and would've leapt to her defence if he'd been sure the mountainous man wouldn't assault him. Then he remembered something,

'Excuse me,' he said to the girl, 'but have you checked the pockets of your coat?'

She jumped up and dragged her coat down from the rack above her head. She checked first one pocket – nothing; then the other.

'Here it is!' she cried triumphantly.

The inspector did as his job suggested and inspected the ticket closely. He clipped it churlishly and went on his way.

'Oh golly, I can't thank you enough,' she said to Adam and gave him the widest of wide smiles. It was a powerful smile and one that Adam found rather inviting.

'My pleasure,' he grinned back.

At that moment the steward came through the carriage announcing that the dining car was now open for lunch.

'Would you care to join me for lunch?' asked Adam spontaneously.

'That's very kind, but I have sandwiches.' She pointed at her handbag.

The steward was next to them now. 'Excuse me, sir, would you like lobster? I have only two left.'

The girl smiled broader still. 'Gosh. Lobster on a train. How decadent.'

Adam pressed his invitation. 'Let's have a lobster each. My treat. I'm off to start a new job and you can help me celebrate.'

She blushed and thought of how little money she had and how she hadn't had lobster since her grandmother used to take her and Henry to Rick Stein's Seafood Restaurant for birthdays.

'Gosh, if you put it like that . . .'

'Well, that's settled,' interrupted the steward. 'I'll put a bottle of the Sancerre to cool if you should require it, sir.'

Kit arrived at Bodmin Parkway station with fifteen minutes to spare. He parked and wandered onto the chilly platform. A keen wind was blowing and he pulled his coat a little closer. The small railway café, situated in the old signal box on the down line, was open and he found a nice woman behind the counter cutting huge slices from a lemon drizzle cake. 'Good afternoon, sir, what can I get you?' she asked in what he thought might be a Polish accent.

'A latte and a slice of that delicious cake, please.'

'Our deluxe lemon layer cake? It was made fresh this morning. Sit at one of the tables and I'll bring it to you.'

As Kit settled by the window, he congratulated himself again on the move to Cornwall – this really was the life.

Adam and Ella had thoroughly enjoyed their lunch. Over lobster and wine they got to know each other.

'So what's the new job you're going to?' asked Ella, tucking her napkin onto her lap.

'I'm a GP and I'm joining a new surgery by the sea. A bit different from my old south London practice.'

'And do you have a family to move down with you? Are you the advance guard?' she smiled.

'Just my cousin, Kit. He's been down in Cornwall for two or three weeks now. Setting up our rented cottage.'

'You're being spoilt. Is he a doctor too?'

'No, he's an artist. Rather good apparently but I don't know my Turner from my Tina.'

She laughed pleasingly at his little joke. 'Well, he'll have lots to paint down there. Where's your cottage?'

'A tiny place, erm, Pen something or other.'

Ella laughed again. 'Well, everywhere in Cornwall is Pen something or Tre something. Is your surgery in the village?'

'No, it's a couple of miles away in a lovely spot. Trevay. Do you know it?'

Ella almost choked on her potato. 'Trevay? I grew up there. It's where I'm going now.'

Adam raised his wine glass. 'Here's to happy coincidences. Cheers.'

Ella picked up her glass and chinked his. 'To happy coincidences.' They drank.

'So,' she said, enjoying the cool wine as it slipped into her tummy, 'if you need to know anything about Trevay I'd be happy to tell you. It's small but has everything you need. A great fish market, good restaurants, and a fabulously chichi hotel called the Starfish. The stars of the Mr Tibbs television series stay there. They shoot it nearby in a village called Pendruggan.'

Adam put his hand to his forehead and tapped it. 'Pendruggan? That's where the cottage is.'

'Oh it's a lovely place. You can walk across the fields and down to Shellsand Bay from there. Do you surf?'

He laughed, thinking about the surfboard his colleagues had gifted him. 'A bit, but not for a long time. I'm hoping to hone my skills.'

'You must! My brother Henry and I grew up surfing. I'm a bit rusty now, but in our day . . . And Shellsand is a great beach to start on.'

Adam looked interested. 'Good.'

The steward came and took their plates. 'Can I tempt you with desserts? Tea? Coffee?'

They agreed on two coffees before Adam asked, 'Are you going down for a holiday?'

Ella scratched her head. 'Not a holiday, no. My grandmother brought us up in Trevay. Our mother was a bit of a wild spirit and left us with her. I don't know where she is now but Granny was an amazing parent and friend. She died almost three years ago and I've come down to see our old solicitor because she died intestate and they have to track down potential beneficiaries, including her daughter, my mum. It's taken for ever.' She took a deep breath, aware that a huge amount of personal information had just gushed out of her mouth. She peered at him with concern but he was looking concerned for her.

'I'm sorry to hear that. It must be hard.'

'Yeah.' Ella turned and looked out at the wintry landscape whizzing by. 'It is. But,' she turned to Adam, 'there may be a nice little windfall. My brother, Henry, has been looking after me and I can't live off him for ever.'

'What do you do?' asked Adam.

'I'm trained as an illustrator and I would like to write and illustrate my own books. Children's books preferably. One is with a literary agent now, but who knows?'

'Another artist! You and Kit will have a lot to talk about.'

Kit was on his last mouthful of coffee and final crumb of cake when the London train came into view.

He saw Adam, head and shoulders above anyone else, leap from the train with his briefcase and a suitcase.

'Adam!' Kit called, jogging down the steps of the café. 'Adam.'

Adam had his back turned and was holding his hand up to someone who was getting off the train. And wow, what a someone! Her Titianesque curls, wide smile and air of simple loveliness blew Kit away.

Adam turned and saw him. 'Ah, Ella. Here he is, my cousin Kit. Kit, this is Ella. She's an artist too.'

Kit shook her hand. 'Pleased to meet you. Can I take your case for you?'

She shook her head and began to say no, but Adam passed it to him before she could grab it. 'Thanks, old chap. Perhaps you'd give Ella a lift into Trevay? Not far from us, is it?'

10

It was a gorgeous winter day. The sky was clear and blue and Penny could see the white crests of the waves as they drove the coast road to Newquay airport. Outside the air was fresh and clean. But inside the car, it was anything but.

'Please don't be cross with me,' pleaded Penny.

Simon was driving, stony-faced. They'd had words over her sudden flight to London.

He turned into the airport entrance and parked at the departures drop-off point, pulling the handbrake up just a little too hard.

'What do you expect? You came out of hospital two days ago having tried to kill yourself. Now Jack Bradbury snaps his fingers and you go running.' He turned away from her and stared into the middle distance. 'I care about you, Penny, but you don't seem to be caring about yourself.'

'It's not that. It's business, and you know how much my work means to me. I'll be back tomorrow evening.'

'And that's another thing. Have you given up on breast-feeding?'

Penny lowered her eyes and bit her lip. She'd been advised not to breastfeed Jenna for a few more days to let the overdose leave her system. She'd been expressing her milk ever since but Jenna was missing her and getting fretful. It was breaking Penny's heart.

'You know I haven't. I just need a few more days. I've made up bottles of formula. They're in the fridge.'

Simon softened and turned his chocolate-drop eyes back to her. 'I love you, Penny. Jenna loves you. We don't care if you never make another television programme again. We just want you well and happy.' He put his arm around her shoulders and held her to him

'Thank you,' she whispered. 'I know. And I love you. This is the last time. I'm so sorry.' She pulled the door handle and stepped out of the car with just her overnight bag. 'See you tomorrow,' she said as she shut the door.

She watched until Simon's car left the car park and disappeared from view. She was nervous about this meeting with Jack. She felt instinctively that he was calling her in to give her a bollocking, but why did he need to do that in person unless he thought he still wanted to work with her? Surely he wouldn't have brought her up to London unless it was something worthwhile. She felt her optimism rise. She was absolutely gutted that Mavis Crewe had vetoed any kind of new Mr Tibbs series, written by her or not, but this wasn't the end of her career. Jack had wafted large amounts of money under Mavis's nose but it had been useless and Penny's confidence had taken a severe knock, but she was squaring her shoulders for the next big project that Jack was sure to be waiting to discuss. She thought of how her mother and sister would enjoy her fall from grace. The thought of her mother brought a spasm of pain and grief that literally stopped Penny in her tracks. She had to place her free hand over her heart and take several deep gulps of air. Her father had died and left her, her mother had disowned her then died, her sister had shut her out but now wanted to be back in her life. The very people who should have loved her and delighted in her success had despised it. She took another deep breath, lifted her head and restarted her walk towards the small terminal building. *Keep going, Penny, keep going.*

The following morning, after a restless night in her hotel bed, she showered and did her hair and make-up very carefully, grateful to Helen for getting her to the spa. She had chosen to wear a long cream chiffon shirt over her ankle grazer, narrow black trousers. She threw a scarlet poncho on the top and vertiginous heels on the bottom. Looking in the mirror she barely recognized herself. Penny Leighton, Director of Penny Leighton Productions was back – everything else had just been a tiny setback. Some of her old power and confidence trickled into her veins. She looked at her watch. Perfect. Plenty of time to get a taxi and arrive looking cool and purposeful. Exactly why she'd stayed in a hotel close by rather than her flat. She packed her bag and checked out. The doorman gave her an appreciative sweep with his eyes. 'Good morning, ma'am, would you like a cab?'

'Yes, please. The Channel 7 building, Shoreditch.'

'Certainly, ma'am.'

Walking into Channel 7 filled her with adrenaline. This was her world. It was the meat and drink that had kept her going for over twenty-five years. The receptionist beamed at her.

'Miss Leighton! We haven't seen you for a long time. How is your daughter?'

Penny smiled, thrilled that this woman should remember. 'She's adorable. The apple of her parents' eyes.'

'I'll call Mr Bradbury's office. He's expecting you.'

The sleek, smoked-glass lift always had surprised her with its speed and this morning was no exception. She held on to the rail to steady herself.

The doors opened onto the eighth floor. It was early and the workstations were still unoccupied. There was no one to meet her. She took it as a compliment and walked confidently towards Jack's office. The door was open. He was working on his laptop.

'Hello, Jack.' She smiled and strode into the self-conscious luxury of the room. He looked up but didn't get up.

'Penny.' His smile didn't reach his eyes. 'Take a seat.'

He closed his laptop and arched his fingers under his chin, watching her as she sat down. 'So, how are you?' He looked her over and she was immediately grateful that the poncho was hiding her baby tummy.

She was nervous. She felt a prickle of sweat on her top lip. 'Good, yes. I mean, thoroughly disappointed by Mavis's behaviour – but onwards and upwards.'

'Hm,' nodded Jack, now fiddling with a paperclip. He stood up and came round his desk and sat on the edge nearest Penny.

'The problem I have is: what do I replace my highest rating drama series with? Any ideas?'

Penny felt her anxiety recede. He still wanted her.

'I've been thinking hard. Running all sorts of ideas with my team,' she lied, 'but the bottom line is: what sort of shows do you want to commission?'

He smiled. 'Exactly. I want exciting documentaries, a really good sitcom that is relevant to the twenty-first century. A game-show format that we can sell around the world – and I want it all wrapped in a beautiful warm glow that says "family". Do you get me?'

'Yes, totally.' She didn't. 'I know exactly where you're coming from.' She thought on her feet. 'You know, now that I live in the West Country I see the day-to-day soap opera that surrounds me: the eccentrics, the farmers, the fishermen, the holidaymakers. I think I can deliver you a reality soap opera that combines *Doc Martin* with *Jeremy Kyle*. *Panorama* with *Countryfile*, and all tied up with a chunky ribbon of *Gogglebox*.'

Jack crossed his arms over his pink linen shirt and dropped his head onto his chest, thinking.

'Interesting.'

'It could be. Very.' She kept her face neutral while her heart hammered. What the hell was she saying?

'Yeah.' He looked up at her. 'But are you the woman to deliver it?'

'Absolutely,' she said emphatically.

'I'm not so sure.'

'What do you mean?' She felt her diaphragm knot.

'I get the feeling you've lost your edge. Not as sharp as you used to be,' he said, standing and turning his back on her to look out of his window.

'That's not true!' Penny said indignantly.

'Well, you lost us old Mavis and Mr Tibbs. You haven't been seen around the industry for months, stuck in Devon.'

'Cornwall.'

'Wherever.'

'Well, I have my daughter to care for. But as soon as she's old en—'

'Exactly. Once a woman becomes a mother she's

unreliable. She gets tired. Emotional. Has to cancel meetings because of whooping cough. In short,' he span to face her, 'their hearts are lost to their hormones and not the industry.'

Penny stood up. 'What you're saying is sexist and definitely illegal.'

'Do you and I have a contract?' He pulled at his lower lip with his manicured fingers.

'No, but we did. And we both made a lot of money of it. The *Mr Tibbs Mysteries* play around the world and made huge stars of David Cunningham and Dahlia Dahling.'

'Yes, but do *we*, you and I, have a contract?'

'No but—'

'Penny, we've had fun, but to be honest, I can't see Channel 7 working with you again. I have to encourage new *young* talent. I'm certain you'll find work, but not here. You've had your turn.'

Penny felt her legs shaking with anger and shock. She picked up her bag and, with as much dignity as she could muster, held out her hand. He ignored it and returned to his desk.

'Well, may I wish you luck?' she said as she turned for the door.

'Thanks,' he said smiling with the lips of a snake. 'And by the way,' he called to her, 'that idea of yours is shit.'

Back in the lift she started trembling uncontrollably. How dare he! How fucking dare he! She knew his reputation as a misogynist but had never witnessed it in its most pure form. Bastard. Bastard. The lift stopped and she stepped out onto the shiny marble floor of the reception area. Whether it was her trembling limbs or perhaps a spill from a coffee cup, her heel slid sideways away from her and she staggered forward, her bag banging against her hip as she fell forward onto her wrist. She heard the bone snap and, without thinking, put her other hand around it to push it back into shape. The pain seared through her and she began to retch. The lady behind reception ran towards her and someone else knelt by her saying something that she couldn't hear. Voices were coming and going but she felt the dark spots of unconsciousness creep up and she fainted.

*

ELLA

Ella had set up her easel on the headland above Trevay. It was a beautiful December day. A few cotton wool clouds were now scudding like candyfloss across a forget-me-not sky. Below, the sea wrinkled and rolled invitingly. A small scarlet lobster boat was bouncing through the waves and the sea gulls circled its wake.

She shaded her eyes with both hands and drank in the beauty of Trevay nestled in the cleft of its surrounding cliffs. It was all so familiar. She scanned the streets and lanes working her way towards her grandmother's old house. Yes, there it was. The slate roof with its two chimneys, the whitewashed walls standing out against the granite of its neighbouring cottages. Her home. Only it wasn't her home any more. When Granny had died the old house had been sold along with the few other assets she'd owned and somewhere that pot of cash was sitting in a bank waiting to be claimed. Ella didn't know how she'd feel about her mother turning up now. She didn't really care about the inheritance. Her mother could take the lot. No. It was how Ella would feel about meeting a woman she remembered so little about. What sort of relationship would they have? Would she love Ella? Would they have mum and daughter fun together? Gossip and shopping? Did they share the same tastes in food? Films? Or would she be a stranger who flew in, collected her dues and flew out again? She couldn't talk to Henry about any of this. He'd made his feelings very clear. He couldn't forget the hurt she'd caused all of them. 'If she turns up now I'll bloody well tell her exactly what I think of her. How could she dump us onto her own mother and just piss off without a word? What kind of mother would do that? No, I don't want anything to do with her.'

Ella dropped her gaze and sat on her three-legged canvas stool. She'd wrapped up well against the sea breeze and had packed a thermos of tomato soup, just as her grandmother had always done. 'Come on, Granny,' she said into the wind, 'I'm here now. You guide me to whatever you want me to do and I'll do it.'

She took out her pencil and began to sketch the view in front of her. Time became meaningless as she absorbed herself in catching the glint of the sun against the hull of the lobster boat. She felt all the tension of the last few days slip away. All her senses were concentrated on her work, so when her mobile phone began to trill, she almost dropped her pencil.

'Hey, little sis. How's it going?'

'Hi, bro. It's heavenly. Just as it was when we were little. Granny's house has changed a bit, but guess what?'

'What?'

'It's a bed and breakfast now!'

'How horrible.'

'No, it's really nice. I booked in. And guess what?'

'What?'

'They gave me your old room.'

'Really? Still got the bars at the window?'

'Oh no, it's all double glazing and wooden plantation shutters now. Oh, and the bathroom has been halved so that your room has an en suite and so does the spare room. And, get this, it's got underfloor heating!'

'Bloody hell, Granny wouldn't approve of that!' laughed Henry from his office in Knightsbridge. 'Have you seen the solicitor?'

'Not yet. I was supposed to have seen him yesterday but he's got the flu. His secretary said she'd ring me in a day or two.'

'The poor old bugger must be ninety by now,' said Henry. 'How was the trip down?'

'First class is the only way to go! Thank you for treating me, and,' she paused for dramatic effect, 'I met a very nice man called Adam who bought me lunch. We had lobster and Sancerre.'

'Oh, hello,' chuckled Henry, 'is this the beginnings of a romance?'

'Oh God no. He's ancient. Must be well into his thirties. He's a doctor and he's come to live here with his cousin who is an artist.'

'Is she pretty? Is she desperate?' joked Henry. 'If it's yes to either I'm on my way down.'

'Neither. His name is Kit and they are much too posh for us,' she laughed, before saying, 'thanks H, for the loan of the money for my stay here.'

'I just wish I was with you,' he said sincerely. 'But we're

so busy in the office just now. If the solicitor had given us a bit of notice I could have booked some leave.'

'Supposing he *has* found Mum?' she asked.

Henry hesitated. 'You know how I feel about that.'

'Yes, but I think I'd like to see her,' Ella said tentatively.

'What the hell would you say to her?'

'I'd want to know where she'd been. The life she'd had.'

Henry couldn't agree. 'I'd want to ask her how she could abandon two little children and leave them with her mother, no forwarding address, no contact. Just run off and disappear.' He picked up his pen and clicked the end of it angrily. 'No, I wouldn't want to see her.'

'Well, we might have to. If they've found her.'

Henry remained quiet, then changed the subject. 'So what are you doing tonight?'

'Having dinner with Adam and Kit.'

'In Trevay?'

'Nope. At their cottage in Pendruggan. Cousin Kit is a very good cook, apparently, and Adam thinks that as fellow artists we will have a lot in common.'

Henry was sceptical. 'If either of them make a move on you in any way, they'll have me to deal with.'

'I'll tell them that. It might make them nervous. My feeling is they are too arty for a punch up with my brother.'

In the kitchen of Marguerite Cottage Kit was a bit nervous. The windows were steaming up and his shirt was sticking uncomfortably to him. He leant over the sink to open the small window that faced onto the church-yard and welcomed the gust of December night air on his damp face. Adam should be back with Ella in about ten minutes and he wanted to make a good impression.

The steam clearing, he ducked through the doorway that led into the snug dining room and checked the table. The brilliant yellow mahonia flowers in the blue and white Delft jug in the middle of the table were perhaps a bit overwhelming but the string of fairy lights around the mantel mirror were perfect. They were a small nod towards the impending Christmas. Back in the kitchen he remembered to take the long loaves of foil-wrapped garlic bread out of the fridge before going into the lounge to straighten the cushions he'd straightened only an hour before. Terry and Celia opened an eye each but remained elegantly slung over 'their' sofa.

Kit spoke to them. 'So, Adam's bringing this gorgeous girl for supper. I want you two to behave. Terry, do not stick your snout into her groin for at least half and hour, OK?' Terry looked at him disdainfully. 'Celia, no sneaking into her handbag and pulling out anything personal: we hardly know her yet and we've got to make a good impression.' Celia waved her beautiful feathered tail in acknowledgement. 'Good,' said Kit. He looked out of the window and saw Adam pulling up in the small silver Peugeot that Kit had hired for the time being. 'They're here! Best behaviour!'

11

For the second time in three days, Penny found herself in the back of an ambulance on her way to A & E. The pain in her wrist was making her feel sick again and she was furious with Jack Bradbury, with Mavis Crewe, with Simon, who should have stopped her from going to the bloody meeting in the first place, and, most of all, with herself.

At the hospital she waited her turn for the triage nurse, the X-ray, and the confirmation of a fractured wrist.

'Are you right-handed? asked the young doctor who broke the news.

'Yes.'

'Well, you'll have learned to be ambidextrous after six weeks.'

'Six weeks?'

'Yeah.' He was adding her notes onto a screen. 'You'll be in plaster for six weeks.'

She felt sick again. How was she going to work? To bathe Jenna? To drive? 'Shit,' she said.

'You could say that. Want to call anyone to come and get you?'

Out in the waiting room she steeled herself to make the call to Simon.

There was no answer from the house phone and his

mobile was switched off. She phoned Helen. 'Helen, hi. It's me.'

'Hey, you. How's the meeting gone?'

'I'll tell you later, but something has happened.'

She could hear Helen's sigh, 'Oh Penny, you don't have to stay in London, do you? Simon is so worried about you. He told me earlier today that he feels he should have stopped you from going.'

Penny sounded sheepish. 'Well, as it happens, I wished I hadn't come either. The meeting with Jack was awful and now I've fallen over and broken my wrist. I'm in St Thomas's A & E right now.'

'Oh Penny, darling!' said Helen. 'What would you like me to do?'

'I can't get hold of Simon.'

'He's in Exeter, at the bishop's thing.'

Penny caught her breath, tears looming, 'I want to come home.'

'Of course you do. What time is the next train?' asked Helen.

'I'm not sure,' sniffed Penny pathetically.

Helen was thinking. 'If I can get hold of Simon, he could drive up to get you. He's closer to London in Exeter.'

Penny heard the laugh of a baby coming down the line. 'Is that Jenna?'

'Yes. I'm looking after her for Simon. Don't worry; I'll look after her until you both get home. I'll go round to yours and get her bathed and suppered later.'

Penny cried a bit more. 'Thank you, Hels. I'll try Simon again now. Give Jenna a kiss from me.'

'Phone me as soon as you've spoken to Simon,' said Helen.

*

Penny texted Simon, thinking that once he turned the phone on it would be better to receive a text rather than a garbled, self-pitying voicemail.

The text read. '*Darling, could you call me on the mobile asap?*'

He called in seconds. 'Hi, just finished. You OK? Meeting go OK?'

She started to cry again. 'I've . . . oh Simon, I'm in hospital in London . . .'

'*What?*' Simon sounded anxious.

'I've broken my wrist . . .' She started to sob like a small child.

He calmed down; thoughts of a second suicide attempt receding. 'Where are you?'

'St Thomas's. On the south bank, opposite the Houses of Parliament.'

'Are you allowed home yet?'

'Yes.' Bitter tears began to flow again. 'Simon, I want you to pick me up.'

'Darling, it'll take me three hours. Don't you want to take the train?'

'No,' she sobbed, 'I want you to come and get me.'

Ella sucked the last moule from its shell and rubbed her fingers in the bowl of lemon water by her side.

'Adam, you weren't kidding. Kit really *is* a good cook.'

She looked up at Kit sitting opposite and raised her glass. 'To the chef!'

'The chef,' repeated Adam. 'What's for pud?'

'What's your favourite, Ella?'

The wine had loosened her nicely and all her natural shyness, if she had ever had any, had evaporated. 'Crème Brûlée!' she said extravagantly.

Kit's face fell.

'But I like all puddings,' she added quickly.

'Well, that's a shame because tonight it's . . . Crème Brûlée!' he said, mirroring the way she had just said it. He swished out of the dining room and in moments was back carrying a shallow earthenware dish. 'Tah dah!'

Over at the vicarage, Helen was walking up and down in the drawing room with a blanketed and very fractious Jenna on her shoulder. Earlier Jenna had refused her supper. Helen had given up and heated a bottle of formula but after just a few half-hearted sucks she had pulled away from the teat and refused any other attempts to make her take it.

'Come on, my lovely, let's look at a book. Which one shall we have?'

Helen recalled that distraction had often helped with her two children.

Jenna stopped crying for a moment and pointed to a book about insects. 'Bababababababa.'

'Let's have a look, shall we?' Helen picked up the book and settled into a comfy armchair with Jenna cuddled on her lap.

Jenna put a thumb in her mouth and with the other hand started to turn the cardboard pages. 'Bababa.'

'What's that, Jenna? What are you looking for?' asked Helen.

She turned the page and there was a butterfly. 'Bababa,' said Jenna, pointing.

'Oh butterfly,' said Helen. 'Pretty butterfly. Can you point to the wings?'

Jenna pointed. 'Clever girl.' Helen tickled her tummy. 'What's on the next page? Shall we see?'

They turned the page and there was a bee. 'Bumble Bee,' said Helen. 'Look.'

Jenna's face crumpled and the crying began again.

'Oh dear, no, we don't want Bumble Bee do we. Fly away Bee. Lets look for Butterfly again, shall we?' Helen tried to turn the page back but Jenna flexed her little body rigidly and began screaming.

Helen felt the angry forehead. It was hot. Possibly too hot. And now she noticed a large red patch spreading from Jenna's cheek up into her right ear – this was the last thing she needed!

'Is it those naughty toothies? How about a spoon of Calpol?'

'But how amazing to be staying, as a paying guest, in your old family home.' Adam reached over and topped up his wine glass.

'It is a bit,' said Ella, 'but also rather fun. I haven't told the new owners. I thought it might freak them out a bit.' Ella took a mouthful of her wine and stretched her legs out to tickle the prone form of Terry lying at her feet. 'They do great breakfasts.'

Kit came in from the kitchen with a tray full of mugs and a cafetiere. He headed towards the sofa. 'Budge up, Adam. White or black, Ella?'

'Black with sugar, please,' she answered, tucking her gorgeous hair behind her ear.

Kit couldn't stop himself. 'Your hair really is beautiful. I'd love to paint you.'

Ella laughed. 'I promise you, you wouldn't.'

'Oh, he would,' said Adam, goading his cousin to embarrassment. 'He's very good at portraits.'

Kit swerved the conversation as best he could. 'Well, landscapes are my thing. I'm down here to work on some seascapes.'

His diversion worked. Ella leant forward and collected her coffee mug from him. 'Oh my goodness, that's so hard. I was on the cliffs above Trevay this morning trying some sketches. The trouble is: how do you make a flat painting look alive with wind and spray and all the sensations that the sea gives when you watch it?'

'I studied Turner at art school,' Kit told her, 'and I almost gave up painting because I knew I'd never do anything that well, and then I thought, well, all I can do is be myself and do the "Kit Thing" to the best of my ability.'

'I envy you,' said Ella. 'I'd love to have a year down here painting the sea through all the seasons.'

Adam sat up and stretched. 'Well, why don't you?'

She laughed. 'Because I need a job and somewhere to live. At least in London I've got Henry.'

'But supposing the solicitor tells you that your grand-mother was the owner of a diamond mine and you and Henry are now billionaires?' Adam said. 'You may never have to do a stroke of work ever again. Paint all day, every day.'

Ella smiled. 'Somehow, I don't think so. There will be a little money but not much.' She stood up and reached for her coat. 'Thank you for a wonderful supper.'

Kit stood too. 'It was my – our – pleasure. Let me give you a lift back into Trevay.'

'Are you sure? That would be very kind.'

'No problem. Let me get the keys.'

As Kit went in search of the keys Adam helped Ella into her coat.

'Ella, I've had an idea. It may be mad, but how long do you think you'll be staying in Cornwall?'

Ella continued to do up her coat. 'For ever, if I could. There's nothing to keep me in London. Other than Henry. But I'd have to find a job, somewhere to live . . . '

'How about you work for me?' asked Adam.

Ella stopped. 'What?'

'At my clinic in the garden here. Only part-time I'm afraid. As receptionist and my PA?'

Ella was stunned. 'It sounds amazing but—'

'Just say yes. Easy.'

Ella bit her lip and pulled her hair up onto the top of her head. How would she pay rent on a part-time salary? 'Can I think about it?'

The Calpol had given Jenna some respite and she'd eventually fallen into a dreamless sleep.

With her sleeping goddaughter in her arms, Helen sat in the old vicarage kitchen thinking about Penny. She had never seen Penny in such a state of defeatism or mental and physical pain. If Helen had to sit here all night, she would. Penny would be in no state to face a sick baby. Simon had phoned a couple of hours ago to say they wouldn't be back until after midnight and three tired adults and a sick child would be a recipe for angst and recrimination.

Jenna suddenly twitched and opened her eyes.

Helen stroked her cheek in a soothing motion. Jenna felt hotter than before. The Calpol must be wearing off. Should she give her another dose? As she was thinking about the pros and cons of more paracetamol, Jenna's body stiffened like a board in a total muscle spasm. She let out a short, high-pitched cry then vomited and began to twitch and shiver. Her eyes rolled in her head and her lips took on a bluish hue.

'Oh shit! Jenna! Jenna!' Helen lifted the child up and could feel her little muscles tense.

Jenna continued to shiver and shake and Helen's panic rose.

'OK, darling, I'm getting the doctor now. It's OK, darling. I'm here and Mummy's on her way.'

With one hand cradling Jenna, she fumbled in her handbag by her feet and tried to locate her phone in its dark depths. Her fingers found it at last and she pulled it out. No signal. Oh shit, of course there's no signal! She looked over at the landline on the other side of the kitchen. 'OK, darling, we'll get the phone. I've got to carry you. I won't drop you. Hang on.'

Jenna stopped her shaking and lay still in Helen's arms, eyes closed, lips blue, breathing but unresponsive.

Helen went cold. The nearest doctor was in Trevay, a fifteen-minute drive at this time of night. Would an ambulance be quicker? If only there were a doctor in the village. Adam! Adam is a doctor and he's next door. Helen hadn't met him yet, but Kit had said he'd arrived when she'd seen him in Queenie's that morning. She picked up her coat from the back of a chair and wrapped it round Jenna before dashing out of the house towards Marguerite Cottage.

'It's a serious offer,' Adam told Ella.

'Don't badger her,' scolded Kit, rattling the car keys. 'She says she'll think about it.' He opened the front door in time to see a white-faced Helen running like a phantom down the drive towards him, holding her coat bundled in her arms. 'Kit!' she shouted breathlessly. 'Kit. It's Jenna. She's ill. Is Adam here?'

Adam shouldered his way past Kit. 'I'm Adam. What's happened?'

It was after one before Simon and Penny arrived back in Pendruggan and Helen opened the door to them. Penny was grey-faced and Simon was pale with exhaustion.

She hugged them both in turn. 'How's your wrist?'

'It's sore,' said Penny. 'I can't believe I've done it. I won't be able to do anything for six weeks. I can't even bathe Jenna.' Before Helen could say anything, Penny continued, 'Thank you for being with her. Has she been a good girl? Did she go to sleep all right?'

Helen took Penny's good arm and guided her to the kitchen. 'She's still up. She wasn't very well earlier.'

'What?' Penny's face took on a hunted look. 'What happened? Oh, I shouldn't have left her.' Penny walked quickly to the kitchen, Simon and Helen, hot on her heels, then stopped in the doorway. 'Who the hell are you?'

A young woman with vibrant curly red hair was holding Jenna who was wearing only a nappy and had her fingers wrapped in the woman's hair, gently pulling the curls and smiling.

Ella smiled at Penny. 'Hello.' Then she looked down at Jenna and said, 'Your mummy's home.'

'Too bloody right I'm home! Give her to me. Why isn't she dressed? She's getting cold.'

'Oh, goodness, what's happened?' Simon tried to put a soothing hand on her arm as they became aware of another person in the room: a very handsome man. He stepped towards her, holding out his right hand. 'Dr Adam Beauchamp, Mrs Canter. I'm the new doctor at Trevay surgery. I start in a couple of days. How do you do?' Penny ignored his hand and took Jenna from the redhead.

Simon moved forward to clasp Dr Adam Beauchamp's hand in his wife's stead, then Adam politely continued, 'Your daughter has a virus and got a bit overheated. She had a little convulsion.'

'*What?*' Penny was aghast. She covered Jenna's pale face in kisses then held her close to her chest. Her plaster cast was awkward and Jenna began to cry. The redhead came forward again. 'That must hurt your arm. Shall I take her while you talk to Adam?'

Penny asserted her maternal dominance. 'No, thank you.' Simon pulled a chair out from the table. 'Darling, come and sit down. Helen, would you be kind enough to make some tea?' He turned to Adam. 'Dr Beauchamp, thank you so much for being here. What happened?'

Adam was calm and clear. 'Sometimes a child's temperature can get so high that the only way the body can cope is to shut down. It's called a febrile convulsion. It's unlikely, but not certain, that it may happen again, but Jenna is doing fine.' He spoke to Penny. 'She needs to be kept as cool as possible until her temperature is normal and steady. That's why we undressed her. Helen did all the right things and I've checked Jenna over, but you must make an appointment with your doctor tomorrow. In the meantime, keep up the fluids and keep her cool. Ella has some experience of looking after children and if you'd like her to stay tonight she has told me she'd be happy to.'

'I would,' nodded Ella.

'They've both been amazing.' Helen hugged Ella. 'I don't know what I'd have done without them. It was all a little bit frightening.'

Simon went to Helen and hugged her. 'You've been so kind. Thank God you were here.' He stepped towards Ella and took her hand. 'And thank you too. It must have been very worrying.'

Penny was glowering at Helen. 'Why didn't you phone me immediately and let me know?'

Helen was not surprised by the question. 'Because Adam is a doctor and I took Jenna straight to him, and because there was nothing you could do other than fret, and I didn't want Simon to drive with that anxiety.'

'Penny, I think it would be a very good idea for Ella to stay,' said Simon. 'Helen can get some sleep and so can you and Jenna. It's what we all need . . .'

Penny was stony-faced. 'I'm perfectly capable of looking after my own child. I *am* her mother.'

Adam stepped in. 'You are quite right, Mrs Canter. Mums are the best tonic a baby can have, but I am certain Jenna will sleep for a good few hours now and I recommend that, with that sore arm,' he gestured to the plaster cast, 'you must get some sleep too and then you'll both be fresh in the morning. Doctor's orders.' Before Penny could disagree he added, 'How is your arm? I have something to help the pain if you'd like.'

Penny clutched Jenna and thought for a moment. Her arm was hurting and she was exhausted. 'OK,' she said. 'Thank you. But it's only for one night.'

'Absolutely,' said Ella gently.

12

Penny woke early, feeling surprisingly refreshed. Usually her daughter had woken her by now but perhaps she was still asleep, exhausted by yesterday's activities. Penny decided to leave Simon sleeping; the poor man had driven for hours yesterday. She slipped on her dressing gown and crept into Jenna's room, anticipating the joy of seeing her cheeky face and smelling her uniquely wonderful scent.

The cot was empty.

Penny's heart skipped a beat. She ran downstairs to find the bloody redhead in the kitchen, in *her* chair, giving a happy Jenna a bottle.

Ella looked up and smiled. 'Good morning. I didn't want to disturb you when Jenna woke. You needed your sleep. How's your arm?'

'My arm is fine,' Penny said tartly. 'May I have Jenna, please?'

'Of course.' Ella stood and neatly put Jenna into Penny's arms and Penny made a point of settling herself in *her* chair. She examined Jenna's face. The redness and heat had faded and she grinned at her mother in recognition whilst clamping the bottle teat between her little teeth.

'She slept well,' said Ella, busying herself at the sink with last night's tea mugs.

Penny tried to be nice. 'You must be tired. Did you stay awake all night?'

'I dozed a bit in the nursing chair. She's a beautiful little girl.'

'Yes, she is.' Penny softened a little more. 'I'm so sorry, I never got your name last night.'

'Oh, it's Ella.'

'And what are you doing in Pendruggan, Ella?'

Ella told her about last night's dinner party at Marguerite Cottage.

'Did Dr Adam say something about you having some childcare experience?'

'Yes, a little. Nannying here and there. I enjoyed it.'

'But you don't nanny now?'

'No.'

Penny gave an inward sigh of relief that the redheaded beauty wasn't looking for a job. 'So what do you do now?'

'I'm at a bit of a crossroads, really. I'm a trained illustrator but I have yet to find someone who wants me to illustrate their books. I'm only here for a short while for family reasons. But I'd much rather stay here.'

Penny grew alarmed. 'Here? In the vicarage?'

'No, no, I mean in Cornwall.'

'But what would you do in Cornwall?' asked Penny.

'Well, here's the thing. Adam offered me a job last night. As a receptionist.'

'At Trevay surgery? Can he do that before he's even started?'

'It would be separate from his NHS practice. He is an acupuncturist, counsellor, stuff like that, and he wants to open an alternative medicine clinic in his back garden.'

Penny remembered the outbuilding newly built in

Marguerite's back garden. 'Oh yes. I suppose it would be perfect.'

'But . . .' Ella blew out her cheeks, 'there's a lot to think about before I say yes.'

Penny wanted her gone. 'You're too tired to make any decisions at the moment. Let me book you a taxi and get you back to Trevay.'

Later that morning Jenna was given the all-clear by the popular Dr Rachel at Trevay surgery. Motherly and sympathetic, she had looked after Penny during her pregnancy, and now she smiled reassuringly as both Penny and Simon looked at her anxiously.

'Jenna definitely has signs of an ear infection which can cause a *lot* of pain and very high fever. I'll give you some penicillin. If you're still worried at the end of the course, do come back.'

Her printer rattled into life and Dr Rachel handed Penny the prescription.

'Now.' Dr Rachel settled into her chair, her hands folded in her lap. 'How are *you?*'

'I feel awful not being there for Jenna when she was so ill.'

'Maternal guilt is painful but very normal. At least your friend was there.'

Simon chipped in, 'Helen was very quick thinking and ran over to our next-door neighbour who I think is to be your new colleague here. Dr Adam Beauchamp?'

Dr Rachel smiled. 'We can't wait for him to start. Apart from coming with excellent references, he's very handsome.'

'Yes,' agreed Penny before seeing Simon's crestfallen face. 'Not my type at all, but he was very good to Jenna and he gave me something for the pain in my wrist too.'

'I'm glad. But what's going on with you? I have the hospital report about your overdose here.'

Penny coloured and looked at her hands. 'It was a mistake. Stupid. I'm embarrassed now.'

'Have you been overdoing things?'

'No.'

'Well,' said Simon, 'I think you have a bit.'

'I'm fine,' said Penny.

Dr Rachel looked from Simon to Penny. 'How are you sleeping?'

'All right. As much as you can expect with a teething baby,' Penny replied with a light smile.

'You look as if you've lost a bit of weight.'

'It's the breast-feeding.'

'How's work?' Dr Rachel smiled. 'When will we see another series of Mr Tibbs?'

Penny could hold her emotions in check no longer and burst into tears. She told Dr Rachel all about the death of her mother, her sister's threats to visit, her meeting with the misogynistic Jack Bradbury and her failings as a television producer and as a mother.

After forty-five minutes and many tissues, Penny finally left the surgery with Jenna held close and Simon's protective arm around her shoulders. He walked them over to one of their favourite cafés, The Fo'c'sle overlooking Trevay harbour. He found a table tucked away from prying eyes. Penny was in no state to be chatty. She felt numb. Dr Rachel wanted to see her again, tomorrow, for a double appointment without Simon or Jenna, and her wrist was hurting. She was tired, but above all she was scared of what was happening to her. *Keep going, Penny*, her mind told her, but for the first time in her life she was ready to acknowledge to herself that she couldn't.

Simon ordered a latte for Penny and a double espresso for himself.

When the waiter had gone he took Penny's hand. 'Why didn't you tell me last night about your meeting with Jack? We were in the car together for three hours and you said nothing, just slept.'

She shrugged, rocking Jenna back and forth, to comfort herself as much as Jenna.

He sighed. 'You know, breaking your wrist might just be God's way of slowing you down a bit.'

Penny raised her eyes to her husband and said witheringly, 'That's shit and you know it.'

The waiter arrived with their drinks bringing a welcome hiatus. Penny stirred her latte rhythmically.

Simon tried again. 'You are a wonderful wife and mother and highly talented at your job.'

Penny snorted.

'But you are not Superwoman.'

'Funny that,' she said sarcastically, sipping her coffee.

'Darling, if you would just get a little help with Jenna, I think—'

She banged her cup down on its china saucer. '*I do not need anyone's help with my daughter!*' She turned her blazing eyes to him and hissed, 'I'm a failure at work, a failure as a daughter, a failure as a sister, a failure as a wife but I will NOT fail my daughter.'

'You have failed no one, Penny. But I am worried about you getting so tired and, frankly, difficult to live with.'

'Ha!' Penny said derisively. 'Take the plank out of your own eye before you take the splinter from mine.'

*

As soon as they got back home, in silence all the way, Penny took Jenna upstairs for a nap. She settled herself on the nursing chair, unbuttoned her blouse and offered her nipple to Jenna for the first time in a week. Jenna refused it. She tried again. She tried until Jenna became upset. Doing up her blouse she went downstairs and made a bottle of formula. Jenna settled to it straight away.

Penny had never felt such grief. Her breasts were swollen with unwanted milk and her heart was full of failure. She settled Jenna in her cot and went downstairs to her office.

At her desk she lifted the lid of her laptop and booted it up. A stream of messages came through, smeary through her tears. She put her elbows on the desk, her head in her hands and sobbed. What was happening to her? Where had her joy for life and living gone? What was the point of Penny Leighton?

She heard the house phone ringing in the hall and Simon's feet walking towards it. She heard him answer, 'Pendruggan vicarage, Simon Canter speaking.'

She sat still and quiet as a mouse. Please God, in whom I don't believe, please don't let it be for me. She listened, straining her ears.

'I see. Yes, it has been a terrible shock for Penny . . . and you too, of course . . . She's not here at the moment . . .'

Penny sent another silent prayer of thanks for Simon's white lie.

'Can I take a message? . . . Well, let me take your number . . . Yes, yes, got it . . . I'll talk to her . . . Well, that would be a good idea. Our address is The Vicarage, Pendruggan, Near Trevay, Cornwall . . . Yes, I'll be sure to tell her . . . OK, Suzie, goodbye.'

Penny was rigid with fear. Suzie? Her sister, Suzie?

What did she want? Penny buried her head in her arms, her hands clamped over her ears. Go away. Go away.

There was a knock at the door and Simon came in. She knew it was him and she pictured him standing looking at her with pity.

'Yes?' she said into her arms.

'That was your sister.'

'And?'

'She's going to write to you, explaining about your mother. She wondered why you hadn't replied to her email. She would like to come here to talk to you.'

'No!' came the muffled but clear reply.

'That's what I thought. She wanted to speak to you but I told her you were out.'

'Thank you.'

Simon looked at the huddled body of his beloved wife and, for one of the few times in his life, didn't know what to do. 'Can I get you anything?'

'No.'

'Call me if you need anything.'

'Yes.'

Left alone, Penny's thoughts turned to her father. He had been on his own when he had had the final heart attack and died, waiting in his car for a couple who wanted to view a house. She'd gone to school and never seen him again.

She was the last child waiting in the playground, no one to pick her up.

A teacher took her to the school office and the secretary rang her home.

No answer.

Penny settled to some colouring and waited while the

school secretary finished off typing the day's letters. 'We'll try again in ten minutes,' she said, wearing a reassuring smile.

Moments later the phone rang. 'Hello, Sunbury School for Girls.' Penny looked up and saw the secretary flick a worried look towards her then back to her notepad. 'I see.' She began to drum her biro on the paper. 'Yes, she's here. I can drop her off. No trouble at all. What shall I say? . . . We are on our way.'

Penny, who'd stopped her colouring to listen, said, 'Is it Daddy?'

For the second time in her short life, she was told she would have to be brave.

Penny turned her face into her arm and wept hot tears for the father she'd lost so very long ago.

13

Adam fiddled with the key in the lock of the summer house. 'Are you sure this is the right key?' he asked Kit.

'Try it the other way.'

'I have, but the blasted door won't open.'

'Try pulling instead of pushing,' answered Kit laconically.

Adam pulled and the door opened smoothly on well-oiled hinges. 'Stop smirking,' ordered Adam.

'Just helping my little cousin, that's all,' smirked Kit.

Adam stepped into the wooden cabin and looked around. They were standing in a bright and airy space with windows and glass doors to three sides. It was painted in cream with a chequerboard tiled floor.

'Perfect,' breathed Adam. 'The desk over there, seating for waiting clients here, coffee table and magazines right there . . .'

Kit was checking the power sockets. 'There's a point here for the computer and phone.'

Adam was already opening a door on the one blank wall. 'And here's my consulting room.'

The entire rear wall was windowed and had French doors out onto the back garden with a view to the church-yard and the fields beyond leading down to Shellsand

Bay. 'It's even better than I thought.' Adam rubbed his hands together gleefully.

'I nearly had it for my studio,' said Kit, knowing full well that once Adam had seen it there would be no chance of that.

'Dear boy!' exclaimed Adam. 'You still could, but it would be a waste, don't you think? And you do have that lovely room upstairs with the new roof lights that Coughing Kevin put in, hm?'

'*Gasping Bob*. Yes.'

'Whatever.' Adam found another small door leading into a kitchenette. 'I can see the lovely Ella in here, brewing my coffee just the way I like.' He was gleeful.

Kit scratched his ear. 'She's too good for you.'

'Nonsense.' Adam stopped opening kitchen cupboards and looked at his cousin. 'Oh, I see. You want her for yourself?'

Kit changed the subject. 'You chanced your arm telling her about this place before you'd even seen it for yourself.'

Adam was pleased. 'She'll be very happy here.'

Kit shook his head at Adam's confidence. 'She might not take the job.'

'She will, old boy. She will.'

*

ELLA

In Trevay, Ella woke from a deep and satisfying sleep. She'd got back from the vicarage just as the other B & B guests were settling to breakfast. 'Had a good night?' asked the landlady with a whiff of disapproval. 'Want a fry-up to soak up the alcohol?'

'Just need some sleep,' she'd smiled, and moved swiftly up the stairs and into bed. Now she sat up and stretched and could see the familiar childhood view from the window. Seagulls were cocking their beady eyes at anything that might mean food; the tide was high and the boats in the harbour were swinging gently on their moorings. She checked the time. It was after lunch and her tummy was rumbling.

'Well, Granny,' she said, 'what are you up to? Should I take Dr Adam's job, which means I could be living back here and able to paint to my heart's content? Or do I go back to London and find a boring but well-paid job and forget all about my painting and books?'

Her phone beeped from her bedside table. She jumped. 'Blimey, Granny, I didn't know you had a mobile up there.' She answered it. It was Henry. 'Hey, Ell's Bells, how's it going?' he chirped.

She told him all about dinner with Adam and Kit, the emergency babysitting for Jenna and the job Adam had offered her.

'What should I do?' she beseeched. 'Boring London job, or the Cornish air and fun?'

Henry laughed. 'Well, put it like that and it's clear! Boring London job every time.'

'You're no help at all.'

'Can you live on what the doctor might pay you?'

'I don't know.'

'Where will you stay?'

'Um, hadn't thought about that.'

'Ah well,' said Henry breezily, 'all those small things like sleeping and eating will sort themselves out. Go for it.'

'Oh Henry, it's wonderful to be back here. Can you come down?'

He looked at the report he was writing, detailing a huge, and hugely boring but lucrative, industrial site in north London. 'Maybe. But not for a while.'

'Well, soon as possible, please. I want you to meet Adam he's really lovely. Funny and clever and—'

'You fancy him.'

'Shut up!'

'Yes, you do.'

'I can look, can't I?'

'Yes, but I need to give him the once-over first.'

She flopped back onto her pillow. 'I'm so happy. I can't believe so much can change in a few days.'

'Anything from the solicitor yet?'

'No. I'll phone tomorrow to see how he is.'

'Don't decide anything until you know what he's going to tell us.'

*

Adam and Kit were having a late lunch in the kitchen when the phone rang.

Kit got up to answer it. 'Hello? Yes, he's right here. Who's calling? Just a moment.'

He passed the phone to Adam. 'It's the Trevay surgery for you.'

Adam dabbed the corners of his mouth with a piece of kitchen towel and took the phone. 'Hello?'

Kit sat back to his lunch of cheese and warm baguette while he waited for Adam to return.

'What did they want?' he asked.

'They want me to go in this afternoon. Two docs are off – one's got shingles, the other some personal crisis.'

'You OK with that?'

'Fine, but it means that you and Ella will have to get the garden clinic fitted out together without my expert eye to help.'

Kit raised his eyebrows. '*If* she takes the job.'

'She will.'

The phone rang again. 'That'll be her,' joked Adam helping himself to a tomato. 'Answer it.'

Kit did as he was asked. 'Hello.'

'Hi, It's Ella. Is that Kit?'

'Hi, Ella.' Kit felt something jump in his chest. 'How are you?'

'Fine. Thank you for a lovely dinner last night.'

'You're not too tired after your paediatric nurse duties?'

'No. I slept like a baby myself. Can I speak to Adam please?'

Kit's smile slipped a little. 'Oh yes. Of course, hang on.'

Kit passed the phone back to Adam. 'It's Ella, for you.'

He followed Adam as he took the call. 'Hi Ella, have you had a chance to think about . . . oh, yes, I quite understand. That's very sensible . . . Of course. By the way, a bit cheeky of me to ask, but what are you doing this afternoon?'

*

A day later, after another bad night's sleep, Penny was glad to get up. Her appointment with Dr Rachel was at ten twenty so she had to get a move on to get herself and Jenna ready for the day. Helen was coming over at nine forty-five to babysit because Simon had a funeral to conduct and Penny was feeling resentful. How could he put a dead person, someone whose problems were behind them, ahead of her, his living, breathing wife who was quietly going insane. 'Oh stop it!' she said loudly enough to wake Simon.

'Stop what, darling?' His voice was muted with sleep.

She rubbed her temples furiously. 'This horrible inner dialogue I have going all the time. I'm so angry and horrible and I want it to *stop*.'

Simon sat up and took her in his arms. 'Dr Rachel will help you, I'm sure she will.'

Penny pressed herself against him and hugged him. 'I'm so horrible to you. I love you so much and I just wish I could stop these horrible feelings. And it's only just over two weeks to Christmas and I haven't done a thing.'

'You don't need to, my love.'

'Yes, I do. There's the shopping, the cards, the decorations, the lunch—'

'I promised I would help and I will.' He kissed her head. 'You know, we don't really need to do anything. It's only the three of us.'

She relaxed a bit. 'You wouldn't mind?'

'I think it would be lovely. You, me and Jenna. A log fire. No one to worry about. Eat what we want, when we want. Afternoon naps.'

'That sounds amazing.'

'Not at all.'

'Thank you.'

'My best gift would be to see Jenna and you at the Nativity service. It'll be all by candlelight and very special.' He squeezed her. 'Deal?'

'Deal.'

After breakfast and when Simon had left the house, Penny was getting ready for the doctor with Jenna sitting on the carpet playing with her hairbrush and a set of plastic cups. 'Mumumumum,' she said, looking at Penny.

'What, darling?'

She made as if to reach out to her daughter but before she could move, Jenna struggled to her feet and tottered a couple of steps towards Penny before plopping back on her bottom. 'Oh my God! You walked!' gasped Penny falling to her knees. 'You walked!'

Jenna started to giggle and so did Penny as she hugged her blessed daughter to her. 'Do it again!'

'More?' asked Jenna.

'Yes. More.'

Jenna stood and got her balance. She took four more steps before tipping over and shrieking with laughter.

Penny felt a crack of sunshine almost reach her soul. She took Jenna in her arms and together mother and daughter lay on the carpet in pure love and happiness.

Helen had let herself in through the back door and saw the breakfast things still on the table. She knew Penny couldn't do much with her arm in plaster, so she began to load the dishwasher. Job done she walked into the hall and called up the stairs, 'Penny?'

'Helen!' cried Penny excitedly, 'Jenna has something to show you.'

Helen walked up the stairs, noticing the unvacuumed carpet. She made a note to do it later when Jenna was sleeping.

'Come in to my room,' called Penny.

Helen pushed the bedroom door open and saw a roughly made bed, two cups of cold tea on the bedside tables, and a pile of clothes that hadn't made it to the washing machine yet.

Amongst the chaos sat Penny, her tired face glowing. 'Watch this. Jenna, up you get. Show Auntie Helen what you can do.'

Jenna concentrated and staggered to her feet again and walked towards Helen.

Helen grinned and clapped her hands. 'You clever girl! When did you start this?'

Penny got to her feet. 'Just two minutes ago.' Penny hugged Helen. 'Isn't she clever?'

'Very clever. Now, how about I get Jenna washed and dressed while you finish getting ready for the doc?'

'What? Oh shit, yes. Taxi's coming at ten.' She waved her plaster cast. 'I haven't done the kitchen yet.'

'I'll do it.'

'Or put the laundry in.'

'*I'll* do it. Just get ready.'

With the plaster cast on, Penny hadn't been able to wash her hair. But she'd managed an awkward shower and a little blusher. She scrunched her hair into an untidy bun and hid her eyes with large sunglasses. Dr Rachel would understand.

Penny's taxi grumbled its way up the hill towards Trevay, through the village and down along the harbour side past the fish market to the doctor's. The surgery's small car park was full and the cabby had to park a short walk away. Penny looked at her watch. One minute to get there. She could feel sweat prickling her scalp and her armpits. Had she remembered to put deodorant on after the shower? She'd just have to keep her arms clamped to her sides.

'I'll be waiting 'ere for 'ee, Mrs Canter?' said the driver. 'Yes please.'

She raced down the street and into reception and stood breathing heavily at the desk.

'Morning, Mrs Canter,' said the nice receptionist. 'I'm afraid Dr Rachel isn't in today. A family problem.'

Penny's shoulders slumped. 'Oh no.'

'Yes, but don't worry, our new doctor is taking her surgery today. Take a seat.'

Penny slumped into the uncomfortable plastic chair and wondered whether to cancel today and wait for Dr Rachel. She really didn't want to be fobbed off by a new doctor and certainly didn't have the energy to retell her medical history.

'Mrs Canter?' A man's voice, deep and well-spoken, called from the corridor to the consulting rooms. She looked up. It was Adam. Looking even more handsome than he had at the house the other night. 'Do come with me,' he said, stepping aside and opening his hand towards his room where she sat in front of his desk.

'How is Jenna?' he asked.

'Better. Thank you for all you did the other night. She took her first steps this morning.'

'Did she? That's wonderful.' He looked at his computer screen where she presumed Dr Rachel had written her notes. 'Now, how can I help you?'

'I think I'm a bit tired. A bit of trouble with work and stuff.'

'What trouble is that?'

'I make a television programme. The *Mr Tibbs Mysteries?*'

'My mother loves it.'

Penny smiled weakly. 'Thanks. I don't think my mother ever saw it.'

'Oh?'

'She died. Recently. I hadn't seen her for a long time.'

He nodded. 'Go on.'

'Well, the woman who writes Mr Tibbs has decided not to write any more stories, so I can't make any more episodes which means I don't have any work and my company is going to go down the Swanee.'

'And how old is little Jenna?'

'She's one and wonderful, she just doesn't sleep.'

'And how are you coping?'

Penny's voice started to wobble. 'Fine, fine. I'm just tired.'

'Hmm.' He turned to the computer screen once more and scrolled through some more notes. 'Tell me, do you find as much joy in life as you used to?'

'Not really.'

'Do you look forward to things as much as you used to?'

'I don't want to do anything.'

'I see from your notes that you had a little trouble with some pills recently.'

She nodded dumbly, watching the tears now splash onto her gripped hands.

She heard his chair creak as he rolled it towards her and took one of her hands. 'Reading Dr Rachel's notes I can see she's concerned for you. She thinks, and I agree with her, that you have a lot on your plate at the moment. Work worries, the loss of a parent; all very difficult things to process. Add to that the responsibility of a young child . . . Anybody would be overwhelmed.'

Penny nodded again, wiping her nose with the back of her hand. 'I feel I'm going mad.'

He rolled his chair back to the desk. 'I can assure you, you are not mad, but you *are* suffering from depression.'

Penny's heart sank further. 'Depression?'

'Yes. Coinciding with Jenna's birth it can be called postnatal depression, but in my experience depression is depression whatever has triggered it.'

She sat rigid, intensely aware of the noise of her own blood buzzing in her ears. 'Oh *bugger.*'

14

As the taxi wove its way slowly back along the quay, Penny quietly watched out of the window. The ships bobbed effortlessly in the harbour, the gulls chuckled and swooped against the stiff sea breeze, and Penny pondered over what a difference half an hour can make to a life. She'd left the house hoping to have a womanly conversation with Dr Rachel about feeling a bit tired and a bit less able to cope than usual, maybe given a prescription for a tonic or something, and was returning with a huge label attached to her. Depressed. A depressive. What does *that* mean? Someone who gives depression to those around them?

How did you tell people you were depressed? It wasn't as dramatic as saying, 'By the way, I have an exotic tropical disease that requires me to do exactly what I like.' People would be sympathetic to that. But this? What would she say? 'Oh, hi. By the way, I'm depressed?' What had she to be depressed about? She had everything. Helen had drummed that into her. But then . . . why did she feel so bleak.

She paid the taxi driver and plastered on her biggest Penny Leighton smile. 'Hi, I'm home!' she sang as she closed the front door behind her. She could hear the dishwasher churning so she walked down the long hallway to the kitchen. The winter sun was pouring through the big sash windows and the air smelt of bleach and pine. Helen was mopping the floor.

'Bloody hell, Pen! When did you last clean this floor?' she laughed. 'I found last year's Christmas-tree needles behind the bin.' Penny was irritated. It was *her* kitchen and if she had Christmas-tree needles on the floor, so what? 'Where have you put my magazines?' she asked peevishly.

Helen stopped mopping and looked up. 'Sorry. I thought they were for recycling.'

'There were articles in them I wanted to read.'

'Sorry. They were months old so I—' Penny had taken her sunglasses off and Helen could see she'd been crying. She put the mop down. 'Pen? What's happened?'

'I need a glass of wine,' said Penny. 'And don't lecture me.' She went to the fridge and poured herself a large glass and sat down.

Helen took a seat next to her and put her arm around the bony shoulders of her best friend. 'Talk to me,' she said.

Simon returned from the funeral full of beans and sherry. It had been a true celebration of the deceased's life. Uplifting, thoughtful, amusing and emotional. Even spiritual, which was increasingly rare these days. Just the sort of funeral Simon would want for himself. One or two of the mourners had even congratulated him on his eulogy. Now, as he walked from the wake and across the village green towards the vicarage, his cassock rippling in the light breeze, he thanked God for his calling and for the beautiful day ahead.

As soon as he stepped into the kitchen he grew tense.

An empty bottle of wine with an empty wine glass sitting next to it stood on the table.

'Penny?' he called out. 'Are you OK, darling?'

He heard footsteps coming down the stairs but it was Helen who appeared.

'Is she all right?' he asked, anxiety coursing through him.

'She's in bed. A bit pissed. Simon, we have a problem.'

Penny was in free fall. She'd slept for a while then woken to the sounds of movement downstairs. She lifted her head from the pillow in order to hear more clearly. Helen must have gone home and Simon was talking to Jenna.

'Let's go down to the beach and find some shells, shall we? You can show me how well you're walking.'

'Mumma?'

'Mummy's in bed having a little sleep.'

'Mumma?' Jenna asked more insistently.

'Mummy will join us later, when she wakes up.'

Penny heard the front door open and close quietly behind them.

Silence.

So, this was a depressed woman's life? Lying in bed. Family tiptoeing with hushed voices, left on her own with only her memories.

After her father had died, Suzie and she didn't go to the funeral. In those days children didn't. Well, that's what her mother told them. She didn't even know when it was until the day the house filled with flowers and her mother was in black with a confetti of white tissues around her.

Her father's friends were kind and one in particular, Patrick, a widower himself, would often take them out for drives and picnics. They even went on holiday with him to Brighton, which Penny remembered as being fun, but whatever he wanted from her mother she wasn't prepared to give.

The day the house was sold and they downsized to a modern housing estate on the outskirts of town was one Penny wished she could forget. Her mother was incapable of doing anything. She sat in the kitchen, removal men working around her, berating Mike for his sudden death.

It was left to a nine-year-old Penny to make tea and direct which pieces of furniture were coming with them and which were going to auction. A colour-coding system was in place. Green stickers for the new house, red to auction. She tried to stop her father's armchair from going to auction but her mother was adamant. 'Why would I want to keep that old thing? I'd burn it if I could.'

At the end of that day, sitting amongst the boxes in their new house, Penny wondered if anything of her father's had survived . . .

She pulled herself back from the memory. *Keep going, Penny.*

Her head was throbbing a little and her mouth was dry. She made a decision. No more drinking. No more self-pity. She had to think about Jenna and Simon.

She got herself dressed, brushed her hair, and cleaned her teeth. She was going to the beach to find her family and tell them how much she loved them.

She could see them at the water's edge, both wrapped in scarves and anoraks against the December nip. Simon was holding Jenna by the tummy and pretending to dip her wellies into each oncoming wave. The wind was blowing their laughter towards her. Penny began to run and breathlessly called their names.

'Mumma!' said Jenna, holding out her arms.

'Simon, let her go. She can walk.'

Simon beamed when he saw Penny and kissed her cheek as soon as she was close enough. 'I know. Helen told me.'

Penny was disappointed. 'I was keeping that as a surprise.'

'Darling, she didn't mean to spoil things, she was just as excited as you are – as I am.'

'She was cleaning the house today. Made a few snide comments about my housekeeping skills.'

'She tidied the kitchen, that's all.'

'Well, it pissed me off a bit. I know it shouldn't and I'm glad she did it really.'

Simon bent down and took Jenna's mittened hand. 'How was the doctor?' he asked.

'Fine.'

'What did he say?'

Penny's head dropped. 'Ah. So you know it wasn't Dr Rachel, then? Helen told you everything, did she?'

Simon picked up Jenna and settled her on his hip. 'Yes, she did. Want to talk about it?'

'Did you and Helen talk about me?'

Simon felt his heart twist. 'Stop it, Penny. Please stop it. We spoke about you because we love you, not because we're conspiring against you, for goodness' sake.' He stared at her, daring her to carry on. She looked away.

'Right,' he said, 'we are going home. We are giving our daughter some dinner, a bath, a story, and then she's going to bed. After that, we shall talk about you. OK?'

So while Penny put Jenna to bed, Simon knocked up a mushroom omelette for them both and brewed a pot of tea. No wine.

Penny came down the stairs and watched him as he washed a salad and made up a French dressing. She went towards him, put her arms round his waist and placed her cheek on his back. 'I love you so much,' she said.

'Well, that's a start,' he replied.

She let go of him as he slid the huge omelette onto the serving plate surrounded by salad. 'Get this down you and tell me all about it.'

'Adam has diagnosed me with postnatal depression brought on by all this stuff that's happened. Mum. Work. Blah blah. And he's given me a prescription for antidepressants and a course of acupuncture, which he's going to give me.'

Simon listened carefully. 'Have you got the pills yet?'

'No. I was going to get them this afternoon but I had a glass of wine and I forgot that I couldn't drive the car, so I had another glass and . . . you know the rest,' she finished limply.

'And do you want to take the pills?'

'I asked him all about them and he said they were like taking a little bridge over troubled water. Just for a few months.'

'I don't want you spaced out all day.'

'They aren't tranquillizers, Simon. Adam said they won't space me out. They'll just help get me back to me again. It's rebalancing the chemicals in my brain or something.'

'Are they addictive?'

'I don't think so. He's going to keep reviewing me to

make sure I don't have any side effects and if I do we'll think again.'

Simon thought for a moment. 'I don't want you taking them. You just need to focus on the good and positive things in your life and we'll get through this.'

Penny was amazed. 'You mean pull myself together? Is that it?'

'It's just that . . .' Simon was trying to pick his words carefully. 'Is it really depression or are you just a bit stressed at the moment? How about a little holiday?' He looked at her beseechingly.

Penny narrowed her eyes. 'Are you embarrassed that your wife has a mental illness? Are you? Because *I'm* not and I wouldn't be if the boot were on the other foot.'

'Stop being so dramatic. You haven't got a mental illness.'

She stood up and walked over to Simon, her hands resting gently on his shoulders. 'Yes, my love, I have. Although I'd prefer to call it an emotional illness. I'm not mad in the "put her in a straight jacket" sense. Taking the pills will hopefully help me get better. Oh, and maybe a little sympathy and understanding from my husband would help. Who knows?'

Simon ran his slender hands over his bald head. 'Penny, you're a strong woman. A couple of weeks of early nights, walks on the beach, no alcohol . . . you'll be fine.'

Penny looked at him with disbelief. 'Thank you, vicar. Is that your advice to all your parishioners? Or just for your wife?'

15

Kit had picked up Ella and was driving her over to a huge second-hand furniture warehouse in St Austell. Adam had given them a list and a budget.

'I don't want any old tat,' he'd ordered. 'The new clinic needs a clean medical feel to it, but with a contemporary twist and the traditional feel of Cornwall too.'

Ella had laughed when Kit relayed this.

'In other words, he hasn't a clue,' she giggled.

'Precisely,' smiled Kit, stealing a glance at her. He loved to see her laugh and this morning her hair was like burnished copper in the sunshine. God, he fancied her.

'Does Adam have a girlfriend? Or ex-wife? Or anything?' she asked in a too-casual way. Kit knew the signs and felt his hopes fade. 'No. No. No one special. Never been married.'

'Golly. But he's so handsome and charming there must be plenty of women dancing around him?' Ella probed.

Kit didn't know how to reply. If he confirmed that his cousin was a womanizing roué with a bad case of commitment phobia he'd sound heartless, and possibly jealous. If he said that women didn't flock round Adam, he'd be a liar. He dodged the whole thing. 'We Beauchamps are known for our charm and good looks you know.' And he leant forward to turn the radio on. Carly Simon was singing 'You're So Vain'. He laughed, and accelerated down the lanes towards St Austell.

The warehouse was huge. The space was divided up into sections: bathroom, kitchen, dining room, etc. They headed for Living Space.

Kit opened his arms to take in the jumble of furniture in front of them. 'What would the number-one employee of Dr Adam's Garden Clinic like in her reception area?'

Ella gazed around and over the various leather sofas, velour recliners and hard-backed chairs until she found what she was looking for.

'Look.' She pointed. 'See that pair of two-seater sofas? In the mulberry linen?'

Kit looked. 'With the cream piping and cushions?'

'Yep. We'll have those.'

'Good spot.' Kit looked at his list and ticked them off. 'Now we need a desk for you.'

Ella was already on it. 'There. The simple one.'

'Pine?'

'Yeah, but I'll paint it white and sand it a bit to look shabby chic. Next?'

Ella was unlike any woman Kit had ever shopped with before. She knew what she was looking for and made up her mind quickly. They gathered together a coffee table decoupaged in old copies of *Cornwall Life,* a Perspex desk for Adam, two ergonomic office chairs that Ella said she'd re-cover, two pretty rugs and a couple of lamps.

Kit paid the bill and arranged delivery. 'Coffee?' he said.

Ella tucked her arm under his. 'Deffo. Then we'll look for curtains, candles, towels, kettle, mugs . . .'

*

Kit was enjoying his day with Ella and wasn't looking forward to it coming to an end but his car was bulging with all the extras they'd picked up and his shopping list was done.

Ella yawned as she got into the car. 'It's amazing how exhausting spending other people's money is.' She stretched her arms against the ceiling of the car. 'Do you think Adam will like the Tibetan Bell?'

'Why wouldn't he? What did the woman say? "A bronze repro of an eleventh-century treasure to resonate with the spirit and soul thereby releasing the negative drama accumulated from life within the twenty-first century?" He'll love it.'

She pinched his elbow.

'Ow!'

'Serves you right. You'll see. Sound therapy is very big now and will add an extra dimension to the treatments Adam offers.'

'You're sounding like the mad witch in the shop. I think she'd been inhaling too many joss sticks.'

Ella giggled beguilingly. 'She was a bit eccentric but sweet.'

Kit spotted his chance while she was so relaxed. 'Fancy a spot of lunch before we head back to Trevay?'

'God, yes. I'm starving.'

'There's a place in Fowey I've heard good things about. Fancy that?'

They found the pub, overlooking the water, and went in. They were instantly assaulted by gaudy Christmas decorations, piped carols and a strong aroma of mulled wine.

'Looks like Christmas has arrived,' said Kit sardonically.

'Can I 'elp you?' asked the pleasant barmaid.

Kit gave her their drinks order and asked to see a menu.

'Blackboard's up there with today's specials.'

The menu offered home-made game stew, roast pheasant, fish pie or traditional Christmas lunch.

'Shall we go mad and have the roast turkey with all the trimmings?' asked Kit.

'It would be rude not to,' laughed Ella.

They found themselves an alcove table with a view of the harbour and settled in.

'This is nice,' said Ella. 'Bet they do a good trade with the holidaymakers.'

Kit chuckled. 'There've been a few holiday romances conducted in here, I'm sure.'

Ella sipped her mulled wine and asked innocently, 'Do you have a girlfriend?'

'Not at the moment, no.'

'Have you left some poor girl heartbroken in Surrey.'

He hesitated before saying, 'More like the other way around.'

Ella was all sympathy. 'Oh poor you. Did you get badly hurt?'

'It was a bit tricky for a while.' He drank his beer and said, 'What about you? You must have your pick of men.'

She pulled at one of her ringlets, curling it around her finger. 'Not really. I don't seem to meet any good ones, anyway. Me and Henry, my brother, we are very useful to our friends who keep setting us up at dinner parties with totally unsuitable people.'

'Oh dear,' said Kit sympathetically whilst actually being delighted. 'What sort are you looking for?'

'Someone normal. Kind. Funny. Someone who'll share

the same kind of music, films, art. He doesn't have to be rich and handsome.' She sipped her mulled wine again. 'What about you?' she asked.

He took a deep breath and blew his cheeks out. 'I'm looking for a drop-dead gorgeous woman with a spectacular bank balance and a generous nature,' said Kit seriously before laughing at her stricken face. 'I'm joking, I'm joking.' He pushed his beer mat around a small pool of spilt beer. 'I don't know. Same as you I suppose.'

'Right, well I'll look out for you and you look out for me. Deal?' she asked

'Deal,' he said.

Later, after a huge lunch, Christmas pudding and all, they walked up through the town's steep and narrow lanes to where they had left the car. It was an effort on the hill so Kit reached back and held Ella's hand, pulling her up with him. At the top they turned, panting, to look at the view over the harbour. Ella snaked a hand around his waist without thinking and said, 'Thank you for a great day. You know, I think I *will* say yes to Adam's job offer.'

'Hi honey, I'm home!' shouted Adam when he came into Marguerite Cottage that evening.

Kit was in the sitting room with a gin and tonic. 'I'm here!' he yelled.

'Good day?' asked Adam, dropping his briefcase on the carpet and loosening his tie. Celia and Terry were lolling in front of the fire and managed a small wave of a tail each.

'Really good. Ella and I got everything you wanted for the clinic and I got to take her out for lunch. She's great fun.'

'Well,' said Adam, sitting down, 'if you want her you'd better grab her quick, unless she has another boyfriend lurking somewhere.'

'She hasn't,' smiled Kit.

'Oh,' said Adam, raising his eyebrows, 'good. Got one of those for me?' He pointed at the gin and tonic. 'And I'm starving. What's for supper?'

'We are going out for dinner. The Dolphin. Helen says it's very good. In fact, she's invited us. Seven thirty. We're going to meet her man, Piran.'

'He must be very old,' sniggered Adam. 'I've been reading up on St Piran to impress the locals. He floated here from Ireland on a millstone, to prove his miraculous powers, he discovered tin, he liked a drink and he lived to be two hundred and six.'

'Well, Helen's Piran is the local historian and archaeologist. He also catches great lobster.'

'I like him already.'

Kit drove them into the Dolphin car park bang on time. 'Is Helen the one who came over with the baby the other night?' asked Adam who recalled very little about her.

'She's sweet. She's Penny Canter's best friend.'

'Oh, is she?' said Adam, thinking back to his consultation with Penny Canter that morning. There was a woman who *needed* a good friend.

A soft-top Mini drove into the car park.

'And here she is,' said Kit. Adam watched as she got out of the car. This was not what he remembered from the other night at all. That woman was make-up less, distraught and wearing shapeless jogging pants and baggy jumper. This one was tall and slender with pale skin and a smattering of freckles on her nose, her strawberry blonde hair cut into a bob whose curls tickled the nape of her neck. She was dressed simply but well, a silk sheath dress exposing her freckled shoulders and shins. Around her shoulders hung a well-cut coat.

Adam knew he'd been staring. Kit hailed her, 'Helen, you've met my cousin, Dr Adam Beauchamp. Adam, Helen Merrifield.'

Adam took her elegant hand and gave her his most devastating smile. 'Lovely to see you again.' At once he became aware of a brooding presence looming behind her.

Helen turned. 'And this is Piran Ambrose. My partner.'

Piran was giving Adam a very dark look. ''Ow do,' he said.

'Fine, thank you,' a flustered Adam replied.

'Shall we go in?' asked Kit.

They arranged themselves around a table and Adam found himself opposite Helen and next to Piran. Kit was next to Helen.

A woman in jeans, with short spiky platinum hair came out of the kitchen with menus in her hand.

She welcomed Helen and Piran with kisses. 'This is Dorrie.' Helen introduced her to Kit and Adam. 'I wouldn't be living at Gull's Cry if it weren't for her and her husband Don. They found the cottage for me, really.'

'Lovely to meet you,' said Dorrie, leaning over and shaking hands. 'You're the new doctor?'

'I am,' smiled Adam.

'How are you finding Marguerite Cottage?'

'Very nice indeed.'

'That's good. My Don will be pleased. He was the one who did the rebuild. How's the shed in the garden?'

He told her he loved it and what his plans for it were.

'You'll get lots of customers round here,' she laughed. 'All those stressed-out second-home owners, they'll pay a fortune for any of that spiritual stuff.'

Adam was affronted. 'Acupuncture and homeopathy aren't just *stuff*. They are recognized complementary therapies from thousands of years of practice. And I certainly won't be excluding the locals with my prices.'

Dorrie was unembarrassed. 'Get Queenie down there and have a look at her hips. If it works for her she'll be the best advert you could have.'

'What a good idea!' Helen beamed. 'Queenie is the oracle around here. Mind you, if she doesn't think you're any good she'll tell people that too.'

'Aye, she will that,' growled Piran who put his large paw of a hand on Adam's shoulder. 'She always speaks her mind.'

Adam wasn't sure that he liked these people. 'I'm starving,' he said as a way of changing the subject.

Dorrie unclasped the menus that she'd been holding to her chest. 'I can recommend the ribeye and the lobster's pretty good.'

'Is the lobster yours, Piran?' asked Kit. 'Helen tells me you've got a few pots down.'

'Aye. I brought six in for Dorrie this afternoon.'

'So, enough for one each,' smiled Kit.

Adam loved lobster but decided to be awkward. 'Well, I'm having the ribeye.'

Piran put his menu down and said, 'Ribeye for me too, thank you, Dorrie.' Dorrie jotted it all down on her pad and went back to the kitchen.

'What do you drink, Adam?' asked Piran with a growl. 'A gin-and-tonic man? Or do you want a pint?'

Adam heard the gauntlet go down. 'Pint, please.'

'A pint?' Kit laughed. 'You're not normally a pint man, Adam.'

'I'm thirsty.'

Piran chuckled. 'Aye. 'Tis thirsty work being a doctor, mind.' He took Kit's and Helen's orders and strode to the bar, acknowledging old friends as he went.

'Never mind him,' said Helen to Adam. 'He's the original unconstructed male. Infuriating, but a good man.'

'I'm sure,' nodded Adam. 'So, Helen, how long have you been here?'

'Gosh, years now. I love Pendruggan. So does Penny, Jenna's mum. She came down and made the village famous with her Mr Tibbs TV series, but it looks like we won't be having any more of those now.'

Penny had told Adam about her career crisis in the surgery that morning. Helen continued. 'The writer, Mavis Crewe, won't let anyone else write the stories, so Channel 7 have dropped Penny, poor girl. And she loves her work. What with that and having a baby, her mum dying and her estranged sister threatening to get in touch, she's well and truly got her plate full.'

'She'll need a good friend,' said Adam.

'Yes. And I'm trying. I cleaned her kitchen for her today. The house is an absolute mess and she doesn't see it. She used to be a neat freak but she's let it all go. And I think she's being rather difficult to live with. I feel sorry for Simon.'

'Does she have any help in the house?' asked Adam.

'No. Refuses it. She's a control freak as well as a neat freak. What she really needs is to run the house as she used to run her office: delegate everything. She needs a cleaner, a nanny and a PA. I was her PA for the first Mr Tibbs and she's a very exacting boss. More than once I wanted to tell her to shove it, but . . . you don't with friends, do you? Then she fell in love with Simon and she changed into an earth mother. The only problem is, she isn't a very good one.'

Piran arrived with a tray of drinks. 'Cheers one and all,' he said, lifting his glass then downing a good mouthful.

Adam took a sip of his pint and, to his surprise, the beer was rather good.

So was the food. The ribeye cut like butter and tasted sublime. The lobsters were plump and juicy.

Don the landlord came out and introduced himself to Adam and Kit. 'Dorrie says you're comfortable at Marguerite?'

'Very,' smiled Kit.

'Any problems, just come to me. There's nothing in that house I haven't fixed at some stage.'

'That's very kind of you,' said Adam. He was ready to go. He'd had enough of all this jollity. 'Well, it's a pleasure to meet you all and thank you for a lovely dinner, but I'm afraid we must leave. Work early, you know.' There was the time-honoured arguing about paying the bill, but Helen and Piran won. Handshakes and kisses over, Kit and Adam walked to their car.

On their way back down into Pendruggan Adam said, 'Can that lovely woman really want to be seen with that hairy ape?'

Kit gave him a sidelong glance. 'Now, don't be setting your sights on Helen Merrifield.'

'Who said anything about setting my sights? You make me sound like a big game hunter.'

'Piran would marmalize you.'

'Marmalize? *Marmalize?*' Adam tipped back his head

and roared with laughter. 'I haven't heard you say that since we were about seven.'

Kit started laughing as well. 'But that's exactly what he'd do to you!'

'Well, I'd better get down to the gym. Do you have any Lycra at home?'

They laughed all the way into Pendruggan, around the green and down the drive to Marguerite.

16

'So, how have you been this last week?' Adam was sitting behind his desk at Trevay surgery looking impossibly attractive.

Penny sat bolt upright in the chair opposite him, the plaster cast resting in her good hand, her shoulders hunched. 'I didn't cry yesterday. The first day for a long time.'

'And what made yesterday different?'

'Simon and I took Jenna down to the beach. She's getting very good on her feet now. We had a coffee at the new little coffee shack on the cliff and then went home. Simon stayed in all day so I had a little sleep in the afternoon and he looked after Jenna. Then later I cooked him some salmon and sauté potatoes and we watched television together. We hadn't done that stuff for a long time.'

'After I last saw you, did you tell him that you are depressed?'

'Yes.'

'How did he react?'

'A bit shocked, I think. Didn't want me to take the tablets. Said that a break, a holiday, was all I needed.'

'Why didn't he want you to take the medication?'

'He thought I'd get addicted or be stoned all day.' She gave a bitter laugh. 'If only!'

Adam ignored her remark. 'But you told him that I was reviewing you once a week?'

'Yes.'

'Well, as I told you, the medication may take up to four weeks or so to get into your system and have an effect, but you will start to feel a lot more like yourself. You'll get perspective back and be able to cope with things much more easily.'

'I hope so.'

'What are you doing for Christmas?' he asked. 'It can be a difficult time, the first without your mother.'

Penny sighed and dropped her head to look at her hands. 'I'm fine. I've got lots to do. I haven't put any decorations up or bought any presents. But Simon has been really sweet. He says the only thing I have to do is be at his Nativity service. He's going to cook for the three of us and everything.'

Adam listened. 'And when is the Nativity?'

'The day before Christmas Eve.'

'Well, that's the day after tomorrow.'

Penny frowned. 'Is it?'

Adam smiled kindly. 'Yes.' He stood up. Her time was at an end. 'I'll see you after Christmas, but any problems before that, don't hesitate to call. You're doing well, but remember to pace yourself. Don't get overwhelmed, especially with Christmas guilt.'

Penny left the surgery with a small spring in her step. Adam had given her a little confidence. She mulled over an idea that was forming in her head and decided she was on a mission.

When she finally got home, Simon was in his study. She poked her head round the door. 'Hey, darling, have you had any lunch?'

He looked up from his writing. 'Hello, you. How was Adam?'

'He says I'm doing OK, and I feel better too.' She smiled reassuringly. 'But I'm starving. Fancy a sandwich?'

'No thanks. Would there be a coffee going?'

She made her sandwich and took it to his study on a tray with his coffee.

'Here you are,' she said, placing the hot mug on the Oxfam coaster with a picture of a robin on it. Simon was astonished. Normally she would put a hot cup down on any surface. Mind you, he thought, recently she probably wouldn't have brought him a cup of coffee at all. Maybe the pills he was so uneasy about were beginning to work.

She settled herself in the shabby leather armchair by the crowded fireplace and tucked into her sandwich. 'What are you writing?' she asked.

Simon picked up his coffee and turned his attention to his wife; after all, she never asked him about his work any more. In fact, some days, Penny made him feel as if he'd failed an exam he didn't know he'd taken.

'Revising my Midnight Mass sermon.'

'Good.' She drank some of her coffee. 'I'm expecting a delivery this afternoon. I hope it won't disturb you.'

'Not at all.' He had already returned to his writing.

'OK.' She popped the last piece of bread into her mouth. 'See you in a bit.'

The large Transit van arrived while Penny and Jenna were watching two male robins fight out their ownership of the bird bath in the front garden.

Penny waved at the driver. He got out and walked to the side of the van and rolled the sliding door back.

Lying sideways in the back was a huge Christmas tree and boxes and bags from the best shops in Trevay.

Jenna pointed at the tree. 'Dree. Dree.' She giggled excitedly.

Penny's mood was rising higher. She instructed the driver where to put the groceries and the presents and then got him to set the tree up in the drawing room, next to the baby grand. As he left she pressed a twenty-pound note into his hand. 'Happy Christmas,' she said.

'Aye,' he answered, 'you too.'

In the drawing room she unwrapped new baubles, tinsel and lights with Jenna tottering about, her hands into everything. Penny ordered Jenna to pass the decorations as she placed them on the tree. Finally, she and Jenna opened a large and glossy box and found, amongst the tissue shreds, the most beautiful angel.

'Isn't she pretty?' Penny asked. 'If you press the button under her dress, her wings light up. Here, I'll show you.'

Jenna clapped and laughed. 'Come on, you hold it and I'll lift you up so that we can pop it onto the top of the tree.'

When it was all just as it should be, Penny called to Simon to come and see.

'Look!' She hugged Simon with glee. 'Jenna did it all, really.'

Penny was so happy that Simon didn't have the heart to tell her that it looked gaudy and overloaded. If this was what she liked, then he would love it too.

'It's wonderful. What a surprise.'

'Do you like it? Honestly?'

'I love it.'

'I've got all the shopping done. I felt so bad about not having done anything, and I know you said you'd help me but I decided to do it all this morning. Now don't go into my office for a bit because there are things in there that I need to send off to Father Christmas.' She gave him a huge wink.

He smiled at her. 'You're crazy, but it's good to see you so happy.'

'And I've got some gorgeous red wine. I'm going to open it now and we can have a glass.'

He looked at his watch. 'It's a bit early for me.'

'Nonsense. Christmas starts now.'

Her good spirits lasted into the following day. She wrapped all her presents, putting them under the tree, and then wrote a load of Christmas cards. Queenie was not impressed when Penny took them to the post office.

'They'll never get there in time.'

'Stick first-class stamps on them,' smiled Penny. 'They'll be fine.'

Queenie narrowed her eyes. 'You doing OK, me duck?'

'Much better, thank you,' Penny said. 'Tomorrow is the Nativity service and I've bought Jenna the cutest reindeer outfit to wear. Are you coming?'

'Never missed it yet.'

'Oh, Simon will be pleased. He's worked so hard.'

But the following morning Penny woke up with a small black stone in her heart. She didn't know why and she tried to shake it free but it stayed with her. She tried to ignore it. Smiling. Laughing. Playing with Jenna.

She was very good at hiding it. Simon suspected nothing and was just happy that Penny seemed more like her old self.

All day Penny tried to keep the darkness at bay.

Helen came over about twenty minutes before the Nativity

service so that they could go together. She found Penny bright-eyed and excited, getting Jenna into her reindeer outfit.

'Oh, I must take a picture,' said Helen, delving into her bag for her phone. 'She looks gorgeous. Mum and daughter together. I'll show her this photo to embarrass her at her eighteenth.'

Penny felt the black stone in her heart weigh a little heavier. She hadn't seen *her* mother on her eighteenth birthday. She smiled for the photo.

'There,' said Helen, showing it to her. 'Isn't that sweet?'

Penny looked. 'I'm so lucky, aren't I?'

'Yes, Penny, you are,' said Helen.

'Would you just keep an eye on Jenna? I need to get my purse.'

In her bathroom Penny sat on the closed lid of the loo and breathed deeply. What *was* this? What was wrong with her? She stood up and, with shaking hands, added a bit more blusher to her pale cheeks and brushed her hair. She went back downstairs.

'You've forgotten it,' said Helen, smiling at her.

'Forgotten what?'

'Your purse.'

Penny went to her bag and pulled it out. 'It's here. Stupid of me.'

'Right, we'd better get to the church for a good seat,' said Helen. 'Come on, Jenna.' She swept Jenna up in her arms and walked towards the front door.

Penny took a deep breath and followed.

In the church, everyone wanted to speak to Penny. The vicar's wife was a glamorous presence and not often seen at church, so the parishioners liked to make a fuss of her and Jenna.

'Isn't she a darlin'?'

'My, 'asn't she grown?'

'She looks like the vicar, don't she?'

'When are we 'avin' some more filming, then? We love Mr Tibbs, don't we.'

Penny managed to keep smiling and thanking the well-wishers for all their kindnesses, and made her way down the aisle to the seat reserved for her in the front pew.

The organ was quietly playing the Bach Christmas Oratorio. Helen pulled out a tapestried kneeler and began to pray. Penny, with Jenna sitting between her and Helen, stared at the plaster Nativity scene in front of the lectern. The Virgin Mary's face was turned in wonder towards her newborn son. Joseph stood tall and proud, his hands outstretched, welcoming the shepherds. Two parents, proud as punch of their son . . . Penny began to think. Had her mother loved her? How could she have behaved that way if she did? How her father must have felt trapped to have the responsibility of a baby. What had made her mother do it? Why did she have to leave her with her Dad? Where had she gone? Where was she now?

The congregation around her stood up as Simon made his way to the lectern.

He was followed by a group of preschoolers dressed as shepherds and angels. Mary and Joseph, holding hands and clutching the baby, came behind. Parents waved and took photos as their little ones made their way.

Once everyone had settled Simon spoke. 'Welcome to this, our Nativity Service. Not only are we celebrating the birth of Jesus, we are also celebrating the miracle of our own families and the joy that lies within. This Christmas I have my own child here, Jenna.' The congregation gave an appreciative hum and heads craned to see Jenna standing up on the pew, chewing a hymn book.

Simon continued, 'Like Joseph, the surprise both Penny and I had at Jenna's impending arrival, was immense, although I have to admit, not entirely immaculate.' There were chuckles.

'I speak now to all mothers who have given themselves selflessly to parenthood. It is not an easy path, tiring, but rewarding, in equal measure. We think of our own mothers who gave us life and we thank them for the nurture they gave us, and the love to let us go when we were ready.'

Penny felt her eyes swim and she held Jenna's warm hand a little tighter. How could her mother not have wanted her?

Simon was saying, 'So let's all sing together our first hymn "Once In Royal David's City".'

The organ rumbled a deep bass note before giving the congregation the first four bars. Everyone stood up and began to sing. Penny could not sing for her threatened tears. She picked Jenna up on to her hip and collected her bag. 'Helen, I must go, I'm so sorry,' she whispered.

She edged her way out of the pew and keeping her head down, avoiding the questioning stares, she walked as quickly as she could to the door and out into the cold air. Helen was only a little way behind.

'Penny!' she called. 'Penny?'

Penny didn't stop until she was back in her own kitchen. She put Jenna down and leant her head on the fridge.

Helen came in, breathless and full of concern. 'Pen. What's happened?'

'I had to get out.'

'Why?'

'What Simon was saying, it made me think about my mother.'

Helen put her hand on Penny's shoulder. 'Of course it made you think about her. I thought about mine too, although my mother has been dead a long time, but yours only so recently. You're grieving.'

'Yes, I am grieving. But not for Margot.' Penny pulled out a chair and sat down. 'She wasn't my mother. It was all a lie.'

Helen started to bustle with the kettle. 'Pen, she was a useless mother but—'

'No, *she* wasn't my mother. That's why I stopped seeing her and my sister – my half-sister.'

Helen's jaw slowly dropped. 'What on earth do you mean?'

*

The very last time Penny had seen her sister and her mother, it had been her birthday and she'd taken them out to lunch.

Penny had been running late and as she walked into the restaurant she saw them both, chatting together.

'Hi,' she said, bending to kiss each in turn. 'I'm so sorry. Traffic. You know.' She sat down to catch her breath and removed her jacket. A flunkey glided over and took it from her whilst another produced three menus and the wine list.

'Champagne, girls?' asked Penny expansively.

'Just an apple juice for me,' said Suzie primly. 'Mummy?'

'I'll have a glass of champagne.'

'Are you sure?' asked Suzie. 'You know what the doctor said.'

'And I say yes please,' answered Margot.

'Oh good. Let's have a bottle,' said Penny, ignoring Suzie's lemon-lipped stare and ordering her favourite. 'Bring three glasses, just in case.'

When the champagne arrived, Suzie relented. Penny took her mother and her sister's hands in each of hers. 'It's so lovely to see you both. Thank you for coming. It's been too long. Let's raise our glasses to us.' She lifted her glass and chinked it against the other two. 'To *us*,' she said and took a satisfying mouthful.

They ordered their food and Penny asked about their news.

'Suzie and I have booked a cruise,' said her mother. 'Just ten days. The Mediterranean.'

'How lovely.'

'Mummy needs a bit of sunshine,' said Suzie.

'Don't we all?' said Penny.

'We would have asked you, but you're always so busy,' her mother said.

'Oh, when are you going?' Penny asked. 'I might be able to squeeze it in.'

Her mother told her.

Penny was disappointed. 'Damn, I'm filming.'

'I told you she'd be too busy,' sniffed Suzie.

'Maybe another time, eh?' Penny smiled. 'If you let me know far enough in advance, I'd love a holiday with you both. '

Her mother tucked into her starter. 'How is your work coming along? It's been so popular, hasn't it? Lots of my friends watch it but Suzie and I haven't caught it yet. It clashes with that wonderful David Attenborough series on the other side.'

Penny absorbed the hurt.

Her mother continued, 'June loves it, though. She asked me to ask you what David Cunningham is really like?'

Penny gossiped about the cast and crew and finished by telling them her news. 'We've been commissioned for a new series and . . . I've met someone.' Her eyes gleamed with pleasure.

'Oh?' said Suzie, not looking up from her food.

'He's so kind and gentle with the warmest brown eyes. He was keen on Helen at first and I wasn't very kind to him but then . . .' Memories filled her brain. 'We just fell in love.'

Her mother sniffed. 'Helen? I thought she had another boyfriend in tow.'

'She does now. Piran. He's mad and handsome and difficult and devoted to her so she was never interested in Simon romantically.'

'And what does Simon do?' asked Suzie.

'Well, don't laugh, but he's a vicar.'

'You're joking?' choked her mother.

'Nope.' Penny was grinning from ear to ear. 'Isn't that amazing?'

'Miraculous,' said Suzie sourly.

'But what about your background? All those boyfriends? You're not whiter than the driven snow, are you?' opined her mother.

Penny bristled. As always, her mother went for the jugular. 'What do you mean by that?'

'Vicar's wives mustn't have a past. That's why Lady Diana had the sense to keep herself tidy.'

The waiter hovered with the champagne to top up glasses. Her mother nodded to him. 'Yes, please.' It was her third.

'Mummy! Simon isn't a royal,' smiled Penny, trying to laugh off the insult. 'Thank goodness it's the twenty-first century and not the eighteenth. Simon and I have no secrets and he's as proud of me as I am of him.'

'Has he been married?'

'No.'

'So no children?'

'No.'

'Well, that's a relief. Taking on another person's child is not easy as well I know.'

Suzie flicked her eyes in warning at her mother. 'Mummy! I think you've had enough to drink.'

Penny sat still, picking up a new and horrible vibe. 'What do you mean?'

Her mother flapped away Suzie's protesting hand. 'Suzie, stop it. Penny is a grown woman. It's all old history.'

'What's old history?' Penny's heart was running cold.

'Surely you've always known?' said Margot, looking appraisingly at Penny.

'Known what?' Penny said.

'That I am Suzie's mother but not yours.'

Penny's heart began to hammer. Her breathing was shallow. 'What – what do you mean?'

'Well, when I met Mike, he already had you. He made it clear that you came with the package.'

Suzie had the decency to look warningly at her mother. 'Mummy! Stop.'

'No, carry on,' said Penny.

'I brought you up as my own, of course. His family were so grateful to me.'

Penny could hardly speak. 'You're not my mother?'

'Of course I am. Ever since you were tiny. Your father had had a stupid fling and your mother didn't want you so your father took you in.'

Penny blinked rapidly. Her mother hadn't wanted her?

'But – who is my mother then?'

'He never told me. In the beginning I asked him, of course. I was a bit jealous, perhaps. But he couldn't have thought anything of her, could he? A woman abandoning her own baby? What was there for me to be jealous of? And then, of course, we had darling Suzie.'

Penny turned to Suzie. 'Did you know I wasn't your sister?'

Suzie looked at her hands in her lap.

Penny shouted, 'Did you know I wasn't your sister?'

Suzie looked at Margot who smirked. 'Of course. I had to tell her. If only to explain why Daddy had to be so nice to you.'

Penny's heart was breaking. 'Fuck you! Fuck you both,' she said and pushed her chair from the table. 'I'm sure you will understand why I have to leave. Enjoy your lunch.'

She blundered her way through the maze of tables as Margot called plaintively after her, 'But what about the bill? Who's going to pay the bill?'

Stumbling out onto the street, Penny put her hand to her beating heart. Her world had tilted and was in danger of capsizing her.

*

'Oh Penny.' Helen grasped Penny's hands between her own as she rapidly assimilated this new information. 'Do you think that's why Margot behaved that way then?'

'I don't know. When Daddy married Margot she took me on for his sake, but then Suzie arrived and I was only second best.'

Helen sat on the chair next to Penny.

'And Margot told you this the last time you met?'

'Yes. My birthday lunch. She got tiddly on the champagne and she just came out with it. As if it didn't matter. And Suzie knew – had done for years, as far as I know.' Her face crumpled. 'How could they do that to me?'

'And your father never told you?'

Penny shook her head. 'No. Maybe he would have told me when I was older. I know he loved me. I know Suzie was a bit jealous of our closeness. That was my defence when I was hurt by being left out of things.' She started to cry, her head in her hands. 'And I was glad that Suzie knew he loved me more.'

'Have you heard any more from her? Since the letter she wrote after your mum's funeral?'

'No.'

'And you haven't contacted her?'

Penny shook her head vehemently. 'No. I don't want her in my life.'

'Does Simon know any of this?'

There was a rustle at the back door and Simon stepped in, still in his robes. 'Forgive me but I've been listening from outside, so I do know now, and Penny, I'm glad I do.'

Another figure stepped in behind him and Simon said, 'Oh Adam, thank you for coming.'

Adam appeared. 'My pleasure. Hello, Penny. Simon thought you might like some company.'

17

Truth is a funny thing. A person can take the worst kind of truth, as long as it's the truth, and Simon, Helen and Adam were perfect examples.

'Why on earth couldn't you have told me when we first met?' asked Simon.

Penny took a deep breath. 'I was ashamed and full of anger. I think I was afraid that if I told you my anger would explode and you would hate me.'

'It must have been a horrible secret for you to keep,' said Helen.

'No wonder you've been struggling,' said Adam. 'How are you feeling now?'

'OK,' said Penny quietly. 'Tired. No, maybe relaxed, relieved, are better words.'

'Liberated?' asked Helen.

'Oh God yes,' smiled Penny slowly. 'I feel . . . a burden has been taken from me.'

'That's good,' said Simon, taking off his vestments and hanging them on the hook behind the kitchen door.

Helen looked at the clock. 'Oh Simon! The service? What's happening to the children and the play?'

'I've left it all in the capable hands of their teachers. I've asked old Mr Briar to do the readings and Brenda will lead the choir. Everybody is very understanding and sends their good wishes.'

'What did you tell them? Do they think I'm mad?'

Simon reassured her. 'No. I told them that you and Jenna were a little under the weather. A tiny white lie but an expedient one in the circumstances.'

There was a knock at the back door and before Simon could stop her, Queenie bowled in with a tin of her mince pies. She gave Penny the once-over. 'You all right, me duck? I brought some of me mincies for you.'

'I'm fine, Queenie. Jenna and I have a little tummy trouble that's all.'

'Oh well, you don't want to give that to all those little kiddies in the church, do you? Very sensible to come back home.' She eyed Adam. 'I see you've got the doctor 'ere?'

Adam gave the nosey old lady his most devastating smile. 'Just came to see if I could borrow some icing sugar.'

'I've got plenty in me shop.'

'Yes, but you were closed this afternoon.'

'Oh yes. Fair do's. I'll be open tomorrow, though.'

Adam steered her to the back door. 'I'll see you tomorrow then. I've got to collect my Christmas kiss, haven't I?'

She gave him a sharp elbow in the ribs. 'You're a charmer, entcha. You and your fella.'

'My fella?' asked Adam.

'Don't worry about me. I'm very broad-minded. I saw all sorts in the war.'

Adam tried not to laugh. 'I'm sure you did. Queenie, I'll tell you all my secrets tomorrow, in the shop. But for now, I need to see to my patients.'

Queenie gleamed with excitement. 'Tomorrow? I'm open from eight until four. But if I'm shut I'll open up for you.'

'Perfect. Goodbye.'

When she had gone Helen dissolved into giggles. 'Adam, you are awful.'

'But you like me?' he replied. 'Now, I want to have a professional word with Penny.' He turned to Simon. 'Do you have a quiet room where we could talk?'

In the drawing room, Penny switched on the Christmas tree lights and drew the curtains. 'It gets dark so quickly,' she said. 'Are you cold? Shall I light the fire?'

'Why not,' said Adam.

Penny lit the fire and sat down opposite him, the fire crackling between them.

'I do feel better,' she said.

'Good. You may find yourself very up and down over the next few days. Christmas is an emotional time and everything I have said before still stands. Try not to drink too much, eat regular meals, and take a daily walk. I am only a phone call away and in the New Year we'll start the acupuncture sessions and see how you get on. I've had some good results with depression, but it's not for everybody.'

'Thank you, Adam.'

'Not at all. I think that you have made huge strides today. Well done. You are on the road to recovery.'

Meanwhile, at Marguerite Cottage, in the consulting room of the new Garden Clinic, Kit was hanging the Tibetan Bell to a strong hook in the corner of the room. 'This is bloody heavy, you know,' he said as he tried to loop the plaited rope over the hook. 'Ella, can you give me a hand?'

'Sure.' Ella came in from the reception area where she'd been painting the reception desk. She helped him with the heavy bell and a few minutes later they admired their handiwork. 'It looks great,' Ella said. 'Where's the bonger to bong it with?'

Kit reached into his pocket and pulled out the heavy metal cosh that the bell required rather than an internal clapper. She took it.

'Right. Stand back.' She gave the bell a swift tap and it released a deeply resonating, but musical note into the room.

'Well, that'll help the migraine patients,' said Kit.

Adam put his key in the door of Marguerite Cottage and stepped inside. 'Helloo?' he called. He put his head through the door of the sitting room. All the lights were on but no Kit. In the kitchen the radio was on, but still no Kit. He opened the back door and there, in the dark, he saw his new clinic, lights blazing and Kit and Ella moving furniture about.

Celia and Terry, lolling on a new rug, gave him one of their warmest welcomes, a slight lift of the head and a tiny wave of a tail.

'Hello,' said Kit. 'You've caught us. We're nearly finished.' He and Ella put the pink sofa in place and stood back. 'Ta dah! What do you think?'

Adam gave the sofa, then Ella, an appreciative once-over. 'I like it.'

Ella was in a flowered playsuit with her hair tied back in a bright green chiffon scarf. 'I thought pink was just so jolly. And look. Tell me what you think. Honestly.' She pointed to her easel in the corner. On a smart rectangular piece of cream-painted wood, she'd drawn in beautiful script:

The Postcard

The Garden Clinic
Dr Adam Beauchamp. Acupuncture and Homeopathy
Opening hours
Tuesday 3.00–6.00 p.m.
Thursday 3.00–8.00 p.m.
Saturdays by appointment only

And on the bottom left-hand corner there was a portrait of Celia, and on the right, one of Terry.

'It's your sign to go outside,' she added.

Adam stood back, screwing up his eyes to see it better. 'Hmm,' he said.

'Are the dogs too twee?' worried Ella. 'Kit said you'd hate them.'

'They are not what I would have chosen, but . . . I like them, and children will love them. Celia? Terry?' he said to the dogs. 'You have become famous figures in art.'

'It's the illustrator in me,' Ella laughed.

Kit asked, 'Have you any published work that we can see?'

She told him about the woman she'd bumped into at the publishers.

'That's my only copy and she's got it.'

'Have you heard from her?' Kit asked.

'Nope.'

'You should follow her up.'

'Yeah, I will. In a week or two.'

'No news from your Trevay solicitor?' asked Adam.

'No, he's better apparently, but now his office has closed for Christmas. His secretary says I'll be the first appointment he books in the New Year.'

Kit smiled. 'Good. I'm glad you are staying here longer.'

Adam interrupted, 'Have you thought any more about taking the job here?'

'I've done nothing else,' said Ella apologetically, 'but I must find out what the solicitor has to say first. Now come and look at your new surgery.'

So Adam prowled around, Celia and Terry following and sniffing disdainfully into the corners. Adam inspected it all, but said nothing. Ella nervously straightened a cushion on one of the sofas then picked up a bit of fluff from the new rug that the vacuum cleaner had missed.

Adam opened the door to his consulting room and walked in. Although it was pitch-black outside, the room still had a welcomeness to it. He sat at his curved and moulded, achingly chic, Perspex desk. He twisted his chair from what would be the view of the garden, to the black-leather examining couch. Then his eyes rested on the Tibetan Bell.

'That's a Tibetan Bell,' said Ella nervously.

He stood up and walked over to it. He tapped it with his knuckle and it offered a small version of its true resonance.

'Where did you get this?'

'A little shop in St Austell.'

He turned to look at her. 'I've been looking for one of these for years. It's very special.'

'Is it?'

'Oh yes, I can charge an extra five pounds to the bill with that.' He looked straight at Ella. 'I love it.'

Kit butted in. 'All of it? I mean this room and reception and everything?'

'All of it.'

194

18

It was Christmas Eve and Simon, sitting in his study, heard the letterbox squeak on its springs and the thump of the post as it hit the mat.

'Post!' called Simon, getting up. 'I'll get it.'

There were several last-minute Christmas cards, a couple of letters for him and a postcard from Mavis for Penny. There was a letter for Penny too, but he didn't recognize the handwriting. He returned to his study, intending to give them to her, but she was upstairs seeing to Jenna and when the phone rang and he distractedly moved things about during what turned out to be a difficult call, they slipped under his blotter.

Later, while Jenna had her morning nap, Penny started to prepare the next day's Christmas lunch. Not known for her culinary expertise, and still with her arm in plaster, she put her laptop on the kitchen table and googled all she needed to know. She peeled potatoes, prepped some sprouts, wound bits of bacon around dried prunes, and made some brandy butter. She was inordinately proud of her achievements.

At lunchtime she made the three of them scrambled eggs on toast and then insisted that Simon joined her and Jenna for a walk on the beach.

'Doctor's orders,' she said, passing him his warm coat.

'Adam says I must spend time with you in the fresh air.'

'I don't believe you,' he said, 'but I'll come anyway.'

The beach was deserted. The sea was flat and a chill, blue-washed sky floated over them. They walked hand in hand, bending now and again to look at bits of seaweed or shell that Jenna found.

'This is going to be a really good Christmas. I feel it in my bones,' said Penny, tucking a windblown strand of hair under her beanie.

'Even after all that's happened?' Simon said.

'Well, it couldn't get any worse, could it?' she smiled.

'Do you want to find her?' he asked

'Find who?'

'Your real mum?'

She kicked at a lump of sand with her boot. 'I wouldn't know where to start.'

'But if you did know where to start?'

'It's not worth thinking about.' She leant her head against his chest. 'I've got this far without her. She didn't want her family, whereas I have everything I want right here.'

They got home as the sun was setting and the stars began to break through the inky heavens.

Simon made a tray of tea with some slices of Christmas cake while Penny lit the fire. Simon turned the television on. *The Jungle Book* was showing.

'I wonder how long it will be?' said Penny, pulling Jenna onto her lap.

'How long what will be?" asked Simon, puzzled.

'Before someone in the village knocks at our door wanting you to do something for them.'

He sat down on the sofa next to her and handed her her tea. 'They won't. '

'Ha. You wait. I'll give it five minutes.'

'No, they really won't. Brenda asked me if there was anything the villagers could do for us and I said to let us enjoy our first proper Christmas as a family without interruption.'

Penny was amazed. 'Did you really?'

'Yes.'

'And will they?'

'Yes . . . barring a proper crisis.'

She kissed his cheek. 'Thank you.'

Simon took her hand. 'Drink your tea and watch the movie.'

It was the most perfect Christmas Eve Penny could remember. Jenna was happy and giggly and more than ready for bed when the time came.

'Want a story?' Penny teased.

Jenna toddled to her bookshelf to choose one.

'Actually, I have a surprise for you,' said Penny. She pulled out of her pocket a small book that had been hers when she was little. 'My daddy gave this to me.'

Jenna climbed on to Penny's lap and for a moment Penny drank in the smell of her freshly bathed daughter, the newly laundered Baby-gro and felt the softness of her hair.

'Right. Let's read this story, shall we? It's all about Father Christmas coming tonight.' She opened the book and read, '"'Twas the night before Christmas, when all thro' the house, not a creature was stirring, not even a mouse . . ."'

As she continued, Jenna sat spellbound, pointing out the pictures of reindeer and presents, then, more sleepily, sucked her thumb until she finally fell asleep and Penny went to join Simon.

Downstairs, Simon had stoked up the fire and put out a plate of cheese and pickle sandwiches and crisps to eat in front of it.

'Happy Christmas, Mrs Canter,' said Simon, raising his mug of tea.

'Happy Christmas, Mr Canter.' They chinked their mugs and watched the television and no one disturbed them before Simon left for Midnight Mass later. Penny helped him into his coat. 'It's nippy tonight,' she said. 'Thank you for letting me stay at home.'

He kissed her. 'Don't wait up for me. I'll try not to wake you.'

He opened the front door and a blast of icy air pushed its way down the hallway.

Shivering, she stood and waved him off. Up in the heavens the stars were bright. On a night like that she could believe in Santa Claus.

She made herself a hot water bottle, turned out all the downstairs lights, other than the one in the hall for Simon later, and went upstairs to bed.

She read for a while but when she turned the lights out her mind opened a memory she hadn't thought about for years . . .

She was asleep in bed with Sniffy cuddled tight when a noise disturbed her. The familiar smell of cigarettes and gin told her it was her father. She kept her eyes tight shut.

She heard the peevish voice of Margot. 'Mike. You'll wake her. You've had too much to drink.'

'Shush. Pass me that,' he said.

Penny heard the thrilling noise of paper crackling as her father dragged something heavy to the foot of her bed.

'Santa's done a good job tonight,' her father said.

'Now let's do Suzie's,' said Margot.

'I just want to give my Penny a Christmas kiss first.'

'You're determined to wake her,' Margot sniffed.

Penny lay as still as she could as she felt her father's lips and bristly chin on her cheek. He tucked the bedclothes tighter under her chin. 'Night-night, Sniffy,' he said, giving him a quick kiss too.

'Mike! Come on, I'm tired,' said Margot.

She left the room and Mike followed her, but before he closed the door he turned and whispered, 'Love you, Pen.'

'Darling? Pen? Are you awake?' Simon was standing by the bed. 'It's snowing. Thought you'd like to see it.'

Penny rubbed her eyes. 'What time is it?'

'Just after one.'

'Is there much?'

'Yes. Come outside. It's magical.'

She put on her dressing gown, with a warm coat over the top, and slipped on her sheepskin boots. 'How old are you?' she said to Simon.

'When it snows, about eight and a half. Come on, just for a minute.'

He opened the front door and they stepped out. The whole of Pendruggan looked as if it was in a snow globe. The Christmas tree twinkled on the village green and all sound was muffled.

'Oh my gosh! It's lovely,' breathed Penny. 'Wait till Jenna sees this tomorrow.'

Simon rootled in his deep coat pocket and pulled out a small box. 'Happy Christmas, Penny.'

'What?' she said, both surprised and thrilled. 'What is it?'

'Open it.'

Her cold fingers, fumbled to lift the lid, but when she did she found a bracelet made of three slender interlinked bangles. 'One is you, one is Jenna, and one is me,' he said. 'Do you like it?'

'I don't deserve you,' she said. 'I *love* it.' She hugged him tight, the snow on his shoulders chilling her hands even more. 'Thank you.'

'I just want you to know that you have us, your family, who will always be in your corner and always love you.'

She wiped a tear away and smiled. 'I'm very impressed. Top marks for romance. Christmas Eve. Snow . . .'

'Well, let's just say, I have friends in high places.'

19

It wasn't Jenna who woke them up on Christmas morning, it was the thump of a snowball on their bedroom window and Helen's voice shouting, 'Happy Christmaaaas.' Followed by another thump.

Simon and Penny, spooned together in the warmth of their bed, giggled. 'She's quite mad,' said Penny.

Simon looked at the time, 'It's only seven. It's not properly light yet.'

'You know Helen, up with the lark. She's probably walking Jack with Piran.'

There was another fusillade of snowballs and then singing. 'We three kings of Orient are . . .'

Penny hid her head under the duvet.

'Shall I let her in?' asked Simon.

'If it'll shut her up,' said Penny.

Simon got out of bed and went to the window. 'There's an army of them. Adam, Kit, Helen, Piran, dogs . . .'

He went to let them in and make tea while Penny woke a sleepy Jenna.

The hall was strewn with wet boots and warm coats as they manoeuvred their way to the kitchen.

'Haaappy Christmas,' said Helen, throwing her arms around them. 'Jenna, look what Father Christmas has brought for you!' She took Jenna from Penny's arms and went in search of her present.

'You are all loonies,' said Penny, taking the mug of tea Simon offered her. 'A little bit of snow and you all regress.'

Kit and Adam hugged her in turn and handed out presents to her and Simon.

'You shouldn't have,' said Penny, embarrassed, 'I haven't done anything for anybody other than Simon and Jenna.'

Penny opened her gift. 'It's lovely,' she said, turning the pretty Dartington glass vase in her hands. 'Thank you so much.'

'Our pleasure. It's for the first primroses,' said Kit. 'Come on, Simon, open yours.'

Simon's present was a cashmere scarf in the Cornish national tartan. 'That's very kind of you both,' he said, winding it around his neck.

'Well, it's going to be very useful today,' said Adam. 'I'm thinking we might have to have a snowball fight on the green after church.'

Christmas Day and Boxing Day passed in a blur. With good food, good company, the happiness of Jenna and endless snowball fights, Penny was starting to think that her life had turned a very bleak corner, and on New Year's Eve Adam and Kit hosted a little party at Marguerite Cottage. At midnight, and all rather tiddly, they sang 'Auld Lang Syne' then, inevitably, started to talk of the year ahead and New Year resolutions.

When Penny was asked she said, 'I know this is cheesy, but it's to appreciate my true family, Simon and Jenna, even more.'

'Yes, that's cheesy,' said Helen, laughing. 'And what about me? Your very best friend?'

'Oh, you're all right,' said Penny, giggling. 'You're like my sister.'

Penny stood up and raised her glass, 'I hereby announce that Helen Merrifield is henceforth known as my sister. And to my real sister, well, half-sister, I say: I wish you no harm as long as you don't come anywhere near me. Cheers!'

*

'How does that feel?' Adam asked Penny.

She wiggled her plaster-free arm. 'Cold.' She rubbed at the pale wizened skin. 'But liberating.'

'Good. Now don't go slipping in the slush and breaking it again,' he said, dropping the grimy cast in the special bin and washing his hands.

'I'll try not to.'

'It may have been an inconvenience but it did at least slow you down,' he said, sitting down. 'You couldn't dash here there and everywhere, could you. You had to focus on yourself, which was a good thing.' He looked at her seriously. 'So. How are you?'

'Pretty good. I'm not drinking so much and my thoughts aren't quite so circular.'

'What thoughts are they?'

'Guilt, mostly. Guilt that I'm not a good mother, wife, daughter, sister . . . That I should have done more to stay in contact with Margot and Suzie, then I remember that they could have been in contact with me. Thinking that makes me angry and I don't *want* to see Suzie, then I feel guilty all over again.' She looked at him and smiled weakly. 'Rather pathetic.'

'Not at all. It's good that you can say it. How are you sleeping?'

'Better.'

'Let's begin the acupuncture this week, then.'

*

'Hello, Mrs Canter.' Ella was sitting behind a very attractive white desk and looking annoyingly lovely. She looked at Jenna who was grizzling and struggling to escape her pushchair. 'Hello, Jenna,' she cooed.

'So you took the job?' asked Penny, less graciously than she meant.

'Yes. My first week.'

'How long are you staying for?'

'I'm still waiting for my family matter to be settled and apparently there's been another hold-up. Would you like me to look after Jenna while Dr Adam sees you?'

Penny was in two minds. She very much wanted Jenna looked after, but she didn't want Jenna to be seduced by the lovely Ella.

She decided needs must. 'Would you? Simon was supposed to be looking after her but he had to go out. Men, eh?'

'It'd be my pleasure,' said the delightful Ella. 'In fact, I invested in a small box of toys to keep little ones amused. It's not always easy to get a baby-sitter is it?'

'No, it isn't,' Penny agreed, hating her for being so bloody thoughtful and perfect.

The door to Adam's room opened and there he was. 'Hello, Penny. Come on in.'

Adam made Penny feel completely at ease.

'I already have a pretty good picture of your state of health, emotionally as well as physically, but I'd just like to look at your tongue. Chinese medicine uses the tongue for a lot of diagnosis so stick yours out for me.'

She did so.

'Good.'

'Anything interesting?' she asked.

'Oh yes,' he said, scrawling something on a Smythson's notepad. 'Now, I'll take the pulse in both your wrists.'

His fingers were cool on her skin.

'Good.' He let go. 'Now, go behind the curtain and slip off your jeans and sweater, please, and lie on the couch, face down.'

He looked away and busied himself with choosing a selection of sterile-wrapped needles, which he placed in to a stainless steel tray. She speedily got out of her clothes and lifted the waffle blanket from the top of the couch. Underneath was a cool cotton sheet. She got settled and pulled the blanket over her as Adam began washing his hands.

'Just relax,' he said, approaching, 'you shouldn't feel anything much but tell me if there are any odd sensations.'

Face down on the couch she could see nothing but she heard the unwrapping of a needle.

'I shall start at the top of the scalp and put a few in there and then I'll work down. Possibly the neck, shoulder blades, shin. Just lie still and breathe gently.'

He didn't speak again but worked swiftly, adding each needle with a deft hand. She began to feel deeply relaxed and closed her eyes. She must have fallen asleep quite quickly, long enough to dream about sailing in a beautiful yacht with Simon by her side. A song was playing and Simon was singing . . . 'for you are beautiful, and I have loved you dearly, more dearly than . . .' Another note was playing. The wrong note. Insistently. She wanted to stop it, to get back to Simon singing to her, but the dream dissolved.

'How are you feeling?' Adam asked, putting his hand on her shoulder.

'There was a noise. It woke me up,' she grumbled.

'My Tibetan Bell.' He smiled. 'It gently brings one back to the present.'

'Oh God! Did I snore?'

'I wouldn't tell you if you had, and falling asleep during needling is a good sign. All the needles are out now, so I'm just going to check my next appointment with Ella while you get dressed. But don't get up too quickly.'

He gave her a few minutes before knocking gently at the door. 'Decent?'

'Yes,' she replied, running her hands through her hair in an attempt to smooth it.

Adam smiled. 'Do take a seat again. Now, you may feel tired and possibly euphoric after treatment. I always warn my patients not to drive immediately afterwards, but being next door you should be fine.' He gave her a warm smile. 'So, how do you feel it went?'

'Well, I didn't feel anything painful and I had a lovely dream.' She tried to pull it back out of her subconscious but it was gone.

'I'd like to see you once a week, for four weeks initially, and I think we'll see a big difference.'

'Thank you.'

'My pleasure.' He stood and walked to the door. 'Ella will book the appointment.' He opened the door and let her back into the reception area. 'See you soon.' She was out of the door, which was closed smartly behind her. She turned in a daze and smiled vaguely at Ella.

'How was that?' Ella asked.

'Amazing. I fell asleep,' she replied.

'Well, it must be catching. Look.' Sprawled across Ella's lap lay Jenna, sparko.

Penny was hit with a spike of pure jealousy and panic. 'She mustn't sleep now. She sleeps in the mornings. She won't sleep tonight if she sleeps now. Give her to me.' She was aware she was sounding shrill.

Ella was horrified that she'd done something wrong. 'I'm so sorry. I didn't encourage it. We just cuddled and she fell asleep.'

She passed Jenna to Penny who took her awkwardly and Jenna woke up, startled, then let out an enormous wail that wouldn't stop. Penny got her bundled back into the pushchair, refusing all help, and without saying goodbye or thank you left for home.

Ella watched her go. The door to Adam's room opened and he poked his head round with a comical expression. 'Is it safe to come out?' Ella nodded. 'Bloody hell, what was all that about?'

*

As it turned out, Jenna was ready for bed after her supper and bath and went down as good as gold. Penny felt a little guilty at having been so rude, but still angry that bloody Ella was so good with Jenna. Better than her? She immediately tried to block the thought. The endless circle of guilt and anger towards her mother came surging back. She wasn't her mother, though, she said to herself. Even her mother wasn't her mother.

'Oh, do shut up, Penny!' she said to herself and heard her father's voice again. 'Keep going, Penny, keep going.' She kissed Jenna's sleeping head and crept from the room.

Downstairs she could hear Simon rattling plates in the kitchen. She was starving.

It was only beans on toast, with a large glass of red wine, but it was just what she wanted.

'How was the acupuncture?' Simon asked, his kind eyes blinking behind his glasses.

'Good, I think. Adam wants me to go every week for a bit. I fell asleep and had a lovely dream. You were in it, singing a lovely song. I can't remember it now, but it was lovely.'

Simon put his hand on hers. 'Penny, you are being amazing. You've been through a very tough time but together we are getting through this.'

Penny felt her heart swell for her kind husband and she squeezed his hand tightly.

'I love you, Simon. I don't mean to be angry and horrible. Everything fell on top of me all at once and I wasn't as tough as I thought.'

He leant forward and kissed her lingeringly.

'That's nice,' she said.

'Shall we have an early night?' he smiled.

Turning the light out in his study, Simon spotted the corner of a letter sticking out from under his blotter. Reaching for the envelope, a postcard slid out too. It was the post that had come for Penny on Christmas Eve. He'd forgotten all about them and took them upstairs.

Penny was in Jenna's room, checking that she was asleep.

'Darling,' he whispered, 'I found this post. It came a few weeks ago. Sorry, I forgot to give it to you.'

She took them without looking. 'Thank you.'

Simon slipped his arm around Penny's waist and squeezed her. 'We three,' he said, looking down at his sleeping daughter, 'we'll get through anything as long as we're together. And it's my job to look after my two girls.'

Penny hugged him and went to their bedroom. She tossed the postcard and the letter on the heap of cushions at the top of the bed and undressed. She put on her nightie then went to the bathroom to clean her face and teeth.

Back in the bedroom, Simon chucked the cushions on to the floor, dislodging the letter and the postcard. They slipped quietly off the bed and between the crack of the mattress and the wooden bed frame. And there they stayed, forgotten in the fond and affectionate lovemaking that was happening above them.

Part Two
Spring

20

Spring in Pendruggan was beginning to blossom. In the vicarage gardens the borders, tended by local gardener, Simple Tony, were brimming with primroses and snowdrops. Little Jenna was following Tony around, putting her pudgy fingers into his earth-caked hand and Penny was watching them from her chair outside the back door.

Simple Tony was Pendruggan born and bred and although, to outsiders, his name was anything but politically correct, it was the name his parents had called him, and the name he liked. That, or Mr Brown. He would correct anyone who called him just Tony.

Penny watched as his head, hair black and sleek as a mole, bobbed up and down next to Jenna's, pointing out the woodlice and earthworms. Socially awkward around adults, with Jenna he was himself.

'Jenna? Mr Brown?' called Penny from her seat in the February sun. 'Would either of you care for a drink?'

Simple Tony lifted his head and gave her his childlike grin. 'Yes please, Mrs Canter.'

'Ribena is your favourite, isn't it?'

'Yes please, Mrs Canter.'

Tony enjoyed Ribena and jam sandwiches. Anything not on that list made him agitated.

He lived in a Shepherd's Hut in the garden of Candle

213

Cottage, which was owned by Paramedic Polly. She'd taken him in after his parents died. He lived in the hut peacefully and independently, nipping over the garden wall to use Helen's outdoor privy, which she'd given him as his bathroom.

'Come and get it,' said Penny as she carried a tray outside with the jam sandwiches and Ribena she knew Jenna would love as much as Simple Tony.

She sat and waited for them to join her, lying back in her chair to feel the breeze playing on her skin. She was thinking about the last couple of weeks; of seeing Adam, of how much she trusted and liked him, and how much better she was feeling in herself. She was eating well, had cut back on the booze and she and Simon were getting along really well.

She watched as Simple Tony put Jenna in his wooden wheelbarrow and pushed her towards her.

''Ere we are, Mrs Canter,' he said above Jenna's squeals of delight. 'She's going to be a proper gardener. That's what my dad used to say when he pushed me in his barrow. Only he said he and not she.'

Penny smiled. 'I can see you as a little boy in there.'

Simple Tony looked confused. 'Can you? Where?'

She smiled again and pointed to her forehead. 'In here. In my imagination.'

'Oh.' He gave a little shiver. 'I don't like imagining.' Then his face brightened. 'But I do like dreaming.'

'Oh, so do I,' said Penny.

Tony lifted Jenna out of the barrow and put her on the lawn. Then he tipped the barrow on its side and sat in it like an armchair. Jenna loved it when he did this and she clapped and ran to squeeze in next to him. Penny offered him a sandwich and as he munched he said, 'Sometimes I dream about the time Alan Titchmarsh came to judge the show.'

'Ah yes,' said Penny, smiling. 'That was an unforgettable day.'

'I can't forget about it. That's why I dream of it,' said Simple Tony.

Penny agreed.

The three of them sat in companionable silence listening to the sigh of the breeze in the trees. Penny closed her eyes and listened for other sounds. Sometimes, if the wind was onshore, she could hear the waves of Shellsand Bay. She strained her ears. No, no sea today, but there was the sound of a car, quite sporty she thought, in the distance. It slowed as it entered the village then moved on at a low speed, coming towards her side of the village green. It was definitely coming nearer. It passed the vicarage and stopped somewhere near Marguerite Cottage. The engine idled, then there was the rasp of gears clashing and the whine of it reversing back. It stopped again and turned into the vicarage drive. The engine was killed. Penny held her breath to hear better. The car door creaked open and then shut. Footsteps crunched on the gravel. There was a pause. Then the knocker on the front door thumped hard.

Simple Tony and Jenna looked at Penny questioningly. 'Now who's that?' asked Penny.

She got up, brushing breadcrumbs from her lap, and walked around the outside of the house. Before turning the final corner and revealing herself, she stopped and hesitated. She didn't like surprise visitors.

She heard a small cough and another thump of the knocker. Staying as close to the wall as possible she peeked around the corner and saw a scarlet MGB roadster in the drive. The roof was off and a suitcase plus other luggage was jammed on to the narrow jump seat. She craned her neck a little further to get a view of the porch. What she saw made her heart stop. It was Margot, her mother. She whipped her head back out of view, shivering with shock. She took another look. The familiar slim figure with her silver-black hair pinned into an elegant pleat, stood with her back to Penny. She was becoming impatient and, as Penny watched, Margot stepped over the milk bottle holder on the step and peered into the nearest downstairs window. She tutted and turned back to the door. Now Penny saw the face clearly. This was not Margot, but Suzie.

Penny, her heart bumping hard against her ribs, crept back to the garden. She beckoned to Simple Tony.

'There's someone I'm playing a game with,' she whispered. 'They've come to see me but I want to pretend I'm not here.'

Simple Tony nodded. 'Hide and Seek?'

'Yes,' smiled Penny encouragingly. 'We three are the hiders and she's the seeker, but she mustn't find us. OK? We must be very quiet until she goes away.'

They didn't have to wait long. After one more impatient knock on the front door they heard the car door open and slam again and the gears angrily crunching into reverse. After a few more seconds the roar of the engine ebbed away, heading in the direction of Trevay.

A horrible dread settled over Penny. The sun was still shining and the garden was still glorious, but she was seeing it all through the familiar veil of tiny black spots that danced around inside her head. The three of them had been huddled behind Simple Tony's wheelbarrow.

He was now standing up and helping Jenna who was giggling. Penny got to her feet and stumbled as the ground tilted beneath her. Simple Tony held her arm to steady her. 'You all right, Mrs C? You look awful pale. My mum would say you look as if you've seen a ghost.'

Penny gripped his hand. 'I just feel a bit faint. Maybe it's the sun. I think I'll go and sit down inside for a minute.' The old panic started to flood back. Why was Suzie here? What did she want?

'I'm going to check on the churchyard. See if it needs mowing. Grass is starting to grow again,' said Tony. 'Mind if Jenna helps me?'

'No, that's fine. I'll just be in the kitchen.'

She sat in her chair at the big table and pressed her hands over her eyes. Had that woman really been Suzie? She looked so like Margot: the set of her shoulders, the expression that always signified life's unfair treatment of her, the ridiculous peep-toed shoes that Margot had so admired on the late Princess Margaret.

If it *was* Suzie, what did she want from Penny? Penny had nothing to give. After that terrible, final lunch she hadn't heard from them again until Suzie had sent the news of Margot's death. But if Suzie thought that Penny owed her something, then she was quite wrong. It was surely the other way round. Maybe that was it. Maybe she'd come to give Penny something of her father's? Penny had nothing to speak of: the little Christmas book was it. No watch or photo album, no signet ring or other small memento.

No, Suzie wouldn't come all this way to give her something. She was here to *take* something, but what?

A shadow fell across the kitchen door and Penny took her hands from her eyes.

'Hi,' said Helen, carrying a supermarket bouquet of white lilies, 'I've brought you some flowers.'

Penny pushed her chair back with a scrape and rushed to Helen's arms. 'Thank God you're here.'

'What's the matter?' Helen was frightened by the look on her best friend's stricken face. 'What's happened? Oh God, have you taken too many pills again?'

Penny was shaking. 'No. Nothing like that. But my sister Suzie was here, at the front door. We hid from her.'

'Why?'

'I don't want to see her.'

'Calm down, sweetie. Let me put the kettle on and you can tell me *exactly* what has happened.' Helen put the lilies on the draining board and filled the kettle.

'She scares me,' said Penny. 'What the hell is she doing here? Why has she come to find me?'

Helen swirled some hot water round the teapot before filling it with teabags and hot water. 'Maybe she wants to make friends with you again.'

'Why would she want to do that?' Penny remembered the warning look on Suzie's face when Margot had spilled the beans over the lunch table.

'She's feeling guilty. New year, new start and all that jazz.' Helen handed Penny a mug of tea. 'Got any biscuits?'

'In the tin.'

Simple Tony and Jenna appeared at the back door. 'I'm off now, Mrs C. Thankee for the drink and sandwiches. Tell the vicar I'll mow the churchyard tomorrow. See you next week?'

Penny stretched her face into what she hoped was a smile. 'Yes, lovely. Thank you so much.' Jenna waddled towards her with a broad smile and muddy hands and knees.

Helen intercepted her with a biscuit and lifted her

onto her lap. 'Now, Jenna, Mummy's telling me a story. So you sit here and we'll listen.' Helen had a bite of her own biscuit. 'You shared a father, after all.'

'Yes. And he was a good father to us both. Before he died it felt like we were a family, but afterwards Margot insisted I went to boarding school. She said looking after two children in a small house was too hard. My father's parents helped with the school fees – they lived in Wales and we barely saw them. In fact, after Daddy died I don't remember seeing any of the family again.'

'Did Suzie go to boarding school when she was old enough?'

'No. Suzie had separation anxiety or something and she had to stay with Margot.'

'That was tough on you.'

Penny reached towards Jenna and stroked her face. 'Well, Jenna is going to have as loving and stable a childhood as I can possibly give her.'

Helen patted Penny's arm. 'You're doing it right now.' She looked at her watch. 'Bloody hell, I'm late. Piran is cooking me supper at his tonight. I haven't seen him all week.'

'You're lucky to have him, even though he's a moody old bastard,' Penny smiled.

'Yes,' said Helen, lifting Jenna to Penny. 'And you are lucky too. We've both found kind men and contentment.'

Penny kissed her best friend. 'Thank you, Helen, for listening. I feel a lot better now. I kind of panicked. God knows why. It's only Suzie. She's not Beelzebub come to cast us to damnation.'

'Exactly,' laughed Helen, 'she's only your sister.'

21

She didn't mention Suzie's visit to Simon that evening, or the next morning. There didn't seem to be a right moment and they were getting along so well she didn't want to throw another scary spanner into the works. She would be seeing Adam in a couple of days anyway and would tell him. Her acupuncture sessions were turning into counselling sessions as well and Adam was a good listener and offered sound advice. She put Suzie firmly out of her mind.

Clearing away the breakfast things she chatted to Jenna. 'It's a lovely day today. Shall I put some washing on?'

Jenna banged her bowl on the table of her high chair and blew a raspberry.

'I think you're right,' said Penny, wiping the crumbs from the breadboard. 'It is a gusty day. I might do my sheets and towels. They'll dry well, won't they?'

'Mumumumumuma.'

'Do you want to help me?'

Jenna's fingers went to the buckle on her harness and pulled to get out. She shouted in frustration.

'OK, OK. Here I come.' Penny threw the dishcloth into the sink and got her daughter out of her chair. 'Come on. Does Teddy need a wash too?'

Jenna shook her head. The last time Teddy had been

in the washing machine, Jenna had been heartbroken to find him pinned by his ears to the washing line.

Upstairs, Penny began collecting up towels, socks and shirts, tossing them all into a pile on the landing. She went to Jenna's room and stripped her cot then remade it with fresh sheets. Jenna dragged a book from her bookshelf and climbed onto the nursing chair to look at the pages.

'Would you like me to read that book to you or are you happy to read to yourself?' Penny asked.

Jenna dropped the book and pointed to Penny. 'Mummma.'

'OK.'

Penny and Jenna sat together enjoying the pictures and the story of a little goose that was hatching her eggs. 'How many chicks will the Mummy Goose have, Jenna?'

Penny took Jenna's little hand and moved her finger over the eggs. 'One, two, three, four, five! Five little chicks. What a lucky Mummy.' Jenna began to yawn. 'Is my little chick getting tired?' asked Penny. Jenna valiantly fought sleep for another couple of minutes then eventually went limp. Penny popped her in to the fresh-smelling cot and left her to her dreams.

Back in her own bedroom, Penny began to strip the sheets from the big bed. As she tugged at the bottom sheet she felt something drop on to her foot. She looked down. A postcard was sticking out from under the divan. She tugged it and noticed a letter with it. She recalled Simon giving them to her ages ago. She picked them both up and sat on the edge of the bed. She chose the postcard first with its picture of the Golden

Gate Bridge in San Francisco. She turned it over to read.

Darling Penny,

Having a glorious time. Been playing (and winning!!!) at bridge almost every night. The boat is full of Americans who simply love the Mr Tibbs series. I knew it was big here, darling, but not how big! It's huge. They keep begging me to write more stories but I have explained to them that it is impossible. Although I did wonder about a finale for a few mad minutes, a last episode, tying up all loose ends . . . then I had a gin and tonic and pulled myself together. Haha! Oh, the steward is calling me to dinner. Keep in touch.

With very fond regards,
Mavis

Penny read it again. A big final episode would be a great idea. Amateur detective, bank manager Maurice Tibbs and his secretary-cum-sleuthing sidekick Nancy Trumpet could finally declare their love and be married. A huge and dazzling wedding with guests who had appeared in previous episodes, even some of the villains who had done their time and returned to society as upright citizens, could be there. There had to be a crime committed too, or maybe Nancy would get kidnapped and held to ransom by a desperate individual who needed the money to pay for his daughter's heart operation. Penny stopped her frenzied imagination right there. Mavis was not going to write any more of anything. She put the postcard on her dressing table and reached for the letter.

She might not have seen the handwriting for a few years but she immediately recognized it was Suzie's. This must be the letter she'd told Simon, on the phone, that she would write. Penny's hands trembled and her heart began to race.

She needed a drink.

In the kitchen she went to the fridge and took out last night's bottle of rosé. She collected a glass and began to pour. As she lifted the drink to her lips her eyes caught the kitchen clock. Ten twenty. She hesitated then walked to the sink and tipped the wine down the plughole. She thought of how flattered she'd been when Adam had told her how much better she looked since she'd cut back on drinking. She lifted Suzie's envelope from the table. 'You are not going to get under my skin,' she said.

She walked to her office and opened the big sash window to the garden. The breeze pushed good clean air into the neglected room. She took a deep breath, sat at her desk and opened the letter.

Dear Penny,

My last email must have come as a horrible shock. Is that why you haven't replied?

I am in the depths of terrible grief and miss Mummy so much. I don't suppose her death has affected you as badly. Of course, when Daddy died we were both too young for it to mean very much, but now I know all too keenly what it is to be an orphan.

I am pleading with you to look kindly on me and take me in to your heart as your sister. You are my only family now.

Life has been very hard for me. I was not able to leave Mummy as you did. You were always impulsive. Boarding school made you so very independent, almost impetuous, Mummy said. And when you left for London and the BBC you never really looked back, did you?

It was always a red-letter day when you came to see us. Mummy would have me cleaning the house for days before your arrival, writing out recipes, getting the shopping in, cooking. I could have resented you and your life, your freedom. But I didn't. To me you were just my sister.

Dealing with the funeral arrangements was dreadful. I had no idea of the expense! Then winding up her affairs, the bank and the will and so forth has been absolutely draining. The house is now on the market and the contents sent to charity or auction.

So you see, not only am I an orphan at forty-two, I am also homeless and single. Where else would I head but to my sister? If she'll have me . . .

I shall be coming to Trevay in the New Year when the house sale is complete, although it very much depends on the auction date. I shall be staying in a small hotel that friends have recommended. I'm told it has sea views. I haven't seen the sea for such a long time.

I shall come to find you as soon as I arrive.
With fondest love and the greatest hope,
Suzie

*

Simon read the letter without any comment. Penny watched him carefully but he betrayed nothing. His eyes scanned the words to the bottom of the page then returned to the top and reread.

After the second reading, he put it down on the kitchen table and polished his glasses, a sure sign that he was thinking carefully.

Penny was impatient. 'What do you think? Isn't she ghastly? What does she want?'

Simon spoke, 'She wants her sister. You are her only family and she wants to reconnect with you.'

Penny gave a sardonic laugh, 'Ha! Doesn't she just. But I don't want to connect with her. She wants something other than just a sister.'

Simon rubbed his eyes. 'Why do you think the worst? Why not take her at face value? She's trying to reach out to you.'

'You should be on *my* side,' said Penny truculently.

'I *am* on your side. I know you have been deeply hurt but this is a chance for Suzie's redemption. I think she wants to make amends.'

'Margot told me that I wasn't her daughter and that Suzie had known for years. And that hurt. Then we had Jenna and I was so glad that she'd never be infected by them and their stupid lies.' Penny began to cry. 'It's just shit, that's all. I was so homesick at boarding school and I missed Daddy so much. '

'No wonder you became so self-sufficient. Such an independent woman.' He stroked her hair.

'And when I left school, Margot said I couldn't come home. I had to get a job and look after myself.'

'And you did. Rather spectacularly.'

'And I tried to get them to be proud of me. I gave

them lovely treats and shared my success but it only made them despise me more.'

'I'm sure that's not true.'

'It bloody well is.' She wiped her nose on her sleeve. 'And just as I'd decided to move on with my life, she's here, and I feel I'm back to square one. She frightens me. I have a bad feeling about her turning up. Why does she want to play happy families now?'

'Because she's your sister.'

'*Half*-sister.'

Simon stretched for the packet of wet wipes on Jenna's high chair and gave one to Penny to wipe her face. She did so, pushing black rivers of mascara over her cheeks.

Simon looked at the postmark on the envelope. 'It's dated December twenty-second and it's now February so I think we might be hearing from her soon.'

Penny blew her nose on the wet wipe and said, 'There's something I didn't tell you. She came the day before yesterday.'

22

At that very moment Suzie was in Trevay, sitting in the spa of the Starfish hotel. A pretty therapist with a glossy ponytail and immaculate make-up was rubbing away at the hard skin on the soles of Suzie's feet.

The friend who had recommended that Suzie stay at the Starfish hadn't been wrong; it was comfortable, friendly, classy and luxurious. She had booked a room on the top floor and had a fine view of the harbour with the Atlantic Ocean beyond. How Mummy would have loved it, she thought, and how wonderful that she wasn't able to – this was something Suzie could keep all to herself, she thought meanly, immediately reprimanding herself. But then, she reminded herself, Margot and she had enjoyed many things together. She sighed. That was then and this is now.

The therapist finished her buffing and popped Suzie's feet back into the bath of warm soapy water. 'Have you thought about what colour polish you'd like, Miss Leighton?'

'Scarlet,' replied Suzie.

'I've got a lovely bright one just in, called Boudoir Passion. I'll go and get it for you to see.'

The colour was just right and as the young girl massaged and moisturized Suzie's legs and toes before applying the Boudoir Passion, Suzie settled with a decaf skinny latte and the *Daily Mail*. She'd always loved reading the *Mail*. It was such a bitch. Mummy and she had had many laughs over the stories it raked up over libidinous politicians and the hideous plastic surgery of over ego'd celebrities.

There had once been a particularly nasty review for one of Penny's television programmes. How they had enjoyed that, whilst tutting at how appalling some journalists could be.

Ah, but now Mummy had gone, Suzie sighed again, and at last she had her life back, money in the bank and time to have a little pleasure of her own. It was what she deserved. After all, it was she who had dedicated her life to the care of her mother. Penny had behaved so badly when she discovered the truth about her parentage. Not once had she phoned or written to apologize or even to thank Margot for being the mother she had never had. Dreadful. But Suzie was prepared to be the better person and put all that behind her. She wanted to see Penny and be sisters again. She wondered what Simon, the vicar husband, was like. Penny had never been into wet men, so presumably he must have a bit of oomph about him. And what was the little girl like? Golly, she was an aunt now. Yes, it was just the right time to become a family again.

What she'd seen of the vicarage from the outside and through the window, she'd rather liked. It was clearly large enough to have two, maybe three spare bedrooms so there was no problem with accommodating her. She'd prefer a room at the back of the house as the sun would be glorious on that side and she'd make sure she got it.

Yes, Suzie was looking forward to her next chapter in life. She'd go over to Pendruggan again tomorrow and see if she couldn't catch Penny.

The therapist finished the pedicure with a coat of quick-drying oil. 'How's that for you, Miss Leighton?'

Suzie wiggled her toes prettily. 'Very nice, thank you.'

'Would you like another coffee or a glass of champagne before Marcus does your hair?'

'Champagne would be lovely.'

The next morning was fine and bright with a soft haze over the horizon. Suzie had breakfast on her stylish balcony, wrapped in a deeply piled dressing gown, feeling the morning sun's warmth on her face. She was very pleased with her new haircut. Marcus had taken off all the length that her mother had so encouraged and given her a short pixie cut with superfine silvery highlights through the tips. She felt young and free and ready for whatever the day held.

She intended to catch Penny early, before ten.

As she walked through the Starfish lobby, freshly showered and made-up, she noticed one or two admiring glances and lapped it up. Outside, her little red MGB roadster was waiting.

As she unlocked it and began to unhook the soft roof, a young bellboy raced down the hotel steps to help.

'I'll do that for you, Miss Leighton.'

'How kind.' She flashed a friendly smile at him. 'It's rather ancient. Nothing electric on these.'

'But this is a classic car,' he beamed. 'What year is this one?'

'When were you born?' She twinkled at him.

'Nineteen ninety-four.'

'Ah well, she's a lot older than you. And a little older than me. Nineteen seventy and 1.8 litre. Still goes like a rocket – just like her owner.' She gave what she hoped was a beguiling smile.

The bellboy blushed and didn't reply. He was busy tucking the folded roof down across the back of the car and stroking the paintwork. 'She's beautiful. A beautiful car for a beautiful lady.'

'What a flatterer you are,' Suzie admonished. 'Maybe you'd like a little ride in her one day?'

He looked away, embarrassed. 'That would be great.'

'Well, then, I'll try to make it happen.'

She folded herself into the car and started up the engine. Waving at the bellboy she reversed onto the road and sped off up the hill towards Pendruggan. Flirting with the poor young man had given her quite a buzz. In this mood she could charm the birds from the trees, or at least her sister into taking her in.

The lanes were glorious and the smell of warm fields and new leaves was heady in Suzie's nostrils.

The lane down to Pendruggan was narrow and winding but she kept her foot on the throttle, enjoying the way the car handled and the ruffling of her new, short hair.

A Volvo with a bald and spectacled man suddenly came round a corner towards her. He stopped safely but the little MG, going faster, slewed to a stop on the muddy verge. He lifted his hand to acknowledge her and opened his window. 'Are you OK? These lanes are a bit tricky.'

She was angry and her heart was still pounding. 'I'm perfectly capable of driving in these conditions. You were coming too fast and on the wrong side of the road.'

'This is a single track lane,' he offered politely.

'Well, keep to your side then,' she said rudely before engaging first gear and squeezing quickly past him.

Simon watched her go in his rear-view mirror. 'You

can always tell the ones from up country,' he said to himself.

The vicarage was looking charming in the early light as Suzie parked in the drive. The sun was winking off the large Victorian sash windows and the front garden was full of early tulips. She walked to the front door and knocked loudly. Immediately she heard the sound of a young child crying and footsteps on a tiled floor, approaching.

She stepped back and arranged her face into a grieving yet unthreatening expression.

On the other side, Penny was soothing Jenna who was balanced on her hip after knocking her head on a cupboard. 'Shh, my darling. We don't want to frighten the postman, do we? He might have a nice letter for us.' Jenna rubbed her head and nestled into Penny's neck. Penny kissed her and opened the front door without a thought.

'Penny,' said Suzie. 'It's me, Suzie.'

Penny froze in shock before slamming the door in her sister's face.

The noise made Jenna jump and then start to cry again.

Penny staggered to the stairs and sat down heavily.

Outside Suzie took stock. It was obviously a big shock for Penny to have her arrive like this, unannounced. But she had written to say she would be arriving soon. She had taken her non-reply as a tacit acceptance.

She knocked on the door again.

Nothing. No sound, no movement.

She bent down and opened the letterbox. 'Penny? Please can you open the door? I come in peace. I just want to see you and talk about everything that's happened. Mummy. Daddy. You and me. I want nothing from you but acceptance and the hope we can be sisters again?'

There was no response from within.

She stood again and wondered what to do. Maybe Penny needed half an hour to think it over. Suzie turned her back on the house and faced the village green. There were council houses on the opposite side, and to the left a row of pretty cottages. The church was almost directly behind her and looked Victorian and bog-standard, but the large farmhouse on the right of the green was exceptional. She walked back to the top of the drive and turned right with the intention of taking a closer look at the farmhouse. It must be at least five hundred years old. On her way she spotted a village shop. The sign over the large and fussy front window announced Queenie's Village Shop and Post Office. The door was open and as she passed she spotted an old lady sitting in an armchair, the better to see the village goings on. The woman was staring at Suzie and gave her a nod.

'Morning,' called Suzie, not wanting to stop.

'All right, me duck?' replied the woman. 'Can I 'elp you? Are you lost?'

'No, no thank you. I'm just exploring the village. Lovely farmhouse.'

'Ain't it? It was one of the stars of the Mr Tibbs' telly programmes, you know.'

Suzie looked at it again and realized that was what it had reminded her of.

The woman pulled out a bag of tobacco and a packet of cigarette papers. 'That won't never 'appen again. They've stopped the programme now. Poor Mrs Canter.

She's the one what put us on the map. You may have seen me in a couple of episodes. I was a background artist.' She expertly rolled a cigarette and put it to her lips. 'That David Cunningham was a lovely man. A proper star. Can't believe 'e'll never be Mr Tibbs again.' She lit the cigarette and inhaled deeply then exhaled on a rattling cough. 'Want a pasty? I've got some left.'

Suzie could think of nothing worse but something the old woman had said led her to believe she could get some information from her. 'Mrs Canter?'

'The vicar's wife. Penny Leighton, she is, professionally.'

'How is she?'

'All right. A bit tired with the baby and that. I 'eard 'er mother died as well. That and losing Mr Tibbs . . . not been a good time for the poor girl.'

'No, it can't have been,' said Suzie thoughtfully. 'Is she well-liked here?'

'Why d'you ask?' said Queenie, screwing up her shrewd eyes. 'You ain't a journalist, are you, because you can push off if you is.'

'No. I'm not a journalist. I'm . . .' Suzie gave her most winning smile. 'I'm her sister.'

'Oh my good gawd!' said Queenie. 'Why dintcha say so? 'Ere's me not offering you tea nor nothing.' She got to her feet, excited to be on the brink of receiving fresh gossip. 'Come in and 'ave a cuppa tea with me. Ain't Penny in?'

'I've arrived as a bit of a surprise.'

'A surprise!' exclaimed Queenie. 'I'm not sure she's up to surprises at the moment, what with her broken wrist an' all. Only had the plaster cast off a couple of weeks.'

'Broken wrist?'

'Yes, poor mite. There was that and the accident with the pills—'

'What accident with the pills?' Suzie asked sharply.

Queenie looked sheepish. 'I'll let her tell you about that – if she wants to. Now come on in and 'ave a cuppa.'

Back at the vicarage, and still sitting on the stairs, Penny had watched Suzie walk away, but as her car was still in the drive she obviously intended returning at some stage. Why had Simon had to leave so early? They must have passed each other in the lane.

Jenna lifted her pudgy hand and tweaked Penny's nose.

'OK, my love,' said Penny. 'Let's get you washed and your teeth done then we'll have a story before your sleep. I've got a good one. All about two sisters and a mummy who pretended to be the mummy of one of them but she wasn't really. And the little girl didn't find out for a long time and still doesn't know who her mummy is. Shall we do that story?'

Jenna shook her head. 'Goosie book,' she said.

Penny smiled. 'OK, Goosie book it is. Let's forget all about the other story, for a while at least.'

23

Suzie's chat with Queenie had been most illuminating. It would seem that Suzie's arrival couldn't be better timed. Her sister, the successful, independent golden girl, was having a bad time in her life. Good. What she needed was someone to help her and care for her. Who better than her own sister? Suzie had charmed Queenie into spilling plenty of details without giving anything away herself. Now she was walking back to the vicarage, ready to claim her sister's affection and hospitality.

Upstairs in the vicarage, Penny had put Jenna down for her nap and was quickly applying a make-up that she usually reserved for getting big budgets out of mean broadcasters. Her war paint. She swapped her track pants for black jeans and her stained T-shirt for an ivory silk shirt. She hadn't had time to wash her hair but a spritz of dry shampoo and a messy up-do completed her armour. She was ready.

She didn't have to wait long.

The door-knocker banged three times but Penny took her time opening it. She stood in the kitchen and inhaled slowly and deeply, then checked herself in the mirror and pulled her shoulders down and back. *Keep going, Penny.* She took the first step into the hallway then walked calmly towards the front door.

*

Suzie fidgeted uncomfortably outside on the step. What was her sister doing? Too frightened to open the door? In that case she was in a worse mental state than Queenie had led her to believe. She heard the rattle of a wheelbarrow behind her and turned to see a youngish man with sleek dark hair and a boilersuit standing beyond the drive staring at her.

''Ow do,' he said.

'How do you do?' she responded.

'Mrs Canter playing hide-and-seek?' he asked.

Suzie barked a short laugh. 'Does she do that often?'

'No,' said the man.

The door opened behind Suzie, taking her off-guard. She turned quickly and saw her sister.

'Good morning, Suzie. I'm so sorry about earlier – a small crisis with my daughter. You may have heard her crying? Come in, come in, I've got the coffee on.'

Suzie stared at the confident, groomed woman in front of her who was now turning and walking away towards a room at the back of the house. Suddenly she felt wrong-footed.

The kitchen was flooded with the morning sun. There was a bunch of paperwhite daffodils sitting in a jug on the scrubbed table. The smell of coffee was bubbling from the percolator and there was Penny, looking entirely in control and very much in her domain.

'Do sit down.' She pointed Suzie towards a comfortable kitchen chair. 'Do you take sugar? I forget.'

Suzie sat. 'Black. No sugar.'

Penny placed two mugs on the table and added milk to hers. 'So, welcome to Pendruggan. How long are you staying?'

Suzie fixed a winning smile to her lips. Two could play at this game. 'That very much depends on you.'

'Me?' said Penny, raising her eyebrows in sardonic disbelief.

Suzie kept smiling. 'Yes. I've come to offer my help as a sister and an aunt.'

'Why now? After all these years?' asked Penny suspiciously.

'Oh Penny, darling. This is me you're talking to, your sister. I hear on the grapevine that your television programme has been cancelled and that, on top of Mummy dying and having a small child to look after . . .' She took a beat. 'Well, at your age that must all take its toll on your well-being. I just want to be here for you and help you with all the support you need.'

Penny managed a glacial smile that did not reach her eyes. 'I am absolutely fine, Suzie. My husband and I and little Jenna are a very loving unit. We support each other.'

Suzie sighed and toyed with her coffee mug. 'How lucky you are. When you left home it was just Mummy and me and I had to pick up the pieces – alone.' She looked wanly round the beautiful room. 'How lovely that you have found such happiness.'

Penny felt the pressure of old buttons being pushed. Anger rose in her. 'You're still young. There's a lot of life to live out there,' she said sharply.

'I don't have your confidence, I'm afraid.' Suzie took a sip of the coffee that Penny had made deliberately strong. Penny watched in satisfaction as her sister winced. 'Golly, you do like caffeine, don't you?'

'I like to feel alive,' parried Penny.

The back door opened and startled them both. 'Hello,'

smiled Simon as he came in carrying a loaf of bread and some hymn books. 'Ah, the lady in the red sports car! We met in the lane.'

Suzie apologized at once. 'I am so very sorry. Was it you in the Volvo? I'm not familiar with these lanes. Can you forgive me?' she finished winsomely.

Simon put his hand out. 'Simon Canter, Penny's husband.'

Suzie shook it. 'Suzie Leighton, Penny's sister.'

'Ah. I see,' said Simon, putting the books and bread down on the side and moving to stand by Penny. 'I was very sorry to hear about the death of your mother. My deepest condolences. I know the news knocked Penny for six.'

Penny pursed her lips and gave him a small scowl. Suzie rattled on. 'Dreadful for us both, but at least Penny didn't have to face the challenge of watching Mummy die. That was left to me, and what a privilege it was. I wouldn't have changed a thing.'

'Well, she was *your* mother,' said Penny.

Suzie cocked her head to one side and gave Penny a cool stare. 'She treated you as her own.'

Simon could see tension brewing. He had two choices. Either leave for his office or stay and mediate.

He chose to stay. 'Can you stay for lunch, Suzie? It would be good to talk.'

She gazed at him as if he were a true saint. 'That would be very kind. I don't want ever to be a burden but you see . . .' a small crystal tear dropped from her brimming eyes and slid down her cheek, 'you are the only family I can turn to.'

Simon gave her a measured glance and for a second Suzie thought she might have overdone it, but he said,

'Then you must stay for lunch and tell us your plans for the future.' He turned to Penny. 'Mustn't she, Pen.'

Penny gave a short snort. 'Well, that would be the Christian thing to do, wouldn't it?' She scraped her chair back and went to the fridge. 'I've got some soup and bread and cheese?'

'Let me help you,' said Suzie, jumping up. 'But first perhaps you could tell me where the little girls' room is?'

Penny rolled her eyes as Simon directed her to the downstairs loo. When he came back Penny was banging a saucepan onto the Aga.

'Well, she seems very nice. It's a jolly good idea to get the two of you back together,' he said.

'Bloody marvellous idea,' said Penny sarcastically as she poured a carton of carrot and coriander in the pan. 'Just hunky fucking dory.'

'Shh! She'll hear you.'

'I couldn't give a damn.'

'She's your sister.'

'*Half*-sister.'

'She's been through a lot.'

Penny stopped stirring and gave Simon a sharp look with glittering eyes. A look he never had liked. '*She's* been through a lot? What about *me?*'

'It's not a competition, Penny,' he hissed.

'What's not a competition?' asked Suzie as she returned.

Simon leapt back from Penny who had continued with her vigorous soup stirring.

'The erm, the village garden competition,' he said. 'Well, it *is* a competition or we wouldn't call it one, haha, but erm . . . it doesn't mean to say we have to compete with each other.'

'Doesn't it?' asked Suzie, mystified.

'Well, erm, what I mean is, we all like to take part, do our best, that sort of thing but we don't have to erm . . . win.' He finished lamely.

Suzie furrowed her dainty eyebrows. 'I only ever play to win.'

Fortunately, Jenna woke up in time for lunch and distracted the three adults with her presence. She enjoyed the attention and the conversation remained safe and superficial until at last Suzie gathered up her bits and announced her departure.

'Well, it's been lovely to meet you at last, Simon.' She reached up and kissed him. 'I'm grateful you've taken Penny on. She needed a strong man.'

Simon was immensely flattered. 'Well, she took me on, actually. But I hope I am a good husband.'

Penny, hanging back from this gruesome love-in, huffed a little too loudly and Suzie raised a polite eyebrow.

Penny changed track. 'How's your B & B in Trevay? Did you get a sea view?'

'Oh yes. It's delightful. Now what's it called . . . the Seahorse? Right on the harbour front.'

Penny glowered. 'You mean the Starfish?'

'Oh yes, that's the one.'

'It's the best on this coast – and very expensive,' said Penny, wondering how Suzie could afford it.

'It's not that bad. In fact, I think it's quite reasonable. Mummy would have loved it, wouldn't she?'

'Oh yes, very definitely.'

'Thank you so much for lunch. It's left me lots of room for dinner tonight at the hotel. I'll phone you tomorrow. Maybe we could meet for coffee in Trevay? My treat. I'll phone you.' She leant towards Jenna who was clinging to Penny's hip. 'Bye-bye, my darling little niece. Auntie's got to go now.'

Jenna swung out her fist and bashed Suzie on the nose.

Penny put her hand to the front door, ready to close it. 'Well, bye-bye, Suzie. Thank you for coming.'

Suzie was rubbing her nose. 'Yes. Until tomorrow.'

If she said anything else Penny didn't hear it as she slammed the door shut between her family and that woman.

*

'Did you hear her?' Penny was stomping between the kitchen table and the dishwasher with soup bowls, mimicking Suzie, 'The Starfish is quite reasonable. Mummy would have loved it. I'm grateful you've taken Penny on. She needs a strong man. Grrr.'

Simon put the salt and pepper away. 'I think you're overreacting. I know you aren't the closest sisters but we have to look for the good in people, Penny. She seems fine to me.'

'*Fine?*' Penny stopped stomping and stuck her face into Simon's. 'Judas Iscariot was fine until he kissed Jesus and sent him to his death!'

'I'm not listening to this. You're upset. I can see that.'

'Well done,' said Penny, now slamming the dishwasher door.

'And I can only assume that it's because Suzie's arrival has brought out some old emotions.'

Penny picked up the kitchen cloth and wiped the table of crumbs. She murmured, 'I'm married to Sigmund Freud.'

'And I'm married to a woman who hasn't been well and who I care about very deeply.' He took her by the shoulders and stopped her frantic wiping. 'I'm worried about you. When are you seeing Dr Adam again?'

She pulled herself away from him with force. 'I am not going mad, if that's what you think. Adam is very happy with my progress. Would you like to come to my next appointment and check up on me?'

Simon gave her a disappointed look.

'Oh Simon, I'm sorry. That was a stupid thing to say, but I have been, still am, rather depressed but *I am not mad.* I am hurt. I am scared of—' She stopped and ran her hand through her hair.

'What are you scared of, Pen?'

She went to him and buried herself in his chest. He folded his arms around her. 'I'm scared of *her*. I'm scared of her worming her way in to our lives and taking you from me. You won't be on my side any more.'

He kissed the top of her head. 'That's silly. I've told you: I am always, and will always, be in your corner.'

She looked up at him and he could see the pain in her eyes. 'Will you? Do you promise?'

'I promise. It's you and me and Jenna. Always.'

'I don't want to see her tomorrow, Simon. I want her to go away. I don't want her to take over my life in the way she took over my childhood.'

'Darling Penny, I think you have a little sister who needs you. She looks up to you and the best way for you to stop feeling scared is to get into her corner and trust her.'

Penny shivered. 'I'm not sure that I can.'

'You can.' He lifted his hand and stroked her hair soothingly.

In the silence of the kitchen, safe in Simon's arms, she heard her father's voice. *Keep going, Penny, keep going.*

24

ELLA

Ella was settling into the routine of her new life very happily. She was still staying at the B & B in her grandmother's old house and once she had told the landlady that it had been her childhood home, the landlady had taken her under her wing and treated her as family. 'You stay as long as you like, Ella, and I tell you what, why don't you help me around the house? Changing sheets, doing laundry, washing up, that sort of thing? In return you can live here rent-free, but you'll have to move out of that big bedroom and into the little one. What do you say?'

Ella had fallen on her feet. Two nice jobs and plenty of time to walk the cliffs and do her painting.

'When are you going to come down, Henry?' she asked her brother on the phone that evening. 'The primroses are blooming and Kit and Adam are dying to meet you, '

'Ella, you know I want to but work is just manic.'

'Are you enjoying it?'

'Not much.'

'Then jack it in.'

Henry twizzled his chair and looked out of his grimy London window down to a grey and sodden, dirty street. 'I wish. Anything on the solicitor front?'

'His secretary rang me the other day. Apologized for the long delay but he's up to his oxters in some complicated trust case or something. We're just not a priority right now.'

Henry took a gulp of his cold coffee. 'Probably a good thing. I have no desire to have news about our mother. When we do it'll turn our lives upside down – unless she's dead.'

'Don't say that, Henry, it's not nice.'

'Just saying it as it is.'

Ella changed the subject. 'I'm thinking of advertising myself as a painting tutor. Locals might be interested or holidaymakers. Perhaps families. It could be fun.'

'Great idea. Look, Ells, I've got to go. Speak soon. Love you.'

Ella took the phone from her ear and checked the time. If she didn't get a move on, she'd miss opening up the Garden Clinic for Adam. And she didn't want to lose her job or his friendship. She had fallen into an easy relationship with Adam and Kit and although, at first, she had fancied Adam a bit, she now treated them like older, much-loved brothers.

25

Penny had settled down and absorbed Simon's advice by the time Suzie phoned her that night.

'Are you free for breakfast tomorrow? At the Starfish? I think we need to meet somewhere less emotional,' Suzie said. 'Maybe we can start again? Begin the day on a positive note with a healthy meal and then the day ahead isn't wasted.'

Penny accepted the invitation graciously and called Helen to see if she'd have Jenna. However, when she put the phone down she had a rant.

'She means she can get me over and done with then she can have the rest of the day doing what she wants.'

Simon volunteered to drive her in. 'I have a meeting in Trevay, at St Peter's, so I can wait and pick you up.'

Next morning Penny said goodbye to Simon and strode up the steps of the Starfish looking as cool as a cucumber. Inside she felt like jelly. Outside, Boudicea couldn't have done better.

She went over all that Simon had told her. Suzie was not out to push her way into Penny's life. Suzie was just lonely and bereaved and needed a little comfort before adjusting and leaving for her next chapter.

Penny took a deep breath as the automatic doors into the lobby opened. I'm just meeting my sister for breakfast, she told herself, a perfectly normal thing to do.

*

While Simon was parking the car, he spotted Adam heading towards the surgery. 'Adam!' he called.

Adam turned. 'Hello, Simon, how are you?'

'I wondered if you were free for supper tomorrow night? With Kit? Only, Penny's sister Suzie has turned up—'

'I'll bet that was a surprise,' frowned Adam. 'Is Penny OK?'

'A bit wobbly yesterday, but they're meeting for breakfast this morning, and I thought a surprise supper would be rather jolly.'

'Will you tell Penny?'

'Of course. So, are you free for dinner tomorrow?'

'I'll check with Kit and give you a call later.' He looked at his watch. 'Sorry, I must go. Full surgery.'

'Yes, of course. And how is the Garden Clinic going?'

'Very well indeed, thank you. Ella is a godsend. Very efficient and good with the patients. I think Kit's rather struck on her.'

Simon had an idea. 'Would she like to come too? The more the merrier?'

'I'll ask her. Must dash. Speak later.'

Simon felt very pleased with himself. He was doing a good thing for both his wife and her sister. A dinner party would be just the thing to lower tensions and promote peace. He hurried over to St Peter's, making a mental note to call Suzie later, then had another thought: perhaps Helen and Piran would like to come too?

The breakfast room in the Starfish was a relaxed yet luxurious affair. Most of the guests were rather well-heeled, the women draped in casual cashmere and discreet Cartier earrings, the men in exquisite Italian jeans, relaxed shirts and loafers, while beautiful small children darted amongst the tables before being reined in by attractive Polish or Lithuanian nannies.

Penny navigated her way to a table window where Suzie was already waiting. She stood and embraced Penny.

'Darling, the kedgeree is to die for. Remember how Daddy used to make it?'

Penny nodded, surprised at the sharpness of the sudden memory. 'I do,' she said. 'Mummy was always cross when he made the eggs too runny.'

'Wasn't she!' laughed Suzie. 'On her last day she wanted a boiled egg and when I cracked it open for her she wouldn't eat it because she said it was underdone. I'd cooked it for *eight* minutes, but she was adamant.'

Penny sat down and tucked her bag under her chair, giving herself time to think. Penny, she told herself, this is the moment that you must be the big sister and comfort Suzie, just as Simon told you. She took a deep breath.

'Tell me about Mummy's last illness. It must have been a very difficult time for you.'

'It was ghastly,' Suzie said mournfully. 'Ovarian cancer. She'd left it much too late to tell me about the pain she was experiencing and by the time she was seen by the doctors it was game over. She was very brave.'

'Why didn't you contact me?'

'To be frank, she asked me not to.'

Penny swallowed the hurt. 'Why?'

'Why do you think? After that final lunch when she told you the truth and you walked out and we never heard from you again?'

'I was very hurt myself.'

'How so? She was a good mother to you.'

'A better one to you.'

'And how do you think I felt about our father? Hm? I certainly wasn't *his* favourite, was I?'

The waiter, with perfect timing, arrived to take their orders.

When he'd gone, Penny resumed.

'How long had you known that Margot was not my mother?'

'I was about five, I think. I was going through Mummy's dressing table. Did you ever do that?'

Penny smiled. 'No, but I used to go through Daddy's shed. I loved the oil cans. Don't ask me why. Mad to think about it now.'

'Well, one day, I was looking through her make-up drawer and I found, pushed to the back, a photo of Daddy with another woman and a baby.'

Penny sat very still. 'And?'

'I took it straight to Mummy. She asked me where I'd found it and she was cross that I'd gone through her private things. And then she told me.'

'What?'

'She said that the baby was you and that the woman in the picture was your real mother but that it was a big secret and I was never to tell you that I'd found it.'

'What did my mother look like?'

Suzie tried to recall. 'I honestly can't remember.'

'Did you find the picture again? After Margot died?'

'To be honest, I was looking for it, but no, I didn't see it.'

'You must have liked having a secret from me,' Penny said bitterly.

'Golly, you're still so sensitive. It was years ago.'

The waiter and another waitress arrived with their kedgeree, pots of coffee and fresh granary toast. The hiatus gave Penny time to collect herself, but Suzie spoke first.

'I suspect Mummy destroyed the photo. It must have been very painful for her to know that Daddy had had a previous lover *and* a child.'

'And to have to take that child on as her own?' said Penny archly.

'Quite. I think she was a saint.' Suzie now flapped open her napkin and gave Penny a penetrating look. 'Have you ever thought about how *I* felt?'

Penny shook her head. 'Tell me.'

Suzie thought for a moment and then blurted something that Penny felt she'd been saving for years. 'Don't you think I know Daddy didn't want me? You were enough for him, but Mummy wanted him – and her own child. I've done the maths. Either I was a premature baby or she was pregnant with me by the time he married her.'

Penny was shocked – not just by Suzie's words but also by how hurt she clearly was about their childhood. 'What are you saying?'

'I think she might have tricked him into marrying her. And he couldn't afford to have *another* child out of wedlock with a second woman.'

'But he would have wanted to be married anyway. He loved Margot – and you.'

'Oh, once I'd arrived he was happy enough, but I think the main reason he really married Mummy was so that you, his *precious* daughter, would be looked after.'

Penny reached across the table and touched Suzie's hand. 'Don't say that. Please. I remember when you were born and he came home from the hospital to tell me that I had a sister. He was so happy and proud of you.'

Penny thought she saw a momentary flash of anger in

Suzie's eyes as she answered, 'I used to be so jealous of the pair of you. Always together. Going out in the car. Working in the garden. The shed. Him teaching you to swim.'

'But you didn't like doing any of those things. You and Mummy were good at going to shop for special presents and wearing nice clothes and putting on lovely perfume.'

'Oh, how shallow you make us sound,' snorted Suzie.

'Not at all,' protested Penny. 'I wanted to share those things with you but . . . It just worked out differently.'

The waiter swept up to their table, looking with concern at their untouched plates. 'Is everything all right? Can I get you something else?'

'It's fine. We're just talking too much.' Suzie switched on her sparkle for him. 'Maybe some fresh coffee?'

'Certainly. One moment.'

Both women started to pick at their kedgeree.

Penny had a sudden need to know one thing. She took a deep breath and asked it. 'Did Mummy leave me anything?'

'No.'

'Did she leave everything to you?'

'Yes.'

'Did she have a reason?'

'Your coffee, madam.' The waiter efficiently poured two cups of steaming caffeine for them. Suzie waited for him to go.

'Of course she had a reason. I was the one who sacrificed my life to her. You had left your boarding school and gone to London.'

'She told me I couldn't come home! That I had to make my own way in life,' retorted Penny angrily.

'No. You didn't want to know. You wanted your own independent life and sod us.'

'That's just not true. Why do you think I tried to help as much as I did? Anything you needed, any problems I could solve. I tried to do it for you both.'

'But you had so much more!'

Penny felt beleaguered and accused. 'I can't help my success. I worked – still work – really hard to earn a living. You can't blame me for a success that you enjoyed the benefits of too.'

'Maybe not, but it is your fault that I didn't have the same opportunities. You left me at home with mother, up shit creek without a paddle.'

In the silence that followed, Penny was aware of her quickened breathing and a seething sense of guilt. She pushed the cooling kedgeree away from her.

'I'm sorry, that was not my intention.'

'I'm not saying it was. But the knock-on effect of your independence was the curtailment of mine. Once you'd gone there was no way Mummy was letting me go, I was her everything. Where was my happy ever after? My career? My husband and children?'

Penny felt a sudden overwhelming compassion for her sister. 'What can I do to make amends?'

Suzie thought before answering. 'I want to be part of a family again, and to find a life of my own.'

'Where?'

'Well, here in Cornwall, with you, would be a start.'

Fifteen minutes later, as Penny was walking to the Fo'c'sle café to meet Simon, her mind was a riot of confusion. Suzie had got up inside her head and moved all the furniture around. She could find nothing that was familiar. She had parted with Suzie emotionally. They had hugged and kissed and words of affection were exchanged, but what would happen next, Penny couldn't tell. Simon was sitting inside the café, two cappuccinos waiting. He stood and smiled. 'Darling, good timing. The coffees are still hot. How was it?'

She told him as best she could, remembering things out of sequence or not at all, and finally asking him what he thought.

'I think you have started to communicate and it's going to be a long road but with a happy ending.'

'Really?' she asked wanly.

'Really. I'm delighted for you. It'll make tomorrow night a proper celebration.'

She looked at him questioningly. 'Tomorrow night?'

'I've planned a surprise dinner party.'

'Who for?'

'You and me and Suzie. Adam and Kit. Ella and Helen and Piran.'

'Where?'

'At home?'

'Who's cooking?'

He hadn't thought of that. His smile remained bright as he thought fast. He'd assumed Penny would cook, but from the look on her face he could see that would go down very badly. 'I thought I'd ask Ella. Adam says she's a marvellous cook.'

'Oh,' said Penny. 'OK. For a moment I thought you expected *me* to do it.' She started to giggle. 'That *would* have been a surprise party. Beans on toast for everyone.'

Simon sat smiling and bobbing his head as if it had been a great joke.

'What is Ella cooking? Any menu ideas?' asked Penny.

26

Piran was not pleased. 'Why do I have to go?'

'Because she's my best friend and her sister has arrived out of the blue and she needs some support,' Helen replied patiently.

'Well, I'm bleddy not dressing up and I'm not drinking bleddy prosecco, neither,' grumped Piran.

'No one is asking you to drink prosecco. We'll take a good bottle of red and some beers and you can have those.' Helen found a broken Biro and began to write a shopping list. 'I'll take some flowers and chocs too.'

'It's Simon I feel sorry for,' said Piran. 'I know she's your best mate and all, but Penny is a high-maintenance woman.'

'She is not!' Helen fired back. 'She's having a bad time, what with work, her broken wrist, and her mum dying.'

'She's unstable.'

Helen felt herself getting angry. '*Not* unstable. Depressed. Have you never felt a bit down? Not even when the love of your life was killed?'

'That's a low blow, Helen,' he growled.

Helen was immediately apologetic. 'Yes, I'm sorry. I shouldn't have said that.'

Jenna – after whom Penny and Simon had named their own baby – had been Piran's fiancée years before and had been knocked down by a hit-and-run driver one New Year's Eve. Piran had been left brokenhearted, a state of mind he had hidden well for many years. Simon had known Jenna well and his and Penny's tribute to her had touched Piran deeply.

Helen continued.

'But you can understand that she is vulnerable. Her overdose was a cry for help, I think, and she says that Adam is helping her a lot, but she's still very sensitive.'

Piran put his arms around Helen. 'Yeah, I know. And you've been a great friend to her.'

'Thank you.' She smiled up at him and kissed his nose. 'So you'll come?'

'Yeah,' he said. 'But no bleddy prosecco.'

Over at Marguerite Cottage Kit was working on his portrait of Lady Caroline Chafford. She had insisted on being painted standing on the grand staircase of Chafford Hall, wearing full evening dress and all her jewels.

Kit had spent a morning with her taking photographs to work from back in his studio. She had been wearing a lace, full-length, off-the-shoulder dress in dazzling violet. The neckline exposing her pillowy breasts and her waist was corseted to within a centimetre of shutting down her vital organs. Her face was remarkable only for the amount of Botox and lip plumping she'd embraced with fervour.

'My husband has commissioned this painting to mark our silver wedding anniversary,' she'd told Kit in a voice that still held a trace of the Welsh valleys.

'That's charming,' Kit had smiled.

'He wants to put it over the fireplace in the grand salon,' she said, moving her position to pose and pout over the beautifully carved banister.

'Terrific,' Kit had said, taking another two or three frames.

The front door opened and two black labradors bowled in, covered in mud.

'Lambert!' shouted Lady Chafford. 'I'm having my photo taken. Get the dogs out.'

A large man with a look of an international rugby player strolled in wearing a Barbour jacket with a broken shotgun over his arm. Ignoring his wife he said, 'Ah, you're the artist, are you? You don't have to do much with Carrie. She always looks fabulous. Don't you, my darling?'

Lady Chafford waved her hand. 'Oh, don't listen to his going on. This is my husband.'

'How do you do, Lord Chafford,' said Kit, politely trying to restrain one of the dogs that had his nose firmly in Kit's crotch. 'Labs are such fun, aren't they?'

'Dylan! Come 'ere!' shouted Lord Chafford to the dog, which continued his truffling. 'Sorry about that. Want a cup of tea?'

'No, thank you. I think I've got all the photos I need now.'

'So how often does she have to pose for you?'

'Well, I'm going to get back to my studio and start work on the composition and I can get a lot done before the last one or two sittings to get Lady Chafford's character and expression to your liking.'

'Fair do's,' said Lord Chafford, grabbing the dogs by their collars. 'Make sure her tits look great.'

Now Kit stood back from the canvas and screwed his eyes up. Her tits really did look pretty good, even though he said so himself. He was just putting his brush down in order to get a cup of coffee when the phone rang downstairs.

'Hello?' he answered, slightly out of breath.

'Kit. It's me Adam.'

'Hi.'

'We've been invited to dinner tomorrow night at the vicarage.'

'Lovely.'

'Yeah. Quick favour to ask though – would you ask Ella if she'd mind cooking it?'

'Hi, Ella?' Kit's heart was lifted just by calling her.

'Kit? Sorry, the signal's bad. I'm on cliffs.'

'OK I'll be quick. Look. This is a bit embarrassing, but Adam wonders if you'd cook a dinner party tomorrow night?'

Ella felt a frisson of pleasure. She would do anything for Adam. 'Yes. Love to. How many people?'

'Eight.'

'Eight?'

'Yes.'

Blimey, she thought. But . . . 'No problem. What time?'

'Seven for seven thirty?'

'OK. What does he want?'

'Well, it's not strictly for him.' Kit explained the problem. 'And so Simon had this great idea but forgot that Penny can't cook...'

'Shall I phone Penny?'

'Good idea. Here's her number.'

'Penny? It's Ella, from the Garden Clinic?'

Penny, who was watching CBeebies with Jenna and wondering if she could develop a new television series for children, remembered how rude she'd been to Ella the first few times she'd seen her and thanked heaven that she had apologized to her. 'Oh, hi, Ella. Is it about tomorrow's dinner?'

'Yes.'

'I hear my husband roped you in and it's very kind of you because I'm useless. What's your signature dish?'

Ella was hoping Penny would have had a clear idea for the menu herself. 'I'm not sure I have one . . . Is there anything you would really like?'

'Oh golly,' said Penny airily. 'Erm, well, something to make my half-sister feel welcomed.'

Ella was thinking on her feet. 'What about something quite simple? Like individual tomato and basil tarte tatin to start with, then hot poached whole salmon with crispy roast potatoes and green beans with cashew nuts and for pud, cinnamon pavlova?'

'Sounds marvellous! Can we start with some nibbles and a nice bottle of chilled prosecco or two?'

'Of course.'

'Well, that's great. Thank you so much. Bring me the receipts and I'll settle up tomorrow. What time do you need to be here in the kitchen?'

'About two-ish?'

'Fabulous. See you then! Bring an extra bottle of prosecco – I may need a glass before my long-lost sister turns up. As Bette Davis once said, fasten your seatbelts, it could be a bumpy night!'

Next morning Penny was up early – and not feeling as optimistic about the dinner party as she'd tried to persuade herself she was.

Simon was keeping a very low profile and had whisked Jenna out with him so that Penny could sort out the house and kitchen. 'Bring some flowers, would you? For the table and the hall?' she'd called out to him as he drove off.

She put the radio on and spent the next couple of hours cleaning and tidying as best she could. It was another perfect spring day and she opened all the windows upstairs and down to let in the sunshine and let out the blues. Her final touch was a spritz of Jo Malone air freshener.

Afterwards she went from room to room checking her work and revelling in the pleasure of seeing plumped cushions, freshly vacuumed carpets and a spotless kitchen.

She checked the time: one fifteen. She could just fit in a quick shower before Ella arrived.

She had time to wash her hair and shave her legs, so tonight might be Simon's lucky night, she thought to herself. That would cheer him up. Poor man hadn't had his conjugal pleasures for a while now. She caught a glimpse of herself in the mirror and was surprised at how much better she looked. All she had to do was get through tonight's dinner party without any upset and deal with tomorrow when it came.

Bang on two o'clock there was a knock at the door.

'Coming,' she called, skipping down the stairs.

Ella had arrived with Kit and his car full of shopping bags. 'I hope I've got enough,' she said, standing on the doorstep. The sun was behind her and shone through her astoundingly beautiful curly red hair.

'Oh my God, you look so beautiful,' exclaimed Penny. 'Like a medieval church painting.'

'Doesn't she?' said Kit, carrying several shopping bags in behind her.

'Shut up the pair of you.' Ella clutched her hair despairingly. 'Believe me, it's very hot under all this.'

Finally the bags were all in the kitchen and Ella, tying her hair up into an unbelievably attractive messy bun, got to work.

Kit left, excusing himself for not being able to help. He had to crack on with Lady Chafford's portrait.

'Give me a job,' demanded Penny.

Ella pushed the large bag of potatoes towards her. 'Can you peel these?'

'Yep.'

'Thanks, and then after that how about laying the table? I've bought some rather posh paper napkins to save the laundry and Kit and I nipped up to the St Eval candle factory.' She dug into a bag and brought out a three-wick squat candle. 'Vintage rose. Hope you like it.'

Penny sniffed it appreciatively. 'I love it.'

Together the two women worked and chatted comfortably. To her surprise, Penny really warmed to Ella.

'Where did you learn to cook?' she asked.

'My grandmother was a great teacher. She was sent to a cordon bleu school when she was young and passed on the knowledge. This tomato tart is one of hers.'

'Looks divine,' said Penny. 'I feel like we've never really had the chance to chat. Didn't you say that you were down here on family business when you first arrived?'

Ella groaned. 'It's taking for ever but yes. My grandmother lived in Trevay and brought my brother Henry and I up. She died without making a will and the solicitor has been trying to wind up her estate. The stupid thing is, he asked me to come down in December but he was ill with the flu and so our meeting was postponed. Then he had some papers he thought had been located but actually haven't been and now he's busy on another case, more important than ours and . . .' Ella pushed her hair back behind her ears. 'Well, it's taking longer than he or we thought.'

'What happened to your parents?' asked Penny, starting to fold the napkins.

'My mum was a bit of a hippy back in the day. Henry and I have different fathers and, to cut a long story short, she left us at Granny's and went off to India or a kibbutz or whatever they did in those days, and we didn't hear from her again.'

'That's very sad,' said Penny. 'My mother did the same but I don't know why.'

Ella was interested. 'Do you want to talk about it?'

Penny told her the little she knew. 'And so that's why Simon wants me to play happy families tonight. To be honest, all I want to do is be nice, say goodbye and never see Suzie again.'

'How odd that we share so much in common . . . neither of us know if our mothers are dead or alive. That's what's holding up our solicitor. He thinks he's found her, then the trail goes cold.'

'How very frustrating.' Penny went to the fridge. 'How about a toast to our long-lost, fucked-up mothers?'

Penny liked Ella. Tonight was going to be fun after all. Her sister would be diluted amongst a table of nice people and there would be laughter in the old house again. Something there hadn't been for some time.

There was a knock at the front door and Penny went to answer it with the corkscrew in her hand.

Suzie was on the step. 'Penny, I'm here early, to help . . .'

Penny felt a small chill cool her happy mood. 'No need – we're fine.'

Suzie pushed herself into the hall. 'Nonsense, many hands make light work. Mmh, something smells good. When did you learn to cook?'

Ella called from the kitchen, 'Penny, do you want the Sauvignon Blanc or the Pinot? I got both.'

Suzie gave Penny a triumphant look. 'Oh. Clever you. Thinking of passing the food off as your own, were you?'

Penny was about to explain but Suzie strode off towards the kitchen and introduced herself to Ella. 'Hello, I'm Suzie, Penny's sister.'

Ella was caught at the fridge, a bottle in each hand. 'Hello, I'm Ella. I hear this dinner is in honour of you.'

'Is it?' Suzie beamed a smile at Penny.

'Of course it is,' said Penny, mustering a smile of her own. 'A "welcome to Pendruggan" supper.'

'Wine?' asked Ella.

Penny needed a drink, so added shakily, 'To celebrate?'

'I don't normally drink in the day but I'll have a small one. To keep you company,' Suzie added slyly.

Penny got three glasses down from the cupboard and poured her sister a small one and herself a large one. 'Ella?' But Ella put her hand over the glass.

'No thanks. I'll save mine for later.'

Penny looked around her; the old kitchen table shone with the fresh wax polish that she had used that morning and the worn silver cutlery had appreciated its buff with a clean duster. Nothing had changed in the room since Suzie's arrival, other than the atmosphere. Suzie was taking all the oxygen, chatting to Ella and leaving no room for Penny to join in.

Effortlessly, Suzie had found little helpful jobs to do,

offering culinary tips of her own and Penny could see Ella warming to her charm.

'I think I'll take a little nap,' she said. Suzie and Ella barely looked up.

'Just an hour or so. Tell Simon I'm upstairs when he comes home, would you?'

Penny sloped off to her bedroom.

Lying on her bed watching *A Place in the Country* she heard Simon come home with Jenna. There were voices raised in happiness and the sound of Jenna laughing in the kitchen. Penny closed her eyes and went to sleep.

Simon woke her at six. 'Darling, the girls said you were feeling a bit tired so I left you. Suzie's feeding Jenna and she's dying to give her a bath and bedtime story. Jenna's very excited by her new aunt.'

'I'll bet she is,' said Penny through a dry mouth and headache.

'It means you've got time to get ready.'

'How lovely.'

'She really is a nice woman, Penny.'

'Well, that's good, isn't it,' said Penny with a sardonic glint.

Simon looked at his wife with concern but thought better of saying anything in case he accidentally caused a row. 'Right, well. I'm going to grab a quick shower. We're going to have a smashing evening.'

Penny got downstairs with ten minutes to spare. The vintage rose candle was flickering on the hall table next to a beautiful arrangement of white roses. As she touched their velvety petals, Simon came out of his study. 'You remembered to get the flowers! These are lovely. Thank you,' she said.

He shuffled a little uncomfortably. 'Suzie ordered these to be delivered.'

'Oh,' said Penny. 'That was kind. What flowers did you get?'

'I forgot. Sorry.'

'Ah,' Penny said, pursing her lips and walking towards the kitchen to check its readiness. The table had been re-laid. Gone were her paper napkins tucked into wine glasses. Here were her old linen ones, newly pressed and folded on side plates. At each place setting there sat a small coffee cup filled with narcissi, thyme, and crocuses from her garden, and in the middle of the table three tall, cream church candles in silver candlesticks she'd forgotten she had, shone beautifully.

Ella had worked wonders.

The salmon lay in the fish kettle, looking succulent, one of her blue and white platters waiting to receive it. Fat slices of fresh lemon and a pretty bowl of home-made mayonnaise were ready for the table. And there was the pavlova, just waiting to be eaten.

Simon, with Suzie clutching at his arm, came in.

'Jenna is simply adorable! She ate up all her supper, had a lovely bath and now she's sleeping like a princess.'

Simon saw Penny's face. 'Haven't Suzie and Ella done a wonderful job?'

'Ella is certainly a marvel,' agreed Penny. 'Better than I ever could have done.'

'I hope you don't mind,' said Suzie. 'But I had to really search for those napkins and candlesticks. Your cupboards are in a bit of a state.'

'Well done for finding them,' Penny said quietly.

'And when I found the coffee cups I just knew what I wanted to do with them.'

Penny clutched the back of a chair to keep her hands from strangling her sister.

Simon said hurriedly, 'Ella will be back here in a minute – she nipped home to get changed – but she gave us instructions to get the nibbles out and the wine open.'

'Do you want any more wine, Penny? After this afternoon?' asked Suzie, with an arched eyebrow.

'Oh yes please. A *lot* more,' replied Penny.

There was a knock on the front door. 'Positions, please, everyone,' joked Simon. 'The first wave has arrived.'

27

Penny had to almost race Suzie down the hall to open the door, and she threw it open just as an enormous clap of thunder shook the village to its bones. 'Bloody hell!' said Adam, who was carrying a bottle of good Merlot, 'I hope that's not a portent for the evening.' He kissed Penny. 'You look lovely – and what's that scent you're wearing?'

Penny beamed with pleasure. 'Oh Adam, you're sweet. You look pretty damn handsome yourself.' She reached up and brushed the shoulder of his perfectly cut jacket.

'Stop flirting you two and get us in before the heavens open,' Kit said, bending to kiss Penny.

'I'm so sorry,' Penny laughed. 'Come in. Where's Ella?'

'On her way,' said Kit with joy. He couldn't wait to spend an evening in her company. 'I said I'd pick her up but she's insisting on a taxi from Trevay.'

'Well, come into the drawing room and let me introduce you to my half-sister, Suzie.'

A huge crack of lightning lit the sky

Penny jumped again. 'Oh, I don't like storms.'

Simon and Suzie were busy handing out drinks and nuts as the introductions were made. Suzie's eyes locked onto Adam immediately but before she could get her mitts on him, Penny took him over to the baby grand piano.

'Kit tells me you play – perhaps you could entertain us later?' she said.

Adam raised an eyebrow and said sotto voce, 'And there's me thinking you're trying to avoid your sister.'

Penny grinned. 'Is it that transparent?'

'Is it that painful?'

Penny nodded and sipped her gin and tonic.

Suzie barged herself between them. 'How do you do? I'm Suzie.' She kissed his cheek. 'Penny's *younger* sister.'

Adam gave Penny a quick look of amusement, then said, 'Suzie, I'm Adam. A new boy to the village too.' He looked at her carefully. He didn't know what he had imagined, but it wasn't this. She reminded him of an artlessly chic French woman. Slender, with a cap of feathery hair, good bone structure and sensuous lips. Not what he'd been expecting at all.

'I've heard quite a lot about you,' he said.

'All bad, I expect. The wicked half-sister?' she said, a vampish glint in her eyes.

There was another knock at the door. Penny looked at Suzie but Suzie ignored her and kept staring into Adam's appreciative eyes.

'I'll get it.' Penny stomped off.

Helen, Piran and Ella had arrived simultaneously. Helen was hiding behind a huge bunch of burnt orange roses. 'Surprise!' she shouted, revealing herself. Penny had never been gladder to see her best friend.

'Suzie's here and she's working the room. Be on your guard,' she hissed.

'Ella's just been telling me how sweet she is and what a help she was while you had your nap this afternoon.'

Penny shot Ella a look. Traitor. 'Really? Well, she's not always what she seems,' she said sniffily. 'Anyway, come in.' Another roll of thunder echoed around the village. 'It's about to pour down.' Another slash of lightning rent the heavens and encouraged them into the refuge of the house.

Back in the drawing room, Penny introduced the late-comers.

Suzie was radiant and met each in turn with an open smile and a warmth that made them feel that she was especially pleased to see just them. Adam was in her thrall instantly.

'I've been what you might call a carer and homemaker all my life,' she told them. 'My mother was widowed too young and Penny, being so much older than me, was able to go to boarding school and do well in life, but I was left to look after Mummy. I miss her terribly but I knew that she would want me to find Penny and rebuild bridges.'

Adam nodded. 'Penny has told me a little about your upbringing. I gather things were a bit tough for you both.'

'Yes. That's right. She thought that Mummy was her own mother until just a few years ago. It was Penny's birthday and she would always take us out to celebrate. Mummy had a little too much wine and out it came. I'm afraid Penny behaved like an adolescent that day and it distressed Mummy such a lot. Thinking back, that may have been the day when her illness started. She was never quite the same. Especially when we didn't hear from Penny again. Of course it must have been a terrible shock for her, but you'd think that given time . . .'

Piran was swirling his glass of Merlot. 'That must have been really hard on Penny, though? To forgive and love a woman who wasn't her mother, particularly if she'd kept the truth from her for so long?'

'Oh yes. But harder on poor Mummy to have brought up a daughter as her own and then have all that nurture thrown back in her face.'

Adam asked, 'Did you ever know who Penny's mother was?'

Suzie shook her head. 'Sadly, no. Don't tell Penny, but Mummy always thought it was some old slapper that Daddy had had a meaningless fling with. I tend to agree with her. I mean, what kind of woman would give birth to a child and then hand it over to its father and have nothing more to do with it?'

'A desperate one?' asked Piran.

'Or disparate,' sneered Suzie. She saw Piran recoil from her sharp remark and clutched at her necklace apologetically. 'Have I said too much? Have I told you things you didn't know? I assumed Penny would have told her closest friends . . .'

'Yes, she's told us,' said Piran.

Penny was on the other side of the room talking to Helen. 'I just don't want her here,' she said. 'Look at her chatting up Adam and Piran.'

Helen looked. 'Piran's immune to that sort of thing. But Adam is definitely interested.'

'Is he?' Penny tried to read their body language. 'If anything it's professional interest because I've told him so much about her. He's just working it out for himself.'

'He seems to be laughing a lot and now he's touching her arm.' Helen nudged her. 'See for yourself.'

Penny saw for herself but refused to believe it. 'He's just putting on the Charm Doctor thing for her. That's all . . .'

Simon and Kit were at the French windows, watching the lightning. 'It seems to be heading inland,' observed Simon. 'Bodmin way.'

Kit remembered something. 'I camped on Bodmin Moor once, with the army cadets. My dad was very keen on that sort of thing.'

'Was he in the military?' asked Simon.

'Yeah. It ran in the family. My father, grandfather, great-grandfather all were. My uncle, Adam's father, was killed in the Falklands War.'

'I'm sorry to hear that.'

'Very hard on Adam. He wanted to join up as soon as he could, of course, but Auntie Aileen pointed him towards medicine instead. The army's loss is our gain.'

'Quite so. And has he never married?'

'Total commitment phobe. He adores women but runs a mile as soon as they start talking permanency.'

'Oh dear.'

The two men stood in comfortable silence, listening to a now distant rumble of thunder.

'And you've never been married?' ventured Simon.

'Nope. I have nothing to offer at the moment. Penniless jobbing artist, that's me.'

'Ella is a very beautiful girl, don't you think? I'd have thought you might set your cap at her?'

Kit looked down at his feet. 'Punching above my weight there, I think.'

A sudden wind blew up and with it brought great fat drops of rain. Ella called, 'Dinner is served, ladies and gentlemen.'

The kitchen shimmered in the candlelight and Ella directed everyone to their seats.

'Suzie at the top of the table as honoured guest and Adam and Piran sit either side of her, please. Simon, you're at the other end of the table with me, and Helen next to you, and Kit and Penny, you're in the middle, opposite each other. OK?'

The tomato tarte tatins were as light as air and slipped down easily with a glass, or two in Penny's case, of chilled Chablis. The salmon was oohed and ahhed over and thoroughly enjoyed and finally came the pavlova.

The wine had flowed and the conversation had been lively but not controversial until Adam innocently raised his glass to Suzie. 'I'd like to officially welcome Suzie Leighton to Pendruggan. A new friend.'

'Thank you so much, all of you,' said Suzie. 'I never thought that I'd have the chance to be with my sister again, let alone sit at her table and share such wonderful food and joyous company.' She turned to Penny who was scowling at her empty pudding plate.

'Darling Penny, there's something I've been longing to say and I think – hope – this is the time to say it.' She took a deep breath. The table was hers.

'When we were growing up, you were my idol. Brave, funny and clever. You and Daddy were always the ones who built the best bonfires and chose the best Christmas trees. Mummy and I did what we could to make the house comfortable but you two were "the doers".'

Penny shifted in her seat but didn't trust herself to look up.

Suzie continued. 'When Daddy died and Granny and Granpa paid for you to go to your lovely school, Mummy and I were left by ourselves, she grieving for her husband, me grieving for my daddy and my sister. The bottom had fallen out of our world.'

Penny became aware of the table shifting their focus from Suzie to her. She picked at a fingernail.

'As your success grew we followed you eagerly, always

watching any television programme you had had a hand in. We understood that you had left us behind, that you had a new and exciting life and we never wanted anything from you. Carrying the secret of your real mother was a horrible burden for me, and one that I honestly didn't want. I hoped I was protecting you and Daddy's memory by not spilling the beans. I see now that it was wrong of me but what could I do? Mummy had sworn me to secrecy and, if I'm honest, it felt good to have her trust, just as you and Daddy shared your little secrets. Was I jealous? What an ugly emotion. But perhaps that is what it was. From the depths of my soul, I am here now to apologize and hope that we can be true sisters once more.'

As her words faded away Penny was aware of a still-ness around the table. She reluctantly looked up and saw Helen looking at her and wiping tears away. Simon had pulled his handkerchief from his pocket and was mopping his nose. Adam was staring at Suzie as if she were the second coming.

It seemed they were all waiting for Penny to say some-thing. 'Um . . .' she started. 'Er, thank you, Suzie. I, erm, don't know what to say without, erm . . .'

Simon helped her. 'I think what Penny is trying to say is how much having you here means to her. And we both welcome you into our home and our family. I know Jenna is delighted to at last have an auntie.'

The table pulled sentimental faces.

Simon went on. 'In fact, it's our pleasure to ask you to stay with us here at the vicarage. Treat it as your home for as long as you want. Tomorrow you can leave the Starfish and come here. We may not have quite the view or facilities that you have got used to at the Starfish, but we *are* your family.'

Adam said, 'Hear hear.' Piran simply rolled his eyes.

'What do you say, Suzie?' asked Simon.

Suzie was wiping away tears of her own. 'Whatever have I done to deserve this kindness? I say yes. Yes please! It's all I've ever wanted.' She looked at Penny. 'If that's OK with you, Pen?'

Penny felt the walls closing in on her. No, it was not OK with her. Suzie was spinning these gullible people a load of bollocks and painting Penny into a corner. What game was she playing? Why did she ever come here?

But what could she say except, 'It's fine by me.'

28

Penny was woken by her hangover. Keeping her eyes tightly shut she rolled over to reach for Simon. She needed a hug and to be held like something that was worth holding.

She crept her hands further towards his side of the bed but the sheets were cold. She opened her eyes, just a little, to find he wasn't there. She rolled back to check the time. It was late. Jenna must be awake and hungry. She staggered out of bed and into Jenna's bedroom. The blast of sunlight coming through the windows was blinding. Jenna's cot was empty and made neatly, the window curtains pulled back and hanging perfectly, and the bin with yesterday's nappies empty and clean. Had Simon done all this?

She managed the stairs and got to the kitchen. What she saw made the possibility of being sick very real.

Simon was sitting at his place eating a full English with Jenna next to him in her high chair, munching on a sausage. Suzie was wearing an apron and squeezing fresh oranges. She must have heard Penny because she turned and smiled. 'Ah, there you are. I've got some fresh coffee brewing for you. Thought you might need it after last night.'

'Mumma!' sang Jenna, waving her sausage. Penny went straight to her to lift her out from her high chair.

'Don't take her out,' said Suzie. 'Have your coffee first. You look as if you could do with it.'

Simon reached to pull a chair out next to him and patted the seat.

She sat and gratefully took the coffee that Suzie handed her.

'Who washed up?' she asked, taking in the spotless room.

Simon looked at Suzie with something like awe, thought Penny. 'Suzie and Ella. They were wonderful,' he beamed.

'It was our pleasure,' said Suzie, placing the jug of freshly squeezed orange juice on the table. 'It really was a marvellous party and it was the least I could do after you'd all been so kind.'

Penny frowned. Had they been kind? It was only a supper. Then the horrible recollection hit her: Simon had asked Suzie to come and stay with them, indefinitely.

Simon was talking to Suzie, 'So what time can we expect you?'

'After lunch? The Starfish people know I'm checking out – I told them before I got the taxi up here this morning – and I just have to pack my bits and I'll be right over. Couldn't do it earlier because I wanted to come back and surprise Penny with breakfast. Oh, I can't tell you how much this all means to me!' She stepped towards Simon and put her arm on his shoulder. 'My new brother-in-law and my new niece.'

'And your old sister,' intoned Penny.

Suzie ignored her and asked, 'Which room may I have?'

Penny was quick with her answer; she was not going to let Suzie have the beautiful back bedroom overlooking the garden and the sea. 'The one in the front is large and has a lovely view of the village green.'

Suzie considered this then said, 'When I got Jenna up and tidied her room, I couldn't help but notice the charming room at the back of the house? With the view over to the sea?'

'But it's so small,' objected Penny.

'But it has an en suite,' argued Suzie. 'I don't need very much room and it's so pretty.'

'You'll be disturbed by Jenna if she cries in the night,' Penny parried.

'No problem at all, I sleep like a log.' Suzie grinned; game, set and match to her. She had got the bedroom she wanted and Penny was vanquished.

'Well, that's that settled then,' said Simon with the satisfaction of a man who had witnessed a fair fight. He kissed the top of Penny's head and Suzie's proffered cheek. 'I'll be in my office. A lot of admin to see to.'

When he'd gone, Penny finished her coffee and pushed her mug away. It was instantly collected up by Suzie and placed into the beautifully organized interior of the dishwasher. 'Would you like an orange juice?' she asked.

'Maybe later,' said Penny. She watched as Suzie whisked out the clingfilm, sealed the top of the jug, and popped it into the fridge.

'There. Well, if you don't need me I'll be off. See you later.'

Queenie was putting up the posters for the Pendruggan May Fayre when Penny came into the shop.

''Ello, me duck,' Queenie said, finishing on one of her rattling coughs. 'How are you?'

'Better than you sound,' said Penny. 'Are you all right?'

'Oh, I'm fine. I need one of me fags, that's all. What can I do for you?'

Penny got the bits she wanted and, as she was waiting for her change, she read the poster for the fayre.

'I'd forgotten we were having a rounders match instead of the tug-of-war.'

'Oh yes. Good idea, ain't it? All the little ones can join in. I was very good in me day.'

'Will you be playing?'

'Just try stopping me,' said Queenie. 'At school they called me Speedy Queenie.'

'Did they?' laughed Penny. 'I can just see you sprinting round the village green.'

Queenie laughed too. 'The boys couldn't get away from me!' She laughed a bit more at her own joke and then sat down on one of the battered armchairs to catch her breath and roll a cigarette. 'Sit with me and give me all your news. How's that little Jenna of yours?'

Penny sat, glad to rest for a moment. 'She's fine. My . . .' She hesitated. 'My sister, well, half-sister, has turned up out of the blue and Jenna's happy to have an auntie.'

Queenie licked her cigarette paper and reached for her matches. 'She came in 'ere the other day.'

'Who?'

'Your half-sister.' Queenie sucked in some smoke and took a strand of tobacco from her lip. 'I may 'ave said a little bit too much to her.' Her shrewd eyes looked into Penny's. 'I'm sorry if I said anything out of order.'

'Like what?'

Queenie lifted a hand to her mouth and coughed nervously. 'Well, when she said she was your sister and had come to surprise you, I told her you wasn't up to a surprise, what with having a baby and losing your mum and that little problem with the pills.'

Penny groaned and put her head in her hands. 'Oh Queenie.'

'I'm sorry, me duck.'

'Oh, it's OK. Everybody knows, I suppose.'

Queenie nodded. 'Whatever did you do that for?'

'I was in a bad place – and I don't really want to think about it at the moment.'

Queenie looked at Penny and saw how much she'd altered in the last few months. 'If you don't mind me saying, Penny, you still don't look right. Maybe having your sister back in your life will help bring your sparkle back?'

Penny doubted that. 'The truth is, Queenie, we've never really got on that well and I'm wondering if we ever will. But Simon has invited her to come and live with us for a bit and she's moving in this afternoon.'

Queenie frowned and thought. 'Are you her only living relative?'

'Yes.'

'So you're doing her a favour, entcha?'

'I suppose.'

'Well don't let her forget it. It's your home and your life. The vicar and Jenna are your priority. By all means get your sister back on her feet, but don't let her get her feet under your table. Know what I mean?'

Penny smiled. 'You wise old thing.'

'Less of the thing,' coughed Queenie. 'I'll keep an eye on 'er for you, don't you worry.'

So Suzie moved in and, to her astonishment, Penny had nothing to be afraid of after all. Suzie was respectful of her place in the family and was good at leaving Simon and Penny to have time together. She was very helpful with Jenna and enjoyed taking her on little outings so that Penny could pick up the pieces of her work in her office. Her antidepressants were working and Adam was starting to occupy a little fantasy corner of her mind, which kept her very happy.

Simon was happier too. The house was being run well and Penny was much more like her old self. They'd even had a chance to have a couple of moments of afternoon passion while Suzie had taken Jenna out. Yes, maybe they had all turned a corner.

By mid-April, the May Fayre Committee, headed up by Audrey Tipton – the most fearsome woman in the village – was strident in its demands of the Pendruggan residents. Everyone had been persuaded (bullied) to donate, work or perform for it.

The WI, the Flower Arranging Group, the Art Club and the Pendruggan Choir – all also run by Audrey Tipton – were working hard on cakes, bouquets and the Cornish anthem, 'Trelawney'. The several holiday cottages in the village were now occupied by retired couples or families with preschool children, taking advantage of the lower off-season rents. Any dogs or babies they had brought with them were encouraged to enter the Dog Show and the Baby Show.

The vicarage had a constant flow of visitors asking questions, dropping off tombola prizes, or wanting to use the drawing room for endless committee meetings.

Suzie was a godsend. She charmed the lot of them and was always happy to put the kettle on or rustle up a few scones.

Somewhere in all this, Penny let go of her duties as vicar's wife and worked on getting her business back in shape.

She was always getting programme suggestions sent to her by freelance writers and producers and now she had time to assess them carefully. Three or four were cracking ideas and she had sent them to broadcasters – although not Channel 7 – to test the water. The BBC were interested in a gritty drama serial written by a young woman who had just come out of university. It had a strong message about the problems and pressures young students were under to achieve their potential and Penny was called to a meeting in London and wanted to extend her trip.

'Simon?' she asked as she lay in his arms after a little afternoon delight, 'would you mind if I spent two nights in town? I'll stay at the flat but I'd love to check into a spa and be pampered for a day.'

'I think that's a very good idea. You deserve it. And Suzie has everything under control here.'

The BBC meeting went well. The head of Drama Documentaries seemed to really like the scripts and assured Penny that he'd get an answer for her as soon as possible. 'I hope to let you know one way or another in about six weeks. A couple of the commissioners are away but as soon as they come back I'll be waving this under their noses.' She thanked him and spent the rest of the day in Bond Street, happily exercising her credit card.

Two days later she arrived back in Pendruggan with new highlights, a rejuvenating facial and a scarlet mani-pedi.

She dropped her keys on the hall table and checked herself in the mirror. Pretty damn good.

'Hi,' she called, wondering who was in.

'Hello?' answered a voice she knew but couldn't place, from the kitchen. 'Who's that?'

Penny was irritated. 'Me. Penny.' She walked into the kitchen. There was Ella, doing some finger painting with a delighted Jenna.

'Hi, Ella.' Penny was pleased, if surprised, to see her. 'What news from the solicitor?'

Ella sighed. 'We're still waiting to hear. It's maddening.'

'Do you think she's still alive?' said Penny, putting her bag on the table and kissing Jenna.

'Maybe. The trail has gone over the world. Italy, Morocco, Estonia, then . . .' Ella pulled an apprehensive face. 'She could be back in the UK.'

Penny reached out and took her hand. 'Scary?'

Ella nodded. 'Very. I'm beginning to hope she's gone for good. It would be much easier than this feeling of apprehension all the time. Henry never wants to have anything to do with her again.'

Penny thought for a moment. 'You know, sometimes I think it's best to just let go of the past. For my part, I've decided that I am so lucky to have Jenna and Simon. I am Jenna's mum and she will always know who her parents are, that we are all that she needs and I'm going to look forward, not backwards, from now on.'

Ella smiled. 'That's what I think too. Fancy a cup of tea?'

'You bet,' Penny smiled. 'There's nothing like tea to put a situation in perspective,' she laughed. 'I'll take over with Jenna; you boil the kettle. By the way, why are you here?'

Ella suddenly looked uneasy. 'Oh, ah, Simon didn't tell you?'

'Tell me what?' asked Penny, sticking her own fingers in Jenna's paints and drawing a smiley face.

'Oh dear, I feel a bit awkward.'

Penny looked at her. 'Tell me what, Ella?'

'They've asked me to help out.'

'What?' said Penny. 'Do you mean on the May Fayre committee?'

'No. To help out here.'

She was aware of the front door opening and closing but assumed it was Simon.

'Doing what?' asked Penny, still not cottoning on.

'Erm—' Ella began.

Before she could explain Suzie strolled in.

'Ah, Penny. Welcome home. We've had a little change of plan. What with Simon working so hard and having so much to organize, poor man, and you working and me looking after the house, we, that is Simon and I, decided to ask Ella to be Jenna's nanny,' she said.

Penny was confused. 'Just for the last couple of days while I've been away?'

'We both thought that you need help with Jenna so that you can get your work done. And Ella could do with a little extra job something more than just the Garden Clinic, and she can give up the B & B and live here.' Suzie smiled, daring Penny to challenge her authority.

'Is this a joke?' Penny asked Ella.

'Hasn't Simon mentioned this to you?' Ella asked nervously.

'No. And anyway, Jenna doesn't need a nanny,' said Penny, feeling the floor buck under her.

'Darling,' said Suzie reasonably, 'Simon and I want you to get back to doing what makes you happy: your work. And we thought Ella was the ideal candidate. She moved into the front bedroom today. She can look after Jenna and be right next door to the Garden Clinic and Adam. Talking of Adam, he's taking me out for dinner tonight. Would you mind if I went to get ready? There's a cottage pie in the fridge for supper. I made it this morning.'

29

'Simon and I had a terrible row when he got home. I'm so hurt.' Penny, looking very hurt, was sitting in Helen's cheerful garden at Gull's Cry.

'Where was Suzie?'

'Adam took her out to dinner.'

Helen was all ears. 'Adam took Suzie out for dinner?'

'Yes,' said Penny.

'Where did they go?'

'She didn't say and I was too fuming to ask.'

'I'll bet,' said Helen. 'But isn't she quite a bit older than him?' she asked.

Penny managed a laugh. 'God, yes. At least six years older.' She took a deep breath of the fresh spring air. 'Can I come and live here with you? Me and Jenna? Till the old witch has moved on to pastures new?'

'Darling, you'd be very welcome if I had more than one bedroom.'

'How I envy you this little cottage,' said Penny. 'All yours. No one to answer to.'

'When I left the house in Chiswick, after my divorce, I never thought I could find anything I would love as much but this cottage is everything to me now.'

'Maybe I should buy one. I could buy out Paramedic Polly next door and knock through to you.'

'Polly's is smaller than here,' laughed Helen, 'so no

5

storage space for your clothes and the ceilings are even lower.'

'But the gardens are so pretty,' said Penny. 'Look at Mr Brown pottering about in your vegetable plot.'

Simple Tony's sleek black head was bent over a hoe.

'He's working wonders on my early peas. He wants to enter them for the Fayre,' said Helen.

'Really?' said Penny, wanting to get back to the subject of Suzie. 'Anyway, Ella has been moved in by my husband and my half-sister behind my back, because they think I can't look after Jenna properly.'

'I don't think that's true,' said Helen, knowing how her friend could overdramatize the facts. 'I'm sure they have your best interests at heart. After all, looking after a toddler is exhausting. And won't it give you more time to focus on your work?'

'I'm not defined simply by my work,' said Penny petulantly. 'I'm a wife and mother first!'

Helen gave her a raised eyebrow. 'Really?'

'Yes.' Penny's hackles were raised. 'I always put Jenna first. And Simon.'

'Do you always put Simon first?' said Helen.

'Of course I bloody well do,' said Penny crossly. 'When I can get near to him. Suzie gets his breakfast and makes his coffee just as he likes it. He can't believe his luck.'

'I'm sure he's enjoying all the attention.'

'He is. And so is Jenna. And . . .' She rubbed a hand back and forwards across her forehead, 'selfishly, I'm enjoying having the extra time and space for myself. Should I feel more guilty?' she sighed.

'No, not at all.' Helen thought for a moment then said, 'Actually, I'm rather jealous. I wish I had a sister who turned up out of the blue like a fairy godmother.'

'Do you?'

'Yes,' Helen said. 'Suzie told me how thankful she is and how much she respects you for taking her in.'

'Did she? When?'

'I bumped into her in Queenie's.'

Penny sniffed. 'She's trying to win you over.'

'Win me over to what?'

'Her side.'

Helen tutted. 'Penny, she's a nice person. She's on *your* side.'

'Huh. Time will tell.'

Helen changed the subject. 'Anyway, how long is Ella staying for?'

'I don't know. Until I can't stand it any longer, I suppose. The thing is, I like her – very much – and she is really good with Jenna, and it is handy being able to go into my office and not have to keep looking at the clock. But I hate the way Suzie seems to be organizing my life for me! Still, as soon as I can get one big project off the ground, life will go back to normal and Ella and Suzie can get on with their own lives and get out of mine.'

Helen looked at Penny shrewdly. 'I know you are hurting and it's very difficult adapting to having Suzie back in your life, but maybe you should take things at face value. Suzie wants to make amends. And get to know you, her sister after all, better.'

*

Penny lay on Adam's couch and felt his warm hands on her skin, seeking out the exact position for a needle. The French doors of the little clinic were open to the back garden and she could hear the comforting rattle of Simple

Tony's old push mower working next door and the drone of bees feeding on the blue ceanothus by the window.

A long-forgotten memory floated into her mind. It had been sports day and Penny was playing in the final match of the Third Year Tennis Competition. She'd had a headache and an ache in her stomach for a couple of days but she was determined to make her mother and sister proud of her. She was so happy that they'd agreed to travel up to see her. It was a hot day and Penny spotted them sitting in one of the rows of canvas chairs. Margot was wafting a fan under her white hat while Suzie sat primly next to her.

Miss Davis, head of sports, led Penny and her opponent, Lorna Garrin, on to the court. She had a couple of quiet words with the girls about meeting with triumph and disaster then threw Lorna's racquet in the air. Penny chose rough and won the toss.

She walked to her baseline and smoothed down her white pleated tennis skirt with sticky hands. She had grown quite a bit since it had been bought for her, and it barely covered her white frilly knickers. She concentrated on Lorna's face staring at her from the other end of the court. She bounced the ball once or twice, threw it high and served an ace. She flicked her eyes to her mother who was talking to a man next to her. Had she seen?

She crossed to the other corner and served again. For almost an hour they battled, evenly matched, but as the sun got hotter both girls struggled. Penny's headache grew until finally she made a mistake. Lorna had the advantage. Penny was serving to save the match.

She tossed the ball up into the air and, stretching for it, she felt something hot and liquid running down her inner thigh. She hit the ball as hard as she could, then quickly ran her free hand between her legs. Blood. Scarlet blood, spreading a stain across her white pants. She looked up and saw her mother's face: a picture of horror and disgust. The ball had landed at Lorna's feet and she gave it a powerful return. Penny didn't even see it land.

'Game, set, and match to Lorna Garrin,' called Miss Davis.

Penny had run from the court and back to the changing rooms, the heat of the sun and humiliation burning through her, scorching her soul. She stood under the steaming shower, trying to scrub the shame away.

No one came to comfort her.

Eventually she plucked up the courage to look for her mother and sister. They were in the tea tent and Margot could barely look at her.

'I'm sorry, Mummy,' Penny said, desperate for a hug.

Margot stood as stiff as a board and hissed her reply through lips that were white with anger beneath the scarlet lipstick. 'You have humiliated yourself – and me – in front of all these people.'

'It's never happened before. This is the first time . . .' Penny started to weep.

'Stop crying! You are so ugly when you cry.' Margot nodded grimly at the passing headmistress before continuing, 'I shall never forget this.'

Suzie was standing next to her mother, smirking. With vicious glee she said, '*And* you lost the match.'

*

'There,' said Adam. 'That's the last needle in place. You're shivering. Are you cold? Shall I close the doors?'

'I'm fine. Someone walked over my grave. It's nothing,' she said quietly.

'Right. You rest there while the needles do their stuff. Then I'll take them out and you can tell me how you've been this week.'

When she was dressed and sitting in the chair opposite him, she felt suddenly awkward. This was the man who had taken her sister out for dinner. Would he continue to see Penny if he was seeing Suzie as a girl-friend?

'Penny,' he said, taking his pen in his hand and opening her notes, 'before we start, I must say something.'

'Yes?' she said, feeling a horrible dread. Was he going to refer her to another doctor?

'You may know that I gave Suzie a lift to Trevay last night. We're running a new Pilates course at the surgery and she had signed up. I was going in to catch up on some paperwork and she asked for a lift. Afterwards she was hungry so we shared some fish and chips on the way home. I want you to know that everything you and I have spoken of remains confidential. I would never discuss you with a third party, no matter how charming.'

Penny's anxious face started to smile. 'Fish and chips?' she chuckled.

'Yes. She said the Pilates had made her hungry. Actually, the Pilates might do you a lot of good too. Would you like me to see if there is a place left?'

Penny felt the weight of relief flood through her. So he hadn't taken Suzie out to dinner as Suzie had suggested. Ha!

'I don't think I'm a Pilates sort of person,' she said, and at supper that night she couldn't help but needle her sister.

'By the way,' she said, passing the bowl of potatoes, 'you haven't told us where Adam took you for dinner.'

Suzie didn't miss a beat. 'Dinner?'

Penny nodded innocently. 'Yes, last night. You had cooked a cottage pie for us and you went out to dinner with Adam.'

'Did I say dinner? I have so much to think about I get mixed up. Mummy used to, and I get it from her. If I said dinner, I apologize. No, Adam took me to Pilates. I've started classes. In Trevay. He kindly offered me a lift and I accepted. On the way back we were both hungry so we stopped for fish and chips.' She laughed as if it were the funniest thing in the world. 'Dinner! Hardly.' She spooned potatoes onto her plate. 'It's a long time since any man asked me out for dinner.'

Ella had also heard Suzie say she was going to dinner with Adam. She wasn't going to challenge Suzie's statement, but she was interested to find out more about Penny's half-sister. 'Really? But you are so attractive. When was the last date you went on?'

'I really don't remember. Mummy was ill for almost three years and before that she and I did everything together. No room for romance.'

Ella had the bit between her teeth. 'Tell me about the ones who got away?'

Suzie gave Ella an old-fashioned look. 'Mummy always said that a lady never tells. Not that there is much to tell. And anyway,' she turned to Simon and put her hand on his, 'not in front of the vicar.'

He reached over and patted her hand affectionately. 'We need to find you a good man.'

Penny shot her eyes to the ceiling. 'Oh God! Welcome to Mills and Boon night,' she said, lifting her wine glass to her lips.

Suzie simpered. 'You have been so lucky, Penny. You had freedom – and more than your fair share of unsuitable men.'

Penny glowered, but Suzie looked at Simon. 'Then you found Simon. I am still waiting for *my* happy ever after.'

'So am I,' said Ella.

'Young Kit would suit you,' said Simon. 'He's a lovely chap.'

Suzie interrupted. 'Ah, but Ella only has eyes for the doctor, don't you, Ella?'

Ella pinkened, horrified to think that anyone may have suspected her crush on him. 'No!'

'Sorry. Have I embarrassed you?' asked Suzie.

'Don't listen to my sister, Ella,' said Penny. 'She likes to play her little games.'

Suzie toyed with the stem of her wine glass. 'In the olden days, before Simon, Adam would have been exactly your type, wouldn't he, Penny?'

Penny, almost too quickly, denied this. 'God, Suzie, you are so juvenile.' She drained her glass and, reaching for the bottle, topped it up before adding, 'Oh, I get it. You want the doctor for yourself and you're checking out who the competition is. Is that it?'

Suzie gave one of her tinkling, couldn't-care-less laughs. 'Now who's being juvenile?' She stood up and addressed Simon. 'Beloved brother-in-law, there's rhubarb crumble for pudding. I made it just for you.'

'In that case I cannot resist,' said Simon, adding mischievously, 'I must tell Adam what a good cook you are.'

Penny groaned. 'Chauvinism is alive and well in Cornwall tonight.'

Suzie bustled round with a bowl of crumble and a dish of clotted cream. 'We can't all be strident feminists,' she said. 'Some of us believe that caring for another person, a partner, a family, a mother, is the most feminine thing a woman can do.'

Penny stretched theatrically and yawned. 'And that is why, my dear sister, so many women achieve so little with their lives.'

'Penny!' Simon admonished. 'You've gone too far. That deserves an apology.'

Penny almost choked. 'Apologize for what? For getting off my arse and working hard? For sharing what I've had with others? For paying people good wages in order that they can feed their families and meet their mortgages? For entertaining millions of people with good television programmes? For settling here, in the back of bloody beyond, with you? No. I have done *nothing* to apologize for.'

30

Suzie was thoroughly enjoying her new life. She was drying her hair after a lengthy shower and revelling in the knowledge that no one would call for her or intrude on her. She missed her mother, naturally, but she didn't miss the endless cycle of caring for someone who had been so dependent. As soon as her alarm went off each morning at six thirty it had been a steady stream of mundane and relentless tasks. Slippers, pills, tea just so, the crossword together, lunches barely touched, papery hands pointing and shaking. No, it had not been fun. But it was over. She was released. The sale of the house and contents would give her more than enough with which to live out her days. Not that she would tell Penny that. Penny had quite enough of her own, after all. No, this was Suzie's just reward. She would keep the nicer bits of jewellery – the emerald engagement ring and matching drop earrings, among them – and sell the rest. She'd also keep some personal bits: her mother's photo albums, diaries, and the only remaining things that had belonged to her father. His watch. His briefcase. A silver-framed photo. She hadn't told Penny about any of these things. She knew that Penny would want them but Suzie didn't want her to have them. He had been Suzie's father too. She knew he hadn't loved her as he had loved Penny and something unkind in her wanted to deprive her sister of his things as he had deprived Suzie of his love. So she had tucked everything away in a large, zipped laundry bag, and pushed it under her bed at the vicarage.

She turned the hairdryer off and began doing her make-up. A little mascara, some blusher and a nude lip gloss was all that was needed down here in Cornwall. Yesterday she'd nipped into Trevay and treated herself to a new summer wardrobe. Her Hertfordshire clothes looked much too formal and drab and she'd chosen three linen sundresses, four stripey T-shirts and a pair of not-too-short shorts. She'd added a hoodie as she'd noticed that everyone seemed to wear them and they were very practical. How her mother would have hated that!

Face done, she picked one of the linen dresses, lime green, and added a pair of pretty sandals and tied a soft cotton scarf around her neck. Today was going to be a busy one. She'd decided that this morning she was going to change all the bed sheets and get them out on the line, give Ella instructions to make a frittata and salad for lunch, then go in search of Kit on the pretext of offering to walk Terry and Celia.

Twenty minutes later all the beds were made with fresh linen and she was on her way downstairs with a basket of dirty laundry balanced on her hip. She crept past Penny's closed office but stopped at Simon's study door and knocked lightly.

'Come in,' called Simon.

She opened the door and popped her head round. 'Fancy a coffee? It's almost elevenses.'

Simon took his glasses off and rubbed his eyes wearily. 'You are heaven-sent, Suzie. I'd love one.'

She edged her way round the door and closed it. 'You look tired.'

He gestured to the papers in front of him. 'I'm writing my piece for the parish magazine and it's hard to think of something new every time. Between you and me, I dread it. Audrey Tipton is the editor and she pulls me up on the slightest grammatical error.'

Suzie put the laundry basket down and sat on the arm of the well-worn leather armchair. 'She runs everything in the village, doesn't she?'

'Yes. She'd have been a match for Mrs Thatcher, Genghis Khan and Voldemort rolled into one.'

Suzie laughed warmly. 'Well, I think you're doing an excellent job, not only in your parish, but with my sister too. I know she can't be easy.'

Simon sighed. 'I have been worried about her.' He looked down at his hands, which he noticed were steepled as if he were praying. He shifted them to a clasp. 'I'm sorry she was so rude to you over supper the other night.'

'Water off a duck's back. Just sisters giving each other a ragging.'

'Perhaps. I know things were hard for her in her childhood. Losing her father affected her deeply.'

'I know. It was terrible for Mummy and me too.'

'I'm sure it was.' He thought for a moment. 'May I ask you something? No need to answer if you don't want to.'

'Of course. Ask away.'

'Why did your mother never reveal that she wasn't Penny's mother?'

Suzie said with sadness, 'Who knows why parents do anything?'

'But you knew. Why didn't you tell Penny?'

'As a child you have no power and if a grown-up tells you to keep a secret you do. And as we got older I almost forgot about it.'

'It must have been very hard on you.'

'Yes it was, but . . . what's done is done. I hope that by being here I can build bridges and let you all see how sorry I am.' She pushed herself from her perch and stood up. 'Starting with a nice cup of coffee.' She picked up her laundry basket and went to the door. 'A couple of digestives?'

He held his hands up. 'No, no. I'll never get into my wetsuit again if I keep eating all you give me.'

'You look fine to me,' she smiled.

He patted his small belly. 'Got to stay fit for Jenna. And by the way, is that a new dress? It suits you.'

Suzie smiled again and closed the door behind her with delight.

The last of the sheets was flapping on the line when Ella called from the back door, 'Lunch is ready.'

'I'll have mine later,' said Suzie. 'Just nipping over to see Kit . . .'

Kit opened the door of Marguerite Cottage with a paintbrush between his teeth and a turpentine rag in his hand. Terry stalked up behind him and sniffed Suzie with a nonchalant disinterest.

'Suzie, to what do I owe this pleasure?'

'I could do with a walk and I wondered if Terry and Celia would like to join me? You too if you're not busy?'

He hesitated, thinking, then, 'You know what? Bugger Lady Chafford. She can wait.'

'I beg your pardon?' laughed Suzie. 'Poor Lady Chafford! May I see her?'

Kit had told the story of Lady Chafford when he'd come for the 'welcome to Pendruggan' dinner party thrown for Suzie, and she had been intrigued to see his work ever since. Not to mention the pleasure of having a good nose inside the cottage.

'She's upstairs. Follow me,' said Kit, leading the way.

On the landing Suzie did her best to see into the two bedrooms and bathroom before entering Kit's studio, but could see very little other than unmade beds and an overflowing laundry basket in the bathroom.

'It's so lovely and light in here,' she said.

'Yup. Had the roof lights put in when we took on the tenancy. Gorgeous light to work in. Here she is.' He walked to his easel in a corner of the room.

Suzie studied it. 'It's fantastic. Is that staircase for real?'

'Oh yes. Staircase and jewels are all real. The breasts and face maybe not.'

'You mean she's had . . .'

'A little assistance I believe, yes.'

'Well, they certainly are quite a focus.'

'Do you think she'll like it?'

'She'll love it. Mummy always wanted to have her portrait painted but it was beyond our means,' Suzie said wistfully.

Before Kit could respond the dogs started barking at the front door.

'That'll be the postman,' said Kit, leaving the room and heading downstairs to collect the post.

There was quite a breeze on Shellsand Bay, enough to brush long, white, whiskers of spray off the tops of the rollers.

'I haven't seen white horses like that since I was little,'

said Suzie, pulling her scarf around her neck. 'They're so beautiful.'

'I'd love to have my paints here now. Seascapes are my thing.'

'Then why aren't you painting them instead of Lady Chafford?

'Needs must. But as soon as I'm finished with her, I'll get down here.'

Suzie rubbed at the goose bumps on her arms.

'Would you like my jacket?' Kit asked.

'That would be very kind. Thank you. I should have brought my new hoodie.'

'You! In a hoodie?' smiled Kit, holding out his corduroy jacket for her to slip her arms into.

'I'm embracing the Cornish life,' she laughed.

The two of them walked the wide length of the beach, Suzie picking up shells and little pebbles, Kit stopping to skim a stone or call the dogs back who were racing along the damp sand.

'They love it here,' he told her.

'So do I,' she said. 'I can see why my sister came here.'

'How is she?' asked Kit. 'Is she feeling a lot happier now?'

'Adam is doing her the world of good.'

'I hope so. I know he likes her very much and admires her strength and optimism.'

Suzie stopped and picked up a small pink shell, rolling it between her fingers. 'Doesn't he have to be careful? Not to send out the wrong signals?'

'What do you mean?'

'Penny is very vulnerable just now. Supposing she developed feelings for him?'

'Has she said anything?'

'No, but I know she thinks a lot of him.'

'Do you want me to mention it to Adam?'

'Gosh no. No need for that. It's just that she is so very needy. And what with Simon working all the time . . . well, I just worry about her that's all.' She put her hand on his arm. 'Forget I said anything.' She pulled his coat tighter around her. 'The wind is getting up. Shall we go back?'

Later that afternoon, Kit phoned Adam and suggested he meet him after work so that they could have a pint at the Golden Hind pub on the harbour front. 'It would be nice just to chill and chat without all of Pendruggan knocking at the door,' he'd said.

'Great idea,' said Adam.

In Trevay, holidaymakers with pushchairs and dogs, were ambling through the narrow streets licking ice creams and stopping to stare through the windows of gift shops and estate agents, each dreaming of a life living by the sea and killing the time between lunch and supper.

'Two pints of Doom Bar, please,' Kit asked Pete the landlord and while he pulled their pints, Kit looked around the bar. Low-ceilinged, a comforting smell of beer and a log fire – and, thankfully, quiet.

'Here you are,' said Pete, placing the full glasses on a bar towel.

'Thanks.' Kit paid then took them outside to where Adam was sitting in the evening sun.

'God, what a day,' Adam said as he pulled his tie loose and undid the top button of his shirt. 'Cheers.'

'Cheers!' responded Kit, tipping the cool clean ale down his throat. 'That's bloody good,' said Adam, wiping the foam from his lips.

Kit did the same. He was stalling for time, not knowing how to ask the question he'd brought Adam here for. He decided to jump in. 'Adam?'

'Yes.'

'That trouble you had last year. With the complaint.'

'That loony woman? She made my life hell. Renewed my faith in the NHS, though. I was exonerated. Pity the poor bastard who gets her as his next patient.'

'So, why did you feel you had to leave the practice when your innocence was proved?'

Adam looked sharply at his cousin. 'I told you: because I wanted to get away from it and start afresh. It was a terrible time. Like a bad smell that just wouldn't go away.' He took another mouthful of beer and looked around the harbour. 'Anyway, this is a much nicer place to be.'

'How would you protect yourself from anything like that happening again?'

Adam gave Kit a suspicious look. 'By being bloody certain that there is always a nurse in the room for intimate examinations. Why do you ask?'

'Nothing. I had a walk with Suzie today and she mentioned that she thought Penny was vulnerable and liked you and I wanted to make sure that you—'

'Didn't do anything?' Adam was angry. 'Do you really think I'm that sort of man? Do you really think I am capable of sexually assaulting a patient? Particularly one who is emotionally vulnerable? God Kit, you of all people.'

'Of course I don't! But I want you to protect yourself. You're a handsome single man,' said Kit apologetically, 'and some women may read a situation wrong.'

Adam drained his pint. 'I am a professional. Even in

the Garden Clinic, where I don't do intimate examinations, Ella is right outside the door. And I never book
out-of-hours appointments. After that bloody woman
who almost ruined me, believe me, I protect myself.'

'I believe you.'

'I couldn't go through that again. And as for being
single, well, if there was anyone who attracted me it
would be Penny's sister, Suzie, but I'd never get involved
while Penny was my patient. Now, get me another pint.'

31

'How many?' Penny asked in exasperation.

'About a dozen,' said Simon patiently.

Penny threw herself on to the sofa in a huff. 'But why do they have to come *here*.'

'Because this is where they've always come.'

'But the village fayre isn't for ages yet.'

'It's in two weeks. You know as well as I do that tonight is when all the individual committees come together to discuss how the whole thing fits together.'

'But why do they always have to come here?' Penny was sounding like a petulant toddler.

'We've got the space.'

'Arrgh,' said Penny truculently. 'This is the last time, OK?'

'OK.'

'*And* they'd better not ask me to run the cream teas in the garden again just because I'm the vicar's wife.'

'Understood,' he said as the door to the drawing room opened and Suzie came in carrying an arrangement of vivid pink rhododendrons from the garden. 'What's understood?' she asked, placing them on a mat on top of the piano.

'Penny and I were just discussing the committee meeting tonight,' said Simon.

'Ah yes. I've got some sandwiches and biscuits ready,'

Suzie said. 'And I dug out the tea urn from the vestry. They'll want a hot drink.' She looked at Penny. 'Should I provide them with pencils and notepads, Pen?'

'Why ask me?' snorted Penny

'Because you've been doing this for a few years now but it's my first time and I don't want to forget anything.'

'If you give them too much you'll never get rid of them. All they got from me was half a glass of cheap sherry. Good luck.' And with that Penny left the room.

Simon covered up for his wife. 'They're a pretty self-sufficient lot, actually. Usually a biscuit and a cup of tea is enough.'

'Well,' said Suzie, plumping the squashed cushions on the recently vacated sofa, 'I think we can do better than that.'

Mrs Audrey Tipton, with her husband, Geoffrey, in tow, was the first to arrive. Suzie opened the door to them. 'You're rather early,' she said, 'but do come in. I'm all ready for you.'

Audrey Tipton narrowed her eyes and said, 'That sounds rather like a challenge.'

Suzie met the steely gaze fearlessly. 'Oh yes, I like a challenge. May I offer some refreshment?'

She took them into the drawing room. 'I have tea, coffee or squash.'

Mr Audrey Tipton's eyes leered at the meagre drinks table. 'Penny usually offers a sherry.'

'Well, I'm so sorry,' said Suzie, sounding very unsorry, 'but I can only offer soft drinks tonight.'

'He'll have a coffee. Same as me. Splash of milk two sugars,' commanded Audrey.

'Excellent. Do take a seat.'

Suzie bustled out of the room and knocked on Simon's study door. 'The harridan has arrived. Would you mind listening for the front door for newcomers while I make the coffee?'

Soon the drawing room was filled, with bodies balancing on the sofa, armchairs and kitchen chairs brought in for the purpose.

Audrey Tipton was in Simon's chair, commanding the room.

'Order! Order!' she called, tapping a teaspoon on the side of her cup. The room quickly settled.

She looked over them sternly before speaking. 'This year is my silver anniversary – twenty-five years as chairman of the Pendruggan Fayre.'

The room mumbled its awe and appreciation.

'And whilst I am at the helm, I want this to be the best year in its history. I want other generations to use us as a benchmark for years to come. In light of this, I have asked the vicar to collect the records of all our planning, execution, and achievement to be placed in the village archives for posterity.'

Suzie let out a laugh, which she quickly attempted to turn into a cough. 'So sorry. Dreadful hay fever.'

Audrey glowered at her and continued her lengthy and self-serving, speech, setting out exactly how marvellous she had been for the last twenty-five years and how she hoped to be chairman for the next twenty-five too. Finally she opened the floor to the others, who had to fully explain all that they had done, were doing, and would do.

It was a long night.

The rotary club were in charge of the beer tent and the barbecue.

Horticultural tent went to Mr Audrey Tipton, assisted by Simple Tony.

Polly the paramedic would man her Psychic Polly stall along with a new sideline of herbal remedies.

The WI members were all over cakes and jams.

The Stitch and Bitch group had been crafting endlessly all year.

The Scouts and Guides would run the Bowl for A Pig and Ferret Racing.

And the pipe band from Truro and the Trevay Drum Majorettes would play and give two marching displays.

'I must say this is all looking very heartening,' nodded Audrey to the group. 'For the art competition I have decided the theme is to be The Spirit of Cornwall and The Sea.' She looked over at Ella. 'I hear *you* are interested in Art. You can be in charge of that.'

'Oh,' said Ella a little shocked. 'What does it entail?'

Audrey gave an impatient sigh. 'Getting artistic people to bring their paintings. Then you hang the pictures in the church. The best one gets a prize.' That was all Ella was going to get and Audrey returned to her notes. 'That just leaves the rounders match. Should be huge fun. Used to play at school and I was pretty good.'

'So was I,' Queenie chirped. 'Very fast runner in me day.'

Audrey looked bored. 'Yes, well it's your day no longer.'

'Are you saying I can't be on the team?' argued Queenie.

'Well, would it be wise? A woman of your age?'

'It ain't the bloody Olympics.'

Audrey waved her hand dismissively. 'Do as you please. But don't expect any injury to be covered by the public liability insurance.'

Suzie stood up. 'Well done, everybody. Now, who would like a cup of tea? Coffee? And I have some sandwiches if anyone is peckish.'

The room broke into sounds of gratitude and relief.

'Just a moment,' boomed Audrey. 'I have not closed this meeting yet. We still have several things to discuss.'

Her steely, piggy eyes swept across the assembled faces. 'Where is Mrs Canter?'

Simon rubbed his hand anxiously over his bald head and stood up. 'She sends her apologies but cannot be here due to work commitments.'

Mrs Tipton sniffed. 'Well I hope her work commitments won't keep her from hostessing the Vicarage Cream-Tea Garden.'

Simon was cornered. 'I'm sure that, work permitting, she'll be here.'

'Work permitting?' Audrey smelled a rat. 'Work permitting? I'm sorry, vicar, but that is just not good enough. I need commitment. I *demand* commitment.'

The room fidgeted uncomfortably. Eyes were downcast. Fingers were fiddled with.

'Well, you see,' started Simon, 'Penny has—'

Before he could finish, Suzie spoke up. 'Penny has passed the cream teas on to me.'

Audrey shifted her raptor gaze to Suzie, whom she disliked immensely for no better reason than that she saw a rebel. A dissenter. A competitor. 'You? And what qualifies you?'

Suzie smiled sweetly. 'Well, it's not that difficult is it? Hot water, teabags, a spoon of coffee . . . I have a hundred scones already in the freezer. I'm doing batches of twenty a night.'

'Are you?' asked Simon, surprised.

'Oh yes. I knew Penny would be overwhelmed with other things so I've been busy.'

'What about the jam?' asked Audrey triumphantly, spotting a weakness in Suzie's plan.

'I've been coordinating with the Women's Institute and they've kindly sold me enough jars at a cut price,' Suzie replied.

Audrey, shocked that *her* women in the WI could be so treacherous, was not about to be defeated and played her trump card. 'That's all well and good,' she smirked, 'but you can't have a cream tea without proper Cornish clotted cream. You won't be getting *that* at cost price.'

Mr Tipton shouted, 'Hear, hear.' And Audrey gave him a little a smirk.

'Ah yes,' said Suzie, frowning a little. 'That could have been a problem.'

The room, whose eyes had been swivelling like a Wimbledon crowd from one opponent to the other, turned to Mrs Tipton who was surely about to claim the match. 'Aha!' she said. 'No cream, no cream teas.'

Suzie stayed calm. 'Exactly. Which is why I phoned Trevay Dairy and asked if they would sponsor us. They provide the clotted cream and in return they have a stall, under the trees in the garden, selling their cheese, milk and butter and taking orders to post the clotted cream anywhere in the country for the holidaymakers.'

The room gasped in admiration.

Audrey, puce, sat down.

Suzie rubbed her hands together. 'Right, I'll get the sandwiches and tea on, shall I?'

32

J enna and Penny were rolling together on the lawn and laughing more and more the giddier they got.

'I'm coming to catch you!' said Penny, reaching out her hands in an attempt to tickle Jenna.

Jenna shrieked with joy and rolled over twice more. 'No, Mumma. No!'

'Yes, Mumma, yes,' said Penny, stretching her hand out again and catching her wriggling daughter. She lifted her into her arms and covered her in loud kisses.

Jenna stopped wriggling and looked up into Penny's face. 'Love Mumma,' she said, and placed her sweaty little hand on Penny's nose.

'Love you, Jenna.'

Ella appeared at the back door. 'Time for a snoozies,' she called.

'Oh good,' said Penny, 'I'm ready for my sleep.'

Jenna giggled. 'Silly Mumma. *Jenna* sleep.'

'No, Mumma sleep.'

'No, *Jenna* sleep.'

Ella walked towards the two of them. 'I'll put you both in bed in a minute. Come on.' She helped Penny and Jenna to their feet then took Jenna in her arms.

'Have a good snooze, darling,' said Penny. Then to Ella, 'I'll put some coffee on.'

When Ella came back down she sat at the kitchen

table with Penny and cradled her cup of coffee. 'You and Jenna have a really special bond, don't you?'

Penny said anxiously, 'Do you think so?'

'Absolutely. You clearly adore each other. You're a very good mum.'

'Am I? I wasn't very good a couple of months ago when I was so tired and unwell.'

'Who could be! You were having a rough time. You won't be the first and you won't be the last.'

'You know I tried to . . . well, I took too many pills one night and now, when I think about it, it's as if that was another person.'

Ella reached out her hand and put it on top of Penny's. 'You had a hell of a lot on your plate.'

Penny smiled. 'Thank you.'

'What for?'

'Being here and being so good with Jenna. You being here has done us all good.'

Ella pursed her lips comically. 'One good thing that Suzie has done then!' Then she stopped, horrified. 'Oh I'm sorry, I didn't mean to say that about Suzie.'

Penny giggled. 'My sister is a bit bossy, I agree. But hiring you was the best thing for all of us.'

They heard a key in the front door lock and Suzie came in. 'Helloo!' she shouted down the hall.

'Hi, we're in the kitchen drinking coffee,' called back Penny.

Suzie came in looking frazzled and loaded with several shopping bags. 'The supermarket was packed with holidaymakers. I wouldn't mind, but they clog up the aisles with their children and husbands, mooching along the sections as if they'd never been in a shop before.' She dumped the bags on the table and began to unpack. 'I should have known better than to go when it's a bit cloudy. If they're not in the shops, they're in the restaurants, the car parks and – oh, hark at me. I sound like a local.'

Ella and Penny exchanged a knowing look and tried not to laugh. Ella got up and put her empty mug in the sink. 'I'll get some lunch on. I was thinking of cheese salad?'

'Lovely,' said Penny. 'I've got an hour or so to do in the office.'

Suzie, emptying the last of her bags said, 'No, Penny. I am taking you out to lunch.'

'Suzie, there's no need, I've got some emails to do and I'm seeing Adam later.'

'The emails can wait and I'll have you back in time for Adam,' Suzie said. She put her hands on Penny's shoulders and rubbed them affectionately. 'You work too hard and I want to spoil you. There's a new café restaurant opened on the beach near Watergate Bay. We are going to try it out.'

Penny, surprised by Suzie's sudden kindness, protested but to no avail.

'Well, this is nice,' said Penny, sitting at a round table on a veranda overlooking the beach and the sea.

'Adam was talking about it the other day,' said Suzie, then added conspiratorially, 'I think he wants to bring me here for dinner.'

Penny raised an eyebrow behind her sunglasses. The last time she'd spoken to Adam about Suzie he had been clear in letting her know he wasn't interested in her. Hadn't he? 'Really? When did he mention this?' she asked.

'Just in passing.'

'In passing?' frowned Penny. 'Where were you passing?'

Suzie pulled her sunglasses down from her head and pushed her hands through her hair. 'So many questions, Pen! Can I help it if he seeks me out?'

'Does he?'

Suzie put her glasses back on top of her head and narrowed her eyes at her sister. 'As a matter of fact, yes. But I am mindful of him being your doctor and so I am keeping my distance.'

The waiter brought their drinks and Suzie toyed with the slice of lemon in her lime and soda before saying, 'Anyway, I thought you were keen on him.'

Penny blushed. 'Not at all, although he is very handsome. But the more I've got to know him, the less that means. He's just a nice man and a good doctor.'

Suzie leaned forward and with a pantomime wink whispered, 'As soon as you're better, I'll tip my cap at him.' It was so comical, and reminded Penny of secrets and jokes they'd shared as children, that she laughed.

'Oh Suzie, I'd forgotten how funny you could be.'

Suzie smiled back. 'It's good to see you laughing, funny face.'

'God, no one has called me that for years.' Penny thought back. 'Not since Daddy died.'

The sisters sat without speaking, each with her own memories, watching the ocean sparkling in the sunshine. Several surfers were paddling their way out to the curling rollers. Penny watched as they pointed their boards to the beach and waited to catch a good wave. Suddenly they were alert to a big one rearing behind them and in one fluid movement they were up on their boards and riding the water into the beach.

In the shallows, the smaller children were splashing on their boogie boards, shrieking with pleasure.

Penny remembered an unhappy holiday after her father had died. Margot had taken them to a rented cottage in Devon, inland from the sea. Every day she pleaded with Margot to take them to the beach, and every day Margot said no.

Penny broke the silence. 'Why didn't you tell me about Margot's last illness? I could have helped, would have wanted to know.'

Suzie fidgeted awkwardly with the cutlery in front of her, then said, 'I am sorry. I wanted to get in touch but Mummy was absolutely adamant. If I mentioned you she would get very het up and in the end I stopped. The doctor said it was best. You know how stubborn and unforgiving she could be.'

Penny nodded, waiting for the sudden mixed emotions of loss, pain and loneliness to subside.

Suzie leant her elbows on the table, something she would never have done if Margot had been there, and said with all earnestness, 'Penny, I am so sorry. For everything. It's part of the reason why I'm here, in Cornwall. I want you to know how sorry I am.'

Penny dipped her head for a moment then fiddled with her drink. 'What's there to forgive?'

'You were hurt. We hurt you. *I* hurt you. I should have got Mummy to tell you about us being half-sisters. I should have been kinder to you when Daddy died. I've thought about it so much. Wondering why, how, I could have been so unkind.' Suzie brushed what looked like a tear from her eye. 'I think perhaps Mummy and I were jealous of you.'

'Jealous?'

'You were Daddy's favourite and a reminder of the fact that Daddy had loved another woman before he met Mummy.'

'But that's silly. He loved you both very much. I know he did.'

'But he loved you best.'

Penny's eyes were filling with tears too. 'Thank you for saying it.'

Suzie's tears were flowing steadily now; she pulled a tissue from her bag and offered one to Penny too. 'I am so, so sorry, Pen. You have been very generous. Not just in the past, but from the moment I turned up on your doorstep. I haven't felt this happy for a very long time.'

Penny dabbed at her eyes and then at her runny nose. 'Do I have my sister back?'

'If you'll have me – but there's something else I haven't told you. You might hate me for it.' Suzie's face was etched with pain.

'What is it?' asked Penny gently.

Suzie, crying more now, was finding it hard to get her words out. 'I have been so spiteful. I told you that Mummy had kept none of Daddy's things, but – please try to understand – I *have* got something.'

'What?' asked Penny, her heart beginning to pound. 'Tell me.'

'It's his briefcase. I honestly forgot all about it.'

'His briefcase?' Penny immediately had an image of her father coming home from work and walking up the drive carrying his well-worn, buckled leather case. She remembered the smell of the leather and his name written inkily inside on the bobbly suede lining. Michael Leighton Upper Sixth. A present from his father to encourage him in his final school exams. 'I remember it. Where is it?'

'At home.'

'The vicarage?'

'Yes, under my bed. I swear I forgot all about it until the other day. I want you to have it.'

Penny's breathing was shallow and fast. The adrenaline was flowing. 'I want to see it now. Let's go.'

'But what about lunch? I wanted to treat you. To thank you.'

'We haven't ordered yet. Please, Suzie, let's just go. I've waited long enough.'

The drive back was agonizingly slow. The narrow lanes were blocked with caravans and mobile homes and even a double decker bus.

Penny nibbled at her nails and tapped her feet with impatience. Eventually they turned into Pendruggan, rounded the village green, and pulled up in the vicarage drive.

She ran upstairs ahead of Suzie and threw the door open to her sister's bedroom. Diving onto her knees she scrabbled under the bed.

Suzie reached her. 'Here, let me.' She grabbed a laundry bag and took the briefcase out, making sure Penny didn't see the rest of the contents – her father's watch and silver-framed photo.

Penny touched the edged stitching of the leather case and brought it straight to her face to breathe in the scent she had longed for. Yes, it was still there. Leather, saddle soap, tobacco and – was she imagining it? – her father's unique smell.

Suzie looked ashamed. 'I'm so sorry.'

Penny hugged her. 'Darling, it's OK. It's OK. I can't thank you enough for this precious precious gift. It smells of Daddy. Sniff and see.'

Suzie pushed her nose towards the briefcase and sniffed tentatively.

'It's him,' said Penny joyfully. 'It's like he's in the room.' A sudden thought hit her. 'Is there anything in it?'

Suzie wrinkled her brow. 'I don't think so, but why don't you check?'

Penny sat on the bed with the briefcase on her knees and began to undo the two buckles.

As soon as she flipped it open she saw his name inked exactly as she had remembered it. Then slowly, almost reverentially, she opened the case further and slipped her hand inside.

There was nothing in it. 'Oh,' she said, her shoulders slumping. She tried the front zipped pocket, but it wouldn't open. 'It's empty.'

She was utterly deflated. 'He used to bring us a Fry's Chocolate Cream bar every Friday. Do you remember?'

'Yes. I hated it.'

'I loved them because he loved them.' Penny looked up at her sister. 'Thank you. Really. From the bottom of my heart. Thank you. May I keep it?'

'Of course. It's yours.'

Penny brought the case back up to her lips and she kissed it.

At her appointment, Adam was very surprised and interested to hear about this new development. He sat at his desk listening intently as Penny recounted the story. 'And so now I understand my feelings towards Margot and Suzie,' Penny told him. 'Unconsciously I was jealous of them for having each other while I was sent off to boarding school and then straight out to work. Unconsciously I was jealous that they had memories of Daddy that I couldn't share with them. And now Suzie tells me that she and Margot were jealous of *me*. How weird is that? God, what a lot of wasted time. And now Suzie has given me the best gift of all. A memory of Daddy – and a sister.'

Adam rubbed his chin. 'And how does that make you feel?'

'Like shit. I have been so selfish and I hurt them greatly when I walked away from them. No wonder Margot didn't want to see me. And poor Suzie. I left her with all the responsibility of looking after Margot while I had an easy life and she had no life.'

'That was her choice. And let's not forget your life hasn't been a bed of roses,' said Adam.

'Maybe not, but Suzie didn't have a choice because I'd walked away.'

'I think you're being too hard on yourself.'

'I've got a lot of making up to do and I am just so thankful that I've been given the time. Simon is always saying that God moves in mysterious ways. He certainly has this time.'

'Have you told him yet?'

'I phoned him from the car. He's so happy. As happy as me.'

'That's good.' Adam leaned forwards and pulled her file towards him. 'How's the medication going?'

'Wonderful. I feel back to normal.'

'Good. Do you have enough or shall I write you a new prescription?'

'I have plenty. Actually, I was wondering if I needed

to take them any more. Your counselling and acupuncture have worked wonders and I am so grateful to you.'

'Oh I think we'll keep you on them just a little longer and then slowly start reducing the dose when I think you're ready.'

Penny stood up, ready to leave. 'By the way, Adam, the restaurant Suzie took me to, in Watergate Bay?'

'Hmm,' said Adam, already thinking about his next patient.

'I think it would be a great idea for you to take her to supper there.'

Adam frowned and was about to say something but thought better of it.

'It's OK,' said Penny smiling, 'I don't expect you to breach any confidences. Bye.'

33

Ella had a day off and was in her bedroom at the vicarage, lolling on her bed.

Penny, who was in an unusually good mood, had taken Suzie and Jenna out for the day. 'Darling, you have a break from looking after us,' she'd said to Ella. 'Go for a swim or something. It's a lovely day.'

'Are you sure?'

'Of course. Off you go – and don't worry about supper, we'll bring in a Chinese,' she said, collecting up her bag and ushering a grinning Suzie out of the door.

'Where are you off to?' asked Ella.

'We're going to spend a girlie day together. Jenna and I are going to spoil Auntie Suzie a bit. Byee.'

Ella wondered what had happened between the two sisters. For the last couple of days they had been very close and affectionate with each other.

Ella's phone buzzed. A text message from Kit. She opened it.

Beautiful day. Am delivering the finished Chafford portrait. Like to come? We could have a pub lunch on the way back?

Ella couldn't think of a reason why not. She typed: *What time?*

He replied: *Ten minutes?*

As she arrived at Marguerite Cottage Kit was sliding Lady Chafford's portrait into the back of the car.

'Hi,' said Ella, taking a look at the finished picture. 'She's going to love it.'

Kit looked at Ella and took in her beautiful flame red curls dancing in the breeze, and her slender freckled legs looking adorable in her white shorts. His heart skipped its usual beat whenever he saw her. He hid his reaction by carefully covering Lady Chafford's likeness in an old sheet. 'I bloody well hope she does.'

The interior of the car was scorching – the beginning of May had brought a sudden heatwave and taken everyone by surprise. Kit started the engine and opened all the windows. 'I hope you don't mind the fresh air. I can't stand air conditioning.'

'Fresh air is best,' Ella said, slipping on her seat belt. 'We can smell the hedgerows and the sea.'

'Your hair might blow about a bit,' said Kit, worried suddenly that she might be more high maintenance than he'd expected.

'No problem.' She delved into her soft cotton handbag and pulled out a pencil. She twisted her hair into a bun and anchored it, using the pencil as a hairpin. 'Ta dah!'

'How resourceful,' said Kit, feeling himself take yet another step towards falling in love with her.

They drove out of the village and Ella rummaged in the glove pocket looking at the handful of CDs he had. She pulled out *Graceland* by Paul Simon and stuffed it into the CD player. 'At school we spent a whole term listening to this. Do you mind if I turn it up?'

Kit couldn't think of a happier car journey. They sang their way through each song, Lala-ing over lyrics they couldn't remember and laughing at each other's mistakes. The sky was almost violet in its blueness and the sun lit up the moorland hills, picking out the white sheep grazing on the golden gorse, and sparkling on the many small bodies of water.

Eventually they turned in at the gates of Chafford Hall and drove through the dappled tunnel of rhododendrons. The house itself lay in the sunshine, with its circular drive of gravel crunching under the tyres. Kit stopped the car and killed the engine.

'Wow,' said Ella. '"Last night I dreamt I went to Manderley again".'

Kit looked at her. 'I love that book.'

'Really?' exclaimed Ella.

'Oh yes. My mother had all Daphne du Maurier's novels. She read *Rebecca* to me when I was recovering from chickenpox.'

'Mrs Danvers was my favourite character. So evil,' said Ella.

Kit laughed, then said in a chilling voice, 'I can hear the rustle of her bombazine black dress coming down the stairs to terrorize the new Mrs de Winter.'

Ella was delighted. 'Ooh, shall we see if we can get the DVD and freak ourselves out?'

'It'll be my mission to seek it out.' He looked at her smiling eyes and the freckles sprinkled across her nose and wanted to kiss her. He had almost made up his mind to do so when Lady Chafford threw open the heavy front door of Chafford Hall and called out, 'Yoo hoo!'

'Well, that was a success,' said Kit, helping Ella into the car forty-five minutes later. 'I think she really liked it.'

'She loved it,' said Ella. 'Why else would she commission you to paint one of Lord Chafford next?'

Kit patted the cheque in his top pocket. 'Maybe we will have champagne for supper after all.'

'A half of lager and a pub lunch will do me,' smiled Ella.

'Good. I know just the place.'

The car park at the St Kew Inn was pleasingly full and Kit parked in the shade of the trees by the river.

The bar was dark against the bright sunshine, but welcoming with its low ceiling and friendly atmosphere. They ordered drinks and food. Ella chose the Porthilly Mussels and Kit picked the beer-battered goujons with peas and chips.

'Would you like to eat outside?' asked the barman. 'I'll bring it to your table.'

In the pretty garden they chose a table in the shade and sipped their drinks.

'What time have you got to be back?' he asked her.

'No time. Penny gave me the whole day off. She's taken Suzie and Jenna out for the day.'

'Really? That's good. Are relations between them warming up?' asked Kit.

Ella's loyalty to Penny and Simon kicked in and she didn't want to say too much. 'Maybe.'

The barman arrived with their food and for the next few minutes they busied themselves with cutlery and ketchup.

Kit offered his chips and tomato sauce to Ella before asking, 'How *is* Penny?'

'Fine,' said Ella neutrally.

'I hope she's happier after her, well, shall we call it her cry for help?'

'She's doing well. She's a great mum to Jenna.'

Kit felt awkward to press on with this questioning but he was worried for Adam. 'How are things with her and Simon?'

Ella was annoyed. 'I'm sorry, Kit, but I don't feel comfortable answering these questions. She's my employer.'

'Sorry.'

'She and Simon adore each other.'

'Good, good.'

They continued their lunch. Then Ella asked, 'Why do you want to know?'

'It's nothing, really. Forget I asked.'

'Well, now I think there's a reason you asked – come on, what is it?'

'Um, this is a bit awkward but, well, Suzie said something the other day.'

'What?' asked Ella.

'She said that she thought . . .' Kit rubbed his forehead with anxious fingers. 'This is hard! Erm . . . she said that she thought Penny might be developing feelings for Adam.'

Ella burst out laughing. 'Jealous cow!'

Kit felt relieved. 'Is that what it is?'

'Almost certainly. I mean, Adam is a good-looking man and I think every woman – and maybe some men – have fallen for his looks and charm. But Penny? Nah.'

'Well, that's all right, then.'

Ella looked at Kit with suspicion. 'Why are you asking?'

Now it was Kit's turn to play his cards close to his chest. 'No reason.'

'Yes there is,' probed Ella.

Kit thought for a moment, then looked her square in the eyes. 'If I tell you something, can you promise me not to tell another living soul?'

Ella nodded, touched by his sudden solemnity and sincerity. 'Of course.'

'Adam would be furious and very hurt if he knew I'd told anyone.'

'I promise not to say a word – if you are sure you want to tell me.'

'I do want to tell you. You see, Adam was almost struck off at his last surgery because a woman, a patient, accused him of inappropriate behaviour.'

Ella's eyes were wide. 'What? What happened?'

'The woman was suffering episodes of anxiety and was later diagnosed with a bit of a personality disorder.'

'Oh dear, poor woman. And how awful for Adam.'

Kit nodded. 'Her mind got fixated on Adam. He's a very good doctor and treated her like any other patient, but then she started to send him small gifts. He returned them all. But after that she began putting notes on his windscreen. Invitations for drinks, her mobile phone number, dates when her husband would be away on business. Naturally, he threw them all away.'

'Was he still treating her?'

'Yes. That was a big mistake, which he regrets now, but he was concerned for her and thought he could deal with it and get her better.'

'Did he mention it to anybody at the practice? The other partners?'

'No. Not until after she sent him photos of her, naked, in his own home.'

'Whaat?'

'She tricked his cleaning lady into letting her into his house one day. The cleaning lady had finished and the woman had told her that all she needed to do was to drop off some files from the surgery and then she slammed the front door behind her. She was very convincing. Once she was in the house she left bits of her own worn underwear in his laundry basket and under his bed, then took the photos of herself lying in his sheets.'

Ella was shocked. 'What did he do when she sent the photos?'

'He told his practice manager immediately and the woman was advised to find another surgery. But she took the photos to the police, told her husband that Adam had taken them, and that started the worst twelve months of his life fighting to prove his innocence.'

'Shit.'

'Yeah.'

'Is that why he's come down here?'

'Yes.'

'Well, I can tell you he's never done anything untoward at the Garden Clinic. I see and hear everything.'

Kit smiled gratefully. 'Thank God. It caused him so much heartache and gossip.'

'I'm sure it did.' Ella sat, thinking for a bit. 'So that's why you're worried about what Suzie said? That Penny has feelings for Adam?'

'Yes. Adam doesn't need any more trouble.'

'Nor does Penny.'

'No.'

'But Suzie can't know anything about what happened to Adam, can she?'

'I can't see how.'

'Which brings me back to what I said. She's jealous of Penny. She fancies Adam and wants to clear the way for herself.'

Kit put his head in his hands. 'Do you think so?'

'Women's intuition – and keen observation! Suzie turns on the charm when she needs to but, now that I know her a lot better, I can tell you that there's something "off" about her.'

'Can you keep an eye on things at the vicarage? Or does that sound as if I'm overreacting.'

'Maybe, but you just want to protect Adam, don't you?'

Kit smiled and took her hand. 'Yes. I'm so glad to get that off my chest. You don't think I'm crazy?'

'A bit but, hey, I like crazy.'

Kit dipped his head and blushed. 'Thanks.'

Ella smiled back at him. 'My pleasure. Now, how about pudding?'

On the way back in the car Ella asked him if he'd like to come out on the cliffs and do some painting with her over the weekend.

'I'd love to, but I have another project I need to have finished for the Fayre.'

'An entry for the Spirit of Cornwall and The Sea competition?'

'Yep.'

'Tell me about it?'

'It's a little bit top secret at the moment.'

'Oh, go on, you can tell me. I'm supposed to be in charge of it.'

So he did, and Ella promised, for the second time that day, not to say a thing.

As he dropped her off at the vicarage he said, 'Can I ask you something?'

'Fire away.'

'How attractive is Adam?'

Ella giggled. 'If I'm truthful, he is very good-looking, but the more I know him, the more I see who he is as a person: a very nice man, a dedicated doctor – but not a man who's looking for a commitment. And now I understand why.'

'You're a very smart woman, Ella.'

'You're not so bad yourself.'

Ella let herself into the vicarage and was met by an anxious Suzie in the hall. 'Can I have a word?'

'What's happened? Did today go OK?'

'Yes, it was lovely, but I'm very worried about Penny.'

'Where is she?'

'She's upstairs, bathing Jenna. Come into the drawing room where she can't hear us.'

Ella followed Suzie. Her mind was whirring. What was going on?

'Shut the door,' said Suzie.

Ella did as she was told. 'Tell me what's happened. You're worrying me.'

Suzie sat on the sofa. 'I'm so concerned about Penny's vulnerability. You must have noticed.'

'On the contrary, she seems perfectly fine to me.'

Suzie was wringing her hands. 'She's so good at hiding it. I remember when Daddy died. To the rest of the world she looked as if she were coping marvellously, while Mummy and I were heartbroken. But underneath she was utterly distraught. Looking back, I can see now that she had a sort of breakdown. She became very withdrawn and remote. Her temper flared without warning and more than once Mummy and I were scared she'd hurt herself – or us.'

Ella didn't recognize the woman Suzie was describing. 'I see no signs of that person. Penny is coming through a difficult time with flying colours.'

'That's what they said when she was little, but today she told me something that really rang alarm bells.'

Ella narrowed her eyes, and sat down. 'Oh yes? What?'

'She told me that she has a bit of a crush on Adam.'

Ella almost laughed in Suzie's face. 'Whaat?'

Suzie was indignant. 'That's what she said.'

Ella stood up. 'Absolutely not! I see them together when she comes for her acupuncture and they have a great patient/doctor relationship, but that is it. All that separates me from Adam and his patients is a flimsy partition wall. I can hear him pull a tissue from its box.'

'Well, I'm worried for her.'

'Don't be. And don't go repeating that story to anyone else. Most of his patients have a crush, but that's all it is, a crush. Nothing serious. Imagine if Simon was to hear any of this nonsense?'

Suzie dropped her eyes and became meek. 'I'm so sorry. I should never have said anything. Maybe I have overreacted, but only because I care so much for her well-being. Mummy always said I put my foot in things. Should I say anything to Penny?'

'No,' said Ella firmly. 'Let her be. She's getting better. She's a good mum, a good wife, and a good business-woman. Let's keep supporting her so that she can keep doing those three things to the best of her ability.'

34

Helen was tucked up in bed with Piran and a Sunday morning cup of tea when someone knocked loudly on the Gull's Cry door.

'Who the bleddy hell is that?' growled Piran. 'Don't 'e know 'tis Sunday?'

Helen couldn't think who it was. 'If it's Audrey Tipton tell her I'm away and yes, the collection of tombola prizes is all under control.'

'I'm not bleddy opening the door to 'er,' said Piran.

Helen sighed and put her tea mug on her bedside table. 'I'll go then, shall I?' she asked sarcastically.

'There's a good girl.' He smiled slyly at her. 'And while you're at it, bring up a fresh pot of tea.'

'What did your last servant die of?' she said, pulling on her dressing gown and finding her slippers.

'Boredom. 'Tis why I like to keep you busy.'

Piran was exasperating and borderline misogynist, but he was also kind and loyal and Helen loved him.

The door-knocker banged again.

'All right, all right, I'm coming,' she muttered.

On the doorstep she found a red-eyed Suzie.

'Oh my God, what on earth has happened?' she asked.

'Can I come in? I'm sorry if I've woken you,' Suzie said miserably.

'Of course, come in and sit down.' Helen put an arm round Suzie and steered her into the cottage.

She led her into the kitchen and pulled out a chair next to the Aga. 'Now, let me make you tea and then you can tell me what's happened.'

Suzie was shaking and looked so pale. 'I'm sorry to barge in like this. I didn't know where else I could go.'

'Is it Penny? Is she OK?' asked Helen.

This provoked more crying. 'I'm so worried about her, Helen. You're her best friend and the only person I can turn to.'

Helen handed Suzie a fresh mug of tea. 'There. Now start from the beginning.'

'It's all so silly. I think Ella may have got hold of the wrong end of the stick. Promise you won't say anything?'

'My lips are sealed,' said Helen, pulling a chair out for herself.

'It's Adam.'

Helen was intrigued. 'Adam? What's he done?'

'Well, I mentioned to Ella that I'm concerned about Penny's reliance on him. She sees him at least once a week and talks about him all the time. The other day she mentioned that she had a bit of a . . . oh it sounds so silly, I shouldn't say it.'

'Say it!' said Helen impatiently.

'Well, she told me she had a bit of a crush on him.'

Helen sat back in her chair astonished. 'Penny said that?'

Suzie nodded miserably. 'Yes.'

Helen sat up a little straighter. 'Suzie, Penny has had "little crushes" on men as long as I've known her. It's nothing.'

'I see,' said Suzie slowly.

Helen frowned. 'Is there something else? Do you think anything has happened between them?'

'I wouldn't know. I don't think so.' Suzie took her gaze beyond the window, and added slyly, 'Not yet . . .'

Helen was flummoxed. 'I don't believe Penny would ever be unfaithful to Simon. What did Ella say when you told her?'

'Told me not to interfere. She said that Adam was a very good-looking man and was making Penny happy.'

'I believe that. Don't you? He's a good doctor and a nice man, but not a marriage wrecker.'

Suzie continued, 'Ella said she heard and saw everything that went on in the Garden Clinic, but I've seen her sitting in the garden, on her phone, when she should be at her desk. Maybe there are things going on that she doesn't see or . . .' She hesitated.

'Or what?' prompted Helen.

'Or that she turns a blind eye to.'

There was a creak on the stairs and Piran loomed in the doorway, wearing an old blue terry towelling robe.

'Right, you two, I've been earwigging and I must say that the doctor doesn't strike me as a fool and Penny would never do anything to hurt the vicar.' He gave his empty mug to Helen. 'Top this up, maid, while we get to the bottom of this.' He turned to Suzie. 'Isn't it possible that Penny may be having a little bit of wishful thinking? Enjoying the sight of a fine young man? You women do get fanciful ideas in your heads.'

'Well, she did get very emotional the other day.'

'Why?' asked Helen, handing Piran his mug.

'Well, with all the strain I've been under in the last year, Mummy dying and having to see to all the arrange-ments, I forgot that amongst her things was Daddy's briefcase. Nothing special. But as soon as I remembered it I told Penny and said I'd give it to her. Well, you should have heard what she said. She really flipped. Insisted we left the restaurant I'd taken her to, even before we'd ordered our lunch, so that I could get her home to show her the bag. Anyway, I calmed her down and she began to see that it really was a genuine mistake on my part. She apologized and thanked me. It's the only thing of Daddy's that remains and I really didn't imagine that an old worn-out briefcase would mean so much to her.'

Helen felt some sympathy for Suzie. 'I've been on the end of Penny's rants more than once and I know she can make you feel very small. But how marvellous that you gave Penny that briefcase. It will mean the world to her.'

Suzie gave a teary smile. 'Thank you. She's just so up and down at the moment and I'm trying so hard to make her life easier . . .'

'You've been wonderful,' said Helen, 'but I am concerned for her emotional state. One minute up, one minute down.'

Piran made a noise of derision. 'Penny's a tough maid but she's not mad. Simon wouldn't have married her if she were. And he'd have told me about it. No, I don't believe any of this nonsense about her falling for the doctor, neither.'

'Do you think I'm making it up?' said Suzie defensively.

'It's a storm in a teacup. Leave Penny be. She's doing fine,' said Piran firmly, and he added, 'If I were you I'd keep it to yourself, just as Helen and I will keep it to ourselves. Understand?'

When Suzie got back to the vicarage, Penny was hyper with excitement. 'You'll never guess what's happened!'

'Tell me,' said Suzie with a beaming smile.

'I've just had an email. They've commissioned my series!' Penny clapped her hands.

'The one about the university student?'

'Yes. I'm so excited! Penny Leighton Productions is back in business. Oh, I can't wait to tell the team.'

'I didn't think you had any of the team left. Haven't they all gone to different jobs since Mr Tibbs was cancelled?' said Suzie casually, heading off to the kitchen.

Penny frowned. 'Yes. Some have. But as soon as I tell them about this they'll all come back.'

'I wouldn't be so sure if they are already in new jobs.'

'In that case,' said Penny, refusing to be crushed, 'I shall hire better, younger, more talented people.'

'Oh good. Have you had breakfast?'

'Not yet. Where have you been, by the way?'

'Out for a walk.'

'You should have said. Jenna would have loved to come with you.'

'I thought it was too early.'

'It's never too early for Jenna. She doesn't understand the meaning of the word.' Penny watched Suzie go to the fridge and take out some bacon. 'Ooh, bacon sandwich, Jenna's favourite. She's watching CBeebies at the moment. It's so good that if I understood children's programming I'd have thought of it myself!' she laughed. 'I can't wait for Simon to come back from church. He's going to be so happy for me.'

Suzie unwrapped the bacon and put a frying pan on the Aga. 'Adam will be pleased too.'

'Oh yes. He'll be pleased for me. If it wasn't for him I wouldn't have had the energy to pitch for the job.'

Suzie put the bacon in the pan then sat at the table with one hand shielding her eyes.

Penny stopped rabbiting for a moment and noticed that Suzie looked a bit pale. 'Are you OK, darling?'

'Bit of a headache, that's all.'

'Let me look at you.'

Suzie took her hand from her face and Penny looked into the red-rimmed eyes and pale face. 'You don't look well, Suzie.'

'I didn't sleep very well.'

'Poor thing. Have you got stuff on your mind.'

Suzie gave a brave smile and shook her head. 'No, nothing.'

'It must be something. Is it me? Being so horrible to you before?'

'Nothing like that. I think I'm just starting to understand that Mummy isn't coming back, that's all.'

Penny said sympathetically, 'Grief takes a while to make itself known. I didn't properly grieve for Daddy until I was away at school and it hit me more as soon as I became a parent.' Penny had an idea. 'You must get an appointment with Adam. He's so good at putting things into perspective and his acupuncture has helped me no end. I sleep better, eat better – and drink less.' She winked. 'Even my libido has started to blossom again, much to Simon's delight.' She laughed happily. 'Or is that too much information?'

Suzie managed a smile. 'Much too much. Go and get Jenna. The bacon will be done in a few minutes.'

'OK, but think about Adam, won't you?'

'Yes. I'll think about it.'

Ella answered the phone at the clinic.

'Ella? It's Suzie Leighton. I'd like an appointment to see Adam.'

Ella felt her hackles rise. 'May I ask what it's about? Adam likes to have an idea of what the problem is before he meets the patient,' she asked.

'Of course,' said Suzie coolly. 'Tell him that I am having trouble sleeping.'

'OK. Anything else?' said Ella, scepticism rising in her tone.

'No. Nothing else,' Suzie snapped. 'I'm simply very tired.'

'Three on Tuesday any good?'

'Perfect, thank you.'

'Hello, Suzie,' said Adam, coming out from behind his desk and shaking her hand warmly. 'Amazing, isn't it, that living in a small village like this you can still not see people for days. Do sit down and tell me how I can help you.'

'I'm having trouble sleeping.'

'Why is that?'

'I keep thinking of my mother. I think I see her. I might be in Trevay or on the beach and I see someone who looks a bit like her and I catch up with them only to find it's not her at all.'

Adam listened thoughtfully. 'Grief catches us all in different ways. What you are describing is a very common but, nonetheless, unsettling part of the process.'

'There's something else,' said Suzie, bringing a tissue to her eyes.

'Take your time,' said Adam gently.

'It's so silly. But I feel unsettled in general and it's stirring up so many worries. Old problems. I was never as popular as Penny at school – before she went to boarding school and left me with Mummy. She's so clever and funny and bright, everything I'm not.'

Adam said kindly, 'Grief can remove one's confidence and self-esteem. You have done nothing to feel this way. I hear only good things about you from the villagers and I can recommend a good therapist to talk these feelings over with.'

Suzie looked up. 'Can't *you* be my therapist?'

'I'm sorry, no. Penny is my patient right now and I don't like to treat close family members at the same time.'

'Oh.' Suzie looked down at her lap and sniffed, lifting her tissue to her eyes again.

'But what I can do is to offer you acupuncture. It can be very beneficial for sleeping. Would you like to try that?'

'Yes, please.'

'Well, just go behind the curtain. You'll find a couch there. Slip off your dress and I'll be back in a couple of minutes.'

Adam stepped out of the room into the reception where Ella was sitting drawing.

'That's good,' he said, looking at it. 'You've caught Marguerite Cottage beautifully.'

'Oh, it's just a doodle really. Is Suzie having acupuncture? Do you want me to sit in?'

Adam hesitated – but he didn't usually have Ella sit in on acupuncture – before saying, 'No, it'll be fine, but do stay right here, won't you?'

Suzie found the acupuncture very soothing and the way Adam slid his fingers over her skin rather sensual. He was very professional and she was almost disappointed when he made no inappropriate moves.

'There,' he said, removing the last needle. 'I hope you find some benefit tonight. You might want to go home now and have a little rest. It can make you feel a bit dopey.'

'Thank you, Adam, you're very kind.'

'Not at all.' He went to his desk and sat down, smoothing his tie as he did so. 'Is there anything else I can do for you?'

'Well, there is one thing,' she said from behind the curtain as she pulled her dress back on. 'Would you consider letting me have some sleeping pills? Not many, just enough for a week or so. I am *so* tired.'

She pulled the curtain back and sat in the chair opposite him.

He fiddled with his fountain pen then looked at her. 'I will, but only enough for six days. They are highly addictive.'

'I know. Mummy had them in her last weeks. I kept them hidden from her.'

He smiled. 'Just promise me you'll be sensible. Just ONE a night.'

'I promise. It'll get me over this little hump.'

He wrote the prescription and handed it to her.

She read it. 'These are the ones our old doctor gave Mummy. They are very good. Don't worry. I shall be sensible.'

As soon as Suzie had left the Garden Clinic, Ella went in to check on Adam. He looked relaxed and unconcerned. 'Everything OK?' she asked.

'Yes, fine. Is Mrs Askew here?'

'Yes.'

'Send her in please.'

Suzie was elated. She clutched her prescription, determined to get to the chemist before the day was out, but as she passed through the garden of Marguerite Cottage and under the boughs of a sweet-smelling orange blossom shrub she heard the front door open and instinctively stopped, hiding beneath the branches. The mad old cow from the village shop, Queenie, was coming out with Kit. He hugged her and kissed her on both cheeks.

'Bye, darling,' he said. 'Same time tomorrow?'

Queenie broke into one of her cackling laughs. 'Oh my good gawd, it's a long time since a young man said that to me. You're gonna wear me out.'

'You're dynamite, Queenie.'

'You make sure you respect an old lady,' she said.

'Always.' He kissed her hand. 'Tomorrow then?'

'Tomorrow, me duck.'

Queenie turned away from him and began her trundle down the cottage path towards the village green.

'Queenie!' Kit called.

She stopped. 'What now?'

'You've got your skirt tucked in your knickers,' he giggled.

'Oh Gordon Bennett. Whatever would people think if they saw me like this! Coming out of 'ere wiv me drawers on show.' She hoiked her skirt out and settled it back where it belonged, mid-calf. 'Cheers, me duck.'

'Cheers, Queenie.' Kit gave one final wave before closing the front door.

Suzie hurried out from behind the tree before anyone saw her. Now what was *that* all about?

35

The day of the May Fayre dawned bright and sunny. A cool onshore breeze meant that it wouldn't get too hot and the vicarage was a hive of activity.

'Can you get the door please, darling?' Simon said to Penny as he struggled past her carrying a large trestle table destined for the garden.

'I'm expecting a phone call from my locations manager,' she huffed.

'It'll just take a second,' he pleaded.

On the doorstep was the local police constable. 'Hello, Jan,' said Penny. 'Come in. It's Bedlam here. Simon's out in the garden if you want him.'

PC Jan was no sooner out in search of Simon, than the door-knocker went again. Penny answered it.

'Hi, Pen,' said Helen, giving her a kiss. 'You OK?'

'No. I'm waiting for an important call but I've become the Harrods' doorman,' said Penny crossly.

'Oh dear. Give me a job.'

'Make me a cup of coffee.'

'A please would be nice,' said Helen.

'Piss off. I haven't time for nice.'

Helen laughed. 'That's good! The old Penny is back. Now I *know* you are better.'

Penny had the grace to laugh too. 'Sorry. But I really need to wait for this call.'

'Yes, madam. Coffee on its way, madam.' Helen went towards the kitchen.

Ella and Suzie were in the centre of controlled chaos. Village helpers in pretty aprons were dashing about stacking saucers and folding paper napkins and Suzie was barking orders. 'The tea urn needs to be switched on at least an hour before we start. Who's in charge of that?' A small woman called Monica put her hand up.

'Good,' said Suzie, ticking something off her list. 'Who's doing bunting?'

Two teenage girls, lounging against the dishwasher, put their hands up and giggled.

'What are you giggling for?' demanded Suzie. 'Bunting can go very wrong. Follow me and I'll show you how I expect it to be done.' Suzie led the two giggling girls out into the garden.

Helen went to Ella who was spooning jam into egg cups and gave her a kiss. 'How is it going? Fancy a coffee? I'm making one for Penny.'

Ella pushed a red curl across her forehead and blew her cheeks out. 'We've been up since five and I'm knackered. She's like a sergeant major. And yes please, I'd love a coffee.'

'Did someone say coffee?' asked Simon, coming back in through the back door. 'Hello, Helen.' He bent to kiss her. 'Has anyone seen the first-aid kit? PC Jan has smashed her thumb while hammering up the bunting.'

The morning rattled on in similar vein with dramas and triumphs, an inspection from Mrs Audrey Tipton, and a crisis surrounding the loss of the Pendruggan Cup, a tarnished piece of history awarded annually to the Champion Horticulturalist. It was eventually found in the boot of Mrs Tipton's car, under the fetid behind of her ancient labrador.

The official opening of the Fayre was at two and the clock was ticking. Penny (who had had a very satisfactory phone call with her locations manager) and Simon and Jenna were to cut the ribbon. As they left the house, Penny admired her husband. 'You do look handsome.'

He blushed. 'It's only my old linen jacket.'

'I know, but you look good in it.' She kissed him.

He scooped up Jenna in one arm and put his other arm around Penny. 'I'm a proud man to have my two beautiful girls to show off.'

Suzie, who was standing behind them, hurried them up. 'Come on, you two. I don't want my scones going dry in this heat.'

The village green was chock-a-block with colourful stalls, invitingly bedecked in streamers and yet more bunting. Cars were parked three deep in one of the fields and the crowds were flocking in.

Mr Geoffrey Tipton was, as always, the voice of the PA system as he said, 'Welcome to Pendruggan Summer Fayre.' His electronically enhanced voice boomed with enough feedback to make the dogs waiting their turn in the show ring bark and cower. 'Ladies and gentlemen, boys and girls, take a ringside seat for our cuddly canine competition, the Pendruggan Dog Show.' There was some scattered applause. Audrey Tipton nudged him and hissed, 'Tell them Dr Adam is the compere.' Geoffrey did as he was told. 'Compered by Dr Adam Beauchamp.'

Adam stepped into the ring and waved to the crowd. His dark floppy hair, candy-pink striped shirt and tanned arms had quite an effect, not to mention his trim behind caressed by tight jeans. He received a barrage of wolf whistles from some of the bolder women. 'Thank you, ladies and gentlemen,' he said. 'Let's meet the contestants for our first category, the Dog Who Most Looks Like Their Owner.' There were more cheers as several dogs and owners made their way into the ring. Suzie, standing on the sidelines in the shade, watched him for a few minutes. The familiar feeling of being undervalued and ignored brewed in her stomach. Adam barely noticed her and Penny and Simon had the whole village in the palm of their hands. What did they have that she didn't? Why did no one care for her in the way they cared for Penny? No one saw her standing in the shadows and no one saw her leave as she returned to her duties at the cream teas.

The afternoon wore on, joyful and good-natured. The fancy dress competition went without mishap or too many tears; Simple Tony won gold for Helen's peas; and Queenie's pasty stall sold out.

Children with painted faces, fuelled by E numbers, chased each other through the legs of strangers.

Fathers sat on the grass outside the beer tent, pleasantly merry and mothers were queuing up to get their palms read by Psychic Polly. The sun was cooling down and the stalls were running out of stock. The Vicarage Cream-Tea Garden was now closed. Suzie, her feet aching and her hands sore from washing-up, came over to the green to share the two final events of the day. She'd spent all day gritting her teeth while the villagers gossiped about what a good job Penny had done on the cream teas this year. How light the scones were and how beautiful the garden looked. She'd pointedly mentioned to a couple of people that the scones had been hers and that Simple Tony was responsible for the garden, but that didn't seem to stop everyone thinking that she was nothing more than a skivvy when it had been all her own hard work and Penny hadn't lifted a finger!

Geoffrey opened up the PA system for the final judging of the day. 'This year's Art Competition is entitled The Spirit of Cornwall and The Sea. The judges have been over to the church and have made their decision and all entries are now available for public view. However, we have brought the winning painting out of the church and over here for all to see.' He pointed to two men carrying a painting that was hidden by a large blanket. 'Bring it over to the stage, gentlemen,' ordered Mr Tipton.

The two men settled the covered picture on an easel and stepped back. Mr Tipton opened an envelope. 'Ladies and gentlemen, I can announce that the judges have awarded this year's Art Competition prize to . . .' He gave a dramatic pause which was filled by a group of young farmers shouting, 'Get on with it, fatty.'

Geoffrey coughed. 'To . . . Kit Beauchamp!'

Kit and Ella standing in the crowd stared at each other open-mouthed. Queenie, next to them said, 'Oh my good gawd.'

'Would Kit please come to the stage and unveil his painting,' said Geoffrey.

Kit grabbed Queenie's hand and pulled her towards the stage. They both arrived flustered. Kit took the mic. 'Gosh thanks,' he said. 'Thank you to the judges and more especially to my muse, Queenie.' He held her hand up to the crowd. An enormous cheer went up. 'OK,' said Kit, 'are you ready for this?' He took a corner of the blanket and pulled. The crowd gasped then fell to silence, then laughed and whooped and hollered. The picture was of Queenie, stark-naked but for strands of mermaid's hair seaweed hiding her essentials, standing in a giant mussel shell with the breakers of Shellsand Bay behind her. 'I call her Queen Aphrodite of Pendruggan, with apologies to Botticelli.'

Queenie grabbed the mic. ''Asn't he done me lovely?''

Suzie watched with a curled lip as the villagers roared their love and appreciation of the old crone. So that was what she had seen at Marguerite Cottage, she thought to herself. Not a sleazy assignation after all. Just a sleazy sitting for a sleazy painting.

Penny tapped her on the shoulder. 'Isn't Queenie brave? I wouldn't have done that in a million years. But she looks so good. Kit's done a wonderful job, don't you think.'

Suzie smiled thinly. 'Wonderful.'

The PA system howled back into life. 'And now, ladies and gentlemen, we saved the best till last,' said Mr Tipton. 'The inaugural Pendruggan versus Trevay Rounders match! Come on, everybody. Young or old, everyone is welcome. Step into the showring and find your teams.'

Piran put himself forward as umpire and scorekeeper.

'Can the two captains come here for the toss, please,' he said loudly.

Gasping Bob stepped forward for Pendruggan and Dr Adam for Trevay.

Piran took a fifty-pence piece out of his pocket. 'Doc, heads or tails?'

'Heads,' said Adam decisively.

Piran flipped the coin. 'Heads it is. You want to bat or field?'

'Field.'

Adam put himself in as bowler and Gasping Bob faced

him, bat in hand. Adam rolled his shoulders and moved his neck from side to side to warm up. Bob spat out his cigarette.

'Ready?' shouted Piran.

Bob and Adam stared each other out and nodded.

'Right, off you go,' said Piran, settling into a deckchair next to a blackboard with a piece of chalk in one hand and a pint in the other.

Adam swung his arm and let go of a fast ball. Gasping Bob never took his eyes off it and smashed it out of the showring. His sinewy legs in his very short denim shorts powered him round first base, second, third. Someone in the crowd picked up the ball and threw it to the man on fourth base who missed it and Bob easily scored the first rounder for Pendruggan.

Adam retrieved the ball and bowled again, this time to one of the young farmers. Again it was smashed out of the park and Piran chalked up another rounder for Pendruggan. Even Queenie hit it hard enough to get to second base, albeit with Kit doing the running for her. At the end of the first half Pendruggan had scored twenty-seven.

Piran called for a refreshment break before the teams swapped over.

First to bat for Trevay was Adam.

Gasping Bob did the honours as bowler and Adam missed the first ball.

'Too low,' said Piran.

Gasping Bob rolled his cigarette from one corner of his lips to the other, narrowed his eyes and let the ball fly. Adam hit it high. The crowd fell into a hush as they watched the ball arc into the sky then plummet down, straight into Simon's open hands.

'Out!' shouted Piran.

'Oh, jolly bad luck. So sorry, Adam,' Simon called as he tossed the ball back to Bob.

Bob bowled again, this time to a fit-looking young woman in trainers. She swiped it hard out to third base where Queenie was standing, musing about her portrait. 'Look out,' yelled Bob, running backwards to catch it, but, too late. Queenie looked up just as the ball and Gasping Bob's head were coming right at her.

As she lay on the ground Adam sprinted towards her. 'Are you OK?' he asked, feeling for her pulse.

She took a couple of fluttering breaths and opened her eyes. 'Oo, better now you're 'ere, doc.'

'You've got a real shiner coming up there, Queenie.'

'Thank gawd it's after my painting's been finished,' she said, trying a smile.

'Better get you off to A & E to be checked out,' said Adam, stroking the paper-thin skin of her hand.

Psychic Polly, now in her official ambulance uniform, arrived panting. Adam filled her in and Queenie was loaded on to a stretcher and taken off to hospital with Helen accompanying her.

'Shall we play on?' said Piran matter-of-factly.

'Aye,' said Gasping Bob, lighting another cigarette. 'I'm just getting into my stride.'

The game continued but in a slightly less gung ho manner. Trevay were now eighteen rounders to Pendruggan's twenty-seven.

Bob stepped down from bowling and Simon stepped up. Suzie took over as backstop.

Ella went into bat. 'Golly,' she said, 'I haven't done this since I was at school. I wonder if I can remember how to do it?'

Simon aimed a nice clean bowl at her and Ella whacked it hard. The ball soared off to left of field and Ella ran, flinging the bat behind her as she'd been taught at school. Ella heard something and turned, just in time to see it land squarely on Suzie's nose, and Suzie collapse to the grass with blood all over her face. 'Oh my God!' Ella screamed. 'I'm so sorry.'

Adam and Penny were on the scene at once and examined Suzie's nose.

'Oh you poor thing,' gasped Penny. 'You poor darling. Are you OK?'

'It's not broken,' said Adam, feeling gently along the bridge of her nose. 'I'll take you back to the Garden Clinic to patch you up. Can you walk?'

'Yes,' said Suzie in shock. 'Thank you.'

Penny helped her to her feet, catching her other arm as Suzie swayed once upright. The crowd murmured around them and Suzie caught the words 'bless Penny, that poor sister'. It was always Penny that got the attention.

Ella was in tears. 'It's all my fault,' she sobbed.

With Suzie's arm now looped through Adam's, Penny took Ella off to the refreshment stall. 'You're in shock, darling. You need a drink.'

Once they'd gone, Piran took charge again.

'Right, teams. We've twenty-six minutes of play left and there's only nine points in it. Let's play on.'

Adam unlocked the Garden Clinic and guided Suzie into his room. 'Is it still bleeding?' he asked.

Suzie took away the wad of tissues she'd been holding and Adam saw a fresh trail of blood snaking its way out of her nostril. 'Oh dear, yes. Here.' He handed her a fistful of paper towels while he found an enamel kidney dish, sterile swabs, and some sticking plaster.

'This might sting a bit,' he said as he mopped her up, stemming the flow. 'You're going to have quite a bruise by the morning. You and Queenie will be in competition.'

Suzie smiled up at him. 'Shall I put a raw steak on it?'

'Leave that to Tom and Jerry!' he laughed. 'You'd be better off eating the steak than wearing it. Does it hurt much?'

'Yes.'

'Headache?'

'Yes.'

He flashed a penlight in her eyes and took her pulse.

'You're going to be fine, but just sit here quietly for a few minutes.'

Sitting there, alone with Adam, Suzie could hear the match still being played. The thwack of the ball and a man's voice shouting, 'Tommy Tommy Tommy! RUUUUN!' Then cheers and applause.

'What a funny old day,' she said.

'They must have raised a lot of money,' said Adam. 'How did your cream teas go?'

'Sold out. Every one of *my* scones gone. Not that I got any bloody credit for it, of course. Blessed Penny did it all, don't you know?'

'Well, the scones were the best I've ever eaten. I'm sure people know who the real hero of the day was, don't you worry,' he winked supportively.

'Thank you.'

'Let me just check that the bleeding has stopped.' He came close to her and put his hand to her nose and pulled out the wadding. 'There, it's stopped,' he said peering closely at her injured face. He was just inches away.

She leaned forward and kissed him.

He jumped back like a scalded cat.

'What do you think you're doing?' he said.

'You feel it, don't you? The attraction between us?'

He looked at her with a frown. 'Suzie, I'm going to put this down to your injury and too much sun. As far as I'm concerned this never happened. I think we'd better get back to the Fayre, don't you?'

There was a noise out in reception and Ella appeared, anxious and apologetic. 'Oh Suzie, I'm so terribly sorry. At school we never had enough bats and so we always had to throw them down. Are you OK?'

Suzie started screaming. 'Get him away from me! Please, Ella. Get him out of here.'

'Wha-what's happened?' asked Ella. She looked from Suzie's bloodied face to Adam's terror-stricken one.

Suzie was hysterical. 'He tried to kiss me!'

Ella looked at him. 'Did you?'

Adam shook his head, his face pale. 'No! You must believe me, Ella, I would never do that.'

'He did!' shrieked Suzie. 'Then he said that I was to forget it had happened.'

'Did you?' Ella asked him again.

'Yes, but it was because *she* kissed me.'

'Did you kiss him?' Ella said to Suzie.

'I—' Suzie gulped. 'I'm feeling very faint. I can't really remember.'

Ella said, 'What are you saying? That Adam assaulted you? That's a very serious allegation. Or, are you saying that there's been a misunderstanding?'

Suzie turned her eyes to Adam and stared at him. He

looked down at his shaking hands. Eventually she said, 'Maybe it was a misunderstanding.'

Adam breathed a deep sigh of relief.

Ella went to help Suzie up. 'Right, let's get you home.'

36

Ella took Suzie home and put her on the sofa. 'If Adam behaved inappropriately then you must speak up,' she told Suzie firmly. 'However, if he didn't, please, please don't speak about it. It could cause him a lot of trouble and be very upsetting for both of you.'

Suzie lay wanly on the sofa, her nose swelling and her eyes black-and-blue. Ella almost felt a compassion for her. Almost.

'I shall keep quiet about it,' Suzie said, in what she hoped was a brave voice.

Ella nodded and crossed her fingers that Suzie was telling the truth this time.

On Monday the vicarage had its quiet hum of normality back. The garden was cleared of its tables, chairs and bunting, the kitchen was spotless, thanks to Ella, and Simon could move freely around his office and drawing room, now that the endless boxes of posters and prizes had been taken away. He sat at his desk and sent a prayer of thanks and relief that it was all over for another year. Penny brought him a cup of tea. 'God, I feel knackered,' she said, perching herself on the edge of his desk and dislodging his carefully organized papers. 'Don't you?'

Simon caught the papers as they headed to the floor. 'A bit. My shoulders ache.'

'That'll be the rounders. Cracking match and a good win for us.' Penny sipped her tea. 'It's going to be an annual event now, isn't it?'

Simon reached a hand up to rub his aching neck. 'I need to get some more exercise in if it is. I've rather let it go, this year. I haven't been out on the surfboard since last summer.' Simon was a very good surfer; he'd been a lifeguard in his youth and still had a great physique.

'How about a run around the green every morning?' asked Penny. He gave a small laugh. 'You'll come with me, I suppose?'

'Good God, no,' said Penny. 'My idea of sport is to lie on a hot beach reading a magazine.' She stood up, dislodging a few more papers, and started to massage his shoulders. 'Then watch my handsome husband as he catches yet another wave, looking all sexy in his wetsuit.'

Simon had a feeling he knew where all this physical affection was going and he really didn't have time for it at the moment. The fayre always seemed to create more admin than you'd think, and besides which, they had a house full of people.

Penny bent and nibbled his neck. 'How about you and me . . .' He was about to make an excuse when, miraculously, there came a knock at the front door. Simon sent another prayer of thanks.

'Bugger,' said Penny. 'We never get a minute to ourselves. I'll get it.'

It was the Trevay florist who was holding an enormous bunch of flowers. Lupins, phlox, sweet peas, roses, bright green mint and honeysuckle arranged in a glorious tangle of scent and colour. 'Miss Leighton?' asked the florist. 'Yes. How lovely. That's me.'

'Here you are. Print and sign here, please.' Penny took the bunch and balanced the delivery pad on her knee as she scribbled her name.

The florist checked. 'Oh, these are for a Suzie Leighton, not Penny.'

'Really?' said Penny, rather annoyed. 'That's my sister. I'll make sure she gets them.'

Penny took the flowers up to Suzie who was lying in bed nursing her sore nose. 'Hey, darling, only me,' said Penny as she pushed the door open. 'I have a surprise for you.' She produced the bouquet from behind her back. 'For you hoo!'

Suzie's smile lit up her tired and bruised eyes. 'Oh Penny, you shouldn't have.'

'They're not from me. There's a card. Here.'

She passed the small envelope to Suzie and waited as she prised it open. Suzie's smile crept slowly and blushingly up her cheeks. 'Oh, how sweet of him,' she murmured.

'Who's it from?' Penny said impatiently.

Suzie handed her the card. 'Take a look.'

Penny took it. On a plain white card was simply the letter 'A' with a single 'X'. Penny was puzzled. 'Who is it?'

Suzie looked coy. 'Adam, of course.'

'Oh,' said Penny, feeling more than a little put out. 'Why is he sending you flowers?'

'To say sorry, perhaps,' said Suzie.

'Say sorry?' asked Penny mystified. 'What the hell for?'

Suzie didn't miss a beat. 'Sorry that I'm the one who has a bashed-up face, I suppose.'

'Oh. Well, that's very sweet of him,' said Penny.

'Isn't it?' said Suzie innocently.

'Do you want me to put them in a vase? Only I'm off to London soon. Meetings about the new programme and all that.'

'Only if you have time,' said Suzie limply. 'How long will you be away for?'

'A couple of nights should do it.' She took the bunch of flowers. 'I'll bring them back in a vase.' As Penny got to the top of the stairs Suzie called out, 'Could I trouble you for a cup of tea and maybe a slice of bread and butter? I think I could manage that.'

Penny gritted her teeth. 'No trouble at all, Suze.'

Penny had said her goodbyes to Jenna and the rest of the household and was putting her overnight case into the back of her Jaguar, when she saw Adam drive into Marguerite Cottage. She waited for him to get out of his car then called over, 'Hi, Adam. How are you after all of the Fayre's excitements?'

She thought she saw a fleeting anxiety cross his face. 'Excitements? What do you mean?'

'Well, all those casualties you had to deal with.'

'Oh. Yes . . . How – how is Suzie?'

'Lolling in bed and treating us all like servants. Your flowers really cheered her up.'

'My flowers?' he frowned.

'Don't play the innocent with me. We knew they were from you even though you only put your initial. Very James Bond.'

Adam was looking eager to get away. 'Actually, I'm in a bit of a hurry. Can't stop.'

'Me too. I'm off to London for a couple of days,' she said, closing the car boot, but when she turned back, he'd already gone.

Adam slammed the front door of Marguerite Cottage. His pulse was racing and his breathing had become shallow. He recognized a panic attack. They had started during the investigation into the allegations that were thrown at him by his last crazy patient. He groaned. 'Oh God, don't let this happen again.'

He definitely hadn't sent Suzie flowers.

He went upstairs and took a long hot shower to calm himself down. Right at the end he turned the tap to cold and shocked his body into vitality.

He knew what he had to do.

Ten minutes later he was dressed in fresh clothes and was knocking on the vicarage door. Ella answered. She was shocked to see him and blocked him from entering the house.

'I don't think you should come in,' she whispered.

'I want to see Suzie,' he said clearly.

'She's resting.'

'Ella, please let me in. I just want to talk to her about what she said.'

'That's not a good idea,' said Ella, 'I think you should just keep clear of Suzie for a bit.'

'I intend to,' he said. 'After I've got the truth from her.'

Ella thought she heard Suzie's bedroom door open. She looked quickly behind her, at the stairs, but no one was there. She whispered to Adam, 'Let me get to the bottom of this. She's a bit wobbly and seeing you might make things worse.'

Adam's shoulders dropped and he looked haunted. 'Ella, please believe me. I did not try to kiss her, whatever she might say.'

Ella looked into his eyes and wanted to believe him. 'I don't think you should have sent the flowers,' she said.

'They're not from me! I *have* never and *would* never send flowers to a patient.' There was another noise, this time a stair creaking. Suzie was standing weakly at the bottom of the stairs. She smiled sweetly at him. 'Adam, it was a very kind gesture but you musn't send flowers again.'

'Oh good God, this is madness! I did *not* send those flowers.' He ran a frustrated hand through his hair. 'Suzie, I want you to know that from this moment I am no longer and will never be your doctor, either at the Trevay surgery or the Garden Clinic. I shall refer you to one of my colleagues.' He turned on his heel and stomped off down the path.

As Ella shut the front door Suzie said, 'Well, I think he's got the message, don't you?'

Ella didn't know what the hell was going on. 'Suzie, are you playing games with him? If you are you must stop it. Now. Adam could lose his job.'

Suzie's bruised eyes flashed with anger. 'Are you accusing me of lying? I bet you'd be on Penny's side if it had happened to her.'

'I would ask her the same question,' said Ella. 'I just want to understand the truth.'

The two women observed each other in silence, then the phone rang. Ella answered it. 'Hello?'

'Hello, this is just a courtesy call from Trevay florist. Are you satisfied with the flowers we delivered earlier? Only we are using a new supplier and as Miss Leighton is a new customer we wanted to make sure she was happy with them.'

Ella looked at Suzie. 'It's the florist. Did you like the flowers?'

Suzie nodded. 'Yes, they are lovely.'

Ella said into the phone, 'She says they are lovely.'

'Oh good,' said the florist. 'There's just a little problem with the credit card Miss Leighton gave us. The expiry date hasn't been accepted.'

Ella's mind turned somersaults. 'I think there's a mistake. They were *for* Miss Leighton, not from her.'

Suzie reacted with speed and grabbed the phone, running upstairs with it, and Ella heard her say, 'Hello. This is Miss Leighton. How may I help?' before slamming her bedroom door.

Ella was troubled. Suzie's accusation had a ring of truth. Adam had history with this sort of thing, but Ella felt she knew him too well to believe that he was guilty in any way. She had spent plenty of time alone with him at the Garden Clinic and had never felt uncomfortable once. And what the hell was all that with the florist? Could Suzie have sent the flowers to herself? She needed to phone Kit.

Kit was as disbelieving as she was. 'He would never put himself in that position again,' he said. 'It almost destroyed him last time. But even though he was found innocent there were still people who said there was no smoke without fire. That's why he came down here. Thank God I came with him or he'd have no one to fully believe him.'

'Well, he's got me too,' said Ella loyally. 'It's Suzie who's odd, not Adam.'

'Do you think I should tell him that we have spoken?' asked Kit.

'Yes,' said Ella. 'And tell him that you've told me about the accusations at his old surgery and that I won't say a thing?'

Kit found Adam on the outside of a few large gin and tonics, sitting on the grass and hugging Terry and Celia.

'Hey, mate,' Kit said gently. 'You OK?'

Adam looked at him with red-ringed eyes. 'I'm fine,' he slurred, clearly not fine. 'Celia and Terry and I are having a chat. Terry agrees that most women are mad, but don't say that in front of Celia or she'll get all huffy. You know what she's like.'

'Oh, I do,' said Kit, settling next to his cousin. 'But Celia is a piece of cake compared with some women we have known.'

'You're so right,' nodded Adam slowly. 'So very right. Ella's all right, though. What a nice girl. Pretty, too. You should take her out one night. She'd be good for you.'

'I've just been talking to her, actually.'

'Ah yes. I saw her earlier.' Adam finished his drink. 'Get me another would you, old boy? And have one yourself. What was I saying?'

'That you'd seen Ella.'

Adam gave an involuntary shiver. 'Yes. Had to see that bloody mad bitch too. Tell her what's what.' He put his arm on Kit's shoulder. 'It's only gone and happened again. But I didn't do anything. She started it.'

'You mean Suzie?'

'She said I sent her flowers. I bloody didn't!'

Kit chewed his lip, thinking how best to phrase what he said next.

'Look, Ella has told me everything. If it's any consolation she believes you and thinks Suzie is a bit barmy.'

'A bit barmy? Good diagnosis. See? What did I tell you? Take that girl out. She's like Celia here. Slim, lovely teeth, gentle eyes and loyal. Nice hair too. Did you get me another drink?'

'I will in a minute. But I want to ask you a straight question first, while you're drunk. Did you kiss Suzie? Or do anything inappropriate?'

'Nothing. Nada. Nyet.' Adam hugged the dogs too him and tears sprang to his eyes. 'Please believe me.'

Kit was certain that Adam was telling the truth. 'I believe you. Now I'll get you that drink.'

37

Penny was easing her Jaguar through the clog of Chiswick's early morning traffic. The last couple of days had been very productive. The BBC was as excited as she was with her new drama, which they'd decided to call *A Degree of Learning*. It was being slated for the evening slot on BBC2 on Tuesday nights.

Kezia Watson, the young writer, was busy fleshing out her scripts and Penny's casting director was searching for actors to play the five leading characters, three young women and two young men who meet at university then graduate in to the real world with all its harsh realities. It would make stars of them if she got it right.

Now Penny was on her way home to Cornwall. She smiled at her words 'home to Cornwall'. It sounded so good to her. She couldn't wait to see Jenna and hold her and sniff her. She couldn't wait to see Simon either. He'd been a rock to her while she'd been so ill. She could see that now, even though at the time she thought he'd been useless. If someone had told her five years ago that she'd be living in Cornwall, married to a vicar, mother to the most wonderful daughter in the world, *and* reconciled with her sister, she'd have laughed in their face. How quickly a life can change.

The cars in front of her were bumper-to-bumper and crawling slower than a very old tortoise with a brick on his back. How had she put up with London for all those years? She looked to her left and saw a spotty young man in a pimped-up Corsa picking his nose. To her right was a young black woman applying her make-up in her rear-view mirror.

In front was a dirty lorry with a sign asking her to tell the bosses if he'd driven well and behind her was a red post office van with some kind of drum and bass music drowning out her own radio. To think that she'd thought this was all quite normal five years ago. Now it was alien and rather aggressive. She longed to feel some sand between her toes with the sound of the ocean swelling in her ears.

Her phone rang and as she pressed the hands-free button, the postman behind her blared his horn. The traffic in front had moved two yards and he was anxious for her to push on. 'All right, all right,' she mouthed at him. 'Patience, dear.' He gave her an unusually rude hand gesture, which she returned with relish.

'Hello?' said a woman's voice from the phone's speaker.

'Hello. This is Penny Leighton.'

'Hi, Pen, it's Kezia.'

Penny pulled a face of annoyance at the familiarity of the young woman calling her Pen. 'I was going to phone you later, Kezia. How are the scripts coming?'

'They're good. I've got drafts for the first two episodes and I'm working on the third.'

'Great. Can you email them to me? The BBC are very keen to see how you're getting on.'

'I'm calling because I don't like what they're calling it,' said Kezia in a slightly aggressive tone.

Penny sighed. Why the hell were writers so difficult

to deal with?' 'I think *A Degree of Learning* is rather good. What were your thoughts?'

'I like *Vitae, Erudio, Universitas.*'

Penny raised her eyes to heaven but said patiently, 'And what does that mean?'

'It's Latin for Life, Education, University.'

'OK . . . Well, that's great – if you don't want anybody to watch the thing. People won't know what it means.'

'I knew you wouldn't get it,' said Kezia sullenly.

Penny bit her tongue. 'You and I are very lucky to have had your scripts taken up by the BBC. Now listen very carefully, Kezia, because I'm going to give you an important piece of advice that you should take heed of.'

She heard Kezia tut sarcastically.

'Compromise, compromise, compromise,' said Penny with emphasis. 'Get it?'

'I don't need to sacrifice my talent for compromise,' Kezia sputtered.

'Well, you're not going to get very far then. Have a little think – then when you realize I'm right, email the scripts. You have a month to get all of them done. If that's a problem, I can always call in an experienced writer to help. OK?'

She hung up and laughed at herself. The old Penny was well and truly back.

The traffic was beginning to move again and she finally got onto the M4 and headed west. She called home, wanting to share all her news with Simon. Suzie answered. 'Hello, Pendruggan vicarage,' she said.

'Nice phone voice, darling,' said Penny brightly. 'You really are bringing some tone to the vicarage.'

'Penny! How is your work going?' Penny told her all

her news then remembered to ask about her sister's black eyes.

'Still painful,' said Suzie bravely. 'I've been staying in, not wanting to frighten the neighbours.'

'Has Adam been over?' asked Penny.

'Yes, he came over the day before yesterday.'

'Well, that was kind of him.'

'Mmm,' Suzie said without elaborating. 'So when are you home?'

'I'm on my way right now. Tell Jenna and Simon I love them.'

'Will do.'

Penny hung up and tuned the radio to Magic FM. The rest of her journey was spent singing along to songs from her youth.

Ella watched Suzie as she put the phone down. 'Before Penny gets home, why don't you tell me the truth about why you sent the flowers to yourself and why you would accuse Adam of something so damaging? Hm? You'll feel a lot better.'

Suzie crumpled visibly.

'Oh Ella! I did send those flowers to myself. I thought that they would let Adam off the hook – an apology for the misunderstanding between us, evidence that he would never take advantage of a woman. I thought it would help.'

'Did he really try to kiss you?' Ella pressed.

'Yes, he did. It was one of those moments. We were alone and he was so close to me. He kissed me and I kissed him back.'

'So why did you scream blue murder when I walked in?'

'I panicked. I didn't want you thinking badly of me. At that moment he made me feel special. I haven't felt special for a long time. I've had relationships, but they've fizzled out. Well, I had Mummy to look after, you see. I couldn't leave her . . . unlike Penny. Could I?'

Ella led her to the kitchen. 'Sit down. Have you eaten today?'

Suzie shook her head.

'I'll make you a sandwich.' Ella made a ham sandwich and a pot of tea. 'Now, eat that and talk to me. Why have you come here? To Cornwall?'

Suzie took a tiny bite of sandwich and wiped a crumb from her lips before speaking. 'I missed Penny. I had been angry with her for such a long time and I wanted to see if we could be friends.'

Ella sat back with her mug of tea. 'Well, I'd say you've been successful in that. You and she have a good relationship from what I see.'

'Thank you. You and Simon have been a part of that healing. You've given me the benefit of the doubt when Penny didn't.'

'And what are your plans, Suzie? What do you see in your future?'

Suzie smiled wanly. 'I see myself happy. Married to a nice man. Living in the country. In a nice house that I'll enjoy looking after. I'm a natural homemaker – Mummy always said so. I don't have Penny's career ambitions. I just want to look after someone who appreciates me. Maybe even have a child if I haven't left it too late.'

Ella smiled. She was still not convinced Suzie had told the truth about Adam kissing her – but she was touched at hearing Suzie's simple list of desires, which had a real ring of truth. 'We all want to love and be loved. Nothing wrong in that. We must find a good man for you.'

Suzie looked coy. 'I *have* found him.'

'Really?' said Ella, surprised. 'Who? Someone in Cornwall?'

'I'd rather not say just yet. It's very early days, but we get on very well and I know he likes me.'

'Well, good for you. What a dark horse you are! What does Penny think?'

'I haven't mentioned it to her yet. I don't want her getting all excited and going out to buy a hat.'

'Good point,' laughed Ella.

'Yoo hoo!' Penny called as she dragged her overnight bag through the front door. 'Anybody home?'

Simon came out of his office. 'Hello, you. I've missed you – oh, and Jenna's out with Ella, before you ask.' He took her bag and hugged her. 'Tell me all about it over a cuppa.'

He made a tray of coffee with chocolate Hobnobs and they went into the garden and sat on the swing seat under the trees.

Penny was so happy telling Simon all about it and he was happy for her. 'It was such fun and the new team are all excited by it too. The casting for the main roles starts tomorrow and Jamie – remember the casting director from Mr Tibbs?' Simon didn't but said yes anyway. 'He's just great,' Penny continued. 'He has such a talent for it. I can trust him absolutely. Hobnob?' she said, passing Simon the plate.

'No, thank you,' said Simon.

'I'm having one. I'm starving. Where have Jenna and Ella gone?'

'Rock pooling with Kit. I think there might be a budding romance there, by the way. Kit seems to be over here an awful lot these last couple of days.'

'Really?' said Penny thrilled. 'Good, we could do with a bit of romance round here. In fact . . .' She leant over and kissed Simon softly and seductively. 'How about a little romance of our own?'

He slipped his hands around her waist and looked into her eyes. 'I've missed you, Mrs Canter.'

'How much?'

'Quite a bit, actually.' He returned her kiss.

'Where's Suzie?' said Penny breathlessly.

'In her room. She hasn't really left it since you've been gone.'

'Well . . .' Penny pushed herself off the seat and said over her shoulder as she headed towards the house, 'why don't we have a quiet moment on the sofa in the drawing room with the door shut?'

'This is just like old times,' Penny said, lying back on the cushions.

As he made sure the door was firmly closed, Simon looked down at his beautiful, successful, sexy, happy wife and said, 'I love you, Penny.'

'I love you too. Now get yourself on this sofa and let me show you how much.'

Simon gently lowered himself onto Penny and expertly they removed only the most vital of each other's clothing.

Soon the familiar melody of their lovemaking made them oblivious to anything but themselves, and they didn't hear Suzie open the door until she spoke.

'Goodness! I wouldn't have come in if I'd known,' she said rather crossly.

Simon lay face down on top of Penny, wondering how much of his nudity was apparent. Penny wriggled her top half free and looked at her sister who was standing in the doorway and resolutely not moving.

'Suzie, dear,' said Penny, with mild embarrassment, 'would you be kind enough to leave the room?'

'I remember catching Mummy and Daddy once. Daddy wasn't half as polite,' said Suzie, without moving.

'I can imagine,' Penny said. 'But please, would you just give us a moment?'

When she'd gone, Simon said, mortified, 'I must apologize to her. This is terrible.'

Penny pulled the zip up on her jeans. 'Apologize to her? Don't you dare! She needs to apologize to us. Making us feel uncomfortable in our own home. She's outrageous.'

'I'm sure she didn't deliberately set out to catch us,' said Simon, putting his socks back on. 'It was an honest mistake.'

'Right, well, I'm going to open a bottle of wine and get her to apologize,' said Penny, running her fingers through her tousled hair. 'You can come with me.'

'I'd really rather not,' said Simon.

'Perhaps you're right. You'll only make out it was our fault not hers. I need to draw a few boundaries for her.'

Penny found Suzie in the kitchen. She had two wine glasses out on the side and was unscrewing the cap from a bottle of Sauvignon Blanc. She looked up. 'What was all that about?'

Penny couldn't believe her ears. 'I beg your pardon?'

'In the middle of the day? Jenna might have come in.'

Suzie calmly poured wine into the two glasses and put one in front of Penny.

'I was making love with *my* husband. In *my* house. And it's nobody else's business.'

Suzie took a seat and with shaky hands drank some wine. 'This is good. Try some.'

'I will,' Penny said, sitting down and picking up her glass. 'What's this about? Have I embarrassed you? Married people have to get their fun where they can, particularly in this house: half the village walking in and out, Jenna looking for us – it's hard. Ask any married couple with kids.'

'I wouldn't know on either score, would I?'

'Oh Suzie.' Penny was full of compassion and guilt. 'I'm sorry. But it's not too late. Look at me. I found Simon, had Jenna, and all when I had pretty much given up on the idea of settling down. And I'm so happy. You'll find the right person.'

'Actually, I have,' Suzie said.

'Oh, how wonderful, darling! Do I know him? Who is he?' asked Penny.

'It's early days. And . . . there are complications.'

'Oh dear,' Penny said.

'Yes but I know he'll be free soon and then . . . happiness.'

'Is he in another relationship?'

'Something like that.'

'Hmm. Well, I'm always here for you, Suze, if ever you need to offload or want some advice. I've done most things I shouldn't have, so I have some experience.' She tried an encouraging smile. 'Sisters help each other and I've been no angel.'

'Like Daddy,' said Suzie. 'He was no angel, was he?

He had an affair with a woman and you were the result. The woman didn't want you so she gave you to Daddy. Daddy couldn't look after you so he found Mummy and married her so that *she* could look after you. And how did he repay her?' Suzie looked at Penny as if she had the answer.

'I don't know,' said Penny, reeling slightly at the sudden turn in conversation.

'By dying and leaving his bastard child with her and with me, his true daughter. What a charmer.'

'Don't speak about Daddy like that!' Penny said angrily.

'Oh, boo hoo,' said Suzie sarcastically.

'Suzie!' Penny was shocked. 'What's brought this on? Don't speak to me like that.'

Suzie stood up abruptly. 'I'm sorry. I'm a bit stressed, that's all. I'm going out for a bit. I need to get some fresh air. And you need a shower,' she added, slamming the door behind her.

Penny put her head in her hands. She had never wanted her father more. Poor Suzie was a damaged person. What other reason could there be for her saying those horrible things about him? If only he hadn't died so long ago, he would walk in the door with his familiar smell and hold her, tell her it would be all right. Keep going, Penny, keep going. Then she thought of his briefcase on a shelf in her wardrobe. She went to get it and ran her fingers over the well-worn handle, dark with the sweat and oil of his hands. She opened up the case and plunged her face inside, took a deep breath. The smell of leather and masculinity filled her nostrils. As she drew herself out of the bag, the zip of the outer pocket caught on the side of her nose. She had tried to open it once before but the zip was so stiff. She clenched and unclenched her hands before slowly trying the zip's tag again. It wouldn't move. She ran her fingers over the pocket to feel any contents. There were no obvious lumps or bumps but a feeling of certainty, something like destiny, coursed through her. She almost felt her father's presence around her. She went to Jenna's room and found her bottle of baby oil. She dripped a little on to the zip and rubbed it in with her fingers. Then she wiped it from her hands and tried again. The zip slowly undid. When it was fully open she put her hand into the pocket and felt a piece of stiffish card. She pulled it out and found a photo stuck to a postcard. She took it to the window to see it in a better light. Her father was standing in a park by a boating pond. He was wearing high-waisted, bell-bottom jeans and a mirrored-velvet jacket over a black T-shirt. He was holding a very small baby with his left arm and a pretty girl with long dark hair and a flowing hippy dress in his right. The girl wasn't looking at the camera. She was holding the baby's hand to her lips and gazing with a loving intensity that Penny could feel coming through the faded photo.

Penny turned the photo over. On the back of the glued on postcard was a message addressed to her father.

> *Darling Mike and Lope,*
> *My little family*
> *I love you both SO much.*
> *I will never forget you.*
> *Be happy. Don't forget me.*
> *Jax/Mummy xxx*

Penny turned the picture over again and studied the young woman. Her mother. This woman had shortened her name from Penelope, to Lope. She ran her fingers over her mother's face. 'Hello, I like the name Lope,' she said. She studied the picture for any sign of family likeness with her mother but it was hard to tell. It was such an old photograph, yet the emotion Penny felt holding it was brand-new. She sat there clutching the only photo of her mother that existed, treasuring every word she had written on the tattered postcard. Her mother loved her. *Her little family*.

Slowly her bedroom door opened and Suzie came in, her face pale.

'Ah. You found it.'

'Did you know this was here? Why didn't you tell me it was here?'

'I put it in there. Years ago. Mummy threw it away when I first found it but I got it out of the bin and saved it.'

'Thank you.' Penny held the photo to her chest, her voice breaking. 'Thank you.'

Suzie nodded, all trace of their last encounter gone. She was being a sister, a true sister at last.

'Is this my mother?'

'Yes.'

'What happened to her?'

Suzie shrugged one shoulder. 'Mummy said something about your mother's parents not being impressed that their teenage daughter had got pregnant. She wasn't even eighteen so she needed her parents' consent to get married. Her parents, your grandparents, had total control over her and you. They were going to put you up for adoption. But Daddy came over all Sir Galahad and took you in himself. The rest is history. Mine and yours. And Mummy's, of course.'

'No wonder Margot hated me,' Penny said wretchedly.

'She talked of nothing else for years,' said Suzie softly. 'She and I together, when I was old enough. She'd just about had enough of you, she told me – which is why you were sent to boarding school. Every day that Mummy had to see your face, she saw the woman Daddy had loved.'

'Is my mother still alive?'

'I don't know.'

Penny carefully placed the tattered postcard back in the briefcase and zipped it up. 'How you must have hated me.'

The two women looked at each across years of emotional pain.

'Oh Suzie, we've missed so much of each other. And for what? For ancient history. I'm so glad we have this second chance together. Look, why don't we have a really nice meal together tonight, just you, me and Simon and we can talk about everything. We can even start to make some plans for you staying here longer, wouldn't you like that? I'm sure there must be a little cottage somewhere round here that you'd like.'

'Don't you want me to stay here?' asked Suzie.

'Well, yes. But not for ever. Look at what happened with you walking in on Simon and me earlier? Wouldn't you like your own space? Nearby, of course, so that we can still see each other all the time. I'm sure that when things work out with this mystery man of yours you won't want some boring old married couple breathing down your neck,' Penny laughed gently.

They were interrupted by the ringing of Penny's phone.

Penny looked at the caller ID. It was Mavis Crewe. Penny took a deep breath and answered as Suzie left the room.

'Hello, Mavis,' said Penny as brightly as she could.

'Darling, I'm in London today, flying out very late tonight. But I'm having a meeting with that rascal Jack Bradbury over at Channel 7. Please, can you join us? I need you there.'

'Oh, Mavis! I've just come back from London earlier today. And I've had a drink. It's also a long way to drive and I'm rather tired.'

'I've sent a car to get you. I'm meeting Jack at nine thirty.'

Penny looked at her watch. 'I'll never get there in time.'

'Darling, I wouldn't ask if it wasn't going to be important for both of us and the car will take you back to Cornwall after the meeting.'

Penny's head was spinning. 'Give me twenty minutes and I'll be ready,' she told Mavis.

'I'll give you five minutes. The car is outside waiting.'

Penny looked out of her window and a black Mercedes was indeed sitting outside the vicarage.

Penny grabbed a few essentials and rushed down to Simon's office to fill him in but his office was empty.

In the kitchen there was a note on the table. *Pen, called out to referee the Scouts' five-a-side. Usual ref has put his back out. Won't be long. Hope all is well with you and Suzie. See you later. Love you, S x.*

She'd ring him from the car and scribbled a note to that effect in case he got home first, signing off with a flourish of loving kisses. She picked up her phone and called Ella as she threw some last bits into her handbag. It went to answerphone. 'Hi Ella, it's me, Penny. Hope you and Jenna have had a lovely day with Kit. Sorry to miss you but I've got a bit of a problem. I have to go back to London. Emergency meeting. Suzie is here but

I'm worried about her. She's not herself. Would you keep an eye on her tonight? Tell Jenna I love her. I'm off now but I've got the mobile so call if you need anything.'

She called up the stairs and Suzie appeared at the head of the landing.

'I'm so sorry, darling, but I have to rush back to London. I've just had the most exciting call from the writer of Mr Tibbs!'

'Oh.' Suzie looked crestfallen.

'I know, I know!' Penny knocked her coat off the hook as she scrabbled around for her boots.

'What about our dinner tonight?' asked Suzie quietly.

'We'll have dinner tomorrow when I'm back, I promise. I want to hear all about your plans – and some more about this man! I just – oh, I *have* to go to this meeting! It could change everything! But I will be back by the morning, whatever happens.'

There was a knock at the door. A smartly dressed driver took her small bag and Penny turned at the door to see Suzie vanish back inside her room. She called up the stairs, 'Tomorrow, I promise! Look after Simon for me!' and then she had to run because the driver was holding the car door for her and they needed to go. She slid across the seat and settled back, suddenly overwhelmed by an emotional tiredness and closed her eyes as the car took her on the road out of Pendruggan.

Suzie was upstairs, watching out of the landing window, and she didn't move until Penny's car had disappeared from sight.

'*Look after Simon for me*,' Suzie repeated to herself. That's what Penny wanted, just as she had wanted Suzie to look after Mummy for all those years. All of those years wasted for Suzie but years of glamour and fun for Penny. Suzie thought of how much her mother had wanted to see Penny towards the end, but Suzie always intercepted her letters before they could be posted. She'd enjoyed Margot's upset at Penny's apparent unforgiving coldness. But Penny didn't deserve Margot's love: she'd left them. Suzie was her real daughter. Penny was an impostor. Poor Simon. Here Penny was, running off as usual to do what she wanted to do, leaving Simon alone. Well, Simon deserved much better. He was a man crying out to be loved and happy. The years of loneliness and resentment were boiling inside her, clouding her mind until she couldn't think any more. Then suddenly, in a moment of clarity, Suzie realized she had one chance to finally grab happiness for herself.

Suzie phoned Ella. 'Ella, my love, it's Suzie. Would you mind asking Helen if you and Jenna could stay with her tonight?'

Ella frowned. 'I just picked up a message from Penny, actually. She said you weren't feeling so good.'

'Did she? No, I haven't been feeling good. Migraine. I'm going to have a bath and get into bed. And if I could just have a night without Jenna crying? I know she can't help it, but she does cry so loudly.' She laughed, a hard, brittle sound.

'I'm sure Helen won't mind,' said Ella. 'Is there anything I can bring you?'

'No, no, I'll be fine. I might take one of the sleeping pills Adam gave me a while back.'

'Well, if you're sure. Sleep well,' said Ella. 'And I won't bring Jenna back too early in the morning.'

'Thank you, Ella. You're very thoughtful. Good night.'

38

Suzie took her time, sauntering through the house adjusting the curtains here, scrutinizing the scuffed paintwork there. It would be different when it was her house. She didn't care much for Penny's taste. Too 'arty', as Mummy would say, and she'd be right. The drawing room in particular, with its large 'tart's' sofa, as she would always think of it now, would be the first piece of furniture to go.

In the kitchen she saw the note left by Simon for Penny and Penny's reply. She smiled and ripped them into small pieces before dropping them into the kitchen bin. Tonight was the night she was to look after her sister's husband. Look after him properly, as he deserved. She would show him what a proper wife does for a man. On the table were the two glasses of wine she and Penny had shared. She went to the fridge and poured herself another. She felt rather wicked but thrilled to be so free and at ease like this in her sister's house. She drank her wine then refilled it. Now that she was on her own, with no one to disturb her, she could do whatever she wanted. And what she wanted first was a long hot soapy bath . . . in Penny's bathroom, and to think through her plan. Why should Penny have everything?

When Simon got home, Suzie was preparing a barbecue.

'I say,' he said, sniffing the air appreciatively, 'something smells good.'

' "*Ain't nobody here but us chickens,*"' sang Suzie. 'Good game?'

'Some of those boys are very dirty players,' said Simon. 'Very rough. And huge! No wonder the usual referee has a bad back.'

'Would you like me to run you a bath? Ease your muscles?' Suzie asked.

'That's kind, but no thanks; I can do it myself. Where's Penny?' asked Simon, hoping that Penny and Suzie had had a civilized conversation after the earlier embarrassment.

'She's had to go back to London. She'll be home tomorrow.'

'Oh? What for?'

'She didn't say. Oh, and about earlier. Simon, I am so sorry if I caused you any embarrassment. This *your* home and you have made *me* feel so at home that I forgot I am just a guest.'

Simon was relieved. 'Not a guest, Suzie; this is your home for as long as you want it.'

She dropped a kiss on his cheek. 'Thank you.' She handed him a glass of wine. 'Now, go and have that bath. Supper in half an hour.' She watched him mount the stairs then swiped his phone from the sideboard, switched it off, and hid it in the back of the cupboard under the sink. That would stop any calls from Penny.

The bath was hot and curls of steam enveloped Simon before they floated through the open window and out in to the garden. He wondered what was so important that Penny had to return to London so quickly. She'd obviously had time to have a bath as bubbles were still gathered round the plughole when he filled it up, but he knew better than to hassle her with a text. She'd tell him all about it when she came home tomorrow. He submerged his head under the water and wallowed in the pleasure of an uninterrupted soak. Life was so busy now with Jenna and everything else that he'd come to forsake baths for fast showers. He came up for air and began to lather himself. Outside he could hear Suzie singing again. '*Ain't nobody here but us chickens*'. That's a point, he thought, where's Jenna? She should be home by now. It was close to bedtime.

Out in the garden Suzie was laying the table. She'd picked a small posy of scented azaleas and had arranged them in a pretty milk jug. The dauphinoise potatoes were cooling and the decadent aroma of cream and garlic was mingling deliciously with the smell of the hot ash in the barbecue. She'd taken a few minutes to put some make-up on, covering her bruises as best she could. She'd brushed her feathery hair dry and it sat beautifully in a loose cap around her head.

She would make sure that this evening was perfect.

She heard Simon come down the stairs. 'I'm in the garden,' she called out. 'Bring the wine bottle with you, would you?'

'What's cooking?' he said, filling up her glass.

'Lamb cutlets. I believe they're your favourite?'

Simon clasped his hands and rubbed them together. 'You angel! Shall I pick some mint for the mint sauce?'

'I knew I'd forget something,' laughed Suzie.

'Where's Jenna, by the way?' he asked, grabbing several stems of mint from the large herb sink by the back door.

'She's at Helen's. Ella said that Auntie Helen was desperate to have them both for a sleepover.'

'Well, she'll be spoiled to death that's for sure,' said Simon. 'So *that's* why you were singing about the chickens.'

'Yep. It's just us.' She topped up his glass of wine.

Simon was tucking into his lamb cutlets with gusto, holding them in his fingers and chewing every scrap of flesh from the bones. 'These really are delicious, Suzie.'

'I like to see a man eating,' Suzie said. 'Daddy had a good appetite and Mummy cooked beautifully – she was cordon bleu trained. I learnt a lot from her.'

'It's a pity Penny didn't,' said Simon, licking his fingers. 'She can do a good Sunday roast or a full English breakfast, but I've never known her to make potatoes like these. They are heavenly.'

Suzie laughed prettily. 'Penny was a tomboy, always outside with Daddy. They enjoyed gardening and tinkering in the shed. He'd take her to the cinema to see all the latest films. They both adored the Bond movies and any cowboy films. I think that's what got Penny started in television and drama.'

'Did you never go to the cinema with them?'

'No. Mummy and I loved the old Sunday afternoon movies on the television – Bette Davis, Joan Crawford, Bing Crosby, Gene Kelly. The women were so stylish and the men so debonair. Not like today's films where sex and nudity seem to be the norm.'

She picked up the almost empty wine bottle. 'Finish this off; there's only a drip left.'

'That bottle went quickly. Too quickly,' said Simon. 'I'll have a headache in the morning.'

'You'll be fine,' she smiled. 'What's your favourite film?'

Simon ran his hand over his bald head and thought.

'I rather like a good western, actually.'

'Really?' Suzie looked surprised. 'Is it the shootouts at Dead Man's Creek or the saloon girls dancing in the bar?'

'Neither. It's the whole idea of being a pioneer, a frontiersman. It was a tough life back then.'

'How about sci-fi?' she asked.

'Leaves me cold,' he said, draining his glass.

'Me too,' she agreed. 'We have something in common.' She reached for the empty bottle of wine. 'I think I might open another. Just one small glass. Will you join me?'

'As long as it's a small one.' He yawned.

'You're tired. All that football,' she said.

'Football, wine, and good food under the stars. What could be nicer?' he smiled.

'You make it sound almost romantic.' She laughed, resting her hand on his shoulder. 'Stay there and I'll fetch the wine.'

In the kitchen she went to the fridge and collected the wine. She got two clean glasses from the cupboard and put them on the table then from the pocket of her dress she pulled out a small white pill. She took a teaspoon from the cutlery drawer and crushed the pill under the back of the spoon until it was a fine powder. With a fingertip she brushed the powder into the bowl of the spoon and then dropped it into the bottom of one of the glasses.

She added wine to both glasses, gave Simon's a stir, and took them out. She passed Simon his.

'Cheers,' she said, chinking glasses.

'Cheers,' said Simon. 'And thank you for being here, Suzie. I think you and Penny have built a bridge that will last the rest of your lives.'

'I'll drink to that,' said Suzie. 'And to our parents who did so much to make us what we are today.'

They chatted together until it went dark and the bats came out to swoop across the lawn hunting insects on the wing.

Simon was suddenly feeling very tired. He didn't want to be rude but eventually he said, 'I'm done in. Don't do the washing up. I'll do it in the morning.' He yawned. 'I can't believe how tired I am.'

'Off you go,' said Suzie. 'Sleep tight.' She stood up and gave him a hug. 'Hope the bedbugs don't bite.'

She walked with him to the bottom of the stairs and watched him make his way up and into his and Penny's bedroom until he closed the door.

Suzie took her time clearing the kitchen and loading the dishwasher. When all was tidy she locked the back door, checked the front door, and turned off the downstairs lights. Simon had left the landing light on so that she could find her way easily to her own room. She took her make-up off and cleaned her teeth. From her underwear drawer she pulled out a lightweight tissue parcel. It contained a gauzy slip of a nightdress that she'd bought a few weeks ago, when she first knew that Simon was going to love her. She slipped it over her head and looked at herself in her wardrobe mirror. Yes, it was just right: a classy glamour, both sexy and demure. Something her mother had taught her. 'You are the daughter of a real woman,' Margot had told her, 'a lady. Not the daughter of a whore, like Penny.'

She raked her fingers through her hair and turned off her bedroom lights, then she went out onto the landing and walked towards Simon and Penny's bedroom. She opened the door and stepped inside. In the half-light coming through the curtains she could see the outline of Simon's sleeping body. She stood looking at him, then she reached out her hand and touched his cheek. He would not be disturbed tonight and, with luck, would still be asleep in time for Penny to catch them together in the morning. He lay perfectly still, his breathing deep and even. She padded around the bed to Penny's side. Lifting the duvet she slid under it and rested her head on Penny's pillow. Suzie rolled towards Simon and felt the length of his warm body against hers. He was naked. She put her arms around him and kissed his shoulder. Finally, for the first time since her mother had passed away, she didn't feel lonely any more.

'Night-night, darling,' he murmured.

Penny's adrenaline levels were high. It was after midnight and the M4 was empty. The black Mercedes was speeding her back to Cornwall. 'You need to be with your family. It's the least I can do,' Mavis had said. 'And when you wake up tomorrow you can tell dear Simon the exciting news.'

Mavis's bombshell had definitely been worth going up to London for.

39

Suzie was sleeping soundly. Penny's bed was large and comfortable and the pillows smelt sweetly of her scent. Simon was a warm and solid presence next to her and she slept in a state of ecstasy. This was where she belonged. All she needed now was to be caught in the act and then she could finally step into Penny's shoes and have the life she deserved. The house, the husband, the baby, all would be hers.

Penny was jolted awake by the hard braking of the car. 'Sorry, Miss Leighton,' said the driver. 'We've hit a thick patch of fog.'

Penny could see the thick grey blanket dense in the car headlights. 'Are we on the M5 or the A30?' she asked, unable to make out if they were on the motorway or the dual carriageway.

'A30, Miss Leighton, just turned off the M5 for Okehampton.'

'That'll be it, then. We're on the edge of Dartmoor. It comes down very quickly here.'

'We might not get to Pendruggan as quickly as I hoped,' he said apologetically.

Penny peered at the time on her phone. Three twenty.

'No problem. Just as long as we get there.' She settled herself back down to sleep.

*

Back in Pendruggan, at Gull's Cry, Helen was in bed reading. She was wide awake. A feeling of unease and anxiety had settled on her when Ella had turned up with Jenna. She didn't entirely believe the story she'd been told, but she was delighted to have Jenna and Ella to stay.

After a light supper of spaghetti hoops, Kit phoned Ella to ask her out for a drink.

'I'd love to, but Jenna and I are at Helen's tonight.'

Helen guessed what was being said. 'Go out. Jenna and I will be fine. Off you go.'

And now it was three twenty in the morning and Helen couldn't sleep. Little Jenna lay next to her, clutching her teddy and gently snoring. Helen hoped that Ella was comfortable on the sofa.

Ella was not on the sofa at Gull's Cry, she was at Marguerite Cottage. She and Kit were facing each other, having just had their first kiss. Each of them had been surprised by it. Kit because he'd plucked up the courage, Ella because she had enjoyed it so much. Not knowing what to say, they kissed again.

When they surfaced they began to giggle.

'Shhh,' said Kit, making more noise than Ella. 'We'll wake Adam.'

'What time is it?' whispered Ella.

Kit glanced at the clock on the mantel. 'Coming up for three thirty.'

'Three thirty? I've got to be up early to get Jenna. I'd

better get back to Helen's,' said Ella, making no apparent effort to move.

'Yes. You'd better,' said Kit, 'or . . .'

'Or?'

'Or. My bed is only upstairs. Much closer than Helen's sofa. I think it might be more comfortable than Helen's sofa too. And I promise, no funny business.'

'Well, in that case, I'd best go home,' Ella said teasingly.

'Or . . .' said Kit again.

'Or?'

'Or you could stay in my bed, with me, and have lots of funny business?'

Ella laughed and drew Kit towards her. 'A kiss to seal the deal?'

'Deal.'

The car slowed down and Penny woke again. Home at last.

'Well driven,' she said stretching. She looked out of the window. This was not Pendruggan. They were at a service station.

'Sorry to wake you,' said the driver. 'But I need some fuel and I thought you might like a rest stop?'

Penny looked at her phone. It was coming up to five. She should be home by now, but they were still about an hour away.

'How's the fog? It looks all right here.'

'It's patchy. One minute clear as a bell, the next you can't see the bonnet.'

Penny thought about Simon who wouldn't be awake for at least another hour and a half. There was no real hurry to get home. 'I'm sure a quick coffee would do us both good,' she said. 'I'll get them in. My treat.'

The quick cup of coffee turned into a long cup of coffee, a full English for him, and a round of toast for her, plus a visit to WH Smith for the papers and a trip to the loo. The whole thing had taken forty-five minutes. And they still hadn't filled up with petrol.

When they got back on the road the sun was up and the day looked fresh and bright. Any remaining fog would soon be burnt away. Penny flicked through the papers and attempted the *Guardian* crossword.

Looking out of the window she ticked off all the familiar landmarks that signalled how close to home they were.

Sladesbridge.

Wadebridge.

The Atlantic Highway.

And finally the turn-off to Trevay and Pendruggan.

At the vicarage, Suzie was wondering whether Simon would prefer tea or coffee when he woke up. He was still asleep. She looked at his dear face. Without his glasses he seemed so young and waking up next to him felt so right. She looked over his shoulder at his bedside clock. Just after six. Maybe she'd just have a little more sleep herself. Penny still wasn't home yet . . .

The black Mercedes purred to a stop outside the house. Penny and the driver were as quiet as possible, closing the doors and boot gently before she waved him off and tiptoed up the path.

She stopped and drank in the peace and beauty of the village. Her home, the cradle of her happiness. There was dew on the village green and over at Pendruggan Farm she could hear a cow cough on her way to the milking parlour.

She turned her attention to her home. The vicarage was slumbering, clad in its wisteria and honeysuckle, the front flowerbeds testament to Simple Tony's green fingers, with larkspur, lilies, heartsease and poppies growing side by side in colourful profusion.

Home. She loved it and all it had given her: happiness, stability, security. All the things she now knew she had craved when she was growing up. She had tried to share it with Suzie but Suzie had her own demons to fight. Penny had had a bad year but now she saw the blessings that surrounded her. Once Suzie had found her own place, this really would be heaven on earth.

She found her key and slid it into the lock.

The house was silent.

She put her bag down in the hallway and climbed the stairs softly. Suzie's bedroom door was shut, and Ella's.

Penny looked into Jenna's room just to inhale her wonderful essence. She wasn't there, but the scent of her was. Ella must have taken her into bed with her.

She walked to her and Simon's bedroom. She put her hand on the handle and opened the door.

Simon always slept closest to the door. He was lying on his side, facing away from her, deeply asleep.

She crept towards him to kiss him and saw a minute movement from her side of the bed.

Penny peeked over and her heart missed a beat. Her sister was lying in her husband's embrace.

'What are you doing here and what the fuck's going on?' she shouted, aware that in the high drama she sounded like a bad actress.

Suzie woke up and saw Penny's face. She sat bolt upright. 'I can explain everything. I'm so sorry to hurt you, Penny, it just happened . . .' Penny noted the appalling clichéd dialogue before lunging at the bed and ripping the duvet off it. She dug her hands into the tops of Suzie's arms. 'Does *that* hurt?'

'Owww!' yelled Suzie. 'Yes! Stop it.'

Penny, still holding Suzie's shoulders, began to shake her. Hard. So hard that Suzie's head wobbled like a marionette's.

'Does *that* hurt?'

'Stop it! Stop it, Penny. Owwww.'

Simon woke up blearily then also sat bolt upright. 'Penny, what are you doing?'

'What am I doing?' she screamed. 'What the bloody hell are *you* doing?'

Simon was trying to gather his thoughts then realized that Suzie was in bed next to him. 'Suzie! What are you doing here?'

Suzie couldn't answer because Penny had grabbed a handful of her hair.

Simon jumped out of bed and went to pull Penny off her sister. 'Stop it, Penny, just wait a minute.'

'*Couldn't you just wait a minute before you jumped into bed with my sister?*' Penny attempted to slap Simon with the hand that wasn't pulling at Suzie's hair. He ducked and grabbed both her hands and forced her to let go. He held her arms tight behind her so that Penny was unable to hurt Suzie further. Not to be outwitted, Penny started to kick Suzie instead.

'*What are you doing in my bed with my husband? How could you do this to me?*' she roared.

Suzie jumped off the floor and onto the bed again, rolling towards the door.

Penny elbowed Simon in the stomach and leapt over the bed after her, putting herself between Suzie and escape. 'No you don't, you bitch,' she said menacingly. 'For the last time: what the hell are you doing with my husband?'

In the garden at Marguerite Cottage, Adam had let Celia and Terry out for their morning pee. He heard voices and screaming drifting from an upstairs window of the vicarage. It was Penny's voice, he was sure, and then Suzie's. It sounded pretty violent. When he heard the sound of breaking glass he pushed the dogs back into the house, did up his dressing gown, and ran over to investigate.

As he got to the front door it was suddenly opened and Suzie, red-faced and screaming, was hurled out by Penny.

Simon was trying to intervene. 'Penny, Suzie, come inside.' He saw Adam. 'Adam, please help me. There's been a misunderstanding. Can you get Suzie in here, please?'

Penny gave a suppressed shriek and stormed back into the house towards the kitchen.

Adam picked up a shaking Suzie and followed Simon into the house, closing the front door behind him. They followed Penny.

'Right. What's this all about?' asked Adam reasonably.

'Ask her!' spat Penny.

'OK,' said Adam. 'Suzie, what is this all about?'

'She's mad,' said Suzie, rubbing her sore scalp.

'*Yes I'm mad! What the hell were you doing in my bed with my husband?*' Penny screeched.

Adam looked at Simon, who looked very uncomfortable. 'That's a reasonable question. Can you answer that, Simon?'

Simon shook his head. 'No. I woke up and found these two fighting.'

Adam looked at Suzie. 'What were you doing in Simon's bed?'

'That's want I want to know,' Penny hissed.

Adam shushed her and they all looked at Suzie for her explanation.

She looked at them one by one, gave a choked sob and ran out of the room before they could move, locking herself in the downstairs cloakroom.

Adam sat the trembling Simon and Penny down and put the kettle on. 'Now then: both of you tell me what's going on here.'

Between sobs, Penny explained what she'd found when she came home.

'I *knew* she had a reason to be here, that bloody bitch. I knew she wanted something from me, she's always been an absolute cow.' She went on to explain about the postcard from her real mother that she'd found the day before and the unkind things Suzie had said about her father and her. 'She always was so jealous, but it wasn't just Daddy's love – she wanted *everyone's* love, she always wanted it all to be about her!'

'Suzie said nothing to me about that,' said Simon. 'I swear to you, Penny. When I got back from five-a-side she was here, cooking a lovely barbecue. We had a bit too much wine, I suppose, and I began to feel very tired. I went to bed and must have gone to sleep straight away. I had no idea she was in the room with me or for how long. I promise you, Penny, I would never do anything like that. I love you.'

'What was she bloody thinking?' Penny half-sobbed.

'As if I didn't know! I was right in the very beginning. She wants what I have got. My entire life, including you Simon,' said Penny forcefully.

Simon was appalled. 'Penny, we don't know that.'

Adam stepped in. 'I think she's been telling a worrying amount of lies.'

They were interrupted by a loud knock at the front door.

'I'll get it,' said Adam. He hurried down the hallway and opened the door to two officers, bristling with radios. He looked past them to their police car, lights still flashing on the driveway.

'Good morning, officers,' he said, surprised but polite. 'How can I help?'

'Would you mind stepping inside, sir?'

'Not at all. Come in. The vicar and his wife are in the kitchen. Can I make you a cup of tea? What can we help with?'

The police officers followed him down the hall.

'May I have your name, sir?'

'Yes, I'm Dr Adam Beauchamp and this is Reverend Simon Canter and his wife, Mrs Penny Canter.'

'Is there anyone else in the house?'

'Yes,' said Simon. 'My sister-in-law, Suzie Leighton.'

'Where is she sir?'

'In the downstairs loo, I believe,' said Simon.

They heard the door to the cloakroom unlock and Suzie came out clutching her mobile phone and looking scared.

'You are Suzie Leighton?' asked the female officer.

'Yes.'

'Are you OK?'

'Yes. Thank goodness you're here.'

'You called us to make a complaint about a Dr Adam Beauchamp?'

'Yes.'

'What?' said Adam, clutching the back of a kitchen chair to steady himself.

'Is the gentleman in question here?' asked the police officer.

'Yes,' said Suzie shaking.

'Would you identify him for us please?'

Suzie lifted her hand and pointed a shaky finger at Adam.

'This is the man.'

'You're sure?'

'Absolutely.'

The male officer approached Adam as Suzie fell into the arms of the female officer, sobbing. 'Dr Adam Beauchamp, I am arresting you on suspicion of sexual assault. Do you understand?'

'What?' gasped Adam.

'You do not have to say anything. But it may harm your defence if you do not mention, when questioned, something which you later rely on in court. Anything you do say may be given in evidence.'

40

Penny put the phone down in her office and walked slowly towards the kitchen where she was met by the expectant faces of Simon and Ella. 'Well?' asked Simon.

Penny pulled out a chair. 'Pass me a glass of wine first.'

Ella got a glass down and filled it from the bottle already open on the table.

'Cheers,' said Penny, raising her glass. 'Here's to my poor sister.'

'To Suzie,' said Ella and Simon, raising their glasses.

'So how is she? What did the police say on the phone?' asked Simon.

'They were really nice. Suzie has admitted drugging you, Simon, and is with the community mental health team now who are looking after her. She's to be kept in tonight so that a proper assessment of her can be made.'

'And what about Adam? Is he still being held?'

Penny put her hands in her lap and hunched her shoulders. 'Er, yes. I had a text from Kit actually. He's still at the police station and he said he'll ring us as soon as anything changes.'

Ella looked relieved. 'Kit has been such a brick. He was terrified for Adam when the police found out about that other sexual assault case against him. You don't think they'll reinvestigate that, do you?'

'They're bound to look at it,' said Simon, 'but they'll soon see he was totally innocent.'

Ella chewed her lip. 'I hope so.'

'Look,' said Penny, 'all of us have been questioned and told the police the truth. They'll soon work out that Suzie has been lying.'

'I couldn't believe what she'd said about you and Adam, Penny. As if you'd be jealous of her seeing him – not that she *was* seeing him. And that *I'd* bullied her,' said Ella.

Penny reached out and patted Ella's hand. 'Or that she'd send those flowers to herself and then get me all excited thinking she'd found a man to love, even though he had complications. I was really pleased for her, until it became obvious who she meant.' She looked at Simon and smiled. 'You.'

Simon took off his glasses and polished them. 'Don't remind me. I can still see your face and hear you shouting when you found us in bed together.'

'The biggest shock-horror I've ever had to deal with.'

'I've never seen you so angry or violent before,' said Simon putting his glasses back on. 'I pity any man who bumps into you on a dark night.'

Despite themselves, the three laughed.

Ella's phone buzzed. She picked it up. 'Kit? What's happening?'

Simon and Penny listened to the one-sided conversation and could tell that it was good news. Just before Ella hung up, Penny whispered to her, 'Tell them to bring a curry home for supper.'

Adam looked wiped out when he arrived at the vicarage and Kit not much better. Ella flew into Kit's arms and hugged him while Simon and Penny guided Adam through to the sitting room and the fire.

'Sit down and let me take your coat,' said Penny. 'Simon, get this man a drink.'

Adam sat down and crumpled.

'Adam?' Penny put her arm around him. 'Are you OK?' He looked up and she could see the relief in his eyes.

'I am so lucky to have my friends in Pendruggan. You, Simon, Ella, even old Queenie. Do you know she managed to get a message to me while I was being questioned? She even gave the police a character witness statement.'

'She's a nosy old bat but the dearest thing,' said Penny, smiling through watery eyes. 'She's very fond of you and Kit, you know.'

Simon came in with a large gin and tonic. 'Here you are. Kit said you'd like it.'

'Oh, I do.' Adam took it gratefully. 'Thank you, Simon.'

'It's nothing.'

'No, I mean for everything.'

'Ah well. That's what friends are for.' Simon was embarrassed and quickly added, 'Ella and Kit have told me to tell you the curry is on the table so come and get it.'

*

Penny took the scenic route to the hospital; she needed time alone to think, to prepare for seeing Suzie. After everything that had happened she just didn't know what to expect. Simon had offered to come with her but she had turned him down. 'I think it's best if Suzie and I meet alone. We have a big bridge to build and I want to do it properly.'

She parked the car and walked towards the main doors and reception where the girl behind the desk looked up and smiled. 'May I help you?'

'I've come to visit my sister. Suzie Leighton.'

'Ah yes,' the woman said reading down a list. 'She's waiting for you upstairs. I'll tell the ward you are on your way. Take the lift.'

The lift stopped and the doors slid open revealing a tall male nurse with a big smile. He held out his hand. 'You must be Penny?'

'I am, how do you do.'

'I'm fine, and Suzie is doing well. She is very much looking forward to seeing you. She's a bit dozy, it's the medication.'

He stopped at a door with a window inset and opened it. 'Suzie, your sister is here.' He ushered Penny in and left them alone.

41

Suzie was sitting in an NHS armchair facing a window overlooking the car park. She looked small and fragile in her dressing gown and slippers.

'Hi,' said Penny, moving to kiss her. 'How are you doing?'

Suzie turned her gaze on Penny and said in a slightly slurred voice, 'I saw you drive in and park. I watched you walk towards me. You looked scared.'

Penny decided to tell only the truth. 'I was a bit.'

Suzie smiled tiredly. 'I'm not surprised. I would be too. Have they told you I'm mad?'

'Not at all. They have told me you are going to be fine but you need some help and a bit of a rest.'

'Have you come to gloat?' said Suzie with a sad frown.

'Oh no, Suzie. No, I haven't.' She reached across and clasped Suzie's hands in her own, holding on even when Suzie tried to pull away. 'I've come to tell you that we are all here for you. Simon and Jenna and I, we are your family. And once you get better we'll help you make a future.'

Suzie looked at Penny apprehensively. 'Why would you want to help me? I don't *have* a future.'

'Of course you do.'

'Do I?' Suzie asked, looking like a small and frightened child.

'Yes. You do.' Penny rubbed Suzie's cold hands.

Suzie started to cry. 'I'm frightened. I was lonely when Mummy died and I wanted to be like you. Independent. Happy. I have hated you for all you've done with your life. And look at you! Even after all that you're offering me kindness.'

'I've hated you and been frightened of you too,' said Penny. 'I was so hurt that you knew about my real mother for all those years. How did you keep that a secret from me? It was like a knife. Can you imagine how hard it is to be betrayed like that?' Penny's voice began to falter.

'I'm sorry,' said Suzie, wiping her tears as fast as they fell. 'I can see now how hard it was for you. Do you want to try to find her? Your mother?'

Penny wiped her own tears before answering.

'No,' said Penny. 'Not now.' She looked up at the ceiling and willed herself not to cry any more. 'You see, you helped me to find her. You saved that postcard for me, and so I *have* found her. In my imagination, and in what she wrote on the postcard. I know she didn't want to let me go, and wherever she is now, she has a life that doesn't have a place for me. '

'How can you be so forgiving?' asked Suzie.

'I can forgive but I'll never forget. And I have comfort in my own family, in Simon and Jenna. And you, my little sister. Suzie, we are the only two people in the world who share a common history. Who remember Mummy and Daddy. That's the glue that makes us sisters.'

Suzie sat very still, her eyes darting across Penny's features then leaned forward and placed her arms tightly around her sister and hugged her.

Epilogue

Penny and Simon were walking on Shellsand Bay with Jenna when Penny's phone rang. They were getting some much-needed fresh air after the month they'd had. The gossipmongers of Pendruggan had had a field day for a week or two and then moved on to other victims, and this was the first day when they'd yet to have a busybody 'just popping by' to try to winkle out some more gossip.

'I'll catch you up,' she told Simon and took the call.

Five minutes later when she reached them again, Penny was beaming. 'We've got to get home!'

'Why? What's happened?'

'We need to open champagne because you and I are celebrating. Old Mave has only gone and come good on her promise! She's delivered the Christmas special script for Mr Tibbs *and* the outline for another six stories too.'

She picked up Jenna and swung her round. 'Yippee! I'm back in business. Mavis has told Jack Bradbury that *I* am the only person she'll work with. I'd have loved to have seen his face. Too old for the game, am I? Ha!' She raised her lips to Simon's and kissed him triumphantly. 'Penny Leighton is back in business. Up yours, Jack Bradbury!'

But that's not where our story ends . . .

Ella had cleaned Marguerite Cottage to within an inch of its life and had pasties warming in the oven. Henry was on his way and his taxi from Bodmin station was about to deliver him to Pendruggan.

Kit came downstairs, freshly shaved and smelling of a light, tangy cologne. Ella sniffed him appreciatively as she hugged him. 'You're not nervous about meeting my brother, are you?'

'Yes,' said Kit. 'Supposing he thinks I'm not good enough for you?'

'He won't think that. He'll love you. Especially if you take him for a pint later.'

They heard the rattle of a taxi pulling up. 'He's here,' said Ella, dashing to the front door.

Henry was paying the driver when he saw Ella's flash of red hair as she ran towards him. She hauled open the passenger door and threw her arms awkwardly around his neck, smothering him in kisses. 'I've missed my big bro,' she said.

'Let me get out first,' he laughed and pulled her from him.

Walking down the path to Marguerite Cottage he saw a young man in a checked shirt and shorts coming towards him. 'Hello. You must be Henry,' said Kit, holding out his hand.

Once inside the cottage, Henry dropped his case on the hall flagstones and followed Ella through the sitting room and out to the garden. He grinned broadly. 'Well, Ell's Bells, you've landed on your bum in butter, haven't you.'

'Would you like a pint, Henry?' asked Kit.

Henry looked Kit up and down and then threw an arm across his shoulder. 'With an offer like that, if Ella doesn't marry you I will.'

Ella elbowed her brother in the ribs. 'Shut up.'

'Just saying,' he said, clutching his chest.

'Ella's got some pasties in the oven. What would you like to do first? Pasty or pub?' asked Kit.

Henry looked at Ella. 'Will the pasties keep for an hour?'

'Yes, go on. They'll keep.'

'Yes, definitely pub first. I've missed Cornish pubs and Cornish beer.'

'Do you want to take your bags up to your room?' asked Ella. 'You're going to have to bunk down in Kit's studio for now.'

'Sounds good to me. Oh, by the way, I have a bag full of post for you. You were only supposed to be here for a few days. How was I to know you'd be here for six months?'

Ella declined the pub, saying she'd rather catch up with her letters.

She waved the boys off and settled to her post, most of which was junk mail, but one was franked with the name of the publishers she had taken *Hedgerow Adventures* to all those months ago. She opened the letter quickly, hands shaking. It was dated five months previously.

Dear Miss Huntley,

Re Hedgerow Adventures

Thank you for your submission. Unfortunately this is not the sort of book we would publish. We will return the manuscript under separate cover.

Yours, etc . . .

Ella threw it in the bin along with the junk mail. She sat for a moment, absorbing the rejection. 'Granny,' she said, 'you got me excited there. Ah well, I'll just have to work harder.' She felt her phone vibrate in her pocket and, putting all thoughts of defeatism behind her, she answered it.

'Hey!' said Henry.

'Hey,' she replied. 'I might walk up to the pub in a minute. I could do with a drink after a—'

'Have you looked at your emails?' interrupted Henry.

'No.'

'You better had.'

'I'd rather come and have a drink with you and Kit.'

'I'd rather you had a look at your emails. It's from Granny's solicitor.'

'OK.' She tucked the phone under her chin, opened up her laptop and went to emails. She saw it straight away. 'Got it.'

'Open it.'

'Oh. My. God,' she said, rereading the message. 'It can't be true.'

'It *is* true.'

'Our mother is alive?'

'Yes. And she wants to see us.'

The End